Scota's Curse

To my Bro, + Sur
Love y'all
Dudley

Dudley Sykes

Prologue

The snow was coming down in sheets, at times made parallel to the ground by a gale force wind. The white steed he was riding stumbled periodically, then at his rider's command would resume cantering along the coast road.

His friends had urged him not to make the trip, but his motivation far outweighed the caveats of his friends. The stinging weather, enveloping and enveloped by dusk, would not keep him from his beloved wife, whom he had not seen for a fortnight. He adored his Yolande. To him, she was worth the risk of foul weather and no escort. For now, she was the only family he had.

Yolande was his second wife, his first having died in childbirth. Over the decade, he had seen his entire immediate family die from one cause or another; first his only daughter, then his heir presumptive son.

The wind and snow became less intense just as day was giving way to night. Suddenly, the great steed reared up, throwing his rider to the ground. The snow cushioned the man's fall, but his horse galloped off into the darkness.

Before him stood a small group of men. "You frightened my horse. Now, get him right away!"

One of the group stepped forward. "We'll do no such thing. You are our prisoner."

They helped him to his feet.

"Damn you! I order you to track my horse and let me be on my way. Your prisoner indeed! I am your king!"

A second man from the group spoke. "You have stolen this land from Haakon and now you must pay!"

The prisoner struggled against the men who held him.

"Turn me loose. You have no right! I have stolen nothing!"

His pleas fell on deaf ears. He was led to a sheer embankment, fifty feet below which was a bed of rocks. In an instant he knew what was about to befall him. "Before you do this dastardly deed, allow me to pray."

He dropped to his knees. His last words were uttered in Latin. He beseeched the Savior and all the Saints to open the gates of Heaven for him and to commit his captors to eternal damnation.

Then he got to his feet and in a calm voice said, "Get this thing behind you quickly." In a matter of seconds his lifeless body lay on the rocks; Alexander III, King of Scotland, murdered on a raw winter night. The month was March; the year 1286 A.D.

Chapter One

1823. Settlers were beginning to trickle into the Oregon territory; those who survived the weather, the Indians, and rogue bandits along the way. Their first view of the Willamette Valley was a scene of lush growth. Wild flowers of variety and color dotted the countryside. Ridges of hillocks extended from the coast in the south to the high Cascades, north.

Newly arriving settlers, either from wagon trains or riverboats, passed by an occasional homestead, or fur trapper cabin, whose inhabitants might offer food and water.

The woods abounded with deer, wild turkey and several other forms of life sustaining meat. Not all the animals fit that mold. Once the wagon masters left the settlers near the Willamette River, they were warned to watch for puma and bear.

In 1823, Sven Svenson, his wife and four sons first laid eyes on the land assigned to them by the agent at Yamal Homestead headquarters.

"Mother, we made it!" Sven exclaimed, "We'll build our cabin on this spot. Our cow will give us calves. We'll have milk and some day a dairy farm." The laws of probability and nature assured Sven of a household labor force. Haakon, the oldest was a strapping sixteen-year-old. Isaiah second born was a wiry, intense boy who had read each of the twenty books Sven permitted for the trek from Independence, Missouri. Jagr was the family optimist. Sven had not started to unload the wagons before Jagr headed into the woods, a musket on his shoulder. "I'll get some meat for supper!" he shouted.

Thor, the youngest at age thirteen, was the family agronomist. He had read that the Oregon Territory would produce wheat, rye, barley, oats, buckwheat, carrots, peas, beans, beets, gooseberries, strawberries, apples, peaches, pears and grapes. From the forests of evergreens, there would be timber to build with and fire wood to warm the cabin hearth. In addition to household wares, Brigette Svenson and Thor had nurtured a variety of plants and seeds throughout the long journey along the Oregon Trail.

The Svensons were not unlike many settlers who had come to America around the turn of the 19th century, but there was a difference. Before leaving Sweden, Sven and Brigette had been blessed by a priest from the Brigetine Order. The blessing had included a quid pro quo. The Svensons were to pick up a coffin in Boston, and as directed, to export it to the Oregon Territory. They were told to bury the coffin wherever they settled. In addition, they were given a name and a post address in Edinburgh, Scotland. At the most feasible time, they had been directed to send a letter to the address, indicating completion of the burial. Before departing Sweden, Sven and his family swore an oath that they would never unlock the coffin before placing the corpse into the ground.

Sven was given currency equal to two thousand American dollars. New in Oregon, their immediate task was to set up a camp and commence construction of a cabin.

"I feel the season changing," observed Brigette. "Winter will be here soon. We'll need protection from the elements."

While unloading the casket and other household wares, a musket shot reverberated through the forest.

"Ah, yes! Perhaps Jagr has killed a deer!" Sven exclaimed.

A short time later, Jagr appeared dragging a carcass behind him.

"Well, well, Jagr! That's a strange looking deer you have there," Thor shouted.

"Ain't a deer," Jagr responded. "We'll have to settle for pork. Papa, I saw all matter of creatures. Turkey. Rabbits. Squirrel. Many birds. And the berries, Mother!! I don't know what kinds. I dared not sample them until," he waved to Thor, "until little brother says they're safe to eat."

"You did well, my son." Sven placed his arm around Jagr. "We'll need to dress out your kill. Mother, how would you like spare ribs for supper?"

Each of the Svensons set about their assigned tasks: Sven and Haakon hung and butchered the wild hog. Thor carried water from the nearby stream to replenish that which had been drained from the water keg. Brigette set up the outdoor kitchen, consisting of a table, six chairs and the utensils she had insisted against Sven's will be packed for the long journey. Isaiah and Jagr began the arduous work of digging a grave for the casket.

That night, as the Svensons sat around their campfire, Sven led them in a rosary. Each member of the family took turns giving thanks for their safe passage into the Oregon Territory.

The next morning, the six family members carried the casket to the grave. Brigette led the impromptu burial ceremony. "In the name of the Father, the Son, and the Holy Ghost, we commit this soul to eternity. We pray that he or she, we know not whom, shall reside in Heaven and be at peace with the Blessed Mother and all the angels."

For a brief moment there was silence, then Sven spoke. "Lord, we trust that in committing this corpse to the ground, we have not made a bargain with Satan."

Later that year, Sven traveled to Portland and posted a letter to Thomas Immelman, Edinburgh, Scotland. It read:

> *"My Dear Mr. Immelman,*
>
> *As we were directed, we have buried the remains of the dearly departed. We said words and blessed the remains as best possible without a priest at hand. The grave is located on the land of Sven Svenson, near a large copse of trees, eight kilometers from a settlement named Amity.*
>
> *Yours in Christ,*
> *Sven Svenson"*

Chapter Two

is fingertips moved softly across her cheek. He watched as her eyelids fluttered opened half-way and finally parted, unmasking green eyes, almost emerald green eyes.

"You had that night terror again last night."

"How do you know?" she muttered, burying her face in the pillow.

"It's always the same." He placed his hand on her bare shoulder. "You moan enough to wake me. Then you start to shake. I hold you in my arms until your breathing becomes normal."

She yawned and threw the bedcovers to one side, revealing the naked body of a former athlete, now tempered by just enough Marilyn Monroe flesh, silky, inviting.

"It's too real. Every detail. I've dreamed it so often — you remember the last time — how long ago was it, Al?"

"About six months. You seem to have the nightmare twice a year of so."

"I want to talk about it before I write it up. Okay?"

"Sure. Today's Saturday. I have nothing on my agenda. That's not quite true," he said, fondling her breast with one hand while caressing her hair with the other.

"Stop it, you horny toad! If we do it now, I'll lose the memory traces."

"God forbid that you lose the memory of a nightmare." He turned from her.

She sat on the edge of the bed and watched as he cracked the blinds to peer out at the early morning rain.

"Connie, I'm always surprised to see wet grass and pavement every day. You know why?"

"No, Albert. But I know I'll hear one of your theories."

"Nope," he paused. "Not a theory. It's more like a lack of sensation."

"A lack of sensation?"

"Yeah. The rain doesn't beat on the roof. There's no thunder, no lightening. Some days I'm not sure I'm seeing mist or a low character sprinkler system. These folks call that rain. Hell, they don't know rain. They don't even use umbrellas. I can just see these folks in a Chicago deluge."

He walked around the bed and held out his hand. "So Dr. Constance Nordstram, get your gorgeous butt in the shower. I don't take unwashed women to Starbucks for breakfast."

She grabbed his hand and lifted herself from the bed.

He retrieved a cup of coffee from the night stand, then offered it to her. "Drink up. Wake up."

Several shower minutes and a blow dry later, Connie emerged from the bathroom.

"Al, I want to talk about that dream."

"You bet, Doll. I'll try to fill in for Carl Jung. Any new details?"

"Yes, Mr. Nixon, she chided. "In fact, there was something new. I'll have to check back in my journal to be sure."

"I want to hear about the latest in that dream series. You may not even have to check your journal. Don't tell me the new part. Let's see if it jumps out at me. Okay?"

She smiled up at him. "Okay. Here goes. The countryside is green. There are hills and mountains. I'm in the dream. There are four others, all men. I'm not sure of my gender in the dream. We go up a hill. We're following a horse drawn wagon and on the wagon is a man sitting up, only he's dead. In the dream, I'm terrified. I believe we've killed the man in the wagon. I'm so scared. We come to a house in the woods and we bury the corpse in a yard behind the house."

She paused and shivered. Her voice rose. "Someone is going to discover what we're doing. We'll be caught and hanged. I'm so scared. I try to run, but my legs feel like lead. I see them coming. They're on horseback, coming right toward me. Now, I'm resigned to my fate. Just as suddenly in the dream as I was terrorized, so at its conclusion I'm content."

"I didn't hear the new detail you mentioned earlier. You've just recounted the nightmare you've had before." Al waited for an answer.

"It was a mountain," she said, her voice trailing off. "A big, snow-capped mountain."

"Tell you what," he said. "Let's get breakfast. Maybe by that time the clouds will blow away and we'll see Mt. Hood. There's a mountain that you don't have to see in a dream."

Albert Nixon watched in silence as his wife sipped her latté between bites of an almond scone. Sooner or later, she would look him straight in the eye and say "You want to hear my thinking?"

"Yep," he would say, knowing the drill, knowing not to push himself on her when she was doing, as she, the psychologist described it, "her internal psychological work".

He had been attracted to her from the first moment he saw her in the Notre Dame student union. After a week of observing her walking across campus to her graduate psychology class, he had worked up the courage to speak to her. At the beginning, Constance had ignored his advances.

He would discover that he was competing with Carl Jung for her attention. He would come to know in time that she possessed an intensity of mental focus that disallowed distractions large or small. He could stand the silence no longer. "A penny for your thoughts?"

"Cheapskate. My ruminations are priceless, you know." She covered his hand with her own. "But for you, I'll lower my fee."

She squeezed his hand. "I don't really have to worry about losing the images from that damn nightmare. It's so real! I swear, Babe, I was there!"

"Ok, so now we've been reincarnated."

"I didn't mean that kind of recycling. I was there in a Jungian sense. Something, some event, resides in my collective unconscious."

She grinned. "I guess I'll just have to get over it. Get real. Make do. Move on. That about covers that issue, as you're always telling me."

Most of the coffee crowd had left by the time the wind blew away the clouds and Mt. Hood rose up in all its awesome majesty.

"Look at that, Al. Is it any wonder people move out here, put up with the rain and the damnable traffic? Is it?"

"The wonder, Connie, will be when that white-haired volcano blows its top and every day is Ash Wednesday."

For the moment they became quiet, bound to each other by circumstances, if not intention; she the teaching psychologist, he the engineer, builder of infrastructures. She had never loved him with passionate abandon. She, like a legion of her sisters, had married because he was handy, and she felt it her duty to propagate the species.

All in due time, she had planned. But when the time came, she could not have children by Al. He was sterile. She had, subsequently, immersed herself in her profession.

Along the way, she fell in love with Carl Jung. After four years, following graduation, in her first position at Arizona State, she was denied tenure. She was a neo-Freudian in a department of template behavioral psychologists. A stranger in a strange land.

She next landed a position in the psychology department of Washington State University. It was a marriage made in psychology heaven. She was allowed to flourish. No colleague made fun of her when she held her seminar on Jung and Nazism. Her research into the dreams of schizophrenics was widely acclaimed in the field of abnormal psychology. Her academic restlessness was unabated, even after the publication of three books and twelve research treatises. There was always the dream and the angst around it. This day in a coffee shop in Vancouver, Washington she was thirty years old, childless, in love with an idea, but married to a forty-year-old whose beliefs were buttressed by steel and concrete; "If you can't see it, it ain't there!"

"So, Dr. Connie, what'll you talk about at that anthropology convention?"

"Al, you never listen," her indignation punctuating each word. "It's an archeology convention. Want to know the difference between anthropology and archeology?"

He could feel the pique as it reddened his face and warmed his ears. "Not really. As far as I'm concerned all of them go around digging up old bones. They don't have enough to do."

"I give up," she retorted. "I need to get back to the house and pack. I have an early flight to Albuquerque."

"So have I," he muttered. "Not that you'd give a fuck."

"Not true. I know you're going to build at least a six-tiered bridge over some river, somewhere. Touché."

"You're partially correct. We're finally commencing work on that bridge over troubled water." He cocked his head to one side. "C'mon, give me that Connie Nordstram smile. I'm sorry if, once again, I blew off your work."

"Me, too," she uttered softly.

Chapter Three

Smithfield, Rhode Island was more that a whistle stop, but less than a village. It was a place. Its main claim to road atlas fame was its proximity to a reservoir where people boat and fish and when they were not boating or fishing, more than likely commuting to either Boston or Providence to make enough money to boat or fish.

For the past six months, Jon LeFreaux had been out of work. Daily, he would paddle his canoe up and down the reservoir, then check the mail only to discover that another of his job applications had been rejected. This day was no different. He crumpled the latest letter and threw it across the room. He remembered his father's caveat when it came time for graduate school: "Boy, there isn't much call for archeologists unless you want to do a lot of digging in Egypt or Peru."

Following his graduation, he joined a team and became a grant chaser. Grant chasers scoured government indices and research foundations, hoping always to unearth the holy grail of archeology: a five-year funding, all expenses, plus team salaries.

Fifteen years had passed since Jon joined his first team at the University of Connecticut. During that period he had worked on seven teams, digging up Indian mounds until the wrath of Tribal Councils shut down most mound exploration. No grant ever lasted more that two years, nor paid enough to buy good wine and choice steak.

He had met his first wife on the second dig. She was a paleontologist, who in Jon's opinion, contributed nothing to the dig, except after work sex. He had married her because she seemed easy to please and she enjoyed sleeping in a tent and going without a bath for three days at a time. The arrangement had worked well for nearly a year. One day he came in from the field to discover that his easy-to-please wife had run off with a grant patron.

His second wife was the result of a Bacchanalian drunk in a Gallup, New Mexico bar. Early on that Saturday evening he had driven into town to drown his sorrow on the occasion of one more grant fund having gone belly up. She had been his waitress. By the time he finished his ninth beer, Lisa Flying Squirrel had taken on the appearance of a Dallas Cowboy Cheerleader. The next morning he had awakened to the smell of fry bread and mutton.

"Good morning, husband," she had smiled and waved a marriage certificate. "You are one fine man. I shall call you Goes All Night LeFreaux."

In the light of day, Lisa Flying Squirrel was no longer a Cowboy cheerleader. She was a nine-beer woman: plump, big breasts, the face of Crazy Horse set atop the body of Queen Victoria. Jon had to use all of his savings to bribe an annulment. He had sworn his allegiance to bachelorhood and by now had lived alone for ten years. Occasionally, he would seek out a female companion, hoping to get maintenance sex.

He hated to accept money from his wealthy father. On most occasions he would approach his mother, who would con his father with some flimsy excuse such as needing money for jewelry to match a new outfit. Subsequently, Jon would receive the largesse. His father never allowed either mother or son to suspect that he knew the ultimate destination of the "jewelry money". Jon would use the latest money order to pay the cost of traveling to a conference in Albuquerque, New Mexico.

He walked to the picture window for one final look at his reservoir, then snapped shut his luggage. As he drove away, he waved to the countryside and spoke a final farewell. "Goodbye, you tiny state. I'll miss you even if your taxes are too high and your esteem is too low. You know, you really ought to be a parking lot between Massachusetts and Connecticut." With a feeling of flimsy closure, he drove the Ranger pickup onto the I-95 expressway. Three days hence, he would arrive in Albuquerque to shop for a dig. He was tired of explaining to people why a Ph.D. archeologist would be working on construction gangs, or pumping gas at a service station, or cleaning an office building. He wanted to feel once more the sweat and grime of an excavation. He wanted to feel the elation of finding a long-buried artifact.

Connie strode briskly across the lobby of the Four Seasons pulling her carry on luggage behind her. From the corner of her eye she caught a glimpse of a "computer job fair" name tag, pinned on the jacket of a shaven, well-dressed, MBA type. He ignored her. The scrubby looking bearded fellow with a ponytail and an offset "archeology conference" name tag followed her with his gaze. By the time Connie reached the check-in counter, the scruffy ogler had undressed her to his satisfaction.

Yep, I'm at the right place, she thought. The men have beards and the women are sunburned.

Before the trip to Albuquerque, she did some light reading on archeology. It bothered her that archeologists seemed to require absolute proof of hypotheses as evidenced by shards and bones. Her own profession was laced with opinions, suppositions, and in some cases, outright charlatanism.

As she approached to check in, she felt a wave of uncertainty. She wanted these meticulous diggers and sifters to love Jung as she loved him. But as she looked around her, she wasn't sure Jung and archeology was a match made in academic heaven.

"I'm sorry, sir. If you can't lock your possessions in your vehicle, we can assume no liability."

"So," Jon replied, his arms raised in a futile gesture, "When some enterprising thief steals all of my earthly stuff, you take no responsibility. Don't you have security patrols in the damn parking garage?"

"Sir, please don't make a scene. We'll help you store your belongings in our service quarters. What kind of 'stuff' are we talking about?"

Jon lowered his voice. "Picks, shovel, axes, trowels, tent, books, suitcases"

"I get the idea, sir. Take one of our baggage carts," she pointed, "over there. Bring your, uh, belongings through the service entrance. Someone will show you where to store your, uh, belongings. How long will you be with us, sir?"

"Two nights. Two nights, and I'll be out of your hair. Okay?"

"Fine, sir. Your key. Breakfast in the lobby six to nine. Exercise and swimming area open from six a.m. to eleven p.m. Will you need a wake up call?"

Jon was beginning to feel foolish for his earlier outburst. "Thank you," he said, as he pushed away from the reception counter.

Connie reviewed her notes one last time. She had lost count of the events and places, but her ritual was firmly in place. If a morning presentation; wake up at six, drink a cup of hotel coffee, attend the bodily functions, shower, dress, organize her notes. She would then walk ten blocks out, ten blocks in, followed by a light breakfast. The last review of the notes was done always in an alcove somewhere near the conference auditorium.

Jon's telephone rang once, twice, three times. "Hello." He heard his own voice coming as it did from the depths of a ribald night. His head throbbed. His stomach was queasy. The taste in his mouth was a familiar reminder of Budweiser and peanuts. What was her name? Was it Julia? Anne? Joan of Arc? Mattered not. He had been unable to coax her into bed. A one beer or a ten beer woman?

"Your wakeup call, sir. The time is 8:15."

"Thank you." He cradled the telephone and stumbled into the bathroom. Awake and relieved, he flipped through the conference program.

"Damn! The placement fair doesn't open until 11:00. Bad luck. Now do I go back to sleep or get out and mingle? Well, let's see." He turned to the second page of the program.

"Ah! I think I'll go to the general session. She's a fox, assuming that photo wasn't made twenty years ago. Hmmm. Carl Jung and the collective unconscious. Jesus, she's probably a fruitcake. Good. Maybe I'll wake up by eleven."

He pressed the T.V. remote. "W" appeared on the screen, a sad expression on his face to announce there would be no more drilling in the Alaska National Wildlife Preserve. Channel change, Rug rats. Once more, cute Katie. T.V. off.

"Minnow was right." He stepped into the shower. "A vast wasteland."

Chapter Four

Connie gazed out over her audience while the Master of Ceremonies extolled the virtues of Dr. Constance Nordstram "professor of psychology, who will speak on," the M.C. paused, checked his notes, "on Carl Jung and the collective unconscious."

She gripped the podium. She believed these archeologists would be a tough audience. "Dr. Chambers, ladies and gentlemen. I'll do my best to recruit you into the fold of a man I believe to be the greatest psychologist of all time."

Wake up the hung over guy in the second row. "Just the mention of Jung causes my brain to engage, my spirit to soar, and my nipples to stand erect."

Laughter. He's awake now.

"Carl Jung was truly a towering genius even when we consider the fact that he was in and out of mental hospitals on different occasions. By today's standards he would be considered a workaholic, a bi-polar, manic-depressive, mostly manic. He was said to have analyzed over 68,000 dreams. We don't know what he did in his spare time, except write tome after tome on the human psyche."

Twitter.

"Though his psychological theory branches in many directions, I have focused on his writings about the collective unconscious and how that may manifest itself in our dreams, and I have theorized about Jungian theory and Nazism, among other pursuits."

Consistent with her past experience in speaking to diverse groups, when she mentioned dreams, a noticeable change came over the audience. Now, they sat a bit straighter and listened more attentively.

"Jung believed that deep within our psyche is banked the totality of human experience. That totality gives rise to our intentions and our movements. For example, we move toward cataclysmic events. We are attracted to these events for no rational reason. Think of Mt. St. Helens and the thousands of Homo sapiens who rushed to see that inferno. Just as our caveman ancestors — excuse me, cave person ancestors — just as they were attracted to fire so do we have today at another level, those who set the fires. Most of the time, a fire chaser or setter gives no rational explanation for that behavior."

In the back row of spectators, Jon LeFreaux squirmed in his seat, trying to decide if the Jungian psychologist was worth the rest of his morning. He decided she was pretty and she had a nice voice. Yeah. I'll stick a few more minutes.

"Jung believed that each of us has a personality that is comprised of four functions: thinking, feeling, sensating and intuiting. Three of the four he deemed to be superior functions because they are conscious operations. The fourth one is always an inferior function and resides to a great extent in the unconscious, and is manifested in our dreams. Now a critical point: so much of what is buried in our unconscious is there because our psyche does not wish it to see the light of day."

Jon shifted positions and glared at his watch. Thirty more minutes until the job tables open. His attention to Connie was sporadic. He gave not a didley damn about Hitler having tapped into the collective unconscious of the German people, bringing out their dark, evil, ancestral kinship with the creatures of the Black Forest. As for Hitler's love of the composer Wagner, Jon surmised that only a madman would be attracted to a musician who searched for melodies with limited success.

"For example, current research into dreams seems to indicate that when the feeling part of the personality is inferior, then subsequent dreams tend to be fear ridden, guilt ridden, and may serve as the base for serial night terrors."

"By serial dreams, I mean those which occur several times over a period of years. Okay. How about you folks being my guinea pigs to illustrate the inferior portion of one's personality. On the back of the desk before you, you'll find a card and a pencil. Please write out a brief description of a dream you have remembered at least four or five times over a span of years. Don't sign your name, unless you wish to have fifteen minutes of fame. Just kidding. I'll select from your dreams to make my point."

Twitter. Connie stepped away from the podium. She could see those who were the meticulous sifters of dirt and rock, hunched over their task, probably going beyond a brief dream description, or the skeptics who wrote smart-alecky notes in the margin, and a few who struggled to remember even one dream.

After a few minutes, Connie moved back to the podium. "Please pass your cards to the aisle. Would each of you seated on the aisle please gather the cards and bring them up." Connie smiled broadly. "Ain't it fun being back in Psych 202? Okay, before I look into your collective unconscious, we'll peek into mine."

"Sometime around the time of my twentieth birthday I remembered for the first time the dream I am about to describe to you. That was the first time. Since that first awakening, sweating, my heart pounding, that dream has occurred at least two times a year." She paused. "Without telling you my exact age, I can recall as a small child of hearing a handsome president say, "Tear down that wall, Mr. Gorbachov.""

"Over the years, I have come to dread this particular dream. It is always the same. The countryside is verdant. There are rolling hills. I'm in the dream and there are four others, all men. I'm not sure of my own gender in the dream. We go up a hill. We're following a horse drawn wagon. I'm so scared; we come to a huge castle-like building. It's set on a hill in a grove of trees. In the wagon is a corpse sitting up as if driving the team of horses. We take the corpse from the wagon and bury it behind the building. I always…"

Connie stopped in mid-sentence. Her hands shook ever so slightly and she could feel the beaded sweat above her upper lip. "I always wake up terrified. In the dream, I know that someone is going to discover what we've done. We'll be caught and hanged. I'm so scared. I try to run but my legs feel like lead. Then I see them coming. They're on horseback coming straight toward me. Now I'm resigned to my fate. Just as suddenly in the dream that I'm terrified, so at its conclusion I'm content."

Connie shuffled her notes and waited for her hand to cease shaking. "Let's take a fifteen minute break after which I'll work on one of your dreams."

Jon remained in his seat as the others moved into the lobby for their Danish and coffee. Shortly, he strode to the stage, waiting impatiently for the last hanger-on to step away from the morning speaker, whose name had escaped him. Finally, he was next in line.

"Would you like for me to bring you some coffee?"

"Thank you, yes. Just a touch of cream."

When he returned with the coffee, Connie was pretending to be interested in a pony-tailed pedantic as he explained how artifacts were preserved.

Jon handed Connie the coffee. "You should drink it while it's hot. Sir, please excuse us. We have some housekeeping details to take care of."

Jon placed his hand on her shoulder. "If you don't mind, let's get backstage to work out the honorarium details."

Connie followed him stage left.

"I appreciate the rescue, but at this moment, I'm wary of the rescuer."

"Please," Jon said, "I must have some time with you — maybe two minutes, okay."

Connie's smirk accompanied the frost in her voice. "So in two minutes you're going to convince me that I should spend even more time with you?"

"No. I promise I'm not hustling you."

"Oh, how disappointing. What then do we have to talk about?"

"The dream, Dr." Jon stammered. "I'm sorry, I've blocked on your name. I'm Jon LeFreaux." He held out his hand, which was ignored by Connie.

"Jon LeFreaux, this is quite awkward. You're not trying to seduce me. You wish to talk about my dream but you don't even know my name, your keynoter. How unflattering."

"I'm sorry. I'm an idiot. But, I must tell you — my recurrent dream is almost exactly the same as yours."

Connie glanced at her watch. "Is that a fact? I must say your line is unusual, if not the most creative one I've ever heard."

"Except in my dream, I'm the person in the wagon. Oh, and one other difference — there's a huge white mountain in my..."

Connie tried to remain stoic, but her insides were suddenly in turmoil.

"If the narrative on your dream card supports what you're saying, we'll talk. I've got to get back to the podium, lest the MC conclude that I've been abducted."

"I'm in room 512. Will you call me?"

"Yes, if your card matches." Connie turned to face him. Her smirk had turned into a slight smile. "Maybe we can compare dreams over dinner."

The last of the coffee breakers had drifted in.

"Let's get started. Hope your coffee hit the spot. You know if it wasn't Starbucks, too bad. You'll never know the joy of paying $3.75 for coffee served in a paper cup, wrapped in a napkin."

Laughter. Connie drew a card from the box.

"In my dream, I'm walking in a mall, but I'm wearing a blouse and nothing else. People don't seem to care, but I'm embarrassed, even though my nakedness feels good."

Hoots from the audience. Connie raised her hand. "Tell me honestly, how many of you have recurrent dreams of a sexual nature?"

A few hands were raised.

"Okay. I'll get back to this dream, but let me select... ah, here's one."

"My recurrent dream is about finding a short route to my car in a parking lot among hundreds of vehicles. I had memorized the row and level number, but my car doesn't seem to be where I thought I parked it. In the dream, I keep going over and over my memory of the parking. Finally, I spot the car and now it has mysteriously appeared in the numbered lot I memorized."

"Very well. I'll get back to this card."

Connie lifted several cards from the box and after scanning four commenced to read the fifth card.

"My dream is about a phrase or a formula that will be a major contribution to science. I always write them down as soon as I awaken. When I remember. Here are the ones which occur most often. 'A big slingshot would be a good means of transportation.'" Loud laughter. "'Find a cave that leads to China.'" More laughter.

For the moment, Connie had sat Jon in the rear seat of her consciousness. She had the audience in her hand.

"Very good! Now, let me get back to the person who dreams of walking in the mall with nothing covering her bottom. In Jungian terms, that's an inferior functional sensate dream. The person who owns this dream, in theory, does not manifest her sexuality in a conscious manner. In other words, her sexual activity is limited. She ain't getting enough."

"You're right about that," yelled a woman from the audience, after which followed loud hoots and several expressions of volunteerism from the men seated around her.

Connie waited out the titillation. "Earlier I alluded to the fact…" She paused. "I said 'fact' as Jung used the term. Dr. Jung's publishers were often driven up the wall by his intellectual arrogance. They would send back a manuscript to him with the notation, 'Sir, please back up your suppositions with research facts' and he would write them a response which usually read, 'I have decreed the suppositions you refer to as facts.' The publishers always caved in to his genius."

"Where was I? Oh, yes. Jung's theoretical system was similar to Freud's in that in addition to a collective unconscious, each of us has a personal unconscious. Okay, follow me closely. In that sensate dream, both the collective and the personal unconscious are at work."

"The personal unconscious is sensating sexually and shouting," Connie raised her voice, "Lady, you need to get out more!"

Guffaws and laughter.

"And where does the collective unconscious come into play? A piece of cake, theoretically. Our early ancestors were naked. Even the early clothing styles probably covered only the upper half of the body. It took thousands of years for our forebearers to figure out that it was best to have your derriere covered when seated on a cold rock in a dank cave."

By now, the diggers and the sifters were fully attentive. Connie glanced at her watch. I never seem to have enough time.

"What about my parking lot dream?" a man shouted from the audience.

"Your dream is a functionally inferior thinking dream." Connie moved away from the podium. "Since you've identified yourself, would you mind coming up to the stage? You and I can be even more illustrative to the folks."

The middle-aged, balding man bounded down the aisle and climbed quickly to the stage.

"Let me do some educated guessing." Connie smiled at her accomplice. "You work at a job that requires minimum mental effort on your part. Am I close?"

The man preened for the audience. "I'll say you're close. I work in a museum. I catalogue and file artifacts and such."

Connie breathed easier. God, why do I take these risks?

"I would say that you're a dreamer, that you fantasize about being a hero; you know, doing heroic things."

"Well, yeah." He answered through a sheepish grin.

"According to Jungian theory, your fantasies and dreams are rarely, if ever sexual. Am I correct?"

"Yes, Ma'am," he responded. "I'm married to a, uh, uh — horny woman, and" he blurted, "I love it."

The audience erupted into laugher and Connie knew it was time to quit.

"Thank you, sir. Ladies and gentlemen, we've run out of time. I've enjoyed this session. After lunch, I'll be in the Conquistador conference room to autograph and sell my latest book, which, by the way deals with dreams. Thank you." Through sustained applause, she gathered her notes.

Connie spotted him moving toward her. She was glad. She didn't wish to wait until evening.

"I'll buy you lunch. I know you said dinner, but…"

"I accept. I don't want to worry about your dream all afternoon and I have no desire to thumb through those cards until I find yours."

Chapter Five

N ow about that dream..." Before he could continue, Connie interrupted.

"No, not now. I don't talk psychology during a meal." She never took her gaze from her plate. "I want to know about you. Once I know about you, your dream may make more sense to me. So, what is your life style? Where do you live? What do you do to move civilization forward?"

"Good Lord, Dr. Nordstram! Do I take 'um in order or just grab at random?"

"Call me Connie. Any order you wish."

"Okay. Will I get to do an inquisition on you?"

"Absolutely. I believe in conversational equity."

"Fair enough. Life style, hmm." Jon rubbed his chin and realized he hadn't shaved this morning. "I play poker well enough to keep my knees from being busted by the Atlantic City goodfellas. I played tennis in college and now can last three sets if I haven't stayed out too late the night before. I'm good at collecting old bones from which others can make esoteric guesses. I read biographies of great people. These days I'm walking through English speaking history with Winston Churchill. Oh, and since I can't carry a tune in the shower, I recite Shakespeare aloud." That should impress her.

He paused long enough to take several bites of his taco. Connie waited for him to resume; her silence a green light for him to continue.

"I watch a movie or so each week. When I'm driving a long distance, I do things like rank my favorite movies or actors. For example --- do you really want to hear this?"

"Yes," she smiled. "I do."

"Well, my all time favorite is <u>Lawrence of Arabia</u>. Now don't you go assuming I'm a latent homosexual! Number two would be <u>Gone with the Wind</u>. Number three would be <u>Shane</u>. You get the idea. I'll do something like list in my mind the capitals of the states — alphabetically. Makes the miles go by much faster."

He lowered his voice an octave above a mumble. "I'm not good at marriage. I've blown two and I'm still on the downside of forty."

Connie held herself in check to keep from derailing his train of thought.

"But, I love women. I like the way they think and act. They're farther away from the cave than men."

He waited for her reaction. Nothing.

"I don't like flying. I get queasy in a three story building. I wouldn't mind flying if I were issued a parachute at check-in."

He sipped his coke.

"Until recently, I lived in a small village in Rhode Island. Smithfield. At present I have a Ph.D., but no address except my pickup truck. Hmm. You said something about helping civilization along? Right?"

She nodded.

"I don't know where I've been, or where I'm going. I have a bad habit of living in the moment and damn the consequences. Being an only child caused altruism to be just another word in Funk and Wagnall's. I'm a disappointment to my father. He hates archaeology, but loves Wall Street. He's a multi-millionaire and has always funneled money to me through my mother, his favorite conduit. But all three of us pretend I'm financially independent. Would I like to do something for humanity? Yeah, who wouldn't? But it's too damn difficult."

Connie waited for him to continue. Finally, she asked, "Do you know anything about your background?"

"Are you asking about my ancestry?"

He stared across the table, quizzically. "If so, I can tell you without forethought I don't know squat about my family. Nobody ever told me and I've never bothered to ask. What about you? Hey, it's my turn. What do I want to know about you? Hmm. Let me see."

His voice trailed off. "What's your favorite food? Where is your favorite place in the whole wide world? Do you ever fake an orgasm?"

Her expression never changed. "Hamburgers. Chelan, Washington. Yes, but not often."

"I guess that was pretty shallow."

"Do you want to know about me, or not," she answered, ignoring his accurate self portrayal.

"Okay, let me try again. What are you willing to share?"

"I'm married to a great guy. He loves me and tolerates me as a professional woman. He's an engineer. Builds bridges. He's a stabilizing influence in my life. We live in Vancouver, Washington. Usually when I tell people that, they think I'm talking about Vancouver, B.C."

"Count me among 'em. I was about to ask if you ever got down to Seattle," he laughed.

She took note of his laugh. It was hearty, not a nervous, glossed over giggle.

"My work is my life. My mate tells me I'll never reach retirement if I don't slow down. He says I smoke too much. I do. He says I get too little sleep. He's right. My father was a driven man. He taught high school math for 30 years, tended bar at night, and was a cabinet maker on the weekends. We grew up having it pounded into us that play was a third world activity designed to bring down Western civilization. My oldest brother fit the mold. Went to Cornell, then started his own company. Made millions, then lost it when oil and gas got cheap. Sold all of his exploration equipment and declared bankruptcy. One morning he didn't wake up. That was two years ago. He was forty-seven."

Jon saw the glisten of a tear unshed.

"My youngest brother got our mother's genes. She could turn her back on an un-washed dish quicker than a flash. A vacuum cleaner around our house might as well have been in a museum. Little brother, Benjamin, discounted our father and his val-ues. He decided to live in that third world, the one that scared dad. He's somewhere in Mexico. We get a post card now and again."

"And your parents? Where are they now?"

Connie stared at the table for several seconds.

"Mom divorced my father and married an old high school sweetheart. They live in New Orleans. That's where I grew up. My father never got over it. Two years after he retired from teaching, he put a .45 to his head and, and, blew his brains all over his bedroom wall. Benjamin was the one who found him and to this day, curses my father. Benjy says 'The old bastard could have taken sleeping pills.'"

The restaurant had emptied except for the two of them and a party of five several tables over.

"Jon, you and I share more than a nightmare. I truly believe that. And I'm not just talking about genealogical studies. Did I mention that in my family, we never knew much about our forebearers?"

"No, you didn't."

"I don't want to lose touch with you. We've got work to do."

He gave her a puzzled look. "What kind of work?"

"Genealogy. Are you ready for this? As of this moment I'm convinced that you and I are bonded by a tragic event of some kind."

She watched his reaction as her pronouncement sank in.

"Jesus, you mean…"

"I mean somewhere back there, our ancestors were involved in something hideous, so hideous that it erupts in our dreams like a psychic volcano."

"Dr. Nordstram, you're stretching my belief system to its limits. God, that is far out!"

"Jon, I want you and me to do a blind protocol. Here, Take this." She reached into her handbag and gave him a slip of paper. "I'll cue us with questions. Each of us will write our answer, but not share it with the other until all questions have been asked. Got it?"

"Yep. Fire away."

"In the dream, describe the clothing of the persons."

"If in color, what color is the horse?"

"How many wheels on the wagon?"

"How many horsemen are riding toward you?"

"Can you describe the building? Any distinguishing characteristics?"

"Are the men old, young, etc.?"

"Okay, let's write."

Several minutes passed before Connie ceased writing. Jon had finished the task and was waiting for Connie's next instruction.

"Wow, Dr. Nordstram, uh — Connie, you sure take your time. Me, I believe in brevity, but that always made me a gentleman 'C' in college grammar."

Connie ignored his disclaimer. "You go first."

Jon lifted his paper and commenced to read. "In my dream, the people are wearing what seems to be black robes, like monks or some such. The horse is white. The driver isn't wearing a robe. The wagon has only two wheels. There are four horsemen on white horses riding toward me and I'm running like hell. The building is made of stone; looks kinda like a small castle. The men following the wagon are young, I think. And there is a great white mountain."

He looked up. "That's it."

Connie could feel her heart racing. "My God! Listen to this! In my dream, the men are wearing black cassocks. There are ropes around the waists. Their heads are covered by cassock hoods. In my dream the horse is a large white stallion and the man leading him is not wearing a cassock. The horse is beautiful. Four horsemen are riding toward me and their horses are all white! The building is like a castle, smaller, made of something stone like. Jon, this is unbelievable."

"Unbelievable, hell! It's scary," Jon replied, shaking his head. "So, what now, Madame Jungian?"

"I've got to process all of this. I've got to have time to think. Right at this moment, my emotional state is just one raw nerve ending. Anything I do or say is going to be irrational. I've got to calm down."

Connie rose from the table, clasping and unclasping her hands. Just as suddenly she sat back down. "I've got a plane to catch, after I've done my thing in the -uh- what room? For God sake, I can't even remember where I'm to be this afternoon."

"The Conquistador room."

"Thanks. Okay, I'll want to stay in touch with you. Give me your address."

She reached into her handbag and placed a pen and paper before Jon.

"As I noted before, Dr. Nordstram, I don't have an address. I'm living out of my pickup truck. I came to this conference hoping to catch a dig of some kind. I was going to the placement center, until you put a cork in my plans."

"You mean you don't have a job? You're…"

"Yep. I'm unemployed. At the mercy of a system that has little use for old bones and broken pottery."

For an instant, an awkward silence settled over the two of them. Connie's blank stare was riveted on the third button of Jon's shirt. He squirmed in discomfort, wadding his napkin, first into one hand, then the other.

"Jesus, you'd think I just spit in my wine!"

"No, no! I'm sorry. I was turning over options in my head. I don't think out loud very well."

She paused, then continued. "I want you to come stay with me—with us — until, until — hell, until we figure out our next move!" Her laugh was stifled, adolescent.

"Oh, I'm not sure I can do that," Jon said.

"Look, I know you think I'm acting crazy, most Jungians are viewed as being a bit warped. But, Jon," she shook her finger at him, "What you and I have in common is not beyond rational understanding, uh — if you can give credence to Jungian psychology."

"Hey, I don't understand what is going on. But, I want to. Connie, I came here to look for a job. What'll I do. Should I take up your offer? Work at McDonald's? Pump gas? Go on welfare?"

"I want you to be my assistant," she replied.

"Your assistant? Good Lord! The last time I was a graduate assistant, I dropped a piece of Peruvian pottery. The damn thing broke into several sections. I glued it back together, but the old professor Roche spotted my ignominy and fired me." A sheepish smile covered his emotional ambivalence. "What would I be doing as your 'quote, unquote' assistant?"

"My thinking as of this moment is that I'll put the touch on one of my favorite patrons," she replied. "This is where you come in: I don't know much about archeology, anthropology, paleontology — you know, those dust covered ologies." She grinned and gave a reflexive tap on his hand. "We need some hard research into such things as clothing of different periods, wagons, architecture, huge mountains. We'll need to start genealogical searches into both of our families. So, you see, there'll be enough work to go around."

"What about your husband? What about my quarters? What'll the neighbors say?"

"We have a spare bedroom and plenty of work space in our basement. As for Albert — that's my husband — he's easy. Unless he caught us in bed together."

She commenced to backstroke. "We'll be in bed together in a metaphorical sense, of course."

"Of course," he said, with a straight face, trying to ease Connie's discomfort.

Chapter Six

"**Y**ou did what?!"

"Please, Al, calm down."

"Calm down, hell! You walk in here and tell me a man you met at your conference is moving in with us. How should I react? Oh, Connie, I'm so happy to have a strange man under my roof. Maybe he and I could share you! You slept with him, no doubt!"

By this time Al's face was beet red, much of his blood having deserted other parts of his body to fuel his anger.

"I can't believe you said that," Connie tried to keep her voice even. "You know I have never cheated on you, though God knows I've had opportunities." She eased up behind him and placed her arms around his waist. "Please let me explain this drastic move."

Connie then proceeded to give Al a summary of the conference events. Al listened at first with feigned interest, then as her narrative wore on, he became more focused. By the end of her pacing, arm waving account, Al's skepticism was blunted.

"So, Connie, I give up. Where from here?"

"Are you okay with him staying with us?"

"Yeah, I think so. I'll have to ease into it. It may take time."

Connie pressed her body hard against his. "Thank you, Darling, you can't even begin to guess what this means to me."

"Connie, what you've told me defies statistical probability. Unless that fellow — what's his name?"

"Jon LeFreaux," she answered.

"Unless he is an alien who took over your body, he could not have known your dream." Al stared at the floor. "But I sure as hell know your nightmares!"

"Thank you, Sweetheart. Thank you. Thank you!"

"So, when will Jon LeFreaux be joining us?"

"He's on his way. Should be here by tomorrow. He has all of his belongings in a pickup truck."

Connie took Al's hand and led him up the stairs. On this day, she did not have to fake anything.

Jon took the last bite of his candy bar and checked his map once more. He could make it to Vancouver by nightfall, assuming no highway patrol slowed him down.

"I'll take my chances," he muttered, shifting into second gear, and moving from the rest stop onto highway 84 at La Grande, Oregon.

Try as he might, he was unable to make the miles pass by listing aloud the US Presidents in order of succession. His thoughts were cluttered by the face and ideas of Dr. Constance Nordstram.

He had discovered a new method to make the miles pass: estimating the statistical probability of two serial dreams concurring close to perfect.

The closer he came to Vancouver, his anticipation became tempered by a thin layer of angst. Now he argued with himself over Dr. Nordstram's proposal. Over the years he had been comfortable with theories that were supported by bones, pottery, and dirty sweat. Yet, he laughed at colleagues who believed that a culture that had barely tested the wheel could have built the Great Pyramid of Giza. Perhaps, he surmised, Connie's backward glances at ancestors were no less credible than his conclusion that the Great Pyramid was constructed by a superior alien civilization.

His inner ruminations faded into the reality of the moment when highway 84 led him into the Columbia River Gorge. He was awed by its magnificence. Green mountain walls encased the Columbia River, fed by numerous streams snaking down steep ravines on the Oregon side of the river. On the Washington side he saw more gently sloping meadows, cattle there grazing, not disturbed by a long train running.

The sun was well above the horizon when Jon drove into a parking area which advertised the "Multnomah Restaurant". As he stepped from his vehicle to stretch away the miles of sitting, he glanced up and left and was held breathless for an instant. Water by the millions of gallons cascaded down a sheer cliff; one more tributary to feed the mighty Columbia. He was seeing Multnomah Falls for the first time.

Jon's hunger for food was replaced momentarily by the urge to climb to the bridge half-way to the top of the cliff. Several minutes later, he along with a group of Girl Scouts, stood on the Multnomah Bridge and felt the spray of the falls, cool against their cheeks. Long after the scouts made their way back down the trail, Jon gazed hypnotically at the scene before him.

Sated by an ample helping of salmon, Jon drove onto highway 205. Following Connie's directions, he crossed the Columbia and arrived in Vancouver just in time to witness a golden sunset.

She was digging in her flower bed when he drove up.

"So Dr. Nordstram, was Jung a flower gardener?"

She brushed a strand of hair from her face as she walked to greet him. "I don't think so. He was a thinker. When he wasn't exchanging barbed letters with Freud, and writing books, he was probably being treated in a mental hospital. I'm glad you're here. Come into the house and I'll fix you a drink. Umm, and perhaps a bite to eat?"

"The drink would be great. I just ate at a touch of paradise called Multnomah Falls." He followed her into the living room.

"I have beer, wine, bourbon, vodka. What's your pleasure?"

"Beer's fine, thanks."

"Let me wash off my garden grime," she said, handing him a Corona and an iced mug. "Have a seat. I would guess you're a bit tired from the drive. How many miles today?"

"About 650," he replied.

Several minutes later, she came back and sat across from him. "You know, Al and I have been here five years. I've never been to the Falls. People keep telling me I should see them. Well, what do you think of our great Northwest?"

"Dr. Nordstram, I was awestruck as I drove through the Gorge. Good Lord! How do you keep this country a secret?"

"We don't. We can't. We've got California moving here in great chunks of humanity. Give them time. They'll screw up this land just as they've messed up their own."

He sipped his beer. Even in jeans and a well worn sweatshirt, she emitted raw sexuality. He moved his gaze past her.

"When do I get to meet Al?"

"Not for a week or so. He's an engineer out on some infrastructure project."

Silence. Jon felt a twinge of ambivalence. There before him was an attractive female, perhaps a crackpot unverified, and her mate was off somewhere building something.

So much time had passed since he worked up a sweat, belly to belly with any female, much less a female psychologist.

"What do you say we unload your stuff." She was walking toward his pickup even before he could answer. "We'll stack everything but your clothes in the work shed. Okay?"

"Oh, you bet," he responded "There's not much other than my excavation tools. Remember I was hoping to latch on to a dig."

"Well, my friend, you'll be digging alright," she laughed. "It may or may not be in Mother Earth. These tools won't do you much good in an ancestor search." She paused. "Unless you plan to dig up their bones."

His room in the basement was not luxurious; nevertheless, it was appointed comfortably: bed, work desk, sofa, cushioned chair, lamp, small bathroom with a shower.

"I'm sorry we don't have something more uptown to offer you. I had to argue three ways from a rat lab to convince Al I wasn't bringing in a sex surrogate." Her face blushed just perceptively. "I told him you were rather ordinary looking."

"Well, thank you very much, Lady." He drawled through feigned pique. His first wife had validated that Jon was no Robert Redford.

"Oh, no! I'm sorry!" she tried to back pedal. "You're not ordinary at all. You're craggily handsome. Anyway, you're here, warts and all." She turned as she started toward the stairs. "I'm going to shower and after that prepare some dinner. You're invited. You like hamburger?"

The dinner conversation was light. She told of her love for the outdoors; that she used camping in the Cascades as a time to escape temporarily from her long dead taskmaster, Carl Jung. She dawdled over her food for most of the meal; then as if it were a chore, became silent to finish off the hamburger.

Jon listened less than intently. He was more interested in her animated descriptions; the way she raised her voice ever so subtly at the end of a declaration.

"Well, my new friend, you've been awfully quiet while I yammered on and on. Anything you want to share - - - you, know, of your personal life? What do you do when you're not looking for a dig?"

"Lately, I drank a lot. I'd get into my canoe with a six-pack, row up and down the Smithfield reservoir until the beer was gone, then go to the mailbox to find one more dig application rejected. Oh, did I tell you, I lived on a lake — they called it a reservoir in Rhode Island?"

"No, but the way you couch it, you weren't having much fun."

"Right. Poor little rich boy subsisting on daddy's handouts. To tell you the truth, I've never found my niche. Not sure I'd recognize it even if I found it. I envy you. I envy your enthusiasm for who you are and what you do."

Connie leaned toward him. "What do you want? Where do you want to go?"

He forced a smile. "To the first part — I want to dig up an alien form that came to earth twenty thousand years ago and died before he or she could return from whence he/she came. As for the second part of your question, I'd go to my father afterward and say 'I told you so.'"

"Well, Jon LeFreaux, how would you like to dig up our ancestry? Yours and mine? You dig while I hustle a grant for our little project." She waited for his response which did not come forth immediately.

She continued. "Room, board, expenses. Anything beyond that is on your tab, or your father's. It's a joke! Laugh!"

His next offering caused Connie to sit up straight and gasp audibly.

"Hold off on the grantsmanship. I'll try to get a loan from ol' dad." He laughed softly. "That's a joke in my family. I would always tell mom I'd pay them back. Once my father rebuked me in his stentorian voice. 'Boy, I don't loan money to my children. I give it to them. All I ask is that when you have children, do the same for them.'"

Jon gazed downward. "Then he'd muddy the proclamation by doubting I'd ever have any loot to give to anyone."

"Are you sure you want to ask him? We're talking about a fairly large sum of seed money."

"Yes, Think about it. I'll do my genealogy. You do yours. If your theory is correct, we'll meet smack in the middle of what we discover."

He sipped on his dinner wine. "How much?"

"Uh," Connie stammered. "Low ball, fifty thousand. Lobster and Four Seasons, a hundred grand."

She waited for his reaction. Jon's expression did not change. "I'll call tomorrow. Oh, and there'll be no sneaking the request through dear mother."

"You want to start planning tonight?" she asked.

"First things first," he replied, in true archeological fashion.

Chapter Seven

Raymond LeFreaux buzzed for his secretary, who shortly approached his desk, her notepad in hand. "Janet, get me the names of three private investigators. I want you to call each one. Find out how much they charge as a retainer, their per day charge. If they have a flat fee — you know — a, uh — job with a limited task, uh — you know what I mean."

"Yes, Sir. Anything else?"

"No. Get the information to me soon."

"Yes, Sir. I'll get right on it."

LeFreaux didn't have to wait long. A short time later his secretary gave him a sheet of paper with the data he requested and a telephone number beside each name.

"Is that all, Mr. LeFreaux?"

"Yes, thank you, Janet. Don't go just yet."

Scanning the list, one investigator caught his attention. Jake Lindsey, P.I. was the only one of the three who offered a flat fee contract based upon the job.

"Janet, see if you can arrange an appointment with a Jake Lindsey, P.I., tomorrow if possible. Invite him to lunch with me at Do Manti's, say noon."

———

Jake Lindsey did not fit LeFreaux's preconceived image of a private detective, as he stood before LeFreaux. He was dressed casually: jeans, open-necked shirt, leather coat.

"Please have a seat, Mr. Lindsey. Would you like something to drink? Coffee, tea, cola?"

"I'd take a beer."

"Oh, I'm sorry. No beer here."

"Coffee's fine." Lindsey straightened his six foot, two-hundred pound body, then leaned forward. "So, what's your problem? I know you haven't invited me here just to sample Do Manti's fare."

Before LeFreaux could respond, a waiter approached their table, pad in hand. "Something to drink gentlemen?"

"Two coffees please and I'll take the special."

"Me, too," ordered Lindsey.

"Well, I do say! You do get right to the point. I like that," LeFreaux exclaimed. "First of all, let's talk about your credentials."

"I was a detective in the Boston P.D. for ten years. Set up my own business two years ago. I'm a Marine Corps veteran. Divorced. No children."

LeFreaux waited for him to continue. After a discomfiting pause, LeFreaux asked, "What kinds of cases do you handle? Do you specialize?"

Lindsey smiled. "In this business, I generally have a no-cull policy, except for espionage."

"You noted that you enter into time arrangements and - un-total case contracts. Is that accurate?"

"Yes."

LeFreaux cleared his throat. "Let's suppose I want to give you a total case contract. What's your fee?"

Lindsey wrote some figures on a napkin and passed it to LeFreaux, who took one look then exhaled loudly.

"Man, you are pricey."

"That's because I'm good. If I don't meet your expectations, you have a money back guarantee. Half now, the other half when I've finished. Sixty day maximum."

"You mean —"

Lindsey interrupted. "Yeah, if I haven't done the job to your satisfaction within sixty days you'll get your money back or we'll re-negotiate."

LeFreaux clasped and unclasped his hands, waited several seconds then in a lowered voice, "Fair enough. Here's what I want you to do."

An hour later the meal and the deal concluded, LeFreaux returned to his office. Jake Lindsey left the restaurant with a thirty thousand dollar check and sixty days to earn it.

_____

"Chips, I want you to manage the store," Lindsey directed his associate, Chips O'Donnell. "I don't know how much I'll be around for the next couple of months. I've taken on a surveillance job for a big time operator here in Boston. I mean big time, a suite of offices, top floor. Oh, and Bennie," Lindsey walked over to his secretary's desk, "please deposit the check in our account."

Bennie grinned. "Great, boss. No rubber checks this month."

"So, what are we doing to earn this serendipity?" Chips asked.

"Raymond LeFreaux wants his son followed, protected from a distance. He doesn't know what the kid's into."

Chips gave a soft whistle. "LeFreaux Investments! Wow! You're in the big game, Charley Brown."

If Lindsey was duly impressed, he did not show it. "Bennie, what do I have that's active?"

"That's easy, boss. The insurance case got settled. You'll be happy to know old man Inkman doesn't want his wife tailed anymore. Chips is still on the traffic accident. Right, Chips?"

O'Donnell nodded.

"Okay. Call me on my cell if the Third World War starts, or something like that. I'm on a plane to Vancouver this afternoon."

"Jake, we're not licensed in Canada."

"I know. I'm going to Vancouver, Washington."

"Where the hell is Vancouver, Washington?"

"Across the river from Portland, Oregon. I'll keep in touch."

"LeFreaux, have a beer."

"Thanks, Al. I need a break from this damn computer. Searching for ancestors is a royal pain in the ass. I thought digging in Indian mounds was hard."

"That's one of the things I want to talk to you about. If you and my collectively unconscious wife have the wherewithal, there is an easier way to get started."

"I'm listening," Jon replied.

"The Mormon Church is in the genealogy business. From what I understand they have turned dead people into assets beyond tithing of the faithful."

"Good idea. Thanks."

"LeFreaux, I'm flying to Arkansas tomorrow. I'll be gone for a week or so. Big construction project."

"Oh," Jon asked. "What kind of construction?"

"Bridge over the Arkansas River. The thing was smashed to bits during a recent flood. Ten inches of rain in two hours."

"Yeah, yeah. I remember reading about it." Jon watched the computer icon fade.

"Al, thanks for tolerating my living with you folks. Your wife is persuasive." He paused, "But she may be on to some weird stuff."

"I was against it. I'm still not convinced you two will find anything of substance."

"Yeah, I know," Jon replied.

"Another thing, LeFreaux…"

"Hey, call me Jon, please. LeFreaux makes me sound almost alien to this undertaking."

"Okay, Jon." Al emphasized 'Jon', "I'm not entirely comfortable leaving my wife in the house with a man who is practically a stranger."

"My God, man!" Jon's voice rose. "Don't you trust your wife?"

"It's not her that I worry about. I'm not sure I trust you. I think you're a rolling stone or worse. For all I know you may be a serial killer."

Jon's face flushed. "I'll have my shit packed within the hour and be out of your hair." He turned to walk away.

"Don't leave, LeFreaux. I'll work on my attitude. I love my wife. Whatever she undertakes, I support. Understand my feelings. I'm working on getting to like you. Give me time. Hey, I know you're not a serial killer. I've never heard of an archeologist who put people into the ground." He smiled weakly and offered a handshake. "Okay?"

Jon accepted Al's hand. "Al, I know what's bothering you. I can assure you I have no sexual interest in your wife." Jon felt his facial muscles grow tense, as was always the case when he was entangled in ambiguity. "You're sure you're not gonna anchor me down with your resentment?"

"Yep. And, uh — if and when I feel any resentment, I'll try to cover it up with my usual charm."

"Fair enough."

"So, how long will this search take?"

"In most cases," the genealogist replied to Jon, "We can give you initial findings within a week. We have an enormous data bank."

Jon cradled the telephone and resumed reading the theoretical writings of Carl Jung. He glanced at his watch. He had just spent an hour giving a Mormon genealogist what little information he could recall about his family. For most of his life, he cared not for his own roots, though he had made it his life's work to probe into the ancient bones of others.

The glaring characteristic he shared with Al was an appreciation for substance. With Jon, if it couldn't be carbon dated or chained historically, it was suspect. In Jon's profession, cynicism was the meat of archeology.

As he tried to understand Jung, he doubted his own motivations. Until he met Constance, his only aim was to gain another dig, somewhere, sometime. Today, he wasn't sure he was searching for ancestry, or a way to stay involved with a woman and a project, both of which he considered at best to be a chase for wild geese. At the very least, his cynicism had been blunted.

The more he read Jung, the more fascinated he became. He was beginning to understand how Constance became hooked. Jung, the theorist, had idolized Sigmund Freud early on, but had fractured the friendship when he refuted Freud's notion of a repressed sexual society. Jung's theory was so complex that Jon's reading became laborious and repetitive in an effort to make sense of Jung. But Jung, the man, was becoming a magnet to Jon. Jung, the man, had analyzed over sixty-eight thousand dreams; had treated and been treated in mental hospitals; had steeped himself in medical science as well as Eastern mysticism. Above all, Jung's notion that some dreams were keys to the collective unconscious would drive Jon in his quest for ancestry.

The three of them drank their coffee, safe inside a Vancouver Starbucks, away from a cold, dank morning. The conversation had been light until Connie blurted, "Al, I'm taking a sabbatical to do some research in Scotland."

Al coughed, strangling momentarily on his coffee. "Scotland, good God! I thought the genealogists were going to do the work for you two." He raised his voice to Jon. "I suppose you're going with her!"

"Nope. I'm going to Montreal. The genealogists took my paternal grandfather, several times removed, as far as Canada. The trail faded from there."

"Al, please keep your voice down. I'm going to Scotland to look up a distant cousin on my mother's side. According to the genealogists, Michael MacTavish is a part of that family tree. The genealogists didn't have any luck looking for my father's roots."

Al shook his head slowly from side to side, as if resigning from the moment. "I'm trying to understand what you're doing, but it's damn hard to do. I'm selfish, Connie. I'll be apart from you for longer than I care to think about. Honestly, I hate the idea."

He paused, sipping at his coffee. "Our bed will be empty without your warm body. If I weren't committed to a couple of contracts, I'd go with you."

Connie reached across the table to place her hand against Al's cheek. "I'll miss you, too. I'll call you regularly, I promise. Hey, I may not even have to use all of my sabbatical time."

"Geez, Al. Will you miss me too?" A tinge of sarcasm behind Jon's grin.

"In a weird way, yes," Al replied. "I've enjoyed your cooking and I haven't had to do any housework for the last month."

Chapter  Eight

The Oloroso Restaurant was set atop a roof, offering a view of Castle Street and beyond. Connie glanced at her watch. Michael MacTavish said he would join her for lunch at noon. Already, he was late and Connie was irritated.

Shortly before 1:00 p.m., as Connie was about to give up on him, MacTavish walked to her table. "The maitre d' pointed you out to me." He extended his hand. "I'm Michael."

"I'm Connie and I was about to conclude that you weren't going to show."

The pique in her tone caused MacTavish to grin. "Ah, you said noon. That covers a bit of time in Scotland, don't you know." His Scottish accent came in quick bursts. "So, you're my cousin from faraway shores."

His scruffy appearance belied his gentlemanly manners. "May I sit?" he asked as he removed his tam.

"Yes, please do." Connie's irritation was short-lived. "Thank you for meeting me. I was about to order. Perhaps you can suggest the best fare."

"Well, I dare say, if you wish to experience a touch of the Highlands, you'll try the Haggis."

"Oh," Connie contracted her mouth. "I don't think I can handle sheep gut."

"That, my dear, is a misconception shared by those who believe French propaganda. Haggis is a mixture of sheep internals, heavily spiced, laced with oatmeal, onions and other herbs. You must try it."

"Which internals?"

"If you must know," he teased, "the heart, the lungs, and now and again whatever a chef may decide to throw in."

"Sounds frightening to me," Connie said. "I believe I'll have the cod," she paused. "Assuming the chef hasn't decided to get creative."

"Sure, Lass. But you can't return to your country unless you try the haggis."

"In that case," Connie grinned, "I may just take up residence. By the way, cousin, you're not wearing a kilt."

"I say," Michael retorted, "you won't see me in one without a ceremony of some kind."

"Oh, and when you wear that kilt," Connie teased, "Do you wear, uh — underclothing? I've heard you Scots disdain underwear."

"Well now, Lass, don't believe everything you hear and I'll never illuminate you." He motioned for the waiter.

"So, my long lost cousin, what are we to talk about?"

"A man named Carl Jung and a dream. Are you familiar with Jung?"

"I know he was a psychoanalyst of some repute," MacTavish responded. "That's about the length and breadth of my knowledge. Never studied much Jung at Oxford."

For the next hour, Connie described Jung's theory, concluding with her recurrent dream.

"All very fascinating, cousin. But, what does that have to do with Michael MacTavish?"

"Michael, you're my ancestral thread. I want to know from whence I came. I want you to help me in any way you can. I want you to advise me by suggesting people and places from the past. My genealogy search has hit a dead end. But there must be some way to discover how I came to be in America. I know I didn't just pop out of nowhere."

MacTavish said nothing, seeming to examine in detail the wall behind Connie, while she squirmed.

"I can pay you for your time and effort."

"Oh, no," he countered quickly. "I don't need your money. I'm, how do you Americans say, very well off. My silence was not a discount of your request. I was thinking ahead. Of your request, I say."

"Then you'll help me?"

"Yes, of course. Allow me to rearrange my schedule. Do you have lodging?"

"Not yet. I was about to ask your recommendations."

"We'll have none of that. Our blood ties are a bit diluted, I suppose, but I insist that you lodge at my manor. 'Tis the least I can do. You've come a long way just to look into a dream." He clapped once. The waiter reappeared. "We'll both have the cod. A bottle of your best wine. A bit of sausage for dessert."

Connie reacted. "Sausage for dessert? I'll pass."

"No, no, cousin. That's the thing we call pudding. You'll love it."

As they drove to MacTavish's manor, Connie kept thinking they were due to crash head on with another vehicle driving on the wrong side of the road. It was causing discombobulation to her nervous system, manifested as a flinch every mile or so.

Set atop an archway in cast iron letters was the address of the MacTavish domicile: SONSIE. A short distance from there, the structure rose up before them, more than a mansion resembling a castle without battlements. As the Austin Healy rounded a slight bend, the North Sea came into view. Sonsie was set at the end of a narrow promontory.

"Michael, I'm almost speechless. What magnificence."

"Aye, I daresay, I never take this place for granted. Sonsie is Scottish for 'lucky'."

"Well, have you been lucky, other than living in the most beautiful residence I've ever seen?"

MacTavish smiled. "Oh yes. I was born into fortunate circumstances. All the wealth of my forebearers was passed down through the ages and landed in my lap. I've been able to grow that good fortune."

"Such as?" Connie asked.

"Well now, Lass, you are the inquisitive one. If you must know, my current ventures include shipping, banking, some manufacturing. Just enough to keep me busy."

"Yes, cousin. Inquiry is the curse of a university professor." She gave his arm a playful tap. "We never know enough. At least until we get tenure."

The interior of Sonsie was, for Connie, a walk into a bygone age. Inside the great room were clan flags hanging on the walls and various forms of statuary. Set in the center of the room was a long table, at the end of which stood two empty suits of medieval armor.

"Tell me about this place, Michael. Was it a castle at one time?"

"Yes, in an unusual way. You might say it was and is," he paused, "a poor man's castle. My ancestors were loyal to the English crown. I daresay if you believe Mel Gibson, we were the villains. Oh, allow me to introduce the household staff," he said, as he turned toward a small group to his left. "Chauncey Osgood, our butler. James Miller, who oversees all that transpires here at Sonsie. I believe you Americans would refer to him as the house manager, or some such. Jennifer Harrigan runs the house and her assistants are Mary Scarborough and Molly Jones," he pointed. "And this lady," he placed his arm around a rotund, older woman, "with the help of Oma and Kate," he nodded toward two younger women, "keep this place spic and span."

Michael placed his arm around an older man clad in overalls. "John Marley keeps up the garden and, oh by the bye, he's married to Emma who, as I mentioned, keeps the castle in good order." He turned to Connie. "This pretty lady is my cousin from America."

After a brief tour of the manor, Michael escorted Connie to her room. "Molly Jones will be your lady in waiting." He grinned. "Thought you'd like that, we haven't had a queen around here since my mum passed away. I know you're anxious to know if I'm married. I was. We divorced. End of story. You see that button next to your bed. Press it hard and Molly will be at your disposal."

"Oh, Michael, I want to call my hubby. Any special instructions about the phone?"

"No, no. 'Tis much like your American teles." He proceeded to write a series of numbers. "Once the exchange gives you the go ahead, you simply dial the number you wish." He laughed softly. "That'll get you over Hadrian's Wall."

Later that evening after two misfires, Al came on the line. "Al, can you believe it! I'm near Edinburgh staying at my cousin's manor. Before I tell you all about this place, write down the phone number. Uh, the uh, tele number, if you please."

Connie launched into a blow by blow account of her previous thirty-six hours, embellishing a description of the manor by referring to it as a castle.

Al seemed minimally impressed. "Please find your grail and come home soon. You have no damn business over there."

The next morning a soft knock on her bedroom door was followed by "Top of the morning' to ye ma'am. His Lordship will join you for breakfast at 9:00."

"Oh, God, Molly! It is Molly? Right? I just got to bed."

"Ma'am, ye're on our time, not yours. If ye're gon' to be on the Isle for a bit, ye'll be needin' to adjust them sheep you count. So come on out now."

"Okay. Okay. Tell his Lordship I'll be down shortly."

Set before Connie was a plate of biscuits, two boiled eggs, and a dish of marmalade. "After breakfast, we'll do the five pence tour. Perhaps that will stimulate your dream mechanism. I must warn you, however, we have no great white mountains."

"Not even in the Highlands?" Connie asked.

"Not anywhere on the Isle," Michael responded. "But we have history both actual and contrived."

"Contrived?"

"Yes, by poets whose imaginations blossomed beyond the truth, or so they say. Would you like to visit Perth as a start to your ancestral search?"

"If you recommend such. Any special reason?"

"Absolutely. You and I may be direct descendents of shenanigans as far back as the thirteenth century, or so it seems."

"What sort of shenanigans?"

"I'll tell you, but not all at once. We'll visit the Scone Palace near Perth."

"Scone Palace, built near the end of the eleventh century, is supposedly near the site of the Stone of Destiny. And, what is the scone stone story? Simply stated, it was the rock over which Royal Scottish asses were seated. According to legend, the scone stone was Jacob's pillar mentioned in the book of Genesis. It rather grew into a symbol of Scottish Nationalism."

Connie was transfixed by the enormous castle. "And this is where the stone is kept?"

"Oh, no!" Michael exclaimed. "Only a replica is on display here. The original stone is in Edinburgh Castle. Perhaps."

"What do you mean, perhaps?"

"Ah! Now we'll get to the meat of the matter and maybe just maybe, the involvement of one of our modern day ancestors. You see, cousin, the poetic tentacles of a possible conspiracy reach back through the centuries. A descendent of Patrick Hamilton, 'tis said with some authenticity, was one of four Scots who broke into Westminster Abbey in 1950 and absconded with the original Stone of Destiny, hoping to return it to this place where Scottish kings were enthroned."

Connie interrupted. "But, when you say back through the centuries…"

MacTavish continued, "In 1528 Patrick Hamilton was executed at the gate of St. Salvators College for professing the teaching of Martin Luther. Later we'll see the exact spot where he agonized for six hours at the stake. If you know any Scottish history, the entire Isle was one huge battleground where one clan fought another clan or the Protestants battled the Catholics. But, dear cousin, dig deep enough and it all boils down to Scotland and England vying for supremacy."

Chapter Nine

As Michael and Connie set themselves to tour Sterling Castle, Connie stopped and, hands on hips, asked "Michael, I love these ventures across Scotland, but what about our ancestry?"

"Ah, Lass, you're needin' to be a wee bit more patient. I want you to experience this land, this history. You know, it has taken Scotland several centuries to achieve independence. You and I descend from all that warring and power struggling."

"Michael, I've been here a week. I've interviewed several people who have no information relating to an ancestor who made his or her way to America."

MacTavish frowned. "I wish I knew the answer to your problem. You tell me that your genealogy reached a dead end with me. As I've told you, I don't know of a fore- bearer who crossed the ocean."

In her room that evening, Connie reviewed her notes. The people, the castles, the towns and cities all had become a miasma of events, none of which seemed to relate to her night terror. She had been unable to unearth an ancestor who was involved in a murder.

In a snit of frustration, she tossed her notebook to the floor and reached for the bottle of scotch Molly provided earlier. After pouring the glass half full, she commenced to draw mental pictures from her weeklong stay in Scotland. From Michael, she learned that Michael and she had descended from a family of Mac-Tavishes who had served King James during his reign. Connie could account for her paternal ancestors from that time to her presence in Sonsie Manor. All in the paternal chain could be accounted for and living in Scotland. On the maternal branches of the tree, the trail grew cold in the middle of the nineteenth century.

Shortly after midnight, Connie drifted into a fitful sleep, during which her recurrent nightmare awakened her with a start. She crawled from under the heavy blanket and flipped the switch on the lamp next to her bed. Her heart raced; she was perspiring, even as the Scottish chill permeated the room. She glanced at her watch: 4:37. She lifted the telephone from its cradle and dialed a familiar number. She guessed that Al would be off the road and perhaps at home.

Three rings. "Hello." The voice was that of a female. Connie felt the blood drain from her face.

"Who is this?"

Instead of an answer, there was a click at the other end.

Connie felt queasy as she rushed into the bathroom. She gagged twice. After nothing came up, she splashed water on her face.

"The son of a bitch!" Anger began to replace shock. "I'm barely out of the house and the bastard brings a female in!"

She dialed her home number once more. Al answered after the first ring.

"God, Al. How long has this been going on?"

"Doesn't matter." His voice was angry, unrepentant. "I've made a decision. You made it easy for me when you went off on your wild goose chase."

"You prick!" Connie shouted into the telephone. "All the things you said. All the events we celebrated! Were you ever in love with me?"

"At one time, yes. Before you fell in love with Carl Jung. That's when you left me."

For an instant, there was silence.

"What do you mean? You've made a decision?"

"I'm filing for a divorce," he answered.

"That's it? Just like that. No easing into it. No 'let's talk about it Connie?'"

Al didn't respond.

Connie continued, "I can't believe this is happening to me."

"To us, Connie. That's part of the problem. It's always been about you. You'll get the papers soon. I don't want a damn thing from you, except your signature on those papers."

The telephone went dead.

Connie poured scotch until the glass was full. "Damn! First one nightmare then another!"

By sunrise her anger had subsided. The bottle of scotch was almost empty and she had a splitting headache. She entered the bathroom and turned on the gas heater. She stood motionless as she watched the nineteenth century tub begin to fill. After a few minutes, the water neared the top of the tub. She lowered herself through the rising steam and gave herself to the soothing warmth of a Scottish bath.

I'm not crying, she thought. Why the hell am I not crying? The anger she felt earlier was suppressed now in bath water. Was I angry because Al is divorcing me? She covered her nose and lowered her head into the water. After a few seconds she came up for air.

"By God!" she exclaimed loudly. "I'm rid of the boring bastard!" She knew at that instant the reason for her short lived anger: she hadn't the courage before to make the decision that Al had made.

"Hallelujah! I'm free! Damn him for getting there first!"

A knock on the bathroom door disrupted Connie's oral celebration.

"Mum, are you well? I heard your scream. Are you well?"

"It's okay, Molly. I was letting the world know that I'm suddenly excruciatingly happy."

"Yes, Mum. What would ye like for breakfast?"

Connie pondered a moment. "Cereal, uh — porridge, I think, and uh, rye toast and marmalade. And please, Molly, I want coffee rather than tea."

"Yes, Mum."

Michael was well into his meal by the time Connie walked into the breakfast nook.

"Good morning to you, cousin. Molly tells me you were flowing over with joy. Did you perhaps unearth those ancestors you've been dreaming about?"

"Nope," Connie answered. "Better than that. My husband wants a divorce."

"And that makes you happy?"

"You bet. No more having to tell him where I'm going and when I return, where I've been. He never understood why I couldn't just be a…" Connie signaled quotation marks "normal housewife."

"Then you're okay. Do you need to share anything, or some such, as you Americans say?"

"Not at all, Michael. But I do need to get back to the task at hand. So, I plan to do some Bible reading. I'm not that familiar with the good book. You mentioned something earlier about the Stone of Destiny. Where…"

Before she could finish her sentence, Michael responded. "Genesis. I can't tell you chapter and verse. Mayhaps 'tis a good time to brush up on the scriptures," he chortled.

"Michael, you've kept me in suspense regarding Patrick Hamilton. Each time I've brought his name to the fore, you become dismissive or change the subject. I know from my research that he was executed for preaching the so called heresy of Martin Luther. I know that he was only twenty four years old when he got roasted. I know that he descended from a royal line; one of the James's, as I recall."

Michael gave her a disdainful look.

"You Americans do cut quickly to the chase. Quite grossly, I might add. Roasted indeed!"

"Michael, please don't send me off to more castles or more tomes about Scotland without good reasons. Carl Jung and I have more important things to do."

Michael glared at Connie, but said nothing for a moment. He pushed away from the breakfast table, then stood behind her before he spoke. "I have been disingenuous with you because what I am about to tell you is in statistical terms, extrapolation beyond the data. You Americans sometimes refer to it as an urban legend.

"It has been rumored down through the ages that Patrick Hamilton sired an illegitimate son, whose mother was descended from an illegitimate union of Robert Bruce and a maid of his castle named, perhaps, Lorilane, she of an ancient MacAlpin clan."

Connie interrupted. "So you're saying that you and I may be descended from Patrick Hamilton?"

"Not necessarily," Michael cautioned. "But it was worth my efforts to find if it were so. But allow me to continue. In 1950 when the four energetic young Scots took the Stone of Destiny, they returned it to the High Altar of Arbroath. There, cousin, somewhere on the grounds of those ruins is where William the First was interred. Also, it is the site where the Declaration of Arbroath was written, perhaps the greatest document proclaiming Scottish independence from England, the Pics, the Vikings, all of whom until then had been unable to subdue the Scots."

Michael sat back down and summoned Molly. "Be a dear and bring us more tea."

"Uh — coffee for me, Molly," Connie rejoined, as she and the kitchen maid exchanged winks.

"That declaration of Freedom in 1320 proclaimed a two-thousand year, 113 Feng Dynasty reaching all the way back to Jacob and ancient Egypt. When those lads retrieved the Stone from Westminster in 1950, they affirmed their belief that the Stone of Destiny was proof of Scottish longevity."

"Thank you, my dear," MacTavish said to Molly as she placed the tea and coffee before them. After a sip, he continued. "According to one part history and one part tale told down through the ages, one of our ancestors may have been involved in the murder of the Scottish King Alexander III. The official version of his death at that time was that he fell from his horse while riding at night to see his wife at Kinghorn.

"The more conspiratorial possibility is that Alexander was pummeled to death by four assassins; three Vikings, who were supposedly angry at the rapprochement between Scotland and the Vikings and one Scot who conspired with Edward I of England. Are you following me thus far, cousin?"

"Yes," Connie replied. "And I'm sure that soon you'll get to the bottom line that affects you and me."

Michael ignored the barb. "Thor Amundson, so the legend goes, was a bastard descendent of the Viking king, Haakon IV. Thor was one of the alleged assassins. If we are to believe in the blood line down to us it goes like this: Thor Amundson's daughter was made pregnant by William the Lion's son. That offspring daughter may have been the mother of an illegitimate son sired by Patrick Hamilton."

Michael shrugged. "So there, as you colonials say, in a nutshell, is the ancestral story. All wrapped up in a set of foggy estimates and tales told around servings of haggis."

"Michael, this is absolutely fascinating. But you don't have any idea about what happened to the Jane Doe of my branch in the nineteenth century?"

"Saw no need. My great great grandfather never spoke of her. She was his first wife. The family register indicates that she just up and left. Possibly went to Ireland. Great great grandfather was married to my great great grandmother. Your maternal ancestor in that scenario may have roots to the north, from scraps of information passed on about her. Her maiden name may have been Nordstram, or Nordal, or Andresen. As you can imagine she became a pariah on our family tree."

He pulled a sheet of paper from his jacket and passed it to her. "I've written some names of natives hereabout in whom you may be interested. Don't you know, Connie, so much of the Scottish culture is recorded in history books, but embellished by folklore. You'll be needing to check into the folklore."

He handed her a key. "This will let you in through the kitchen area. I'll be away on business for a few days, but I trust you'll stay with us. You've added a bit of luster to this manor."

Connie arose from the table and hugged Michael effusively. "Thank you. My heavens! When the genealogist gave me your name, I never dreamed I'd be so fortunate."

Michael stiffened, then placed one arm around Connie. "Good show. Good show."

The Bible was old; worn thin by time and use. The cover was embossed in gold. Centered was a coat of arms: red, green, and maize.

Connie opened it carefully to the page Michael had marked with a ribbon of golden silk. It held the entries of the MacTavish family tree. At the very top was "Yolande, widow of Alexander III; child of Robert IV and Conitesse de Montfred. Birthed John MacTavish, a bastard; father unknown; denied officially; father unknown."

Eventually, Connie read through another lengthy tree outlining the MacMalcolm dynasty, the Bruces, King Edward I, David II, James Edward Red Gauntlet, and to the Ian entry: 1842 A.D. George MacTavish married Yolande but there was no entry of the maiden name for George MacTavish's first wife. It was noted that at the time of her flight, she was pregnant.

Connie glanced at her watch. 10:42. She turned the wafer thin pages to Genesis 28:10 - 22 and commenced to mouth the words softly.

"And Jacob went out from Beersheba and went toward Haran. And he lighted upon a certain place, and tarried there all night, because the sun was set; and he took of the stones of that place, and put them for his pillows, and lay down in that place to sleep. And he dreamed, and behold a ladder set up on the earth, and the top of it reached to heaven and behold the angels of God ascending and descending on it. And, behold, the Lord stood above it, and said, I am the Lord God of Abraham thy father, and the God of Isaac: the land where on thou liest, to thee will I give it, and to they seed; And thy seed shall be as the dust of the earth, and thou shalt spread abroad to the west, and to the east, and to the north, and to the south: and in thee and in thy seed shall all the families of the earth be blessed. And, behold, I am with thee, and will keep thee in all places whither thou goest, and will bring thee again into this land; for I will not leave thee, until I have done that which I have spoken to thee of. And Jacob awaked out of his sleep, and he said, Surely the Lord is in this place; and I knew it not. And he was afraid, and said, How dreadful is this place! This is none other but the house of God, and this is the gate of heaven. And Jacob rose up early in the morning, and took the stone that he had put for his pillows, and set it up for a pillar, and poured oil upon the top of it. And he called the name of that place Bethel: but the name of that city was called Luz at the first. And Jacob vowed a vow, saying, If God will be with me, and will keep me in this way that I go, and will give me bread to eat, and raiment to put on, So that I come again to my father's house in peace; then shall the Lord be my God: And this stone, which I have set for a pillar, shall be God's house: and of all that thou shalt give me I will surely give the tenth unto thee.'"

She closed the Bible, muttering to herself as she lit a cigarette. "Ain't that something? Old Jacob also had a dream."

Deep into the night, having gone to bed, then tossing and turning unable to sleep, Connie slipped from her covers to light a cigarette. She was not sure where next to turn. It would take some time for Al to get the divorce papers in the mail, she assumed.

Even if he stalls, she thought, I can take all the time I need to look them over to make sure he doesn't take me to the cleaners.

She strode to her desk, feeling her way in the dark. Forthwith, she located the lamp switch. She scanned the names Michael had written down. To the side of each was a locality and a brief note.

-John Angus; Kinghorn; loves to reminisce

-Mary MacGuffy; Berwick-upon-Tweed; eccentric, wordy, thinks she knows every thing

-Benjamin Smith; Sterling; knows every detail of the Sterling Castle and history; King James executors

At the last, Michael had written:

"Perhaps this will give you a start."

Chapter Ten

The bed and breakfast Jon had selected was built in 1723 and since converted into an inn. The Auberge Les Passants du Sans Soucy offered Jon not only a comfortable living space, but, also, a touch of Ancient Gaul, with mortared stone walls, a skylight, and buffed wooden floors, and upon entering, a French Art Gallery.

Jon had enjoyed his breakfast of chocolate croissants. Now, it was time to go to work. After several rings, a male voice came on the line. "Bon jour, Maison Laforge."

"Mr. Laforge, this is Jon LeFreaux. I spoke to you earlier on the phone. I arrived in Montreal last evening. Will it be possible for us to meet?"

"Oui. Yes, yes. Of course. You are a distant cousin of my wife, I understand. Up from the States?"

"You bet. Tell me where and when."

"Do you know the Auberge du Viex port? No! No! I'm sorry. Of course you don't. Where are you staying?"

"I'm registered at a marvelous little B and B, the Auberge Les Passants du Sans Souci," Jon answered.

"Good! I have a business lunch appointment at noon at the Auberge du Viex Port. It's about six blocks from Sans Souci. I'll meet you in the lobby at, let's say, 2:30. Okay?"

With a few hours to kill, Jon decided to walk around old Montreal. Though the people he passed on the street appeared no different from those in any American city, the banter was mostly French.

"Oui. Laissez les bon temps roulez. So much for my French," he muttered.

Jon's walk along the streets of Vieux Montreal reminded him of the adage that Montreal was the Paris of North America. He treaded softly into the Basilique Notre

Dame. He smiled inwardly as he contemplated the notion of a Canadian hunchback screaming from the battlements "Sanctuary! Sanctuary!"

He marveled at the history set forth in the Pointe-A-Calliere. There he was in his realm: history under-girded by archaeology. Shortly before 2:30 p.m. Jon entered the lobby of the Auberge du Viex Port. He didn't have a long wait. The portly man who approached him gave a tentative "Are you Mr. LeFreaux? Jon LeFreaux."

"Yes," Jon extended his hands. "Thanks for meeting with me. If I'm to believe my genealogical search, your wife and I are kin. Well maybe not kissing cousins, but distant relatives."

Jon felt his face flush. Jesus, that was lame.

Jon was relieved when Martin Laforge laughed. "Well, Jon LeFreaux, I'm always pleased to meet a long lost cousin on my wife's side. And you look prosperous enough that I'm not fearful you are after our fortune. Have you had lunch? This place does a marvelous salmon salad."

"Yes, I had a sandwich at a bistro down the street. Thanks."

Jon was caught up in an awkward silence. Digging up artifacts required careful lifting, handling and dusting. He was an amateur at digging up ancestors. "So," he ventured as he glanced at the artwork in the lobby, "Are you a native — Canadian?"

"Why yes, yes I am. My forebearers and my wife's ancestors also came from Scotland in the middle of the nineteenth century. Tell you what, let's have a drink at the bar and we'll talk a little blood line, eh."

As they slid into the luxurious leather seats of the booth, Laforge inquired, "Is ancestor hunting a full time job, or do you have other pursuits?"

"I'm an archaeologist on sabbatical. As you are probably aware, root hunting is big back in the States. I consider the present to be a good time to search," he paused "and I've always wanted to visit Canada."

"I'm glad you're here, Jon. As I mentioned on the phone we have a pretty detailed genealogy of her branch going back a few centuries. We've been at it for several years."

Jon felt a surge of enthusiasm. "Great. Could I have a look at your genealogy records?"

"You bet. When we leave here I'll drive you to our place. We, that is Annette and I, have an estate out in the country."

"Annette. Your spouse? My kin?"

"Yep. Great gal. You'll love her."

The Laforge residence was an estate like no other Jon had seen or imagined. An electronically controlled gate opened up to a lengthy driveway on either side of which was a variety of flora and beyond that gently rolling grassland. "Nice place you have here," Jon observed with as much savior faire as his nervous system would allow.

"Yes. Yes, we like it. It was my wife's good fortune to have been the only offspring of Adrian O'Shaughnessy. He came to Canada around the middle of the nineteenth century, started a cement business and became obscenely wealthy. He didn't marry until he was fifty years old. Married a young thing. Annette came along when he was sixty."

"Are you still in the cement business?"

"We own sixty percent of the company."

He pushed the garage opener. Jon counted four other automobiles in the garage.

"But that's not my main interest at present. Annette and I own a ranch in Alberta out from Calgary. We raise lots of beef, much of which is shipped to the States via a rail line in which she and I own the controlling interest."

"Well," Jon said, "I suppose you are only partly teasing when you alluded to your fortune."

"Very astute of you, Jon. Let's go in and have you meet Annette."

The woman who greeted them in the great room was straight from the Hollywood back lot: tall, slender, jet-black shoulder length hair, pearl white teeth.

"Nettie, this is the man that purports to be your cousin. He's doing a genealogy search. I've agreed to help him."

Annette extended her hand to Jon. "So you're Jon LeFreaux. What is the purpose of your ancestral venture?"

Jon felt the warmth of her hand and she continued to hold his beyond what Emily Post would recommend. Jon experienced a twinge of discomfort. "I forgot to tell you, Jon," Martin interrupted, "My wife has a habit of cutting quickly to the chase."

Jon eased his hand from Annette's casual grip. "I could tell you a cock and bull story that I have a sentimentally rooted interest in my family tree. The truth is much more interesting. I'm working with a psychologist. We're trying to find the possible origin of a dream. Are you familiar with the teachings of Carl Jung?"

Neither Laforge responded immediately. "This is such a coincidence," Annette responded, "I believe Jung would describe it as an event of synchronicity. I've read most of Jung's works — well, read at them — and I've undergone two years of analysis. I have a journal filled with dream content."

By now Annette's initial stiffness was giving way to guarded casualness. Her smile which did not accompany Jon's introduction, seemed genuine to him. "Do you ever have bad dreams? You know, nightmares, night terrors?" he asked.

"Oh, yes." She turned to her husband, "Martin has been awakened often by my screaming. Isn't that right, dear?"

"Sure as the dickens I have. I know her dream all too well."

Jon was uncertain at first how much he should share with them. As was usually the case, he found it difficult to trust vague suppositions and theories with loose ends. "Dr. Nordstram and I met at an archaeological convention. Oh, did I mention, yes I did," Jon fumbled for wording. "I'm an archaeologist. As a matter of fact, I'm on an involuntary sabbatical. I went to that convention hoping to catch on to a dig or a project of some kind. Anyway, during Dr. Nordstram's keynote address she described in detail her recurrent dream, nightmare, if you will. It was almost exactly the same as the dream I have periodically." Jon paused, uncertain as the amount of information he should give out. Briefly he continued, "We have the same dream set in an era long past. We are gathering as much data as genealogy and personal search will allow."

"Jon," Martin asked, "Would you like a drink? Wine, beer, hard stuff?"

"Red wine, if you have some. I'll wait until you return."

"No, no, go ahead. This is fascinating. I'm anxious to hear all about the dream."

Martin walked behind the bar and emerged with a glass of wine for Jon.

Jon faced a quandary: tell all or give tidbits. Quickly, he decided to open up. In detail he recounted the dreams of Connie and himself. As Jon reached that part of the dream where the four horsemen are riding toward him, Annette Laforge could contain herself no longer.

"Well! This is odd. You're describing that part of a dream that has bothered me all my life!" She turned to face her husband. "Martin, you've blabbed, haven't you? Surely, you've told Jon. Or, you told someone and Jon gained access to the story. Isn't that right?"

"No, no, my dear. I've done no such thing. I've honored your request that I not tell anyone."

Annette stared hard at Jon. "You know my analyst, don't you?"

"I do not," Jon replied, surprised by her sudden inquisition. "I've told you the truth about my reasons for being here. If I've caused you discomfort, I'm sorry."

Martin interrupted, "I'd like to know more about your dream."

Annette ignored him. Her gaze was riveted upon Jon. She waited briefly. "Of course, I'm sorry I reacted the way I did."

"Ah, yes, Jon," Martin grimaced, "My wife is sometimes La Belle Dame Sans Merci."

"And that says? I took Spanish. My French is nonexistent."

Annette touched Jon's arm. "He said sometimes I'm tough when I think my privacy is being invaded. We'll talk tomorrow if you accept my apology and Martin's invitation. Now, I'll show you to your room. Fair enough?"

"You bet," Jon replied, "and thank you."

Chapter Eleven

"LeFreaux, do you have time for a report? This is Jake Lindsey."

"Uh, Mr. Lindsey. Yes I do. Thanks for calling."

"As you recall when I reported to you from Vancouver, Washington, your son was living with a man and his wife, Al Nixon and Connie Nordstram. As per your instructions, I've not been intrusive."

"Where is Jon now?" LeFreaux asked.

"Yeah," Lindsey answered, "I'm getting to that. Two days ago he flew to Montreal. After a bit of inquiry and some bribery, I discovered him meeting with a man, Martin Laforge, who has since put your son up in one hell of a mansion."

Lindsey gave a brief pause. "Mr. LeFreaux, did your son give you any information regarding his travel intentions?"

"No, I've never questioned how he uses the money his mother and I give him. I have no idea what he is doing. Perhaps I should have asked."

Lindsey ignored the obvious. "There's nothing extraordinary about Nixon and Nordstram. He's an engineer with Markum Construction. An outfit specializing in bridge building. His wife is a professor in the Liberal Arts College of Washington State University and she kept her maiden name evidently for professional reasons. I did some checking. Neither has a rap sheet. She got a speeding ticket once. I'll be doing a rundown on the Laforge's this week. Should I approach Jon directly?"

"No, no!" LeFreaux blurted, "Not at all. No. No. It would embarrass both of us."

"Oh, it wouldn't bother me."

"I meant my son and me."

"Of course," Lindsey replied, feeling foolish.

Soon after talking to LeFreaux, Jake Lindsey called his secretary. After two rings Bennie Rochelle answered, "Lindsey Agency, may I help you?"

"Bennie, I'm in Montreal. Is Chips close by?"

"I'll ring him. Jake, we miss you around here. Hope you are having fun cavorting hither and yon."

"You know better, Miss Smarty. I'm working hard."

"I'm on the line, Jake," Chips interrupted.

"Chips, I don't know what's going on in this case. At present I'm trailing around the poor little rich kid of old man LeFreaux, but nothing's happening out of the ordinary. The guy goes from Rhode Island to Washington, meets up with a duo in Vancouver, then flies to Montreal. At this moment he is staying with a couple named Laforge."

"Well now," Chips laughed. "If you get too bored, I'll come in off the bench for you."

"I'll get by, old buddy. Here's what I want you to do. Check all the financial registers that list LeFreaux and Laforge. From Watergate I remember the adage, 'Follow the money'. Get back to me as soon as you can."

"Let me remind you, pard, you're not licensed in Canada."

"I know," Jake countered. "I'll stay out of trouble."

Annette's demeanor had changed. Jon was hesitant to engage her. He sipped at his coffee, waiting for her to converse about anything other than horses and Canadian weather. Abruptly, she exclaimed, "Really, Mr. LeFreaux, why are you ancestor hunting? I doubt your dream story."

Jon was not ready for her quick conversational thrust. "I, uh, why are you so, uh, what can I say, so skeptical?"

"You're traveling about Canada over a dream tests my limits of credulity. You could be just one more grifter after our money. If so, I must say you are creative."

By now Jon's guard was up. He would tell the Laforge's nothing more of his mission, especially the grisly details of the dream. "Annette, I assure you I'm not a con man. I'm an archaeologist in league with a psychologist. I come from a wealthy family in Boston. Your money is the last thing I need. But I would appreciate your help in tracking down our ancestors."

Annette's conclusion to their morning tete-a-tete did not surprise Jon. "You're welcome to stay here one more day, then I want you to leave. I must get to a meeting of a charity that Martin and I sponsor. I wish you well in your quest."

"You don't wish to compare dreams, notes or history?" Jon asked. "Is that correct? Are you willing at least to point me to another relative or a record of some kind?"

"I'm sorry Mr. LeFreaux," she replied. "I can offer you no further assistance. If you are still at our home this evening, you're invited to dinner."

Jon watched her walk to her chauffeured limo. No, he said to himself, I won't be around for dinner. But Annette Laforge had reinforced Jon's archaeological mien. She had inspired him to dig below his new found layer of suspicion.

Chapter Twelve

John Angus, as Michael predicted, loved to reminisce. Once Connie introduced herself and stated her reason for meeting him, he commenced a narrative from which Connie gained scant information. He spoke of his first memories from the time he was five years of age. By the time he had moved himself half way through the twentieth century, Connie was able to work her way into the conversation. "Mr. Angus, you have indeed lived a full life. I want to ask you some specific questions."

"Full life indeed, ah Lass, ye speak as tho me life is over. Not a'tal it ain't. Me health is good. I plan to celebrate one hundred years."

"Forgive me Mr. Angus."

"Call me John."

"Okay, John. What do you know about the Stone of Destiny?"

"Ah yes. The stone. I was home from the war, maybe five years. Woke up one morning and there it was in the morning paper. Three lads and a lass had pilfered the stone from the English and brought it home. One of the lads lived right here in Kinghorn, he did. The way people made over him you would have reasoned for sure he'd be a reincarnation of old William Wallace himself."

"John, do you recall any details of that heroic event?" Connie asked.

"Heroic you say, ha! It was down right looney. That piece of rock they took from the abbey was a fake, so they say. The word is that no Scot in this day and time knows what happened to the real stone."

Connie remembered Michael's account of the fake stone conspiracy. Now, more than earlier, she was enthralled by the old Scot's narrative, even as his rambling probed Scottish history, little of which she believed related to the stone. But she did not want to discount the old man.

"Mr. Angus."

"Call me John, Lassie. Makes me feel young and out in the dell again."

"Well okay, John," Connie teased. "I see you as a young sprout right at this moment. Back to the stone. So why is the rock at Edinburgh thought to be a fake?"

Angus gave her a disapproving look. "Tisn't a rock lassie. It be a sacred stone that Jacob carried across all matter of desert."

"Okay, John. The stone. Do you believe it to be a fraud? The one at Edinburgh?"

"Indeed I do. And do ye want to know why? I'll tell ye. Old Jacob would have had the devil's own time without God's help carrying that Edinburgh stone around. That blessed stone weighs one hundred and fifty kilos. Now, ye don't just pack one of them things around on ye backside. Jacob, as you know, was a mere man. Do you know your Bible, Lass?" Not waiting for an answer he launched into a lengthy discourse on the book of Genesis.

Connie glanced at her watch, took a deep breath, and decided not to interrupt Angus. Drawing upon her knowledge of psychology, she concluded that in his own way he was catharting and would run down sooner or later. As she guessed, he became silent after a while. He stared into the distance. Connie guessed that he was going into his past. She reached across the ancient wooden swing to place a soft touch on his weathered hand.

"John, I'm amazed by your knowledge of the Bible. Also, you are a true historian."

"Thank you, my dear. What more do you wish to draw from me?"

Connie became aware that he was tired and momentarily used up. She decided to ask him one last question. "Can you give me a name of anyone who perhaps knows something about the Edinburgh stone possibly being a fake?"

"Sure, Lass. Old Ben Smith over in Sterling likes to tell folks that he knows everything about everything. He's a pedantic sort. I doubt he knows more than meself."

Yes, Connie thought, the older they get, the more childlike they become. My dog can bark louder than yours. "John, thank you for spending this time with me. I'd love to meet with you again. Can we do that?"

John's expression became animated. "Sure as can be. Any time you say, Lassie."

"How about the day after tomorrow? You and I can drive up to the castle. Would you like that?"

"Surely. But I ain't going to waste much of me time around Ben Smith. He spends too much of his life standing in his own light."

———————————————

"Molly, bring our guest a tankard of ale. I'll have one also." MacTavish directed his servant. "Now, Halloran, you were saying?"

The heavyset man across the table shifted in his chair. "Michael, I know the Lass is your cousin, but she's running around the countryside asking all sorts of questions. It gives me the heebies."

"Yeah, Michael," the second man declared in a strong voice, "The damnable colonials are like bulldogs. They ain't inclined to turn loose a notion. You know, Michael, she's denned up with old Angus."

"Yes, Paul, I know because I put her on to him."

"You did what!" Paul Barker exclaimed.

"Stay calm, Paul. You know as well as I nobody pays any attention to old John Angus. He's a looney of the first order. I gave Dr. Nordstram his name, plus others, because I knew in a matter of time his name would come up. You see, Paul, you allow her to discover a nugget or two and she won't think you are hiding the mother lode. And besides, she's at my place where I can keep an eye on her."

"Sure, and I trust you're right, Michael MacTavish," Patrick Halloran replied. "You know I haven't had a clean night's sleep in years. I have night terrors that we'll be found out."

Once Michael allayed to some degree their concerns, Barker and Halloran drank the last of their ale and bade Michael good night.

Pat Halloran, like Michael MacTavish was landed and wealthy. His associate, Paul Barker, managed the financial affairs of Halloran and was a part owner of Halloran's shipping company. The three of them had known each other from their days at Eton. Paul Barker occupied a peculiar place in the community. His cousin, so rumored, had helped to plan the theft of the stone purported to be the Stone of Destiny from Westminster Abbey in 1950. Periodically, that persistent rumor would bring out an enterprising investigative reporter who would poke around for a fortnight, then go home or be rammed by a train while crossing a railroad track. Nevertheless, the conspiratorial tale would not die.

Late into the night Barker drove Halloran to his estate then headed immediately across town. Orley O'Feely's small cottage was set in the middle of a ghetto where one spent time looking over his shoulder during daytime and hesitated to walk about at night. Barker was in the rogue zone of Sterling where dwelled thieves, pick-pockets and an occasional assassin. Barker had been told that O'Feely was a rogue for hire. Before Barker could knock a second time, he was slammed against the door and he could feel the pistol against his spine. "So, what brings you to me home? You're a dandy for sure. Now, ye might want to speak up, quick like. Otherwise, you'll be a dead dandy."

"That's what I want to talk to you about."

"You mean you want to die here and now?"

"No, No!" Barker whined. "I'm here to seek your services. Please don't kill me before you hear me out."

Paul Barker was frightened. "I-uh-I would like to engage your services," Barker said, as he wiped a bead of sweat from his brow.

O'Feely jammed the pistol hard against Barkers spine at the same time he placed a chokehold on him.

Without warning a terrified Paul Barker commenced to relieve himself, the urine spilling over his expensive Italian shoes.

"So, Dandy! Now you're pissin' on me stoop. Just what service do ye think I perform?"

"Please, you're choking me. A fellow who gave his name as Cinderman Charlie referred you."

O'Feely loosened his stranglehold and pulled the pistol away from Barker's back. "And what service did he tell you I could perform?"

Barker inhaled deeply as the spots before his eyes began to dissipate. "He-uh-he said-uh-you could erase problems."

"He did, did he now, and what matter of problem do ye wished to be erased?"

"A woman. But I don't want her killed. I want her frightened, so she will discontinue a-uh-project she's working on."

O'Feely began to laugh. "I was sure you was a copper afore you pissed you're pants. Come on in to my house. But don't ye seat your wet arse on me couch."

With Barker standing before the table at which O'Feely sat, O'Feely opened a notebook.

"What's your name and your business?"

Barker reached into his jacket pocket and handed O'Feely a card. After a quick perusal of the card, O'Feely asked, "What's her name and where can I locate her?"

Several questions later, O'Feely said, "Mr. Barker, I'll use the tele to reach you tomorrow. We may be able to do business if your story checks out. But," O'Feely jabbed Barker in the chest, "if ye're settin' me up, I'll do ye in. Do we understand one another, Mr. Dandy Barker?"

"Yes, sir, Mr. O'Feely. Certainly so." Barker nodded his head vigorously. "But, please don't do her bodily harm. I just want you to scare her," Barker directed.

"Oh, that'll be a walk," O'Feely replied.

The morning sunrise and Molly Jones awakened Connie following her fitful night's sleep. Her trip to Sterling for the second time had proved to be less than productive. Ben Smith pontificated at great length about the history of the stone, his information a template of every museum in Scotland. When Connie asked for information pertaining to Michael's grandfather and spouses, Smith pleaded ignorance.

The trip to Sterling had not been a total waste for Connie. In the short time she had known old John Angus, she had become enamored of him, as well as fascinated by his eccentric translations of the world around him. Cast adrift in the emotional void of a broken marriage offset by the excitement of a genealogical search, Connie had adopted a new father figure.

"I'll run your bath, Mum. Would ye like your tea now or when ye come down for your eats?" Molly asked as she entered the bathroom.

"I'll come down, Molly, and please call me Connie. Mum makes me sound like a stuffy old spinster. Also, I want you to have breakfast with me, so we can, as you Scots say, gab a bit."

"Why thank you, Mum, er, Connie. I'd like that. We'll have eats in the servant's nook off the galley, if that suits you."

"That's fine with me," Connie replied.

She continued to be put off by the British caste system, covered though it was with a veneer of old world civility. She enjoyed being catered to by Molly, though at times Connie would have enjoyed making her own sandwich or brewing her own tea. She had given up asking for coffee. When Molly reluctantly served it to her, it was usually lukewarm and weak, served through an attitude suggesting the Queen had been offended.

Molly was seated at the servant's table. When Connie walked in, she rose abruptly. "Mum, er, Connie, I have prepared a special breakfast for ye. I know how much ye like bagels and cream cheese and I got ye some strawberry jam. Oh, and I have a surprise for you. A pot of Maxwell House coffee."

"Molly, you are a dear. Thank you. That would be grand. And," Connie paused, "Ye-uh-you will join me for breakfast?"

"Yes, Mum. I'll be having a bit of haggis."

Connie knew at that point to give up on the "Mum" designation, but she was not going to add haggis to her morning fare.

"So, Molly, tell me about you. Have you been working for Michael very long?"

"Yes, Mum. This was me first and only placement. I like it here. Lord MacTavish is good to me."

"And, Molly, do you have a beau, you know — a, uh, male friend — uh, a lad?"

Molly's face reddened perceptibly. "Oh, sure, now. And he's a fine one, too. He's a copper, a constable. You'll see him now and again ridin' his bicycle."

"Molly, I'm being nosey. I'll stop that. What would you like to talk about?"

Molly frowned. "Don't rightly know, Mum. I've never had gab with me betters."

There was the strata thing again that so irked Connie. "Molly, I don't consider myself to be your better. If I haven't told you before now, I don't take your service for granted, though God knows, you do spoil me."

Molly smiled, obviously pleased that Connie had appreciated her work. "Mum, I don't know exactly why ye're here, but the gossip about town is that ye're interested in the old stone."

"I'm interested in my ancestors, dear girl. I don't know squat about stones and such. But you say there's gossip about my intentions?"

"Yes, Mum. And because ye're in my care, matter of speakin', maybe ye ought to know about some devilish happenin' hereabout the stone."

Connie's interest was peaked immediately. "Oh, I know the rumors around the theft of the stone from Westminster. Not much more than that. That's where my ancestor interest comes in. One of my relatives may have been involved."

"Lord MacTavish ain't told you what happened two years ago to some lads who went about the village inquiring about the stone?" She gave Connie a quizzical look. "And the old folks tell about them who comes inquirin' over the ages."

Connie felt her body stiffen. "Molly, what happened to the lads you're speaking about?"

"They met their maker whilst settin' on a track, they did." Molly crossed herself then continued. "The constable made a rulin' that the lads drove their lorry on the track and waited fer the next train to do them in. Suicide it was."

"Good heavens! What a gruesome way to commit suicide. There were no signs of foul play?"

"No, Mum. Not a tad, so they said." Molly glanced over her shoulder, then in a low voice, almost a whisper said, "Some say it was the curse of the stone. Some say back over the years, them who came inquirin' come to a bad end."

Connie was silent for an instant, framing her next question, "Molly, can you give me the names of the lads who were, uh — done in by a train?"

"Surely. They were newsmen, I think you Colonials call them reporters. They traveled from Stonehenge. As I remember, their names were Cornwall and Sittering. That's what I remember."

Later that evening, between main course and dessert, Connie questioned Michael about the men who died on a railroad track. Michael never blinked.

"My, my, Constance, you do roam about. Yes, the lads had been probing up and down the land about the stone. I'm not sure precisely as to the nature of their seeking. I should have mentioned it to you, but I considered it of no consequence to you in your search. You have to remember, dear Constance, the folk hereabouts are a mite superstitious. Ah, the curse of the stone, my eye. Oh, and about the news lads, the post-mortem found excessive drugs in their systems."

He rang the tiny dinner bell. "Please bring our tea. Oh, and coffee for our guest. Now, cousin, have you set your agenda? Where will you go next?"

"I'm going to drive over and pick up old Angus. He'll try to put me on the trail of something, real or imagined."

Molly placed their beverages before them.

"Constance, I regret that your search is not yielding the results you wish. Of course," Michael smiled as he touched her hand, "I'm ambivalent in my hopes for you. On the one hand, I wish you success, but I know, also, that I enjoy having you as our guest."

Connie felt a slight libidinal surge. Until that moment, she had not seen Michael as a potential lover. That was before today. Connie had not had sex for an indecent period of time, and Michael was a relatively attractive man.

"Thank you, Michael. You have been so kind to me. I love it here, and I'm enjoying the search, even though I've hit some dead ends." She leaned across the table and tugged gently at his arm. "I've needed these two weeks not just to look for ancestors, but also to get my personal life reorganized."

"I know," he answered. "I assume you returned the divorce papers you received a few days ago?"

"Yes, I did. How did you know?"

"The large envelope you received had a law firm return address. I took it from there."

Connie waited, not quite sure where the conversation was leading.

"Connie, would you like to attend the opera with me?"

"When?" she asked.

"This evening," he responded.

Connie had been enamored of Puccini from the first time she listened to his work on the Firestone Hour. She sat now enraptured by the aria of an Italian tenor whose name did not slide easily over her tongue. Subtly, softly, Michael placed his hand over Connie's. For an instant, she felt a tingle. As unobtrusively as the situation would allow she withdrew her hand slowly and reached into her handbag to pull out a tissue. She dabbed at her eyes to wipe away a non-existent tear.

"I'm sorry, Michael. That last part was so sad." She was ambivalent about a new intimacy. For now, she could remember only the comfortable sexual routine of the ex-husband she was learning to detest. As deftly as he had ventured into her psychological space, so now he backed away. He saw no need to be pushy. He would be patient.

"I'm sorry, my dear. I didn't realize you take your opera so seriously." His muffled laugh was forced. He had wanted to bed Connie from the first time he laid eyes on her.

She had not fooled him. "Michael," she whispered, "I'm sorry. I'm not ready. But I do find you," she tried to find the right word, "I do believe I'm, uh, fond of you." She felt her face grow warm.

"I'm flattered, Constance. Please don't mistake my intentions. I have no erotic designs on you," he lied. "Oh, and I'm fond of you also."

Chapter Thirteen

A month had passed since Connie arrived in Scotland. Michael had made love to her several times. She was confused by her feelings toward him. At certain times she felt to be the used and the user. At other times she was comfortable in his embrace. But, she was optimistic over the leads given by one villager or another. Days would pass between each faint hope and she would consider ending her search. Occasionally she would curse Jung for sending her to Scotland in the first place.

On this day, Connie was at a dead end once more. She decided to drive to her old friend's house and seek his company for a day. To Connie, John Angus was a stray. From her early childhood, Connie had always collected strays: cats, injured birds, frogs, any living organism that needed a haven. To Connie, John Angus was a lovable old stray who, though not the resource she had hoped, filled for her a day or two, here or there.

When she knocked on the door, Angus opened it immediately. Anytime Connie rang him up, he was always ready to go with her wherever she may lead. This day he was in a state of agitation, that being accompanied by a broad, sparkling smile.

"Aye, Lass. I been a waiting' for ye. Give ol' John his morning hug!"

Connie embraced the old man. She knew he had arisen at the crack of dawn and more than likely had been waiting by the door for the last hour.

"And how is my favorite man this morning?"

"Good, Lass. Good. And I've got a morsel for ye. I'll tell ye all about it in the car. Where do we go?"

"John, I think we'll drive up the coast if that suits you."

"It does, indeed. That way we'll be able to stop off in Arbroath. I have a lass I want you to meet."

"And why would I want to meet her, John Angus?"

"Oh, now, Constance! You'll see. Be patient if your colonial nature will allow."

Connie had learned early on that John Angus moved at his own pace. Even thought it frustrated her, it was a characteristic that charmed her.

"John Angus, you are being awfully mysterious. This lady must be special."

"She is that and you'll know when you meet her."

For the next sixty miles, Connie listened to Angus' narrative about the battle of Bannackburn. Occasionally, he would throw in a remembrance of the village where someone named Kathryn Digbe resided. After his second reference to Digbe, Connie asked, "And, who is this lady?"

"She's the one ye'll be a meetin'. Day afore yesterday, I was tellin' me kinsman about your cavortin' about in your search fer an ancestor. When I mentioned you were a kin of Michael MacTavish, Billy James — that's me kinsman — he told me that Katy Digbe might help you."

"So, what do you know about this lady?"

"Not a whit," he responded. "Except she's got one foot in the grave if I'm believin' my kin."

"She's ill?"

"Oh, no! Says my kin, she's, as you colonials say, a senior citizen."

When Connie drove into the Village of Arbroath, a Seattle style rain, along with a stiff wind, set a Scottish atmosphere for their entrance.

"Park this lorry right over there," Angus directed, as they approached an eatery. "You wait here. I'll inquire as to the whereabouts of Kathryn Digbe."

A short time later, he emerged grinning. Connie opened the door for him. "I thought I might have to go inside and rescue you."

"Ah, Lass, you're actin' colonial again. I had to warm the cockles of a few souls whilst I was seeking the lady lest the natives think I'm up to no good."

Connie laughed. "John Angus, you are a trip." She gave him a peck on his bearded cheek. "So? Did you find where she lives?"

"Now, yes I did. The lads say she lives about a mile down the road. They say to look for an old thatch-roof barn. Her dwelling is across the road from it."

The barn was old, unused, and worn out. Across from it was a small cottage fronted by a hedge row and a small yard filled with a variety of flora. A soft knock brought to the door an elderly woman; gray-haired, distinguished in appearance.

"Marnin' to you. What'll ye be needin'?"

Angus spoke first. "My oh my! You're even more of a beauty than I was told. Name's Angus; John Angus. This lass in an American doin' some genealogy searchin'. We think you may be able to help her."

Connie extended her hand. "I'm Constance Nordstram. So pleased to meet you."

Digbe's handshake was firm; her greeting wary. "Well, now, don't stand in the weather all day. Come in and get warm. I'll brew some tea."

For Connie, Digbe's cottage was an architectural journey back in time. The exterior as well as the interior was constructed of rough hewn stone, housing the signature element of a large fire place.

"Please seat yourselves. I'll have your tea and biscuits very soon."

"Thank you, Mrs. Digbe."

"I'm a miss, not a missus. Never bothered to take up with a lad on a permanent basis. Had me some good times, however."

"Oh, I'll bet you did, a lovely woman such as yourself," Angus gushed as he gave a slight bow.

She set the tea and cookies before them. "Now, what can I do for ye?"

"My kinsman, Brue Single, who is acquainted with ye, says ye may have some information about the lads and lass who kyped the Stone from Her Majesty."

Digbe directed her attention to Connie. "What did you say ye're called?"

"Connie. Connie Nordstram. I'm a distant cousin of Michael MacTavish."

Immediately, Digbe's cheerful mien was replaced by a glower. "The MacTavishes are snakes in the grass. They be nestin' wi' the English as far back as Braveheart. Traitors they were." She smacked her fist into her palm.

"Well, Miss Digbe, I wouldn't know about that. I'm staying temporarily with Michael. He's been kind to me."

Angus moved quickly to steer the conversation in a new direction by repeating his earlier query. "I say now, me lovely, you know some lore about the ones who brought back the Stone to Scotland?"

"Indeed I do. Four of 'em, there was, three lads and a lass. One of 'em was a McEacheren clansman from nearby. The others I don't know."

"Does that McEacheren live around here now?" Connie asked.

"No, no. She's long since passed on," Digbe replied as she crossed herself.

"Any relations?" Angus asked.

"I wouldn't know about that. Might be she had friends."

"Miss Digbe, you seem to dislike the MacTavishes. Is there more to it than their having been, as you say, traitors to Scotland?"

The old woman became agitated. "Indeed! My grandmother twice removed told us the travails of Yolande MacTavish."

"Travails?" Connie asked.

"Indeed. Me grandmother twice removed was a dear friend to her. Old Brody Mac-

Tavish, as told by me grandmother twice removed was a mean one. He laid the belt to her on many an occasion. My grandmother twice removed, told how old Brody would beat her for every little breach such as himself finding a dirty dish about the kitchen."

Connie worked to keep her excitement in check. "Kathryn, was Yolande pregnant at any time during the marriage?"

"Oh, indeed. She was with child when that evil man sent her away."

"He sent her away because she became pregnant?"

"Oh, No! He didn't believe it was his child she was carryin'. He believed she had been bedded by the groomsman. My grandmother twice removed, said that was nonsense."

"Do you have any idea as to where she might have gone?"

Digbe arose from her chair to pour more tea. "Talk was that she boarded a ship and went to America."

Connie's heart was beating wildly. "Miss Digbe, you have been most gracious and helpful. Thank you. I enjoyed your tea and cook — er — biscuits." She walked around the settee and gave the old woman a gentle hug.

"You're welcome anytime, Lass."

"Well, now, what about me?" Angus asked.

"Same for you, you old curmudgeon. Ah, ye do spread it on a bit thick."

Chapter Fourteen

After Jon left the Laforges, he spent the next three days in the Hall of Records searching for any name that might lead him past Annette Laforge in his ancestral chain.

On this day as he walked back to his hotel, he turned abruptly to window shop. It occurred to him that the man across the street in the reflection had been in his presence for the last two hours. Jon, the archaeologist, had once more paid attention to a detail that might have gone unnoticed by the average person. He decided to check the situation to see if he was the mouse being stalked by the cat.

He crossed the avenue. From the corner of his vision he observed that the man had not moved. Jon watched him remove a pack of cigarettes from his jacket. At that point, Jon quickened his pace. After several steps, he turned onto a side street and waited. An instant later Jake Lindsey wheeled around the corner and was suddenly face to face with Jon.

"Okay, mister, if you plan to mug me, I'll scream like hell because you're scaring me."

"So I've been made, Mr. LeFreaux. Time for me to piss on the fire and call in the dogs. I've been on your tail before and since you left Vancouver. I'm Jake Lindsey, private detective." He showed his credentials. "I was supposed to keep you under surveillance without your knowing it. Guess I got careless."

Jon relaxed enough to resume breathing normally. "Why in hell would you track me around for a month?"

"I'm not at liberty to divulge that information. Consider me your bodyguard. Sort of a guardian angel."

"Come on, detective. Do I look like I fell off a turnip truck recently? Al Nixon hired you. That's my guess. You're supposed to catch me in bed with his wife. Right?"

Jake made a snap decision. If old man LeFreaux was willing to pay him for tailing duty and didn't want it known, Al Nixon could be Jake's reason for his tail.

"Believe what you will, Jon," Jake teased.

"Listen man!" Jon exhorted. "Constance Nordstram is in Scotland. I'm sure as hell in Montreal and not sleeping with her."

"Didn't say you were. All I can tell you is that I'm commissioned to see what you're up to."

"Well, if you must know, I'm on an archeological expedition. I'm not cuckolding anyone or doing anything of a nefarious nature."

"Have you had lunch?" Lindsey asked.

"What does that have to do with anything?" Jon was incredulous at the inquiry.

"Well, I think we should have a talk over lunch. Since I no longer have to do a midnight skulker routine, perhaps we can come up with a new surveillance agreement."

"What do we have to talk about, Mister — uh, what did you say your name was?"

"Jake. Jake Lindsey. You could tell me all about archeology and I could tell you some hair-raising stories about peeping through keyholes and such," Lindsey smiled. "C'mon, Mr. LeFreaux, loosen up."

Jon was confused. He said nothing for a brief interlude. He stared at his shoes hoping to cut through his ambivalence toward the man before him. He had never felt so violated.

"Lunch? Okay. Okay, you're buying. I assume Al Nixon is paying you a hefty fee."

Lindsey continued the ruse. "I'm sorry. I can't discuss any of the surveillance details. I'm not sure I believe you when you say the lady is in Scotland. I can't keep an eye on you every minute. I have to sleep occasionally."

The conversation over lunch was flaccid. Jon's suspicion turned his food tasteless. As he drank his third tumbler of wine, he decided not to waste his worry on the detective.

After much small talk, Lindsey decided to give his prey a few tidbits. "Jon, let me tell you about Madame Laforge, with whom you've probably been sleeping while her old man is out of town…"

Before he could continue, Jon interrupted. "Sleeping with her, my ass!! That bitch may be a long lost cousin, but she was as friendly as a snake."

"Anyway, as I was saying, it seems that the Madame's great, great grandpappy was poor as a church mouse until one day he woke up mysteriously rich. That was in 1878. Before that he was in the cement business alright. He drove a mixer truck."

Jon was confounded for the moment. The story told by Martin Laforge did not square with what he was hearing now. "So, if this indeed, is the case," Jon's eyebrows did a subtle wave. "How did you come by this information?"

"Because I'm a private detective trained to dig. As an archeologist, you should be able to appreciate that."

Jon ignored the non sequitur. "Okay, as yet I'm not sure about you. I'll promise to stay generally in your line of vision if you promise to help me with my digging."

"Fair enough. What are you about?"

"Ancestors. I'm searching for my roots. I got as far as Annette Laforge and now I'm at a dead-end."

"Hey man, I do some things quite well and some things not so good. I don't know a thing about genealogy."

"Don't worry," Jon replied. "I'll handle that end of things. I want you to find out everything you can about the Laforges."

As the two of them got up from their chairs and started to exit the restaurant, Jon made a quick decision. "Jake, let's sit back down. I have a story to tell you."

Chapter Fifteen

"John Angus, things are looking up. This lady's information may push me closer to my missing ancestors," Connie declared as she started the auto engine. "But I do want to follow up on the McEacheren list. What do you think?"

The old man tugged at his beard. "Sounds reasonable to me. We'll roam about the village and do a bit of inquirin'."

Three hours later after several conversations with the locals, Connie found no further information about the McEacherens. Each inquiry brought a negative oral response or a silent head shake.

On the drive back to Edinburgh, Connie was glad that she didn't have to respond to Angus' constant prattle. She was lost in her own thoughts and she didn't like what she was thinking.

"John, do you believe those villagers were holding back on us?" Connie asked, interrupting Angus' twenty-minute narrative on Scottish sheep-herding.

"Indeed I do, Lass. Surely, the cat didna get their tongues. But, you know, their caution comes from centuries of dealing with outsiders. To them, you were an outsider. Oh, yes, Lass. They knew more than they were a tellin'."

For a time, Connie sat in the car listening to John Angus' take on the day's activities. She could sense that he didn't want the day to end.

"So, John Angus, do you have any plans in the near future? If not, I'll call you."

The old man framed his answer with a wide grin. "I'll be ready, Lass. Where might we be a goin'?"

"We'll be going seaside, John. I have some ports of call in mind."

"Molly, I want you to tell me everything you know about Michael MacTavish. I realize I'm putting you on the spot. Is there anything I should know that you haven't mentioned?"

Connie tried to be pleasantly inquiring, but Molly detected the sharp, interrogating edge in Connie's question. For an instant, Molly was flummoxed. She stood silent, unmoving. Then, with a burst of uncharacteristic emotion, "Mum, I don' know why ye're here. I wish ye wasn't. Ye're always lookin' behind doors where ye ought not be lookin'. Me, I know very little about his Lordship."

"Molly, I think it's that very little I want you to relate to me. I promise, I'd never give you away for anything you tell me."

Connie's questioning was brought to an abrupt end by Molly. "Mum, I have to return to me duties. Don't ask me more about his Lordship." She walked briskly toward the door.

"Wait, Molly. I apologize for my blundering. I appreciate your loyalty to your boss. Do you know when he'll return from, I presume, his business trip?"

"No, Mum. He never tells me such." And with that curt response, Molly left the room.

Connie changed into her warm-ups and grabbed her iPod. She would do her usual run this evening for more than working up a sweat. She would try to unclutter her thoughts surrounding the day's events.

She had barely cleared the entrance to Sonsie when a ski-masked man stepped in front of her, tackling and wrestling her to the ground. Before she could scream, the assailant placed a gloved hand over her mouth. As he pressed against her, he whispered, "I'll not kill you this night, but be warned. You are to stop your meddling. Pack your belongings and return from whence you came. If you understand, say 'ummm.'"

"Ummm."

"Should you seek out a constable, your life shall not be worth a two-pence. If you understand, say 'ummm.'"

"Ummm."

He rubbed the dull side of a knife across her neck. "If you scream when I release you, I'll slit your gullet. If you understand, say 'ummm.'"

"Ummm."

The masked man took his hand away from her face. She coughed. She gasped for oxygen, much of which had been cut off by the assailant's hand.

"Why are you doing this to me?"

"If you must know, I don't like meddling colonials," he whispered. "Now, resume your evening stroll and do not look back."

Connie got to her feet, then fell and fainted dead away on the grass. A short time later she regained consciousness. The night chill combined with her recall of being assaulted caused Connie to shake spasmodically. Her shoulder ached. Her face and mouth were painful to the touch. When she commenced to walk, the pain from her ankle radiated up her leg. Slowly, she made her way to the door of the servant's quarters.

She knocked loudly. The door opened and she almost fell to the floor before Mary Scarborough steadied her. "Jesus, Joseph, and Mary! What happened to ye? Molly! Molly Jones! Come quickly."

Molly Jones responded. "Oh, dear Mum! What happened to ye?" she asked as the two women helped Connie to a chair.

"I'll bring a cloth and some water," said Mary. "You make the lass comfortable."

"Oh, Mum, ye're a mess, don't ye know."

"Molly, I was jogging too fast and fell on my keister," Connie lied, feeling the discomfort of an aborted grimace.

"I'll fix ye up, Mum. I shouldna' let ye out of me care. Ye won't tell his Lordship, will ye? I'm to look after ye, he told me."

"Oh, dear Molly, it wasn't your fault. I'm just a big klutz."

Molly gave Connie a puzzled look. "A what, Mum?"

"I'm clumsy. I go around tripping over and running into things." Connie decided not to confide in the staff. No good purpose, she decided, would be served by raising their anxiety level.

Molly treated Connie's abrasions on her face and arms, while Mary immersed her injured ankle in a pot of warm water.

"There, there, Mum. You'll be as good as new in a bit. I'll run you a hot bath and fetch you a bottle of spirits."

Connie attempted to assuage Molly's anxiety. "Molly, please relax. I'll be okay. You're not to blame for what happened to me." Connie tried to smile, but the slightest facial contortion resulted in a sharp pain.

"Mum, I shouldna' been short with ye earlier, now should I?"

"Quit your worrying, young lady. Get my bath ready." Connie gave her a playful pat.

With Mary and Oma as escorts, Connie made her way up the staircase. She eased into the tub while Molly hovered nearby.

"Molly, you may go now. Thank you for looking after me."

The young servant wiped away a tear. "Do ye want your spirits while ye're in the tub?"

"That would be welcome," Connie replied.

———————————————

Jon's cell phone played a brief version of Sousa's Washington Post March. "So, hey, Jake. What's up?"

"Who's Jake? This is Connie. Remember me?"

"Connie! How have you been? Good Lord! When did we talk last?"

"Two weeks ago. Never mind. I'm in trouble, Jon, and I'm scared." She proceeded to tell Jon about the attack on her.

"Can you see your way to come over here?"

"You mean, uh — come to Scotland?"

"That's exactly what I mean. Some bad stuff is happening. I don't know where to turn or whom to trust. I do know that what I've learned thus far can benefit, possibly, both of our searches."

"Have you gone to the local police?"

"No, it happened only a short while ago. I'll, uh, report it tomorrow."

"Do it now, Connie. The gendarmes may be able to find some clues!" Jon almost shouted into the telephone.

"You're right, Jon. I'm not thinking straight," she mumbled. "But you haven't answered me. Will you come?"

"What about Al? Have you told him about the attack?"

There was a protracted silence from Connie's end.

"Connie, are you there?"

"I'm sorry, Jon. What I haven't told you is that Al is divorcing me. He's already filed the papers."

Jon's answer was swift. "I'll be there as soon as I can book a flight. What airport, Connie?"

She felt relief flood over her. "Glasgow."

"Okay. I'll call back as quickly as I know flight details."

———————————————

Molly's friend, the constable, assisted by two plain-clothes-men from Scotland Yard questioned Connie in detail. Could she remember anything about her assailant? How tall? How much did he weigh? Anything unusual about his voice? Connie repeated herself. "I don't know. I was so surprised and shocked." She paused, then snapped her fingers. "He whispered, yes, he whispered. He kept telling me he would kill me if I didn't quit meddling."

That recall brought a new line of questions, which resulted in the police becoming acquainted with Carl Jung and Connie's search for ancestors.

Following their interrogation of Connie, the two men and the female lead detective scanned the area of the assault, but found nothing. By that time the moon had gone behind the clouds and complete darkness had set in.

"So, what do you make of it?" asked Maggie Withers, the senior detective.

"Doesn't make much sense to me. No mugging. No robbery. Not a tad," the other detective answered.

"How say you, Constable McCarthy?"

"Me lady-friend, who serves the MacTavish household, tells me the yank has been all over lookin' fer them dead ancestors. Me lady-friend tells me, too, that the lady has become a bit interested in the Stone."

"I'm curious, constable. Why didn't the yank say anything about the Stone!"

———————————————————

Shortly after checking through customs, Jon and Jake Lindsey were met by Connie. Her greeting was effusive. Had Jon doubted her delight at seeing him, her close body hug would have sealed the deal.

"Connie, I'd like to introduce you to Jake Lindsey. He has become my personal bodyguard and caretaker. I would use him as my butler, but since he's a private detective, he would, no doubt, be offended."

"A private detective? When and why did you hire a private detective?"

"Connie, I didn't hire him. I think Al put him on my trail to make sure I wasn't, uh, involved, uh, romantically with you. I'm not, am I?" Jon became aware of his tendency to stutter when he encountered an ambiguous situation.

Connie turned to Jake. "Jake, I don't know how you came to be here, but, as a matter of fact, you may come in handy." She extended her hand. Jake noted that her handshake was firm, somewhere between 'How do you do' and 'I'm not an easy lay just because I'm getting divorced'.

"Well, no," Jake smiled, "I don't know what I've gotten myself into, but since I'm under contract to look after Jon and you're on the same loony trip with him, I'll try to plug in. Hell, lady, it'll sure beat snooping on two-timing spouses."

"So," Connie flared, "Jon filled you in and you feel the same way as my recently beloved husband!"

"I call 'em like I see 'em, Ma'am. The only dreams I ever have are usually wet."

Connie ignored the suggestive repartee.

"Did Al hire you?"

"Sorry, lady. I'm not at liberty to tell you anything." Jake was finding it more difficult to keep up the ruse. Each time he felt the urge to come clean, he remembered LeFreaux's condition of employment. Someday, Jake hoped, Jon would figure out things for himself. In the meantime, Jake would remain the enigmatic shadow of the poor little rich boy.

"Tomorrow, I'll see what I can find out from the local police," Jake offered. "That is if you, Dr. Nordstram, are willing to retain me."

"The hell you say, Jake! You want to double-dip! If Al is already paying you, I see no good reason for Connie to add to your largesse!"

"Cool down, Jon," Lindsey motioned his palms turned downward. "Don't get your shorts in a wad. It's a matter of contract. She can retain me for one dollar. That way I can say to the locals that I'm in her employ." He turned to face Connie. "Okay?"

"What about Al?" Jon asked.

"What about him?" Jake evaded.

"Never mind," Jon answered.

"I'm staying with my long lost cousin," Connie said. "I recommend the Royal Inn. Decent accommodations. I'll set it up if you wish. Two beds, I presume," she said. "Jake, he'll be in your line of vision. Just in case he decides to come to visit me, you'll have something to report to Al."

What a web I weave, Jake thought.

Paul Barker knocked on the door, then gave a quick look over his shoulder. He had no desire to be choked again.

"So, Mr. Dandy, do ye have some queenies fer me?"

"Yes, yes, indeed." Barker reached into his jacket and handed O'Feely a wad of notes. "You remember I requested that you not harm the lady's body."

"Surely and I shant lay a finger on her."

"But, but, uh, what — you attacked her last night didn't you? Oh, I'm not faulting you. Perhaps it was good that you roughed her up."

"Blimey! What in King Billy hell are you talking about! I ain't done a bloomin' thing to her. I wasn't about to risk the slammer until I had me money."

"The local constable reported that Mrs. Nordstram was assaulted last evening. I assumed it was you."

O'Feely braced Barker against the wall.

"Ye're not playin' ring around the rosy with me, are ye? If ye've hired a back up, that means ye're not trustin' me." He pressed Barker against the wall.

"Please, please," Barker pleaded. "I've not hired anyone but you yourself. I haven't the slightest notion about who attacked the woman." He smiled weakly. "Regardless, someone beat you to the task. That's good fortune for the both of us." When O'Feely released his grip, Barker moved away quickly. "Now, about your pay."

"Yeah, what about it?"

"I'm thinking, you know, just considering — I shouldn't be obligated to pay you, uh , what with the event of last evening."

"No, no, me Dandy. It donna work that way. You contracted wi' me to scare the bijesus out of a lass. If ye want to scare her some more, I'll surely do it. But, Mr. Dandy, ye'll not be a gettin' your money back."

Barker lowered his head in resignation, thankful that he was no worse for the wear, considering his proposal. "That's fine, Mr. O'Feely. That's just fine. We'll call it a bargain. I may wish to call on you again."

"I donna think so, Mr. Dandy. I'd prefer ye just put me out of ye're memory. Do ye understand?"

Barker, confused and frightened, made his way to his auto, silently swearing to himself for having bargained with the devil to no good end.

———————————————

"Mum, why didn't ye tell us you were put upon by a masked man?"

"I wasn't thinking clearly, Molly," Connie answered, sipping the tea Molly brought to her. "I didn't want to upset you and the other servants. I'm sorry I was evasive."

"Evasive, Mum? You downright told us a whopper."

"Okay. Okay. I lied to you. After our conversation the other evening, I wasn't sure I could trust you. I hit a sensitive spot when I asked you about Michael. The way you reacted made me suspicious."

Molly stared straight ahead. Connie waited for her to show anger. After a brief silence, Molly crossed herself and blurted. "I donna mean to snoop on his Lordship, but sometimes I do hear things."

"Such as?"

"A fortnight ago, his Lordship met with two men. I had ne'er laid me eyes on either one. They mayhaps was talkin' about you. I was gettin' too close to something, I know not what. I dinna wan' to hear more. I was a bit frightened."

"That's all you can remember, Molly? Are you sure."

"Yes, Mum."

Connie placed a reassuring hand on Molly's shoulder. "Molly, thank you for the information. I regret that I was tart with you."

"But Mum, I'll be needin' to go to confession. I coulda mayhaps warned ye. A lot of penance I'll be a doin."

After Molly left the room, Connie poured herself a scotch. Over and over, she recounted the events of her time in Scotland. Had she misjudged Michael? Why would anyone be interested or threatened by her search for ancestors? Most people, as she had experienced, discounted her dream analysis as so much mumbo jumbo.

Shortly after midnight, unable to cancel out her jumbled thoughts Connie rang the Seaside hotel and asked for LeFreaux.

"Jon, are you awake?"

"I am now. What's up?"

"I know Jake and you had planned to meet with the local police tomorrow. How about we leave that to Jake while you and I do a bit of research up north?"

Connie waited for his response. After a long silence, she asked, "Jon, are you there?"

"Yeah, sorry. I was organizing things with Jake. He thinks it's a good idea."

"Thanks, Jon. I'll meet you in the hotel lobby at 8:00."

Connie could hear Jake's voice in the background. "Jake wants to know if you make all of your plans after midnight," Jon joked.

"Only if he has something in mind," she retorted. "Oh, and I promise not to wake you again tonight."

———————————————

By the time Halloran arrived at their usual meeting place in the park, Michael was seething with anger. He refused the handshake offered. "I told you, dammit, I didn't want her harmed! You've hurt her badly and you've got Scotland Yard stirring! Not only that, Constance has hired two private investigators." Before MacTavish could continue, Halloran interrupted.

"I don't know what you're talking about. I checked with Barker and he doesn't know what happened. We did not commission an attack on the lady."

"I'm not sure I believe you, but I'll listen to what you have to say. If you and your lackey violated our agreement, I'll…"

"You'll what, Michael! Don't you dare try to intimidate me! I don't know what happened to the yankee bitch. Have you ever considered that whosoever put a smacking on her may have done us a favor?"

Halloran told of the O'Feely encounter as Barker had related to him.

"If you have doubts, Michael MacTavish, go to Mr. O'Feely and see for yourself."

"I perhaps may do that," Michael rejoined. "In the meantime, don't try to contact me again. If there are future developments, I'll be the one who contacts you. Are we agreed?"

"I suppose," Halloran pouted. "By the bye, you owe Barker and me for your part of the advance paid to O'Feely."

"Has your brain gone wooly?" Michael almost shouted. "He's done nothing, if I'm to believe you. I don't pay for jobs undone. Am I making myself clear?"

"Yeah," Halloran answered, "But you are the cheeky one. If O'Feely doesn't receive the sum we agreed to — well …" His voice trailed off.

"That's your problem, old boy. So, get it fixed."

Halloran huffed and moved away without telling MacTavish that O'Feely already had his money.

Jake extended his hand to the local constable, John MacCarthy. "I'm Jake Lindsey, private investigator, hired by Dr. Constance Nordstram. My credentials."

MacCarthy gave the I.D. a cursory look.

"Aye, Mr. Lindsey, and what may I do fer ye?"

Jake breathed easier. The man said nothing about Jake's Massachusetts license serving no valid purpose in Scotland.

"And you are…"

"Me name is MacCarthy. John MacCarthy of the Eden MacCarthys."

"I've heard of your clan tradition. My guess is that your clan dates back a long way." Over the years, Jake had learned to schmooze cheating husbands, on several occasions preventing damage to his life and limb.

"Oh, sure now. Back to old Jimmy himself. Aye, we're a proud lot."

"Old Jimmy, you say. And who was Old Jimmy?"

"King James, he was. Crowned as he sat above the Blessed Stone, with the swords of me ancestors to protect him."

Jake made a mental note to do some reading on Scotland. The only King he knew ran a bookmaking operation in Providence.

"Well, Mr. MacCarthy, I understand you're the lead on the Nordstram case. Since I'm also in her employ, perhaps we could share information." Not waiting for an answer, Jake took out a notepad.

"Well, I'm not sure I can do that. You see there's other coppers on the case and I donna want to ruffle their knickers, if you know what I mean."

"Mr. MacCarthy, I'll just ask you a few questions. No big deal. Such as, I want to know about the Stone. I hear there's a mystery about it."

MacCarthy bolted upright, spilling his tea in the process. "Now, I told ye I ain't answering any more of yer questions. If ye're smart ye'll let us do the work. Be gone with ye."

Jake Lindsey had been strong-armed by the Boston mafia, as well as the New York City police. He wasn't about to be intimidated by a Scottish constable.

"Constable MacCarthy," Jake's voice remained calm, "Whether you like it or not, I'm here for the duration. I intend to get to the bottom of the attack on Dr. Nordstram. I think we should cooperate with each other. If not, it can't be helped."

The last thing Jake expected from his question was the constable's reaction. Jake had considered his query an icebreaker in order to discover how the assault investigation was proceeding. But now, his feathers had been ruffled and his curiosity ignited.

MacCarthy sat back down. "Well, now, Mister, er — what was yer name again?"

"Lindsey. Jake Lindsey."

"Well, now, Mr. Lindsey, I can tell ye that we're pinchin' the usual suspects. Ye know, the muggers, pickpockets, and the like. So far we ain't turned up nothin'. Well, now ye know the lady said his face was covered by a black mask."

At that point, Jake decided not to ask more about the stone until he did his own footwork.

———————————————

Connie sat up in bed. Molly placed the breakfast tray across Connie's lap. When she saw the food she realized that she was hungry, having been for the past several hours more than a little concerned for her safety.

"How're ye feelin', Mum?"

"Much better, dear. I'm a trifle sore but the doctor says that will pass. No major damage, other than to my psyche."

"What's your psyche, Mum? Did the lout do damage to it?" Molly gave Connie a puzzled look.

Connie thought for a moment. Molly was not one of her students in personality theory.

"It's — uh — like your spirit, your thoughts, your fears. It's in one's mind. The assailant raised my fear level. I've never been really scared before now."

"I'm sorry, Mum. Sometimes I get frightened. Will it beat up on my — uh, psy - psy."

"Psyche, Molly. P-S-Y-C-H-E.

"Thank ye, Mum. Will ye be needin' anything more?"

Michael entered the room as Molly left. Connie was glad she hadn't questioned Molly further from their previous conversation. She would not breach Molly's confidence.

"Constance, my dear, I trust you are getting on well. Whatever happened to you was not sporting. I don't think much of a lout who attacks women." He kissed her on the cheek.

"Nor do I, Michael," she replied, with minimal enthusiasm for his understated sympathy. She was caught between protecting Molly's confidence and her own urge to confront him.

"So, my dear, I trust you'll not think all Scots go round attacking pretty women."

"Michael, I don't know what to think. Why have I become some kind of threat to some event I hardly understand?"

She stared into his eyes, waiting for a reaction. Michael's expression never changed.

"I wish I knew, dear girl. You're certain the fellow wasn't some sort of mugger who realized too late that you had nothing on your person?"

"No, no. As I've told the police, his exact words were 'You are to stop your meddling'. Michael, I wasn't aware I was meddling into anything other than my ancestral history. Is that so bad?"

"Not at all, Connie, if that's the extent of your inquiries. By the bye, you haven't updated me lately. I do understand you've hired an American detective. Is that true?"

Connie was surprised. "Yes, I have. But how did you know?"

"Oh, Constance, dear!" he laughed. "There aren't many secrets around these parts." Without Michael realizing it, he had raised Connie's suspicions a few more notches. She would, she decided, not tell him any more about Jon and Jake. Nor would he learn from her the information she had gleaned from the Digbe woman. For the time being, each time she encountered Michael, she would remember Digbe's caveat about him. Furthermore, she would not be intimate again with him until suspicions were alleviated.

Chapter Sixteen

"Jake, are you sure this is a good idea?"

"Look, ol' buddy, now and again a body has to go fishing. Just consider this outing a fishing trip."

Jon sat silently for the next mile before he spoke. "I think we should have told her. After all, she and I had planned to do some investigating."

"I understand your concern, Jon. My reasoning goes like this. I want to see how the Digbe woman reacts to queries. You know, Connie inquired about a relative. I want to know more about that damn stone. I've noticed that it seems to come up no matter the conversation."

Jon pointed to the house Connie had described.

"We're here. What's your strategy?"

"Like I say, Jon boy, I'll work that stone into the conversation somehow."

Kathryn Digbe was as Connie had described her; today, however, a bit irascible. "What do ye want? Yer runnin' boys have threatened me already. Now, state yer business and be on your way."

"Mrs. Digbe, we know nothing…"

"I'm not a missus. Ain't never been married, but I know what's what."

"As I was saying, Miss Digbe, we don't know anything about, as you called them, 'runnin boys' who threatened you, but we would like to know more."

"And, Miss Digbe," Jon began.

"Call me Kathryn, if you please. I allow the cute ones to call me by me given name. You're a cute one." She grinned.

"Okay, Kathryn. We work for Dr. Constance Nordstram, whom you met a few days ago. She sends her regards," Jon lied.

"Ah, I liked the lass. Charmin', she was." Digbe paused. "She ain't upset with me about that MacTavish devil, is she?"

"Oh, no. She was quite interested in your observations."

Jake nudged Jon. "Uh, Miss Digbe, or should I also call you Kathryn?" Jake waited for her response. She waited for his question.

"Well, Kathryn, can you tell us about the Stone of Destiny. We hear a lot of rumors about what happened to it."

"Young man, if ye're helpin' Missus Nordstram hunt down her dead relatives, how be it now that ye're all astir about the Stone?"

Jon interrupted. "We had no interest in the Stone until recently. Connie — Dr. Nordstram was assaulted by a masked man. He threatened her. He told her to quit meddling. That was only after she started going about with John Angus, who accompanied her to Sterling and told her all about the Stone, uh, and the rumors around it. We're interested in Dr. Nordstram's ancestry; and concerned for her safety."

"Kathryn, Dr. Nordstram said that you knew one of the lads who took the Stone from Westminster." Jake flipped open his notepad. "McEacheren, I believe was the name you mentioned."

"No, sir. I dinna say I knew the lad. I knew about his kin."

"Can you tell us the whereabouts of the kin?"

Digbe gave a light cackle. "He's underground, he is, long since passed on, so I'm told."

Jake's pen was suspended above his notebook. "Well, now, Kathryn, let me start over. Can you tell me about this McEacheren you know — uh — give me any details you might recall?"

"How do I know I can trust ye?" Digbe didn't wait for an answer. "I can't be sure ye're not a part of the conspiracy and them runnin' boys."

"What con—" Jon started but Jake interrupted before he could continue.

"Kathryn, I can assure you that neither of us is in on the conspiracy. We simply want Dr. Nordstram to be safe from the rascals who were a part of the conspiracy."

Digbe walked to and fro a couple of times. "I'll give ye a name but," she shook her finger at Jake, "Ye mustn't let the cat from the bag that I told ye."

"Fair enough," Jon said. "We'll never mention your name."

"If ye'll drive up to Dundee, there's a lass in the village named Mary Manion."

Jake wrote the name and waited. Digbe offered nothing further. Jon nudged Lindsey. "Thank you, Kathryn. We'll be on our way."

"You lads tell the Nordstram lass to visit me. I like her. I donna get many visitors, you see."

"We'll do that," Jon answered. "I know she enjoyed your company. Thanks again."

As the two of them approached their auto, Jon said, "You drive this time. The left side of the road makes me crazy. I keep thinking I'm gonna head-on some unsuspecting soul."

Jake took his place under the steering column. "Jon, I'm glad you picked up on my interrupting you in there."

"No problem. It worked well. I'm not sure we'd have gotten that name if we'd shown our ignorance."

"Yep. You and I are damn colonials, not to be trusted with the Queen's subjects."

"Jake, why didn't you ask her about the men who threatened her. Runnin' boys, she called them."

"She wouldn't have named them. I've learned to be paranoid in this business. I really believe that if I had asked her about the runnin' boys, she would have suspected we were testing her. In case you didn't notice, she didn't exactly take us unto her breast."

"So, what's our next move, gumshoe?"

Jake shifted into first gear, "Jon, ol' bean, we're going to dangle some bait hereabouts."

"What, if I might be so bold?"

"You and me, pal," Jake shifted into second gear.

"Are you kidding!" Jon exclaimed.

"Nope. I have an idea. Want to hear it?"

"Hell, yes! When someone tells me I'm bait, I get inquisitive."

Jake didn't answer right away.

"Well?" Jon pushed.

"We're gonna do some random inquiring. We're gonna pick some Scottish dudes who might be milling around. We're gonna ask some questions and we're not gonna do it subtly. You get my drift?"

Jon shook his head. "Jake Lindsey, you are a piece of work. But if these random Scots don't wish to help us, what then?"

"Oh, I'm guessing they'll clam up. I don't care. I want the word to get out that you and I are truly a pair of nosy colonials."

Jon felt a slight shiver. "You weren't kidding about the bait thing. Damn, Jake! I don't care to end up like those two fellows who accidentally stalled on a railroad track after they supposedly sucked up too much powder."

"Me, neither," Jake replied offhandedly.

"We going to use our names?"

"You bet. And our address and our telephone number. If need be, I'll give 'em our email address."

MacTavish glared at the man before him. "It would have been sporting of you to tell me about your attack on her."

"I saw no need to tell you anything," Roy Ahern blustered. "You apparently saw no reason to inform me you had incorporated those two idiots into your plans."

Michael fought the urge to strike Ahern. In a calm voice, he said, "So, what do you know of the two Americans snooping around?"

"Michael, I couldn't believe their cheekiness. They were stopping people in the village, asking about the Stone and everything else under the sun."

"Such as?"

"They were inordinately interested in those two from the <u>Mirror</u> who ran into a locomotive." Ahern grinned.

"I understand they have visited with old lady Digbe. You think she knows anything?"

"Perhaps," Ahern answered. "I saw fit to pay her a call. At first I was a country gentleman. But when she went dumb on me, I allowed as how she could stay healthy by losing her memory for things remembered."

"Roy, the more heavy-handed you become, the more suspicion you arouse. Hereafter, I want you to check with me before you, uh, take action. Do we understand each other?"

"Yes, Michael."

MacTavish placed a hand on Ahern's shoulder. "Keep a sharp eye on those American detectives. To whom are they talking? Does anyone know things he shouldn't know? Keep me informed. Good chap, now be on your way."

Connie's departure from Sonsie was not a pleasant one for her. She had become especially close to Molly and to the other servants with whom she had shared breakfasts and morning gossip. Though she had not been intimate with Michael for several days, she felt a touch of nostalgia and guilt. She chose a time when Michael was away on business. She left a note of appreciation, but her trust in Michael had been diminished by his actions. She was proud of her ability to see beyond that which seemed obvious. While Michael had shown affection and the hospitality of his castle, Connie concluded that his assistance had been superficial. His knowledge of her movements had made her uneasy in recent days. He had probed more than once about the activities of Jon and Jake. Three days ago, late into the night, she realized that she had become fearful of Michael.

She rented a small cottage near one of the firths. She invited Jon and Jake to move in and use the two spare bedrooms. She cared not that the villagers, according to Molly, would see her as a "fallen woman".

She was hanging the last of the curtains when Jon arrived with groceries.

"Hey, way to go, girl, you've really spiffed up the place." Jon gave her a peck on the cheek.

"Well, had I left it up to you two, we'd have bisquine covering the windows and the natives would think we were smoking pot, or if not bisquine, you'd probably leave us bared to the world."

Jon had not thought of Connie in a sexual sense, at least for the last day or so, but now, the notion of her being stark naked caused a stir in his groin. Offsetting this urge was his realization that Connie was a woman surrounded by danger. Until recent times the greatest danger he had faced was either having an archeological dig fall in on him, or herding sheep on a Navajo reservation.

Connie paused from her curtain hanging. "Where's Jake?"

"He'll be along. He drove to the constabulary to ask more questions of Molly's boyfriend. Jake's like a flea on a dog. He's there to remind the dog that he is still a dog. I tell you, Connie, I wouldn't want Jake Lindsey on my case. He said not to expect him for dinner."

Connie placed a kettle of water on the stove. "I'm beginning to like tea. Next thing you know I'll be cooking haggis. You want a cup?"

"Thanks, but no thanks. If it's okay with you, I'll pour myself some scotch."

"Oh, I just changed my mind, Jon. Where did you get scotch?"

Jon pointed to the bag of groceries. "It was in there all the time."

"Jon LeFreaux, I could kiss you. I haven't had a drink since leaving the MacTavish castle."

She placed two glasses before them. "Pour away, you keeper of the cache! About three fingers for me."

Jon raised his glass. "Here's to ancestors. May we stay alive long enough to find them."

Connie was startled for an instant. "Uh, I've been apprehensive, but my God, I hope you're not serious about the staying alive thing."

Jon decided not to say more about his concern for their safety. "I'm sorry. I've been able to see the sky falling since I was a kid. Just a habit by now."

"What's going on, Jon? Don't mess with my mind."

Being an archaeologist had trained Jon to assume nothing and to doubt everything until all the bones had been carbon dated. Apprehension and a thin layer of fear were not going to change him at this juncture.

"Tell you what, Connie; I'm not sure I know what's going on. But, even with my limited detective experience, something has raised my suspicion about these folks."

"Me, too," she replied. "I don't believe for one minute that my attacker was a mugger. Somebody wants me to pack up and go home." She sipped at her scotch, all the while staring out at the North Sea. "If such be the case, Jon boy, they're going to be disappointed. The synchronicity which brought you and me to this place is to me more powerful than a bit of angst. I'll not be intimidated, nor will I be frightened out of Scotland!"

For a brief time, neither of them said anything more. Lost in her thoughts, Jon may as well not have been in the room. While Jon poured the two of them more whiskey, Connie reached into the cabinet and placed cooking utensils on the stove. She selected a pork loin and cabbage from the refrigerator, prepared both for cooking and then placed them in a pot atop the stove.

"Dinner will be served in one hour. If you wish more than what's offered, too bad." She shot a mischievous grin toward Jon. "I know I've been uncommunicative for a while. Nothing personal. In the meantime, keep pouring the scotch."

"You bet," he replied as he moved closer to her. "I think we should drown our apprehensions in booze and, uh, make love. What do you think of that idea?"

"Not much," she retorted. "Jon, I appreciate that you want to make love to me. I'm not ready. I'm still sorting out my feelings since the divorce and, uh — Sonsie…" She stopped in mid-sentence. She tapped him on the shoulder. "Not that I don't find you attractive and besides, I'm preoccupied with all that's going on around us. Jon, the events overpower my libido for the time being, but," she bussed him lightly on the cheek, "we'll see what develops."

She lit a cigarette. "Did Jake say when he would return?"

"No, he just said not to wait up for him and when did you start smoking again? You told me you'd quit."

"The pressure. Helps me with the angst."

"That being the case, I'll have one. May I bum one from you?"

She passed him the pack. After several drinks, a pork-cabbage dinner, and a conversation into the early morning, both retired to their separate beds, much to Jon's frustration.

When Jon realized the pounding sound was not in his head, he staggered to the door. "Yeah, what?"

"It's me, buddy. My knuckles are raw from banging on the door. Lordamighty, were you unconscious?"

Jon opened the door to his disheveled protector. "We waited up for you most of the night. I know. I know. You said not to bother. We were more than a little concerned. Want to tell me all about it?"

"Yeah, but first I gotta have a cup of joe. You have some coffee, I hope."

Jon placed a kettle of water over the gas flame. "It's instant; not exactly Starbucks."

"Whatever," Jake agreed, as he pulled up a chair to the table. He gazed around the room. "We're not living in the lap of luxurious square footage, are we? God, I wonder how old this place is."

"Wonder no more, my friend. The lady who leased it to us says it dates back to the sixteenth century. She said at one time it had a thatched roof."

After the teapot began to steam, Jon poured two cups of water, then dipped the coffee bags.

"So, the lady prof is still sleeping. Did you get in her pants last night and don't you give me some cock and bull about what a gentleman you are," Jake leered.

"I'll answer that for him, Mr. Lindsey." Connie had eased quietly into the room. "It's none of your concern. It's my business who, as you so eloquently put it, gets into my panties. So there," she twittered.

"Sorry, Connie. Is there a hole nearby that I can crawl into?"

"Forget it, gumshoe. No problem. Okay, what have you learned?"

Jake passed his cup to Jon, "The bait has made some folks nervous."

"What bait?" Connie asked.

"Jon and I have been making blatant inquiries around the neighborhood."

"And?"

"Last night," Jake took a swallow of his coffee before he continued. "Last night I was out trolling in one of the local pubs. Fella comes up to me and says, 'You're the yank who's nosin' around, ain't ye?' or words to that effect. Before I could answer, he took a swing at me. He missed. I hit. Sent him sprawling into the arms of his buddies. Not taking any chances on who was friend and who was foe, I kicked one in the n— uh, groin and stuck my fist in the solar plexus of the other." Jake paused to swig his coffee. "The three of them forthwith hightailed it from the premises."

"So? What happened then?" Connie asked.

"Somebody called the local gendarmes." Jake paused. "About that time, the lass I was hustling grabbed my arm and we vacated that place, pronto."

"That's all that happened?" Jon ventured.

"Oh, no! The lady in question drove us to her digs." Jake gave them a sheepish look. "Uh, we, uh — engaged in some mutual, uh — fun for a couple of hours."

Connie's retort was cutting. "Jake, I suppose I should be interested in your sex life, but I can wait. Will you, for God's sake, get to the point, unless bedding a barfly was the point."

"Well, now!" Jake's pique rose to the surface. "You are the impatient one. I'm trying to tell you two what happened and drink my coffee at the same time!"

Jon shook his head, "Two hours. I'm impressed."

Connie gave Jon a scolding look.

Jake hesitated over his coffee. Let her wait.

"Sorry, Jake. Don't want you to think I'm a smart aleck. I'm pretty stressed out."

"No problem. Okay, here's what I got. The lady in question knew the amateurs who attacked me. Says they work for a fellow named Ahern. We'll be wanting to converse with him sometime soon."

Connie gave Jake a puzzled look. "I'm not sure I understand what connection…"

Jake interrupted. "There may not be a connection to your mugger. But, I'm guessing that everyone in the United Kingdom by now knows the three of us are working together."

"So," Jon asked, "What's our next move?"

"I want you and Connie to go about your genealogy business." Jake turned to Connie. "Isn't that what you're here for? I'm experienced at looking for folks who crawl out from under rocks. Okay?"

"You're sure you don't need me to cover your back?"

"No, Jon. I can take care of number one. You look after Dr. Nordstram."

"Jake Lindsey," Connie flared, "That is so condescending! I'm not your sorority, helpless female."

"Fine, Lady!" Jake reached into his coat. "I was going to give Jon this pistol. You take it and protect him."

Connie lowered her voice. "I — uh — no, I don't want the gun. I don't believe guns solve anything."

"Okay." Jake handed the revolver to Jon. "I assume, partner, you're not a member of some anti-gun lobby."

"God, no! And thanks."

"Do you know how to use that thing?"

"Yep. I learned in Mexico when it was my turn to stand watch over the dig."

"Good. I'll check in with you two from time to time. If you uncover any vermin, let me know."

As Jake drove away, Jon turned to Connie. "So, professor, where do we dig today?"

"How about we pick up old Angus. He may have more names for us." She grinned. "If not, he'll surely have some Scottish lore to keep us occupied."

Chapter Seventeen

Jake's email from Chips was surprisingly lengthy and detailed. It read:

Jake, I've worn out some shoe leather checking the finances of Laforge and LeFreaux. I'll start with Laforge. The money trail on Martin petered out early. He was just a good ol' French Canadian until he married a gal named Annette O'Shaughnessy. Here the plot thickens. It seems her great great grandfather came over from Scotland around the turn of the nineteenth century. If he was like most young Scottish immigrants, he was probably poor as a church mouse. But guess what? The people who know a bit of his history reported that all of a sudden in the late eighteen hundreds he became a member of the nouveau riche. Seems he went from being a cement mixer to owning the whole works. As time went on he kept on piling up the big bucks. He married late in life and sired one son who later had Annette who lives outside Calgary and who now controls the financial empire. Martin is her boy toy. He's all hat and a herd of cattle. Enjoys his ranching hobby. A fellow named Lamar Kelly is the true power behind that lady's throne. He owns ten percent of the corporation. The parent company retains the original name O'Shaughnessy Cement, Inc. Let me tell you, Jake, those folks are into more than cement. They own a chunk of the railroad industry, the beef industry, the construction industry, the lumber industry. I won't even list several other money makers, plus they invest heavily in U.S. and British markets. As best I can figure, they're in that rarefied atmosphere inhabited by the Waltons, the Mellons, and several Middle East oil tycoons. Would you believe ten billion and change?

Now, about this fellow LeFreaux. He's a player in the market and a venture capitalist. Over time, he's backed some winners and a few losers. He's a babe in the woods compared to Annette O'Shaughnessy Laforge. Unless I missed a few coins, he's worth about fifty million.

You're going to love this, Jake. His ancestor was also named LeFreaux and came to the USA around the same time as Annette's pappy. Our great grandfather LeFreaux had a sister who married a fellow name O'Shaughnessy. That O'Shaughnessy, it seems was no kin to the Laforge O'Shaughnessy. Big Daddy of the poor little rich boy became a millionaire, then did some wise money managing. I haven't a clue as to how LeFreaux's father made his money. No records. No money trail at all. Okay. Steer me onward and upward.

Jake saved and printed the transmission before shutting off his computer. Now he had a name to give to Dr. Nordstram.

———————————————————

Connie rapped gently on John Angus' door. She waited, then knocked again. "Jon, I don't know why we're getting no response. Usually, John is waiting by the door."

This time Jon knocked loudly; still no one came to the door. "He's old, Connie. Maybe he forgot."

"John Angus doesn't forget a day with you and me. Something's wrong." Connie peered in the side window, but the shades were drawn. "Jon, I'm going in if we have to break down the door. Maybe he's had a heart attack or a stroke." She turned the door knob and pushed open the door.

"Dr. Nordstram, I'm glad we didn't have to break down the door. My shoulder started to ache just thinking about it," Jon laughed.

Once inside the small cottage, Connie said, "I've never been inside here before. As I look around, I think I know why he always waited by the door. John!" She spoke in a loud voice. "John Angus! Are you up and about?"

The room was cluttered with articles of clothing, random chunks of coal, and a few unwashed dishes in the sink. Two chairs were set around a small table. A wooden rocking chair was placed next to a sofa which appeared battered from years of use.

Connie opened a door to the side of the living room/kitchen area. "Jon! Oh, my God! Jon!"

The room before them had been ransacked. A chest of drawers had been turned over and emptied of papers and magazines. Shelves holding books had been torn from the wall. The mattress of a small bed had been slashed, its stuffing scattered across the floor.

"Jon, I'm sick to my stomach. I'm scared!"

"Me, too," he replied. "I'm scared of what I'm going to find behind that next door." Cautiously, he pushed the bedroom door open.

"Connie, don't come in here. Good God!"

His warning fell on deaf ears. She took one look and commenced to sob. John Angus, covered in blood, lay dead, his face buried in a pillow.

Connie lowered her head. "I loved that old man. You know, uh — we connected from the first time I met him. I had transformed him into a father. I was going to have him travel with us to check the passenger manifests of ships leaving Scotland around 1850, now..." her voice trailed off.

Jon placed his hand on Angus' neck. "Connie, no need for me to try for a pulse. He's cold. He's been dead for some time."

Jon turned away from the corpse. "We'll need to notify the local authorities." Jon paused. "Someone was looking for something, Connie. My guess is that the old fellow came upon the intruders."

Through muffled sobs, Connie stammered, "It's all, uh — it's — uh, it's probably my fault."

"Ah, c'mon, lady. How could this be your fault?"

"Jon, he was helping me. Don't you see, and well, you know, some bad people have..." She raised her head. "I was scared before. But now, I'm angry! He was special! He was my friend. I want the bastards brought to justice!"

Jon ignored her outburst. "If you lived here and wanted to hide something, where would you hide it?"

"Obviously, not where the killers looked, assuming they found nothing."

Jon commenced to move around the room, tapping the wall at regular intervals. "If I seem over the edge, I learned this routine from years of searching for unknown relics in strange places."

After several minutes, he concentrated his tapping effort on a spot near the corner of the room. "Whoa! Connie that sound is hollow. I believe the wood covering is a veneer over the stone. If my hunch is correct there's a break in the stone."

"What are you saying?"

"I'm saying what if old Angus has a secret compartment behind this wall?"

Connie looked around the room, then walked to a closet off the kitchen.

"I give up, professor Nordstram, what are you doing?"

Connie raised her voice from the other room. "I'm looking for a basher of some kind. You know, like a hammer or a hatchet."

"And?"

"And, we'll break through that wall to see if you..."

"God! Are you sure. Our butts could be in a sling if we do that. Don't you think if there's bashing to be done, we should let the police do it?"

"No. If you want to bail out, go right ahead. I don't trust any of these people and that includes the local authorities. Besides, our prints are all over this place already."

"But Connie," Jon exclaimed in exasperation, "We had a reason to be here. We came to pick up the old man, not to smash in a wall!"

"Jon, think about it." Connie re-entered the bedroom with an axe in hand. "Our story will not be compromised by bashing in the wall. Someone had killed Angus and left the place in shambles. That's what we'll report" She passed the axe to Jon. "Either you do it, or I will."

Jon shook his head in resignation. "Give me the axe. Unless, you wish to save it for the time we break out of a Scottish hoosegow."

On his second swing the paneling shattered, revealing an opening in the stone wall. Jon reached inside the recessed area. He retrieved a time worn envelope, the writing on the outside had become almost illegible. By now, Jon's heart was pounding against his ribs. "You open it, Connie. My hands are shaking."

Chapter Eighteen

Chips O'Donnell walked along Independence Avenue, tired but satisfied that his day had been productive. He had interviewed a number of officials in the Hall of Records. His trail from Montreal had led to Philadelphia where he expected to locate any living relatives of Annette Laforge. He decided to call it a day before checking out his latest lead.

Back in his hotel room, he emailed a progress report to Jake Lindsey, then commenced to undress. The bed before him looked inviting. He would have no trouble sleeping this night. As he was about to enter the bathroom, a knock on his door was followed by, "Room service, sir. I need to give you more towels."

"Give me a minute." Chips wrapped a towel around his waist and opened the door. "Hey, good! Usually, there aren't enough…" He was shoved backwards before he completed his sentence, by two well dressed men pointing pistols at Chips.

"What the hell! Who the hell are you?"

"We'll do the asking. You do the answering," declared the lead intruder, as he jammed the pistol into Chips' abdomen.

"You go to hell."

The second man slapped Chips across the cheek with his weapon. Blood spurted from the deep slash as Chips fell to the floor, his struggle to arise brought kicks to the ribs, first from one intruder, then the other. Chips groaned in pain, then fell back to the floor.

"Now, let's start over, gumshoe. Why are you snooping around here and there?"

Chips grimaced. "I was looking for a ride to Disneyland."

Both men began to kick Chips' face again. The brutalization continued for several seconds.

"Hey, he ain't movin' no more," said Joe Agles.

"He's dead. Damn!" proclaimed Baron Septo. "You know the boss is gonna be pissed! We didn't get shit out of him. We gotta get rid of the body."

"Joe, clean up the room. Make sure you scrub up the blood."

"Ain't no blood. It's all on his face."

"I'm gonna bring the car around to the service elevator. We'll dump him at the quarry."

It had not occurred to the intruders that Chips learned to play possum in a jungle near Da Nang. As his vision cleared, he saw Agles removing a blanket from the bed. Chips took a deep breath, then unplugged the lamp next to his head. In one motion, he launched himself and the lamp. Agles went down when the metal base smashed into his skull.

"Kick me now, you sonofabitch! It's my turn!" Chips yelled as he swung the lamp downward into the chest of the unconscious man.

Moving rapidly, Chips reached inside his jacket hanging from the only chair in the room. He removed his pistol, chambered a round, cracked open the door slightly, then waited for Septo's return.

Jake smiled at the receptionist. "I'd like to see Mr. Ahern if you please."

"Do you have an appointment, sir?"

"No, just tell him an old friend has dropped by."

The matronly receptionist didn't move from her chair. "Your name, sir."

Jake leaned toward her, smiling all the while. "Oh, now, dearie, I want to surprise him."

"I'm sorry, sir. He doesn't like surprises. Who shall I tell him wishes to surprise him?" She rolled her "r's" in Scottish dialect.

"Well, I tried," Jake responded, as he eyed the door over which read "ROY AHERN, PRESIDENT, AHERN ENTERPRISES". He turned as if to leave, then moved quickly toward Ahern's office door.

"Sir, you can't go in there!"

"Watch me, lady."

He pushed open the door and was facing a middle-aged man sitting behind a large oak desk.

Roy Ahern reached into the top desk drawer. "Who the hell are you? I don't recall having an appointment!"

"Mr. Ahern, if you have a pistol in that drawer, I advise you to leave it there. I suspect I can outdraw you and outshoot you."

Ahern placed both hands on the desk. "State your business, then get the hell out of here."

"My business," Jake replied, "is to ask you about three of your employees named Boone, O'Riley and Thornton."

"What about them?"

"Well sir, they attacked me recently in one of the local pubs. I thought perhaps you might help me locate them. I intend to press charges."

Ahern squirmed in his chair. "No one by those names works for me. Where are they? Your guess is as good as mine."

"Ah, Mr. Ahern, you are one for the ages. My informer tells me that three inept goons who work for you attacked me last night. I'm just curious. Do you know anything about that?"

"Hell, no! But if you're so damned insistent." He pressed the intercom button. "Jean, please have Mr. Peters come to my office. Now, Mr. whatever the hell your name is..."

Jake interrupted. "Lindsey. Jake Lindsey. I'm here on behalf of a client, and because my hand is sore from using it as a bludgeon against your goons."

Raymond Peters entered the office.

"Lindsey, Ray Peters is our HR Vice President. What were those names you mentioned?"

"Boone, O'Riley, and Thornton."

"Ray, Mr. Lindsey thinks those fellows are in our employ. Seems they attacked him last night, or so he alleges."

Peters opened the ledger and commenced to scan the names. "We have no Boones on the payroll." He flipped a page. "Nobody named O'Riley." Pause. "Nope, no Thorntons."

Ahern gave a dismissive flick of the wrist. "Thanks, Ray. Now, are you satisfied, Mr. Lindsey?"

"Not really," Jake answered. "Thanks anyway for your time."

Most unusual, Jake thought. He never bothered to ask me for my credentials. Didn't get outraged enough.

"Connie, does this writing mean anything to you?"

'I'm not sure. Let's get out of here. I'm shaking. I can't think straight at this moment." She started toward the door.

"Whoa, girl. Are we gonna notify the local constables or what?"

Connie paced back and forth. "Yes, but not in person. We'll mail an anonymous note. Now, can we get the hell out of here?"

"Not before we remove some prints," Jon said. He walked into the kitchen and returned with two dishtowels and a container of water. "Think hard. What have we touched?"

Connie commenced to list. "The -uh- doors. The ax. The wall where you felt around. John's neck, when you checked his pulse. Oh, and I leaned against the bed frame. Can you remember anything else?"

"No, but we'll need to discard our shoes. Scotland Yard doesn't miss a thing."

"Good thinking. What about our tire tracks?"

"Ah, yes! Rain is in the forecast for today. Oh, and every other day this time of year!"

———————————————

Jake grimaced as Connie and Jon related the events around their visit to John Angus. "I can't even imagine what drove you to be stupid. We have enough trouble with people outside the law. Now, to make matters worse, the local authorities will be all over us."

Jon glared across the table. "What do you mean?"

"I mean we'll be on the short list of suspects because we have been in contact with old John." In the pit of her stomach, Connie's anxiety was turning to raw fear. "Jake, I'm sorry. It's all my fault. I persuaded Jon to smash in the wall. I'll take all the blame if Scotland Yard gets to us."

"How noble!" Jon reacted. "So you're saying that a dangerous female criminal was just leading me around by the nose."

"Hell, no! That's not my intent. If you recall, you wanted to leave before we messed up the crime scene." She shook her head from side to side. "I think I lost my common sense when I saw that old man in a pool of blood."

Jake raised his hand. "Okay, let's not get into a pissing contest. The fact of the matter is that if push comes to shove, we're all suspects."

Jake proceeded to tell them about his visit to Roy Ahern, concluding that no evidence existed to link Ahern to Jake's attackers.

"The fact of the matter is that I can't locate Boone, Thornton, or O'Riley. After a bit of snooping around, those rascals are nowhere to be found. Either Ahern has put them in cold storage, or they really don't work for him."

"My God!" Connie bolted upright. "This fellow, Ahern, would do that? He'd kill three of his own men because they were in a barroom brawl with you. Jake, that's a bit of a stretch."

"I didn't say he killed anyone," Jake retorted. "And, no, I don't believe in the scheme of things, I'm that important. But consider this, you two amateur ax wielders. What if those goons have something on Ahern?"

"For what?" Jon asked.

"For any number of things. When you're a private detective, you also become a conspiracy buff. Think about it. You know, I've been out among the natives. There's a history of folks meeting bad ends, not necessarily on a railroad track. Add to that the email I received from my partner, Chips. He was attacked in his hotel room by two thugs. He had begun bird-dogging some people in Canada. Seems the trail of information led him to New York. He got beat up pretty bad."

Connie winced. "What about the men who assaulted him?"

Jake chuckled. "They didn't realize who they tangled with. Chips says they're under arrest in a local hospital, across the room from where ol' Chips is being treated. Enough about that. Have you two thought through how to notify the authorities about Angus?"

"We thought we'd send an anonymous letter," Jon replied. "We'll wait a day or so, maybe longer. The tire tracks will be washed away by that time." He paused. "Hope the old man won't be too ripe."

Connie shook her head. "Jon, that was gross and denigrating."

Jon ignored the upbraid. "Jake, we're pretty sure we left no evidence of our visit to Angus. We'll use newsprint letters to form the note to the gendarmes. Are we leaving anything out? You're a cop. You should know."

"What I know is that all three of us had better be on the same page when we get the third degree."

He motioned to Connie. "Let's have a look at that paper you took from the Angus place."

Connie passed the envelop across the table. "Jake, we haven't been able to make any sense from it. It's a bunch of gibberish."

"No," Jake responded. "I'd say it's code."

TRYST OMBLAS OFLA BUIE ARFUM LINN HOL BLA NUI TOOZ
DREE FLU ONO DUI XTAT AWA JUS TLE GRE LUN FASH KMT OXY
JEZ BOT G10 HOT HAT ELO OPA VANG GLO 511 VANT ZAY MUIR
1MB OTT ZZY LOM LUNT OK1 MNT RVO LNN WATT DOE RAP
GN1 TLT CESS AUB JAN TLP YOO LEET TZO BYA OMA OTA LYN
ZOO ALB TOM TON WATT OLA ZTA OPA GEE LEAL GYM TOO TAO
ONA EEN

Chapter Nineteen

"Jake, you didn't have to come all the way back here. Hell, I'm gonna be out of here in no time.

Lindsey placed his hand on O'Donnell's bandage. No trouble, Chips. I was concerned about you. Shoot, if those perps had done you in, I would have to get myself another partner. So catch me up."

Chips proceeded to tell Jake of his investigation around the Laforges. He reiterated that somewhere along the highway of history, an inordinate amount of money had ended up in the hands of a man named O'Shaughnessy, and was passed down subsequently to Annette O'Shaughnessy Laforge.

The men who attacked Chips had met bail and one of them had been discharged from the hospital. After Jake left Chips, he eased quietly into the room where Joe Agles was recovering from the beating he received from Chips' lamp stand.

"Hey Joe, wake up!" Jake whispered as he bent down over the prone figure. Agles' lids fluttered for an instant, before he opened his eyes. His right leg was in a cast and elevated. One arm was in a cast. His head was bandaged and his face was covered with contusions.

"My God man!" Jake exclaimed. "What happened to you?"

"I've told you cops all I'm going to tell you. Now, get out of my room."

Jake seated himself on the edge of the bed. "I'm not a cop. I work for Raymond Laforge," Jake lied. It's my understanding that the man who attacked you has been sticking his nose into Mr. Laforge's business. My job is to find out why." Jake held his credentials before Agles. "I'd really like for you to help me and so would your boss," Jake bluffed.

Agles said nothing for several seconds, as he tried to shift his position.

"Who the hell is Martin Laforge?"

"He's a gentleman who is rich, powerful, and can't stand to see a contract botched." Jake glowered "If you get my meaning."

"No, I don't get your meaning. What are you talking about?"

"Mr. Laforge wanted things done clean and quietly. You and your buddy made a mess."

"I ain't sayin' no more."

Jake turned toward the door. "Okay by me. I don't have my ass in a sling."

"Wait a minute," Agles said. "Have you talked to Septo?"

"No, I haven't," Jake replied. "He's already written his statement. He said the two of you just wanted to talk to your victim, but that you went crazy and assaulted the fellow. Septo says he tried to stop you, but you wouldn't let up on the poor bastard."

Agles commenced to breathe heavily.

"What are we charged with?"

"You're charged with assault with intent to kill. Septo is not charged."

Agles tried to sit up. "No, No! Baron wouldn't do that. I know him. He wouldn't do that!"

Jake handed the telephone to Agles. "He's in room 412. Check for yourself."

Agles dialed room 412. He listened to the ring at the other end for a short time. He returned the phone to Jake, who knew that Septo had been released from the hospital.

———————————

Tired and scruffy from his twenty-seven hour stop and go flight, Jake rapped on the cottage door.

"Hey man!" Jon exclaimed, "Am I glad to see you. So, how's your partner?"

"I'll tell you all about it if you fix me a cup of tea."

"You want tea?"

"Yep" Jake answered. "I soaked up gallons of coffee on that flight. It began to taste pretty ordinary."

"Jon, we're in the middle of something big." Jake sipped at his tea. "It seems we're making some very important people very nervous."

Jake told Jon of his visit to Chips; how Chips had come in contact with Agles and Septo; how Chips had managed to prevent his own murder.

"Once I bluffed that dude, Agles, he was ready to spill the entire can of beans. Problem was, he didn't know a hell of a lot. He gave me a name, but it didn't help me much." Jake grinned. "Ol' Agles said that he and his buddy were contacted by a Sylvester, but Agles never knew his last name. Said he talked with an accent that sounded French."

Jon's excitement was tempered by a feeling of angst. "What are we talking here?"

"Well, ol' buddy. Take your pick. If you had your choice, would you look for a fellow with a French accent, considering the situation, in Phoenix or Montreal?"

"Gotcha. So, what now?"

"Chips'll be back in the hunt in a week or so. He's going to question some folks who are concentrically located around the Laforges." Jake became pensive. "It's fish or cut bait time. Are you sure you want to continue?"

"Yeah. Yes, I am." He raised his palm. "Well, only if Connie remains willing."

"Jon, you're not going to like this." Jake lowered his voice to a whisper. "I'm going to need more money, which means I'm going to have to hit your papa for some moola."

Jon didn't flinch. "Do it. He can afford it."

"Before I put the touch on him, let's see what Connie wants to do. By the way, where is she?"

———————————

Connie shifted her eye contact from one detective to the other, all the while trying to prevent her hands from shaking. She leaned across the table. "Why am I here? Have you caught the person who assaulted me, or what?" She forced a half-smile. "Or did I get caught jaywalking again?"

"Not at all Mum," replied Detective Sykes. "We understand that you have spent a bit of time recently with John Angus."

"That's correct. In fact, I was hoping to have him accompany me to Inverness later this week."

Sykes tapped a pencil against his notepad. "What is your business with old John?" Be careful, Connie. "He's a good guide and he seems to know all there is to know about Scotland. I'm very fond of the old guy."

"I see," Sykes said as he made a note. "For sure, old John knows a great lot about our land and what he doesn't know in fact, he stories it up."

Connie did not respond.

"When was the last time you toured with John Angus?"

"If you expect me to remember the exact date, I can't help you there. I've always had a terrible memory for time and dates. A week or so ago, maybe a Monday."

Sykes nodded. "I see. So, he was a guide for you and where did he guide you?"

Connie breathed easier. "You may or may not know, I'm doing a genealogy search. That's big in the U.S." She grinned half-heartedly. "Seems the entire populace is searching for roots."

Both detectives remained silent for what to Connie seemed an eternity.

"Has John done something wrong?" Connie asked, mustering as much sincerity as her angst would allow.

"No, Mum. But someone has done him a terrible wrong."

Connie lowered her chin to her chest. "What, uh, what do you mean?"

"Old John Angus is dead. He's been murdered, Mum."

Connie commenced to sob. The tears were real as she recalled the death scene and remembered the affection she felt for the old man.

"Who would have wanted to kill such a sweet, decent person. Who would do such a thing and why?"

"Mrs. Nordstram, to the best of your knowledge, did old John have any enemies? Did he ever mention any names?"

"Not in a negative way," she replied. "The only people he talked about were those he hoped could help me."

Sykes' pencil was poised. "And they were?"

"Well, let's see. There was Kathryn Digbe and Ben Smith. Oh, and some villagers in Sterling. I don't exactly recall their names. Most were a bit suspicious of, as you folks say, us colonials. Much of the time we visited historical sites."

"These historical sites, Mum, helped you in your search for ancestors?"

Connie blanched for an instant. "Oh, those places I visited to please Mr. Angus."

"I see," responded Sykes. "We have heard a bit of talk that you've inquired about the Stone of Destiny."

"Yes. It's uh, so very — uh fascinating." Over a weak smile, Connie searched for words. "John Angus told me all about it. From his point of view, you understand."

Sykes jotted more notes. "And what was his point of view?"

Connie felt the vise tightening around her. "He seemed to believe that a massive conspiracy was involved around the Stone. He believed that the stone in Edinburgh is a fake. I need not tell you, of course, but that notion is common gossip."

Sykes passed a note to the other detective. He read it quickly then asked, "Mrs. Nordstram, did old John tell you that we suspect he was involved in the theft of the Stone from Westminster Abbey?"

"Heavens no! You mean he — How was he, uh, involved?"

"According to rumors over the years, Mum, he was a planner from the get-go."

Connie grew pale as the blood drained from her face. She felt for an instant as if she would collapse.

"Are ye well, Dr. Nordstram? You seem a bit faint."

She struggled to regain her composure. "I'm okay, thanks. I'm shocked to hear such a rumor. John Angus was a gentle person. I find it hard to believe that he was a conspirator of any sort."

"Well, Mum," Sykes rejoined, "we're not saying the old fellow was involved in a bit of chicanery. We just want you to know of the town talk. By the bye, did he ever give any detail about the theft?"

Connie shifted her weight in the chair, paused as if trying to remember. "Uh, as I told you before, he did mention the Stone and the conspiracy stuff. But, it was always, as I recall, within the context of his long-winded treatises on Scotland's history."

She waited as Sykes scribbled in his notepad. "Thank you, Mum. Should you recall other details, please stay in touch. You will, I trust, not be leaving the Island any time soon?"

"That's correct."

"Very well, Mum. May I have your passport please?"

Connie experienced a rush of discomfiting fear. "Am I a suspect, or what?"

"Should you be, Mum?"

Connie fought to regain her composure. "Not at all. May I go?"

She searched through her purse. As she handed her passport to Sykes, she said, "I think you're treating me as a suspect. That displeases me."

After Connie left the room, Sykes said, "Sergeant Thompson, there's more to that lass than meets the eye. Why would she need two men to help her look for ancestors? Oh, sure, and the big fellow is a P.I."

"Sir," Thompson replied, "I do believe you are correct in your assumptions."

Jake watched as the email from Chips rolled from the printer. "Hey you guys, we've got mail from Chips. Wanna know the latest?"

Connie and Jon moved quickly to peer over Jake's shoulder.

Hey searchers. Hope you're still enjoying a wee bit of Scotland. Here's the latest from this end. I took the smattering of info from Agles, one name that led me to Philadelphia, PA. This fellow named Mabry O'Toole, was not a fan of the Laforges. Get this. He said he had some kin who was party to the theft of something valuable. He knew nothing of the valued object in question. I think he believed his kin was involved in a diamond heist. Anyhow, he wasn't talking about the nineteen fifties fiasco. He said his kin was involved in a heist with a man named O'Shaughnessy way the hell back in the 19th century. Said his great, great grandfather was cheated out of his share of the loot from the heist. At present, I'm searching the records for any mention of a Charliss O'Toole. Happy hunting on your end.

"Well, my children," Jake shrugged. "We're back to square one, if O'Toole knows what he's talking about."

Jon paced up and down in frustration. "What the hell have we gotten ourselves into, Dr. psychology professor?"

"I don't know, gentlemen. I do know that I'm scared and for God's sake I haven't done a thing except search for an ancestor."

"Oh, and by the way, cluttered up a crime scene," Jake added.

"We can't undo that, Jake. I think if I had it to do over, I'd do the same thing." Jon smiled as he put his arm around Connie.

"Connie, do you think you satisfied the local cops when they questioned you?" Jake asked.

"No," she responded. "And the reason I think so is because they took my passport and told me not to leave the country."

Jake was startled for an instant. "What about you, Jon? Have you been questioned?"

"Nope. Why should I be?"

"Because you know our friend, Dr. Typhoid Mary. It's just a matter of time until the three of us are linked. We do hold an ace in the hole. We have that strange coded note. I'd like to have a friend of mine in Boston see if he can make heads or tails of it."

Connie and Jon nodded. "Will you have to use the original?" Connie asked.

"No way. I'll email a copy. My buddy is good. He was a code breaker for the Israeli military." Jake reached for his coat. "I've got places to go and people to see. In the meantime. Jon, any word on your request to Papa LeFreaux?"

Jon walked to the nearby closet and retrieved a packet from his coat. "Here's the dough. I've already had some of it converted to pounds sterling or some such. Take a wad, if you understand the Queen's currency."

"So, I'll see you two later. Be careful. Stay safe. Your dad never questioned the need for more money?"

"Nope," Jon said.

"Jake, Jon and I are going to resume our search for ancestors. Stone of Destiny? What stone?"

"Good idea — ancestor hunt — good. No break in your normal routine."

As Jake closed the door behind him, Connie put her head in her hands and sighed wearily. Jon sat down beside her and commenced to stroke her hair.

"Are you sorry I got you into this mess?" she muttered softly.

"Hey girl! You've got to be kidding. I wouldn't have missed it for the world. I'm having a hard time remembering that we're chasing the roots of a dream. Connie, that stone is in there somewhere. I damn well know it in my gut."

Connie's thoughts were cluttered, under-girded by a lingering angst. Her life had been secure behind ivy covered walls and a dubious science named psychology. Now she found herself in a real world filled with intrigue and murder.

"Jon, are you concerned that we'll be found out? What were we thinking?"

Jon gave his chin a ceremonial rub. "Well, my dear, our curiosity got the better of us. One great failing of our human nature is to know stuff. When we encounter something that doesn't make sense, we dig for an answer. As an archeologist, I listen to all the claptrap, for example, about how a bunch of primitives built a bunch of pyramids. We don't know, so we guess."

Connie walked to the cabinet and brought out a bottle of scotch. As she set it before them, she said, "My friend, I'm horny and about to get pickled. Care to join me?"

Jon was taken aback for an instant.

"Are you sure, Connie?"

"I'm sure," she replied, as she led him to her bedroom.

Chater Twenty

Two days into his quest for an 18th century O'Toole, Chips hit pay dirt. Charliss O'Toole, the record noted, was born in Sterling, Scotland, and had immigrated to the states in 1862. He had served in the Union Army and was honorably discharged in 1865. He had married Mary Gatlin in 1866. Chips' tedious week-long search yielded birth records showing that Charliss and Mary had five children; four daughters and one son.

Back in his hotel room, Chips set himself up with coffee, a telephone directory, and the will to solve a deepening mystery.

He grumbled to himself as he counted 115 O'Tooles in the Philadelphia telephone directory. He began to dial. Two hours and thirty-five O'Tooles later, he ceased calling. The next morning on his second call, a woman answered. "O'Toole residence." Chips steeled himself for another rejection. "My name is Lawrence O'Donnell. I'm a genealogist and I'm trying to locate descendents of Charliss O'Toole. You wouldn't by any chance be on that tree?"

Madelyne O'Toole laughed. "No, but my husband is a direct descendent. His grandfather, three times removed was Charliss O'Toole. You see, my husband, Sam, couldn't care less if he discovered William Wallace was his kin. Me, I love genealogy."

"Hey, great! Do you know about any descendents of Charliss' four daughters?"

"Oh, sure. Let me get my book."

A short time later, she returned to the telephone. "Two of the daughters, Cecelia and May, died in childhood from smallpox. Cheryl never married; died at the age of eighty. Lucy married a fellow from up east, Boston or maybe it was

Providence, anyway his name was Shaunessy. Ethan Shaunessy."

"This is very helpful Mrs. O'Toole…"

"Call me Madelyne."

"Okay, Madelyne. How about current descendents?"

"Oh, sure," she replied. "A great granddaughter married a fellow named LeFreaux from Boston. When I was doing my search years ago, I spoke on the phone with her. Margaret O'Shaughnessy LeFreaux, she was. She surely bragged about her husband and her only son. At the time I talked with her, the son, Jon, was in college studying archeology, if I recall correctly. Don't know about any other descendents of old Charliss."

Chips was flushed with excitement. "Madelyne, how far back were you able to trace your husband's ancestors?"

"Let me see," there was a long pause on the other end. "Oh, I hadn't mentioned that my husband is Scottish, with some Irish and German blood. I know O'Toole sounds Irish, but he's proud to be mostly Scot. Breaks out his kilt now and again." She laughed at her own pronouncement. "Here we are. I was able to go back in history to the time of Alexander III. The German and Irish blood is fairly recent. Not very exciting. Do you want to know about those trees?"

"No," Chips replied. "I'm interested mostly about the Scottish tree. Were you able to identify an ancestor from that time?"

"Possibly. The details are murky. Do you know anything about the Stone of Scone?"

"Somewhat, Madelyne. I understand that Scottish kings and queens over time have been crowned as they sit on the Stone."

Madelyne giggled as she corrected Chips. "No, no. They didn't sit on the Stone. They sat in a chair above the Stone. And not only Scottish royalty was crowned that way. To this day the newly crowned Royals of England are also given their scepter in such a manner."

Madelyne O'Toole felt a touch of smugness. It was not often that she could share her knowledge with an acolyte off the street, on the phone.

"About the Stone… my husband's ancestor, possibly, was party in some chicanery involving the theft of the Stone way back in the 14th century."

For several seconds she was silent.

"Are you still there, Mrs. O'Toole?"

"Yes, oh, yes. I was checking my genealogy journal. When I traveled to Scotland — you know I spent several weeks in and around Sterling, Edinburgh, and numerous other locales — while there, I was on the receiving end of countless rumors. The Scots thrive on rumors and folklore, don't you know. There was one old fellow named Angus who insisted that any Stone of Scone after Alexander III was a fake."

Chips stopped scribbling his notes.

"Mrs. O'Toole, may I call you Madelyne?"

"Please do."

"Where does the ancestor fit in?"

"If you check your Scottish history you know that King Edward manipulated John Bailliol onto the throne. The gossip was that enemies of Edward — in this instance those who wished Robert Bruce to become king — were involved in the assassination of Alexander III. Oh, and that one or more conspirators were loyal to a Dane named Haakon IV, who believed his part of Scotland had been stolen by Alexander."

More silence. "Are you still following me?"

"Yes, ma'am. I think so. Now about that alleged ancestor thief…" Chips was trying to belay his impatience. "Do you have a name?"

"Well, yes." Chips was aware that he had irritated her a bit, as he waited for a response.

"The name bandied about was MacAlpin or McAlpine. Allus or Allan MacAlpin."

"One more question, Madelyne. The old fellow you talked to in Scotland. Was Angus his first or last name?"

"His full name, according to my notes, was John McCann Angus."

"Mrs. O'Toole, Madelyne, you have been most helpful. Perhaps I could call on you in person at some future date?"

"Yes," she answered. "Okay, I've been very rude. I haven't asked you about your genealogical search." Long silence. "Mr. O'Donnell, are you there?"

By the time Chips responded, he came up with the need to know about an ancestor named Jacob Lewis Lindsey.

─────────────────────────

Connie rolled to her side, awakening to a dreary Scottish morning. She became aware of the empty side of her bed, where Jon LeFreaux had slept the night before. For the moment, she was trapped between conflicting emotions. She had needed him and used him. But unlike her intimacies with Michael, she knew that with Jon she had felt secure and comforted. In the dawn of a new day, fear continued to blanket any new emotion.

As she pulled back the bedcovers, Jon appeared in the doorway, nude, holding two cups of coffee.

"Well, now," Connie leered. "Is this your early morning advertisement?"

"No, no. I was hoping to bribe you with coffee."

"Won't work," Connie teased. "You used me up last night. But I will take the coffee. Please give my robe to me and put on some clothes, lest I act tempted again."

Jon tossed her robe, then commenced to dress. "I enjoyed us so much. I haven't felt such intensity, ever."

At first Connie said nothing; then she arose from the bed, placed her arms around him, and ruffled his hair gently. "You are a dear. We'll do this again sometime. Uh, that is, if you're willing. Now, my bedfellow, we have work to do!!"

"Connie, I've been up for quite a while. Got out your Bible and did a bit of research, You want to hear the results?"

"You, in league with the Bible. Go ahead, enlighten me," she replied.

"I got to thinking about old Jacob and that big rock. I read the section about his promise from the Big Man up in the sky. How did that rock come to be? It goes like this:"

'Abraham sired Isaac; Isaac sired Jacob; Jacob sired Judas; Judas sired Phares; Phares sired Esrom; Esrom sired Aram; Jesse sired David; David sired Solomon; Solomon sired Roboam; Roboam sired Abia; Abia sired Asa,'

Jon paused.

"Here is the point at which it gets confusing," he continued,

'and Jacob sired Joseph the husband of Mary, of whom was born Christ.'

"And now comes the New Testament. As best I can decipher, that Rock bypassed a few sireings to arrive in Scotland."

Connie gave a nervous laugh. "Jon, you would have to bring up that damn stone. So much for your Bible reading. Today, we go castle touring for the benefit of the detectives who are following me, or so Jake says."

Jon flinched. "Uh — do you think I should be seen with you?"

"Oh, I'm sure they have you pegged as an accomplice to whatever crime we're supposed to have committed. Remember what Jake told us to do: act normal, move about in a regular routine looking for ancestors. I feel certain they'll show up one day to search this place." She spun around. "Oh, oh! The envelope. You did hide it well?"

Jon's fake smile could not disguise his anxiety, evidenced by his clenching and unclenching his fist.

"Yes, I did."

"But you're not going to tell me the location?"

"No, I'm not. If either of us is ever questioned regarding anything taken from the Angus place, we can say honestly, that we know nothing about it, or where it might be."

Connie gave him a puzzled look. "You mean you don't know where the envelope is hidden?"

"You got it, Dr. Nordstram."

Connie said nothing for a few seconds. Then, "Jake has it, right?"

"Not anymore. He wouldn't tell me where it is for the reason I mentioned."

Connie moved in close to Jon. "If you're lying to me, I'll…"

"You'll what?" Before she could continue, Jon kissed her full on the mouth. "Now, I'm gonna get dressed for our tour."

Within the hour, they were on their way to Edinburgh Castle, arriving there shortly before noon.

After parking near Holyrood Castle, Jon and Connie commenced the walk along the Royal Mile leading up the hill to Edinburgh Castle. As they made their way, Connie read aloud from a tour map.

"Jon, we're starting at Holyrood. You want to hear about it?"

"If you say so. What I mean is, you bet."

"Okay. We're looking at Holyrood which was where Mary Queen of Scots established her court. Mary was a conniving royal slut, according to historians. She was engaged to a French Dauphin pretty early. He was five years old and she was an infant."

"Good lord!" exclaimed Jon. "Puberty must have breezed in early."

"Yes, Jon," Connie replied. "You're funny. Now to continue. She married the Dauphin when she was sixteen and became Queen of France and Scotland. She slept around, she was in the middle of political intrigue and she had a burr under her saddle named John Knox. The Puritanism of Knox and his followers eventually led to all sorts of trouble for Catholic Mary." Connie paused in her narrative.

"Hey, I'm listening," Jon said. "You're a good tour guide and a great lay."

"Ah," she retorted, ignoring the accolades. "Says here, she being Catholic, received a Papal disposition to dump the King of France, renounce being the Queen of France and return to Edinburgh. She then married her cousin; a fellow named Henry Darnley, but took on an Italian lover by the name of David Rizzio. That didn't go over too well with Darnley, so he had Rizzio killed. Later Darnley was strangled to death in a plot in which Mary was perhaps a part. She later married the principal suspect in her husband's murder, the Earl of Bothwell. Earlier, she had moved from Holyrood to Edinburgh Castle, perhaps to protect her from Knox's Protestants or other plotters, including her cousin, Elizabeth. I've got to rest my voice, Jon."

"You know what, Connie? Those folks make our presidential and congressional royalty look pretty tame."

"Uh, huh," she replied between breaths. "Whew, this hill is tough. I thought I was in good shape."

Before joining a tour of the castle, the two Americans stood staring at the magnificent structure, awestruck by its size and prominence on the Edinburgh landscape.

In spite of Jon's constant checks, they were unaware of the two detectives who had followed them from the time they left their cottage.

Jake twice read the message aloud:

Jake, I've done my voodoo decoding on that alphabet soup you sent me. To the best of my magical ability — and with the help of a top of the line computer program — here's what I've come up with. One word, "stone." Nothing else made any sense. That was it, Jake. Whatever you're into, good luck.

Jake gave a quizzical look first to Connie, then to Jon. "I'm disappointed."

Connie shook her head. "The only word that makes sense is stone. It's obvious that someone was referring to the Stone of Scone."

Jake raised his eyebrow. "Ah, but to this skeptical cop, that message could have been about a jewel robbery. You know the Star of India heist was big in the news, as were a number of other cursed stones."

"I don't know, Jake," Jon responded. "Based on the lore around these parts, I think someone wrote old John Angus an encrypted message about the Stone of Scone."

"I'm in agreement with Jon," Connie added. "Otherwise, why would John be murdered just as folks hereabout believe we're stone chasers."

Jake recoiled. "Dr. Nordstram, my advice to you is simple: Keep that damn stone out of your conversations with the locals. That includes Scotland Yard. Okay?" You're ancestor hunting. Nothing more. Nothing less. For your own benefit and mine, don't drop your guard." He turned his attention to Jon. "We're in a dangerous situation. As yet, I don't know why, but I'm working on it."

Chapter Twenty One

An officious receptionist ushered Chips into Raymond LeFreaux's office, there to be greeted with a power handshake and an effusive smile.

"Mr. O'Donnell, thanks for coming. I'm especially inquisitive since our telephone conversation yesterday. So, you're working for my son on whatever mission he has undertaken?" LeFreaux waited an instant, then, "Oh, my. Pardon my manners. Please take a seat." LeFreaux moved from behind his desk to one of the sofa chairs placed around a coffee table. Seated across from Chips, he rephrased his question. "I shouldn't have denigrated whatever my son is doing. What is he doing these days?"

"Well, Sir, its complicated." Chips paused to frame his answer. As he gazed out the picture window, he could see only the tops of the Boston skyline. Were he to look down, he knew that he could see Fenway to the West and the airport to the East. In between would be those who served the likes of Raymond LeFreaux. Chips had never before felt so intimidated by an executive suite.

"I'm a private investigator. I'm a partner of Jake Lindsey." Chips shifted his weight. "I don't know your son, Mr. LeFreaux, except as Jake describes him. It seems that Jon, in his genealogy search…"

"His what?" LeFreaux interjected.

"Genealogy search. He's in Scotland tracking down his family tree."

LeFreaux nodded his head from side to side. "Godalmighty! I've laid out a hundred thousand dollars for him to look for dead people!"

"As I said, the picture has become muddled."

"Muddled?"

"Yes, Sir. Your son may be in danger."

"Why would an ancestor search put him in danger?"

"It seems to be about a stone, Mr. LeFreaux. Have you ever heard of the Stone of Destiny?" Chips watched LeFreaux's reaction. Nothing. No paling out. No nervous shuffle.

"No, I haven't. Perhaps you could enlighten me and get to the point of how my son is in danger."

Chips proceeded to outline the events, as Jake had relayed them to him. Chips neglected to tell LeFreaux about his own investigation into the O'Shaughnessy matter.

"Why didn't he tell me? He knew I would stand ready to protect him. Why?" LeFreaux lowered his head into his hands. "Why?"

"If you want my opinion, Sir, I venture he would be embarrassed about spending your money on a hunt for dead ancestors." Chips said nothing about the concordant dreams of Jon and Connie.

When Jake explained that part to Chips, the two of them had laughed considering the million to one probability that such a phenomenon could occur. Chips had no intention of fueling LeFreaux's doubting of his son's dubious lifestyle.

"Can I help in any way?"

"I don't think so, Sir. My partner and I are on the case, as are several Scottish detectives. Jake Lindsey will protect your son, as you commissioned him to do. We will keep you informed along the way."

Chips hesitated before seeking an answer to the main reason he had made the appoin-tment with LeFreaux.

"Anything further, Mr. O'Donnell?"

"Yes, Sir. I know this is a bit awkward, but it could be pertinent to the safety of your son. Uh, you're a wealthy man. How did you come to make your fortune?"

"And just how in hell could my financial status have any relation to my son's safety?"

"Extortion, Mr. LeFreaux," Chips lied. "Possible extortion."

LeFreaux walked around the desk, once seated, he said, "I was as poor as a church mouse when I met my wife. She had inherited a fairly large sum of money. Over the years, I invested it wisely. More than likely, you know already that I'm worth over fifty million. Our meeting is over," he responded abruptly. "Good day, Mr. O'Donnell. Keep me informed."

No sooner had Chips left the office than LeFreaux was on the intercom. George Cassidy responded quickly to the call of his boss.

"George, I have a job for you. First of all, I want you to learn all about the Stone of Destiny and…"

Cassidy paused in his note taking. "The what?"

"Stone of Destiny. Go on line; that'll give you a start. Then I want you to go to Scotland, track down my son, Jon. I'll give you his Scotland address and telephone. There's a PI named Jake Lindsey. I want you to get a fix on what he's doing. At present, he's commissioned by me to protect my son. Report to me as soon as you have some idea as to why my son is in danger. Oh, and do not let Lindsey know that you're checking up on him, nor is my son to know that I've sent you. See Nora in HR. She'll arrange your resources. Any questions?"

"How about the local authorities? Should I work with them?"

"Yes, of course. Once more, try to stay clear of my son and Jake Lindsey."

Later, in the Hall of Records, Chips wrote the name, Margaret Eileen LeFreaux, nee Magnusen. Birthdate: 10/26/40. The date on the marriage certificate was 6/3/59.

"Well, now, Laddie," the swarthy faced detective inquired, bending close to the face of Jon. "I see you've been in the company of Dr. Constance Nordstram quite a bit of late. We know she was acquainted with John Angus." Detective Elmo Sykes then straightened up. "Tell us what ye found when plundering the domicile of one John Angus?"

Jon could feel his heart pounding. Jake had warned him that Scotland Yard didn't waste time and rarely suffered fools. His throat was dry as he tried to swallow. "I'm sure I don't know what you're talking about. Perhaps you could enlighten me." Never expand your answer, Jake had warned.

"Oh, come now, Dr. LeFreaux. You are a doctor, I'm told."

Jon nodded.

"What matter of medicine do you practice?"

"I don't practice medicine. I'm a Ph.D. archeologist."

Detective Sykes once more got close to Jon's face. "What were you searching for when you smashed a hole in old Angus' wall?"

Jon turned his head aside from Sykes's pungent breath. "I'm sure I don't know what in hell you're referring to." Jon remembered another of Jake's suggestions: show a bit of ire, but not too much.

The Scottish lawman commenced to raise his voice. "What if I told you, Laddie, that your prints are scattered about where you did in the old man?"

Jon smiled. He hesitated briefly. "I would say you witnessed a miraculous phenomenon."

"What do ye mean, uh, by that?" Sykes stammered.

"How could my fingerprints be there when I had nothing to do with a murder of any sort, anywhere?"

Sykes whispered something to the other detective in the room. He turned back to Jon. "We'll allow you to sit here for a bit. That'll give you time to remember all about being in old Angus' domicile."

Once more, Jon recalled Jake's advice. Jon sat quietly. Seconds later he lowered his head to the table and pretended to nap. He began calling to mind the images of Connie's and his search for lost ancestors and the allure of Scottish history. He walked once more along Hadrian's Wall, from Solway to Tyne. He imaged again the Castles of Sterling and Edinburgh. He had wanted to sit above the Stone of Scone where so many kings and queens had been crowned over the centuries.

He was certain that Connie and he had become experts in examining sheaves of history in numerous halls of records. Edinburgh. Dunbar. Aberdeen. Falkland. In his mind's eye, they melded into a single picture of little reward and much frustration.

He raised his head and smiled as he recalled the B & B outside Glasgow, the night he made love to Connie.

Had Scotland Yard tailed them for the fortnight? He knew not.

An hour after Jon had been left alone, his interrogators returned.

"Am I under arrest? If so, I wish to know the charge."

Detective Sykes answered. "Not at the moment. As your FBI often states, you are a person of interest, at present, not a target."

"So — may I go? I have a great deal of research work waiting for me."

"Yes, you may go. You're not to leave the country. And to make sure you continue to enjoy our hospitality, you'll not get your passport as yet."

Jake, it seems that the info I sent you is going to take me on a backtrack. I'll try to find out how Eileen Magnusen came by the dowry she brought to her marriage to LeFreaux. I could just up and ask her, but old Raymond might have serious objections. So, I'll take the long way around.

Jake waited for a response after he read the email to Connie and Jon. "I'm confused and in a mild state of shock," Jon said. "My mother always gave the credit to dad for having made a bunch of money. I don't know what else to say."

"Do you want Chips to try tracing your mother's history?"

Jon thought for a moment. "Yeah. You bet. Now, I'm really curious and slightly worried about what your partner may uncover."

"Are you thinking…" Jon interrupted before Connie could complete her question.

"Yes, I am. I don't think for one minute that my mother was involved in something, nefarious. But…" Jon waggled his finger. "Even a scandal of some kind a generation or so back, could hurt the family name. If you know anything about Boston society, those bluebloods are not a forgiving lot."

"So be it," Jake replied. "Now let me catch you up on my travels hither and yon. I've been unable to lay any dirt on Ahern, but I haven't given up. I'm not convinced that he's as pure as the driven snow. I've had no luck in tracking down the lads who jumped me in that tavern. I'll hit a couple more places to find any trace of those three. I'm not optimistic. Now, Jon, tell me all about your set-to with the local gendarmes."

"Not much to tell. Like you warned me, that detective Sykes was a bulldog. Said he had my prints from the crime scene. When I didn't bite, he left me alone for a hell of a long time. I just sat and daydreamed until he came back."

Jake grinned. "Yep. The old let'em sweat trick. We did that when I was Boston P.D. Paid off occasionally. Was there anything that especially caught your attention?"

"Yeah," Jon answered. "I'm now certain that Connie and I are under constant surveillance. Sykes alluded to stuff he couldn't have known unless he just happened to be in the area where it occurred."

"Such as?"

Jon glanced toward Connie. "Once, out of the blue, he asked how long I had been balling Connie."

Connie could feel her face burning. She moved closer to Jon. "And what did you say?"

"Told him, uh — as I recall — uh, I told him we were doing research together." Jon stared at the floor. "He then ventured his opinion that we surely did a lot of research all night in the same hotel room."

Jake shook his head slowly. "Look guys, use your good sense. I have a deep rooted belief in all-night sex, but please be a bit more discreet. You two are beginning to look tawdry. These spiritual descendents of John Knox will be quick to see you as murderers. It's a short leap from adultery to murder in these parts."

"I resent that, Jake!" Connie flared. "It's not as if we're — uh, doing, you know — having sex all the time!"

"Dr. Nordstram, frankly I don't give a damn who you fuck, when, where, or how many times a day. But you and Don Juan," he glanced at Jon, "are in my care, matter of speaking. Please try not to call any more attention to us." Jake emphasized "us".

"We'll be more careful, Jake," Jon said. Separate rooms on the road and such. No outward displays of guilt."

"Okay." Jake answered. "To the business at hand. I want to visit the lady Digbe again. I think she could have told us a lot more than she did when we met with her."

Chapter Twenty Two

Four flights of stairs and Chips breathed heavily as he walked down the hallway. When he knocked on the door of apartment 424, Jody Obeshi answered in a loud voice, "Who are you? What do want?"

Chips moved to a position which allowed her to see him through the peep hole. "My name is O'Donnell. I'm looking for a man named Septo, Baron Septo. This is the address given to me."

"He don't live here no more. He got pissed at me and took off."

"Do you mind if I come in and ask a few questions?"

"You got sompin' for me?"

Chips brought out his wallet. He extracted a twenty and held it up for Jody to see.

"That's a start," she laughed. "You gonna hafta do better'n that."

Chips dug deeper. "How's this?"

She opened the door. "Thank you. Let me…" before he could finish the question, she interrupted.

"Gimme the bread. First things first."

Chips handed her the money. "Now, uh-you know Septo, you say?"

"Know him? Hell, I been with the bastard for ten years. I was glad to see him go. I'll bet you're a cop."

"No. I work for a genealogist."

"What's a, uh gene — whatever?"

"We track down long lost ancestors."

"Uh-huh," she replied, having little idea of the way Chips had defined himself.

"So, what do you want to know about Baron?"

Before Chips answered, he gazed around the one room flat, cluttered with soft drink cans, beer bottles, clothing strewn about, a sink filled with unwashed dishes, unemptied ashtrays.

She sat down on an unmade bed, then motioned for Chips to join her. More than her dress being slightly hiked above her knee, Chips was interested in the needle marks on her arm.

"Hey, I'm a good lay. I'll show you a real good time for a couple of Ben Franklins." She patted the unmade bed.

"Thanks for the offer. I'm a little short on cash, but to answer your question about Septo…"

"Okay, I'll go for a hundred. How does that sound?"

"Thanks, Jody. You're an attractive woman, but I'm gay," Chips lied.

Her expression changed quickly from an inviting smile to a contemptuous sneer.

"Let me try again," Chips continued. "Now that we've settled our sexual differences, I'll tell you what I want to know about Septo. Where is he now?"

"How much cash you got on you?"

"Hell, lady, I've given you a wad already!"

Obeshi rose from the bed. "You wanta know where Septo is, you gonna have to come up with sompin' more than what you give me so far." She patted the palm of her hand.

Chips reached for his wallet, looked inside it, then responded. "I'll give you my last twenty. That's it."

She snapped up the bill he extended.

"He hangs out a lot at the Cedar Town Tavern over on Lompor Avenue." She gave a high pitched laugh, "You didn't fool me none. You're a cop. You ain't no gene-whatever."

As Chips walked down the four flights, Jody was gazing out her window to the street below. She watched Chips enter his auto, she then picked up the telephone and dialed the number for the Cedar Town Tavern.

George Cassidy was not enamored of his latest task. He saw himself as a realist, and not one who read fairy tales about biblical stones. His function as Raymond Le-Freaux's CFO was to watch bottom lines to make sure outgo did not surpass income and to stay abreast of stock market fluxuations.

Cassidy, as a loyal worker for LeFreaux, had never questioned directions the CEO gave him. Now, as he stood outside his auto observing the small cottage a hundred yards to his front, he regretted not having confronted LeFreaux. Did not the boss know that accountants rarely make good detectives?

Mid-morning. For the third day in a row, he was prepared to tail Jon and his female accomplice. Shortly before 10:00 o'clock Jon and Connie drove away from their cottage with Cassidy not far behind.

As they entered the main thoroughfare, Jon glanced in the rearview mirror. "Well, Dr. Nordstram, Scotland Yard is on the job. Now and again, I'm tempted to get into a car chase. You know, like in <u>French Connection</u> and every adventure movie since."

Connie didn't say anything for a few seconds. She glanced to the rear at the vehicle, several hundred feet behind them. "Let's give those detectives a reason to earn their money. What do you say?"

"You mean…"

"Yes. See if you can lose them. But don't forget to stay on the left side of the road."

"Connie, you do shock me at least once a day. I have to ask you, lady, are you nuts?"

"Nope," she replied. "When stopped, we're late for our next inquiry up the road at Montrose. When we hear the siren, we'll pull over. I want to know if they have anything on us by this time. My guess is they'll be frustrated at having to chase us. Perhaps they'll spill the beans. What do you say?"

Jon answered by pressing the accelerator to the floor. "Okay. But you do the talking when they catch up to us."

The speedometer needle passed the 120 KM mark. "Are they still with us?" Jon almost shouted.

"I don't see the car. We must be putting some distance between them and us. Good job, Dr. LeFreaux."

"Thank you, Dr. Nordstram. I'll pull onto the next side road. The odds are that we're still the fox and they're the dogs."

Behind them, Cassidy saw the flashing light. He eased his auto to the side of the road. He slapped the steering wheel in anger. "Dammit! I'll never find them!"

The policeman peered into the side window, tipping his hat and smiling. "Good day, sir. I do say, ye were moving along rather briskly. May I see your permit?"

"Uh, do you mean my driver's license?"

"Ah, you're yank. Yes, I believe you refer to the permit in such manner."

"I don't have a license."

The highway official grimaced. "Then we have a situation, sir."

Cassidy cursed himself silently for having neglected to place his Massachusetts driver's license in his wallet. A lot of good it was doing back in his Mercedes.

The officer walked to the back of the car. "Please open the rear compartment."

Cassidy did as he was instructed.

"Officer, I have a passport."

"Constable. I'm a Constable."

Cassidy fought to control his irritation. "Constable sir, I suspected I was going too fast, but I'm still learning the metric system."

The Scottish patrolman laughed. "Now, sir, Mr. Cassidy, is it? Ye can't expect me to take ye up on that one." He flipped a page of his notepad. "How in the Lord's name were ye able to rent this carriage without a driver permit?"

Cassidy was in a quandary. He knew that if he told the truth he would cause trouble for the car rental employee he had bribed, and he wasn't sure as to the nature of Scottish law and the briber.

"It's, uh, it's a loan car from a friend."

"I see," responded the constable. "And your friend is associated with the Highlands Carriage Agency. Mr. Cassidy, give me the keys to the carriage. We'll take a ride to me station. Please face the carriage and place your hands behind you."

Jake Lindsey was out of his element. His efforts at conversation with the natives were met with the usual suspicion. A week and several false leads passed before he encountered the first Scot who would speak to him at any length about Ahern or any of his employees. Three beers into his meeting with William Parker gave Jake his first credible lead. Parker told Jake that he had worked for Ahern, but had left his employ five years earlier. He remembered a man named Boone. Didn't know Boone's whereabouts but that Jake should talk to a man named Armistead, who as Parker remembered, was a friend of Boone.

So it was that Lindsey entered the premises of Ahern Industries for the second time, bypassed the office of Ahern and went directly to the Department of Personnel.

"I'm here to see Mr. Peterson." Jake smiled at the secretary.

"And your name, sir?"

"Mike Adams. I don't have an appointment. I'm here to interview for the engineer position you have posted."

"Very good, Mr. Adams." She lifted the telephone and pressed the intercom button. "A Mr. Adams is here about the engineer position."

"Send him in," the voice on the intercom directed.

For a brief time, Peterson did not look up from the file he was examining.

"May I sit?" Jake asked.

"Please do. I'll be with you as soon as I…" as he looked up startled, he exclaimed, "I know you!"

Before Peterson could touch the intercom, he was staring at the bore of Jake's Glock. "Be cool, Mr. Peterson, and both of us will come out of this without a scratch."

Peterson dabbed at the bead of sweat on his forehead. "What do you want? I told you that this company never employed the three men you asked about."

"That's true," Jake replied. "At present, I'm more interested in a person named Armistead. I don't know his first name. I want you to have him come to your office."

Peterson shuffled the papers before him.

"You mean now? Today?"

"That's exactly what I mean. I want him here now. And I don't want you to route him through Ahern's office. Am I clear?"

Again, Peterson wiped the perspiration from his brow as he reached for the intercom button.

"No, no, Mr. Peterson!"

"I was going to have my secretary go through our files to determine whether we even have anyone named Armistead working here."

"Okay. Go ahead. Do something crazy and I'm liable to do something crazy."

After a short wait, Leon Armistead entered the office. He was dressed in the Scottish white collar style of the day: shirt, tie, wool jacket, khaki trousers, brown wingtips.

"You wished to see me, Mr. Peterson?"

"Be seated. Leon, Mister, uh, I'm sorry, I don't remember your name — wants to make an inquiry."

"Adams. Mike Adams, Leon. This won't take long. I understand you're a friend of Peter Boone."

"Yes, I sure am. But I haven't been in touch with him since he left."

"So," Jake said, "He worked here. Is that how you met him?"

"Yes."

"Do you know where he went?"

"No. I was a bit surprised when Mr. Peterson here told me that he had just up and left."

"I see." Jake riveted Peterson with a hard stare. "And do you know of his whereabouts these days?"

"Certainly not" Peterson replied defensively.

Jake turned his attention back to Armistead. "Thank you, Leon. Should you hear from your friend, here's my number."

"Are you a copper? Is he in some sort of trouble?"

"I hope not. Thanks. That's all I need to know for now."

"Mr. Peterson, I'll be in me office if you require me presence further."

As Armistead closed the door behind him, Jake offered Peterson a proposition. "Let's exchange pickles. I won't tell Scotland Yard that you erased employee files provided you don't tell them I pointed a gun at you. Bargain?"

Peterson fidgeted in his chair. "You'll never get away with this."

"Sure, I will," Jake replied. "You better pray that Boone and the other two are alive and well. Otherwise, you're an accessory to murder. Oh, and I want Armistead's home address. One more thing: Don't tell Ahern of our deal. He won't be happy that you cooperated with me."

The bar was tucked away on a poorly lit street several blocks off Independence Avenue. A lone auto was parked in front next to a fire hydrant. Trash littered the area. The neon sign above the entrance read "Cedar Town Tavern" as it blinked off and on.

Chips pulled in behind the 1966 Mercedes. He shoved an ammo clip into the Berretta and gave a cursory look up and down the street. Satisfied that he had not been followed, he walked into the tavern. Three men sat at the bar while the bartender busied himself washing steins, glasses, and pitchers.

Chips glanced at the clock to his front, ten thirty-seven. He selected a bar stool away from the trio to the right of him.

As the barkeep dried his hands, he made his way over to his new customer. "What'll you have?"

Chips placed a bill on the counter. "You got a Corona?"

"You bet."

The bartender set the beer and a glass before Chips. "Anything else?"

"Yeah. I was told I might find Septo here."

"He's in back," the bartender replied, motioning with a head nod. "Through that door. He does some work for me from time to time."

The instant Chips walked into the back room, Septo swung a tire iron to the back of Chip's head. He was unconscious before he fell to the floor. Septo dragged him through the back door and dumped him into a van parked in the alley.

"Is he dead?" the driver asked.

"If he ain't, he will be soon."

"I got the chains," Agles said. "You gonna let me finish him off? That bastard almost killed me and I want to see him bleed like a stuck hog."

"You got it," Septo said.

Late into the night they wrapped Chips in heavy chains. Agles then slit Chips' throat never knowing that he had cut the throat of a man who was near death already from a crushed skull.

Chapter Twenty Three

Connie waited before she knocked on the door a second time. As Jon and she were about to walk away, Kathryn Digbe opened her door.

"Well now, what'll ye be out and about fer, this day?"

"Good morning, Miss Digbe," Connie raised her hand in greeting. "May we speak with you again? I've brought along some sweets if you're in the mood."

The old lady's face broke into a wide grin. "Yes, a tad of chocolate is always welcome. Come right in. I'll brew some tea." She tapped Jon's arm. "Glad ye brought along the cute one. He'll go well with the sweets."

"Why thank you, Kathryn. I'm flattered."

As Digbe busied herself brewing the tea, Connie placed the fruit-filled chocolates on the table. In a low voice she said, "I hope we have better luck than our guardian, Lindsey."

Digbe set the teacups before her visitors. "I'm glad that other fellow didn't come with ye. Misfortune is sure to find that one."

"Misfortune?" Jon exclaimed, raising his voice.

"Ah, yes. The runnin' boys are keepin' an eye on your friend."

"And who are the running boys?" Connie asked.

"They wore masks, the cowardly devils. I dinna tell that Jake lad. I'm not sure I should tell you."

"But Kathryn…" Connie nudged Jon.

"When I dinna come right out and answer his questions, he was frisky wi' me. He was surely, an impatient one. I dinna appreciate that."

"Kathryn, we'll not push you to tell us more than you're willing to share. We understand your position. I, too, am wary — maybe even afraid of MacTavish."

"Ye should be, Lassie. His runnin' boys are the dregs."

"How do you…" This time Connie disrupted Jon with a soft kick under the table.

"So MacTavish's thugs have threatened you?"

"May I ask, in what way?" Jon ventured, hoping he would not be cut short by Connie.

"They dinna come right out. What they did was tell me all about what happened to poor old John Angus."

Connie's anxiety was reawakened.

"Kathryn, why do you suppose anyone would want to kill John Angus?"

"The Stone, Lass. That damnable stone."

"I'm not sure I understand," Connie said.

"John Angus told me once upon a time that he carried a secret about the Stone. But, you know now, all around these parts saw old John as a gossip. Didn't pay much attention to him. I told him if he didn't quit making up tales about the Stone, he would come to some bad end. He surely did that."

"Miss Digbe, did John Angus tell you the secret he carried?" Jon leaned close to her.

"Nae. He would only say that if I knew his secret, I would be in danger."

"And that's why the runnin' boys keep hounding you?"

"I think no," she answered. "Mayhaps that MacTavish devil, so high and mighty livin' in a castle he concocted, as I told ye, he fears me knowledge of his tree."

"His tree?"

"Surely. His ancestor tree."

Connie gave Digbe a quizzical look. "Katy, why didn't you tell me you had known John for some time?"

"Wasn't sure I could trust ye. When John Angus acted like he was seein' me for the first time — ye know, when ye two came over — I didn't know if ye were friend or foe. And when ye said ye were kin of that devil MacTavish, I shut my mouth, matter of speakin'."

Connie thanked Miss Digbe and asked if they might visit again.

"Aye, Lass. I donna get much company. I'll be glad to see you. Perhaps I can trust you. Perhaps!"

Jon put his arm around the old woman. "You can trust us. We're on your side. And if you ever feel threatened by those runnin' boys, please let us know about it." He handed her a card upon which he had written a telephone number.

Connie hugged the old woman effusively. "Thanks for the tea. We'll visit you again for sure. Have you reported to the police about the threats?"

"Ye must be batty! I donna trust them coppers. They try to have us believe they're Scots! Ha!"

Jon drove in silence for several miles, then, "What do you think, Connie?"

"I think the two of us are in a hell of a quagmire. That's another name for a confusing, frightening mess." She paused. "I've made up my mind, Jon. I'm going to confront long lost cousin Michael. If I, we, are in danger from him, I think we ought to know."

"And just how do you intend to confront him?"

Connie slid over close to Jon. "I'll ask him outright if he had anything to do with the attack on me."

"Just like that! Are you nuts?"

"No, I have a big, brave archeologist to protect me." She kissed him on his cheek.

"The old lady hates Michael. That may color her perception. You know — he's Satan and responsible for all bad things."

"Woman, are you trying to run me off the road? It's a strain to remember to drive on the left side. But now," he leered, "I have to keep that libidinal surge in check until I can get you in bed." He paused. "I believe you're right about the old lady's suspicions."

———————————————

George Cassidy had never seen the inside of a jail. Now, for the moment, he was a resident in one. He had become testy with the constable when he was not allowed to call outside the country. He waited, frightened and isolated in a strange land, among people who looked like him, and except for a few burrs sprinkled in their speech, spoke the same language as he. Alone in the darkness of the cell, he prayed that LeFreaux's son would bail him from his wretched station.

He cursed the day Raymond LeFreaux had given him his present assignment. He regretted having insulted the Scottish policeman who arrested him. He lay back on the cot. He kept telling himself to endure that which could not be changed; to learn from the experience. Such rumination did little to calm his fears.

A short time after midnight, the night jailor opened Cassidy's cell door.

"Out ye go. Got a couple of lads here for ye."

After retrieving his personal effects Cassidy moved into the holding area waiting room.

Jon and Jake rose from their chairs. "Mr. Cassidy, I'm Jon LeFreaux."

Cassidy could feel the tears of relief well up.

"Thank you for coming. This is terribly embarrassing for me. Your father sent me."

Jon interrupted. "I know. I talked to him a short while ago." Jon extended his hand. Cassidy's handshake was firm, but sweaty. "This is Jake Lindsey."

"How do you do, Mr. Cassidy? I'm sorry you had to put up with these folks. Their accommodations aren't very upscale." He lowered his voice to a whisper. "They're a bunch of pricks."

Jake's easy manner brought a weak smile from Cassidy.

"Mr. Cassidy…"

"Call me George, please."

Jake continued. "George, I looked over your rap sheet. Jesus, you've been here two days and already you've bribed a car rental guy, cussed out a constable — they call that resisting arrest — you're driving with no permit. God man! How long have you been a private investigator?"

Cassidy didn't answer until they were outside the station. "I'm not. I'm an accountant. Why in God's name your father sent me here is beyond reason."

"I'm sure my father trusts you," Jon responded. "Now, if you don't mind telling us, why are you here?"

"To find out what kind of danger you're in and to work with the local police — uh, on your behalf."

"How did he know Jon has some trouble?" Jake asked.

"I haven't the faintest idea. He just called me into his office and gave me my instructions. I always do as he directs and have done so for nigh on twenty years."

"Shall I call my father on your behalf?" Jon offered.

"No, no!" Cassidy exclaimed. "I don't want him to know I've acted in an incompetent fashion. I'll have my secretary send a copy of my driver's license to me. That way the constable will know I'm allowed to drive."

Jake laughed. "George, ol' boy, your driving days in Scotland are past. You will be lucky to get off without some time in the pokey. When do you go before a magistrate?"

"Three days from now."

"Get yourself a barrister or as we colonials call them, lawyers. I assume they lifted your passport."

"Yes." Cassidy smiled weakly. "They lifted everything except my underpants."

"George," Jon volunteered, "How can we help you to keep me protected from danger?"

Cassidy became defensive. "I know you two are laughing at me. Good Lord, Jon! I'm just trying to carry out your father's wish. He cares for you very much." Cassidy hesitated. "Even though he's never understood your choice of vocations."

Jon gave a cynical laugh. "So, my dear father continues to broadcast his differences with me. So be it."

"No, no Jon! I'm his only confidant. He certainly does not go around airing his disagreement about you."

"Let's drop it," Jon said. "Where are you staying? What's your tele number? I'll go to the magistrate with you if you want me to."

"I'd like that," he replied, handing Jon a card. "And, Jake, could you come along?"

"I'm not sure that's a good idea, George. Let me think about it. My PI license doesn't mean much in these parts. I'm flying by the seat of my pants looking after ol' Jon here."

"So, now, we're both in the scam business."

"You two are making me feel like a piece of prime rib!" Jon laughed as he gave a punch to Cassidy's shoulder.

"Try hamburger," Jake retorted.

Molly led Connie into the massive area, which in Connie's native land, would be called a great room.

"Have you been well, Mum?" Molly asked.

"Yes, Molly, and you? I've missed you and your tea. Bet that surprises you. I've grown to enjoy tea."

Molly grinned. "Many more cups of tea and ye'll be one of the Queen's loyal subjects." Molly looked over her shoulder. "Have ye been hit again, Mum?"

"No. Just that one time."

"I miss you, Mum. I must return to me duties now. His Lordship says he'll be down shortly."

Connie paced around the room for an irritating period of time. She was on the verge of leaving when MacTavish came up behind her.

"I dare say, Connie, you do have a tart way of bidding one adieu."

Startled, Connie spun around to his glowering Lordship.

"Ah, but 'tis good to see you again. Your note was a bit brief and somewhat cold. I was surprised."

Connie clenched her fists at her side to hide their shaking.

"Michael, I was confused and frightened — and," she stared straight into his eyes, "I had grown suspicious of you."

"Oh, dear girl! Suspicious of me. I swear to you, I had nothing to do with the assault on your person. My God, Constance! Why would I do such a dastardly thing? Please sit and perhaps I can allay your mistrust, if not your fear. I've missed you."

He pressed a button at the end of the table. "Molly, dear, please bring tea for my guest and me. Now, what did I do to cause your abrupt departure?"

"I'm uncomfortable even discussing this but once I overheard you speaking to someone. Whether on the tele or in person, I didn't wait to know. As I remember you said, 'She's getting too close to things'." Connie felt her mouth go dry around the lie she had just told.

For a discomfiting moment, Michael stared down at the table. "I swear to you, I had nothing to gain from an attack on you. As a matter of fact, I have let it be known that any mischief toward you will be an affront to me. Believe me, I am concerned for your welfare."

"Michael, I want to trust you. You've been kind and gracious to me. But I keep asking myself the question: have you been straight with me?"

Michael tried to remain calm, even as his face reddened with anger.

"What do you mean?"

"I mean have you told me all you know about your great, great grandfather's first wife, and whom I suspect may be an ancestor of mine?"

Before MacTavish could answer, Connie continued. "You told me that old John Angus was a gossip; that no one paid any attention to and now that old man is dead. Michael, what's going on? Why do unknown people want me out of Scotland?"

MacTavish placed his hand on Connie's arm. "Okay. Truth time. If you heard me allude to a woman getting too close to things, quote, unquote, I was referring to you. Now don't jump to conclusions. I was trying to scare you out of Scotland, because I did not want you to be harmed. But, so help me, God, I did not attack you nor did I order an attack on you. I know that you had grown close to John Angus. Closer than I intended. When I told you about him, I thought you would see him as a busybody, then go on your way."

Connie was at a crossroad of intentions. Should she tell him of the letter from Angus' home? The authorities had never made known all the details surrounding the murder. Specifically, the broken wall had been placed off limits to news people, the Yard's reasoning that any confession by some nut case could be discounted through erroneous details he might give to back up his confession.

"Michael, when you told me about the Stone of Destiny, you glossed over the rumors around it. Are you holding out on me?"

"My dear Constance, you are the persistent one. Are you asking me to consolidate all the rumors into one neat package? If such be the case, you're out of luck. I'll tell you of the fairy tale talk most repeated, and trust it will satisfy you. I must say, dear cousin, I'm no longer sure which artifact you're trying to uncover: The Stone or a missing ancestor."

At that juncture, Connie made the decision not to tell Michael of the coded letter, nor her part in acquiring it.

"Because I was attacked after coming into contact with John Angus, and because of the opposition my cohorts and I have run into when we bring up the Stone in conversations, I'm very interested in that rock. And occasionally, deep into the night, I think: Is it possible that an apple from our family tree fell into some Stone conspiracy? So you see, Michael, those are my reasons for wanting more detail from your point of view."

"Let's see if you'll believe my answer this time around regarding great, great grandfather's first wife. As I told you, no one knows what happened to her when she left these hustings. I want you to believe me. Did she go to Ireland? I don't know. To the colonies — beg pardon, to the United States? That, too, is an unknown."

Connie riveted MacTavish with a harsh stare. "I've been told that great, great grandfather was abusive to her."

Michael's anger flared. "That old bastard told you that!! It's a damn lie!"

Connie backed away. "That old bastard, as you refer to John Angus, did no such thing. My information came from an entirely different source and you don't have to be so defensive."

"I apologize for my outburst. Great Caesar, Constance! How could anyone know anything about how your great, great grandfather and mine treated his spouses?"

Connie smiled. "As you've told me, Scotland thrives on rumor and folklore."

"And anything you've heard about our great, great grandfather being a tyrant is just that, folklore. My research indicates that he was well respected, beloved. Your great, great grandmother left him because she was pregnant by a groomsman. What do you think of that lore? Great, great grandfather could not have been blamed had he scourged her from the premises."

Connie said nothing in response.

MacTavish continued. "You asked for more detail about the Stone. I've told you all I know, Constance. You, no doubt, know as much as I. Oh," he lowered his gaze, "I forgot one detail. Rumor has it that old John Angus planned the heist of the Stone from the Abbey."

Connie tried to suppress a surge of anxiety. In a calm voice she asked, "Michael, why have you waited until this moment to give me this TINY detail?"

"Didn't think it was significant, my dear."

"It was good to see you again, Michael. Thanks for your information." She paused. "And the tea."

"Connie, don't go. I've missed you. I've missed our intimate moments. Please stay."

"No, Michael." As she walked to her car, she knew that she might never trust her bloodline cousin again.

Chapter Twenty Four

"How did it go?" Jake asked.

"As well as could be expected," Cassidy answered.

"You were right about the car thing. I'm not allowed to drive in Scotland forevermore."

Jon's laugh was stifled. "So now, I'll be your chaperone."

"I've got a better idea," Connie offered. "The two of you can look after each other and I," she thumped her chest, "will see to you both."

"Okay, have your fun, but I'm here as Mr. LeFreaux instructed and whatever you're about I'm in."

"How did the hearing go, aside from you not being allowed to drive in Scotland?" Jake asked.

Before Cassidy could answer, Jon spoke up. "The first thing the judge did was inform me I wasn't needed in the hearing room. I sat outside. But a nice young lady brought me a spot of tea, don't ye know. Sorry, George. I butted in."

"No problem. I had to pay a three hundred pound fine. And I'm on probation. Not allowed to bribe anyone for the duration of my stay in Scotland. I feel bad about the young fellow who lost his job at the rental place."

"Did the judge really order you not to bribe anybody as long as you are in Scotland."

"Gotcha, Dr. Nordstram. I made that up. I'm to stay out of trouble for a year."

After two rings, Jake answered his cell.

"How long has he been missing?"

At the other end, Bennie responded. "Three days. I didn't worry at first. But you know that Chips always checked in every other day."

"Yes, I know. Where was he the last time you heard from him?"

"He didn't give me his exact whereabouts. He said he was going to check a lead at some place called Cedar Town."

"Thanks, Bennie. Tell him to call or email me the next time he checks in."

Jake closed his phone and turned toward the others. "My partner hasn't called the office in three days. My guess is that he's hot on the trail of a cheating husband." Jake's lighthearted manner belied his anxiety. He knew that Chips was a creature of habit, one not to stray too far from a lifelong adherence to schedules.

"I'll check with you three later. In the meantime, keep a low profile. I'm going to try to dig up some bodies."

After he closed the door behind him, Cassidy inquired, "What did he mean by that?"

"Who knows, George," Jon answered. "Jake keeps his own counsel."

Tom Benini and his buddy, Jack Dugan got an early start for their fishing trip. The sun peeked over the eastern horizon as they put their boat into the Skukill River.

"Hey, Jack, can you believe how low the river is? That should help us pull in a good catch."

"Keep your voice down or we won't catch anything but trouble. I wish you had remembered to get our licenses."

"Don't blame me, ol' buddy. I had to do a job for the boss. You had time to do it."

"Forget it, Tom. I just hope we don't get caught. Big fine if we do."

Two hours and three beers later, no fish had been caught.

"Let's call it, Jack. I don't know where the damn fish are. They sure as hell ain't here."

The electric trolling motor pushed the boat slowly toward the river bank. Benini continued to cast, even as Dugan laid aside his fishing rod. Ten yards form shore, Benini yelled, "I got sompin', Jack! Hey, hey! It's a big one!"

Dugan flipped the motor switch. The boat bobbed in the water while Benini struggled to bring in his catch. His casting rod was bent almost double, but he kept reeling and pulling. "Man! I don't know what's on the line, but it's big!"

"Probably a tire," Dugan laughed. Sweating profusely, cursing loudly, Benini brought the object to the surface. "Son of a bitch! It's a body, Jack!" Dugan hooked the corpse with his grapplers. "Tom, get this boat to the bank while I hang on to this feller. What's that dangling from his leg?"

"Looks like a piece of chain. I'm guessing this dude aggravated the mob. It sure looks like something the wise guys would do," Benini replied. "So what are we gonna do, Jack?"

"We're going to call the locals."

"Oh, so we're out fishing without a license and we pulled in a dead body. I'm not sure there's a license for dead body fishing, Jack. Jesus! We're in a pickle! They'll bust us for fishing illegally and maybe we'll be suspects." He paused. "And what if it is a mob hit. They ain't gonna be happy that we invaded their burial ground. I think we should just get the hell out of here and let this poor devil go back where he came from."

"Don't be stupid," Jack admonished his friend. "We're gonna call the police, but I won't give them our names. Now help me drag him to the bank."

"So the caller gave no name?"

"That's right, lieutenant. He told us where to find this body. Nothing more."

The homicide detective, Abe Kulaski, bent down to check the corpse. "Did the computer get the number?"

"Yes, sir. One of our guys has already checked it. It was from a phone out near Paoli," the uniformed officer answered.

"This guy was dead before he went in the drink. Look at his skull. His throat's been cut also. Okay, keep this place clean. CSI'll be here soon."

"Yes, sir."

"Why does a dead body always turn up on our shift?" Kulaski inquired of his partner, Nancy Ramirez.

"We're just lucky, Abe," she replied. "Here come the CSI boys."

The crime scene duo, Pete Marelli and John Fleming, lifted the yellow restraining tape then knelt down over the body.

"Abe, you're forever finding work for me. I had tickets for the game today."

"Yeah, John. The bad guys refuse to do their killing around our schedule."

Nancy Ramirez, the youngster in the group, spoke teasingly. "You're a pair of old horses. The city should have put you out to pasture long ago."

"Now, young lady," Fleming rejoined, "that would be great if I had you to chase around the pasture."

"Abe, you heard that. Sexual harassment. Gotta get me a lawyer," she laughed. "What do you think happened here?"

"Here's my first impression," Marelli said. "The death was caused by a severe blow or blows to the head. Blunt instrument I'd say. The killing took place elsewhere. Probably more than one chain was used to weight the body, which means most of whatever chains were attached came loose, perhaps, farther up river."

"The tire tracks indicate two vehicles were here," Fleming added.

"Abe, who discovered the bodies?"

"We got a call. Anonymous. Gave us the exact location. Nothing more."

"I'll give you another educated guess. Someone was fishing here on the river." Marelli walked to the edge of the water. "He probably put in here. Found the corpse, then got the hell out of Dodge."

"If that's the case, why wouldn't he come forward?" Ramirez asked.

"Again, just a guess. He, or they, were doing illegal baiting, probably something like electrifying the water to bring the fish to the top. That's the modern method. Used to be dynamite, but that became too messy, what with urban sprawl and the like."

"At present he's a John Doe. No ID of any kind," Ramirez noted.

"Maybe we'll get lucky with a print." Ramirez walked over to the uniformed officer. "Which one of you took the call?"

A young policeman stepped forward. "I did, ma'am."

"What time did the call come in?"

The officer flipped a page in his notepad. "My partner and I got the recording from central at 1305. We came right out."

"Did you notice anyone near this area?"

"No, ma'am, other than the two of us and you folks…"

"Thanks, and please don't call me ma'am. Makes me sound older and matronly." She held out her hand. "I'm Detective Ramirez."

"This is my partner Patrolman Joe Milan. I'm Benji Adkins, uh, patrolman. We just graduated from the academy."

"When you make your report, try to remember every detail when you drove up," she directed. "Something may seem insignificant, but could fit into the bigger picture."

"Yes, ma— uh, detective. We'll do that," Adkins said, as Ramirez walked away.

"Fucking power-needy female," Milan whispered. "Does she think we're dummies?"

Jake slumped through the door of the pub and joined the others at a nearby table.

"What's your poison?" George Cassidy asked.

"Beer, any beer. To tell you the truth, I need a bottle of scotch. I've got some bad news. My partner, Chips O'Donnell has been murdered. His body was found near the Skukill River in Philadelphia."

"God, Jake, I'm so sorry," Connie grimaced, placing her hand on Jake's arm.

"Anyhow, folks, I'll be going back to the U.S. for his funeral." He turned his attention to Jon. "Hey, man, I regret that I'll be doing some strong inquiry into your father's comings and goings. It's a crappy situation. He hires me to look after you and now he's gonna be a subject of my bulldogging. Can you beat that?"

"Yep, and my cover is blown all to hell. He'll probably fire me. Guess it can't be helped," Cassidy added.

"I wouldn't be so sure, George. I can be a sneaky bastard when I put my head to it. Hell, I know nothing. George Cassidy? Who is George Cassidy?"

"Thanks, Jake."

"So," Jake eyed each one of the three. "Can you stay out of trouble til' I return to me kilts and haggis?"

"We'll try, Jake," Jon replied.

"And I don't believe Mr. LeFreaux is involved in something so awful as murder," Cassidy said.

"Didn't say he was," Jake retorted, irritated and defensive.

"Do what you have to do, Jake. I'm sorry about your partner. Don't stay away from us too long. Remember, my father is paying you to look after me." All three gave a nervous laugh.

Jake turned to leave. "One last thing. Jon, I haven't had time to talk to Mary Manion. Remember, old Mrs. Digbe gave us that name. You might want to check her out."

Connie looked surprised. "Jon, you never mentioned anyone named Mary Manion. Who is she and what does she have to do with us?"

"Connie, I, uh," Jon stammered. "I forgot."

"I wish so much you men would keep me in the loop. I'm not some cotillion debutante!"

Jon ignored the rebuke. "Where is she located? I don't remember, Jake."

Lindsey broke out his notepad. "Dundee. She said the lass was living at or near Dundee."

Cassidy, who had listened with some interest, chimed in. "I'd like to go along. I've been reading about Dundee and St. Andrews."

"You're in," Connie answered.

———————

Jake Lindsey held Benny Rochelle close. She sobbed as the two of them watched the coffin being lowered into the ground. She had been Chips' emotional support when he was going through his divorce.

"Bennie, I want to pay my respects to Amy."

Jake walked to the edge of the small group gathered around the grave. He extended his hand to Amy Caldwell, Chips' ex-wife.

"I'm so sorry, Jake. Chips and I had our differences. He was a good person, Jake, but his work always came first. As you know, I have a hard time being alone." She gestured toward the man beside her. "This is my husband, Tom Caldwell. Jake Lindsey was Chips' partner."

The two men shook hands. Jake whispered, "Sorry to meet you under these circumstances, Tom, and this is Bennie Rochelle, my assistant."

"Yep. Too bad about Chips. Amy cared for him very much. Says he was a good guy."

Jake put his arm around Bennie and they walked slowly to their car.

"Bennie, this is probably not a good time, but I want you to try to remember as much as you can about Chips' last call."

Bennie Rochelle reached into her purse for a tissue. By the time Jake opened the car door for her, Bennie had not responded to his query.

"I know this is difficult for you," he said.

"Jake, I loved him, but he never saw me. I was just someone who answered phones and kept books. I was afraid to tell him how I felt." Her sob was muffled. "Now, I wish I had."

They drove in silence for several blocks before Bennie acknowledged Jake's question.

"He was in Philadelphia following up on a lead of some sort. You know, Chips was never one to give out too much information."

"Oh, how well I remember," Jake added.

"His emails to me were short and to the point. Did he give you a name or a place, any tidbit of info will help me."

Bennie spun around. "What are you going to do, Jake? Don't tell me you're going to put yourself in danger! Please let the police down there take care of the bad guys. I can't stand the idea of losing you both!"

"Bennie, girl, you couldn't get rid of me even if you wanted to. I'll be safe. I promise you I'll work with the Philly police." He paused, "Even if I don't trust them completely."

"You both were always so damn bullheaded! The only thing I remember is the phone number where he was staying. Oh, and he said he was going to Cedarville, I think."

Back at their office, Bennie and Jake began the task of cleaning out Chips' belongings and his files.

"God!" Jake exclaimed. "He was a messy one. How did he know where to find anything?"

"He didn't, most of the time. He left that to me."

"Come over here, please, and help me locate any recent notes or files."

Bennie stopped packing O'Donnell's personal effects and knelt beside Jake.

"When he was working on something current, he placed his notes in the grocery box," she pointed, "Up there on that shelf. I think he did it deliberately in order to keep a few things from you and me."

"Now Bennie, why would he do that?" Jake said as he pulled down the box.

"Because, as he told me once, he didn't want to give you half-assed information."

Jake gave a barely discernible laugh.

"Yep. When he first began working in this office, I had him check out a cheating husband. He came back three days later with his report for our client. You can't imagine how lucky for us that I read over in detail the report. He had the wrong husband under surveillance."

Jake was quiet for a moment. "After I chewed him out, I calmed down, a bit. I'll never forget the hangdog look on his face. He said, 'You'll never catch me again doing something half-assed.'"

Jake glanced at Bennie. A tear made its way down her cheek.

"Yeah, me too, Bennie." He kissed her on the cheek. "I'll keep in touch. I'm taking a puddle jumper to Philly. Gotta get to the airport by four. Can you give me a lift to Logan? I don't see a damn thing in this box that'll help me."

Twenty minutes through town and the tunnel. Neither spoke until Bennie pulled into the passenger loading zone.

"Jake, are you sure you won't change your mind?"

"Can't do it. It's unfinished business. Somebody did my buddy in. Somebody's gonna pay." He pulled Bennie to him and gave her a playful pat on the cheek.

"Hold down the fort."

Chapter Twenty Five

Jon looked to his rearview mirror.

"I don't see anyone following us. You don't suppose they've taken us off surveillance?"

"I doubt it," Connie replied.

"George, now and again, check behind us to make sure you don't see the same car twice. I'll take the upcoming side road. That should be the test."

A mile down the country lane, Jon pulled to the side of the road. "We'll wait here a bit."

A minute later, a Toyota pickup passed, followed soon by a woman in an older sedan.

"Okay, I'm convinced we don't have a tail today. Let's see what Sterling has to offer."

"I've been once to Sterling Castle. It's an awesome structure overlooking a beautiful town." She turned to face Cassidy in the rear seat. "So, George, you said you were a fan of Sterling."

"Oh, I wouldn't go that far," he corrected. "I've read about the castle and the battles in that region. These Scots were always warring with some group over something. When they weren't fighting outsiders, they fought each other. Seemed to be their favorite form of entertainment."

At the outskirts of Sterling, Jon stopped at a petro station for gas and a map. While Jon chatted with the attendant, Connie scanned a telephone directory until she found the name: M. Manion. She dialed the number on her cell phone and after two rings, a woman answered.

"Are you Mary Manion?"

"Surely. What may I do for ye?"

"Mary, Kathy Digbe gave me your name. She said you may be able to help me. I'm doing a genealogical search for my Scottish ancestors. Could we meet?"

"Surely. When are ye thinkin'?"

"I was hoping we could get together today, if that fits your schedule."

"Schedule. Ha! Lassie I haven't had me a schedule since me husband Gogan set me time table."

Connie winked at Jon who had walked up. "Could we meet at your residence or…"

Before Connie could finish her question, Mary Manion interrupted.

"We'll meet at the old church if ye'll not be a mindin'."

"What church, Mary?"

"The only one that matters, Dearie, St. Salvator's College."

"Fine." Connie glanced at her watch.

"Shall we say an hour from now? Oh, and how will I recognize you?"

"Ye won't need to bother. I'll know you right off. You're a yank. I expect your man friend will be with you."

"Good. I'll…" The line went dead. Mary Manion had hung up.

"Jon, that was eerie. She knew we were coming. I'm getting paranoid again."

"Is she going to meet us?"

"Uh-huh." Connie mumbled as she re-entered the auto. "In an hour at St. Salvator's College."

Jon passed the map to Cassidy. He scanned it briefly. "Take the next right. If this map is accurate, it'll lead us directly to St. Salvator's."

Four miles later, the magnificent structure loomed up. Two gargoyles stood guard at a walkway leading to numerous stone steps up to the main entrance.

George Cassidy stood and stared, spellbound at the piece of history before him.

He walked over to a marker on the ground. "Right here," he pointed, "Right here is where Patrick Hamilton was burned at the stake when he came back from the mainland imbued with Lutheranism."

"Why would Mary Manion tell us to meet her at a church? This is a college for God's sake!" Jon exclaimed in a loud voice. He had barely finished stating the obvious when Mary Manion walked up behind him.

"Quite simple, Lad. 'Tis a place that made a martyr of a heretic, a traitor to the Holy Church. Hello." She turned her attention to Connie. So you're the lass Katy spoke about."

"Thanks for meeting us. I'm Connie, this is Jon and standing over there is George. Katy told us you might be able to help me in my search for ancestors."

Mary seemed puzzled for an instant. "Oh, old Digbe was never one to give a body a full story. What would ye want to know about your dearly departed?"

"I think a grandmother, several times removed, was married to a MacTavish. She was kicked out of the manor by her husband, according to Miss Digbe. But nobody knows where she went or what happened to her."

"Well, I declare to all the saints! I was thinking you'd want to know about the Stone. All around these parts know ye have some interest in knowing."

"Mary," Connie started, but was quickly interrupted by Jon.

"Yes, Mrs. Manion. What about the Stone?"

"Well, now. Are you searching for ancestors, also, or might ye be snoopin' about the Stone?" She glared at Jon.

"Both, dear lady. What can you tell us on either subject?"

"Well, I donna know about you, but the lass here, says Katy Digbe, ought to be warned about Michael MacTavish and his ilk."

"And why would that be?" Connie asked.

"Because Michael MacTavish and his ilk come down from old Jimmy. They were a bunch of reformers. Heretics to the Holy Church. They stole the Stone and had it sent to bloody England at the behest of old Jimmy."

"Who is old Jimmy?" Cassidy inquired.

"Bloody King James, that's who!" Manion retorted. "But here's the rub. He didn't take the real stone to that Westminster hell hole. Nae!"

"So," Cassidy interjected, "there's something to the urban legend surrounding the Stone?"

"And just who might ye be? Are ye huntin' too, for the dearly departed?"

"No." Cassidy tried to keep his feelings hidden, even as he saw himself somewhat irrelevant to the conversation. "No, Mrs. Manion, but I have developed an affinity for things Scottish. Especially, history hereabouts."

Manion's voice softened. "Well, now, I could grow to like ye."

While talking, Mary Manion glanced over her shoulder several times. Jon listened impatiently as Manion commenced a lengthy narrative aimed in Cassidy's direction. Jon did an eye roll and was about to interrupt the one-way conversation between Manion and Cassidy. Before he could speak, Connie placed a gentle restraint on his arm.

"Let her talk," she whispered. "Her actions remind me of John Angus. I couldn't rush him either. If George bonds with her, that could be a plus for us."

"Okay, if you say so, but she really makes me nervous the way she keeps looking around."

After lambasting Shakespeare for his portrayal of Macbeth, Manion launched into a tirade about the English and the "bloody" Saxons. She was not prone to go over the battles won by the English, but she flailed her arms enthusiastically when she described the Battle of Bannockburn.

Two battles and three English tyrants later, Mary Manion wiped her brow, then said to Connie, "Now, where were we, dearie?"

"You were going to help me trace my family tree. That's what Miss Digbe said you might be able to do."

"And the Stone. What about the Stone?" Jon added.

Manion pointed to a park-like-bench.

"Let's sit over there. Me legs need a bit of rest."

After they were seated, Cassidy observed, "If my information is correct, these benches date back to the time of John Knox. Notice how worn down…"

Before he could complete his thought, Manion exclaimed, "To mention his name in my presence is sacrilege. He was a mad dog and a reprobate. Took a young thing for a wife when he was in his eighties. For the life of me, I donna know why he wasn't burned at the stake. When our Queen Mary would ride in her carriage, he would run beside and scream filthy obscenities to her. In the name of Jesus, Joseph, and Mary and all the Saints, I pray John Knox is getting his comeuppance." She crossed herself.

Jon sighed loudly. His patience was wearing thin. Once more Connie nudged him. "Don't say a word."

"Then I shant invoke his name again, Mrs. Manion. I apologize." Cassidy moved away from the group. "I'm going to look around. I'll meet you back at the car."

"So, you're kin of Michael MacTavish. Does that be so?" Manion asked.

"Yes. There is a bloodline. I'm trying to trace back as far as possible. I'm especially interested in my great, great grandfather's first wife" Connie answered. "Do you have any knowledge about her. Her name. What clan. What happened to her?"

"Ah, yes," Manion smiled. "It's just like that devil MacTavish not to give you her name. Her name was Yolande Margaret Hamilton MacTavish."

"Mary, are there records to prove what you're saying?"

"Of course, my dear. Yolande Margaret MacTavish descended from Alexander III's second wife, Yolande Contesse de Montford." Manion leaned toward Connie to whisper. "It's all in me Bible. That line came down through the ages. It came down to Patrick Hamilton through much legitimate and illegitimate breeding. Oh, and he was an active one! 'Tis said his seed was planted throughout the kingdom and though he was me ancestor, he was a no good."

"Your ancestor?" Connie was surprised.

"Yes, my dear, and yours also. Isn't that a surprise. You and I have the same blood. You see, someone made Yolande pregnant before Alexander was murdered."

"Murdered?"

"Surely. That bloody King Edward didn't acknowledge the fact that a renegade had impregnated Yolande. The lore passed down through the ages, which I believe to be God's truth — that a Nordic descendent of old King Arthur was the father of Yolande's child. Bloody Edward would have seen his claim on Scotland made nil, because the people would have believed that child to be a descendent of Old Alex. Now, lass, are ye gettin' the picture?"

Before Connie could answer, Manion continued. "The English history books will have you believe that Alexander was thrown from his horse and broke his neck, That's pure balderdash! The lore, which I believe to be God's truth, is that Haakon's son in league with three of Toom Tabard's Scottish traitors did in old Alex."

"Jon," Connie exclaimed, "Did you hear what I just heard?"

"Yep. Mrs. Manion, does history or the lore describe the color of the horse from which Alexander was supposedly thrown?"

"Sure lad. A white steed, it was. But old Alex wasn't thrown from a horse, he was pitched over a fifty foot cliff. There's a spot that marks where he was murdered."

Connie could barely contain her excitement. "Mary, what does your history tell you about the method for transporting Alexander's body to his castle?"

"Well, ye know the hearses in them days were quite plain. Carts they were, pulled by a single horse. The royal dead were treated as warriors all the way to their graves. They were seated upright as if life was in them. That way, the folk saw their king as upright and Scottish to the very end."

An eerie silence settled over the three of them. Mary Manion shifted her weight and stretched her legs. "I'll be needin' to get back to me place now."

Jon held out his arm to her. "Mary, we'll drive you back to your home now, but I want to ask you one final question. Who was Toom Tabard?"

"Ah, sure. That be old John Balliol. He was bloody Edward's puppet."

On the return trip, Mary Manion remained silent. When Connie walked her to her door, Mary asked, "Will ye visit me again?"

"Of course, Mary. We'll call on you again soon. We'll want to know all about the Stone."

Chapter Twenty Six

"Mr. Lindsey, you may be seated in the Captain's office. He'll be with you as soon as he's finished lecturing a group of street tarts." The desk sergeant pointed to a doorway.

Jake pulled a chair up to the Captain's desk. He gazed about the room and noted the area was free of clutter. The desk was clean except for a telephone, an intercom, and a pencil holder. Pictures and awards were aligned with forethought and precision. On a stand in the back of the room, a bust of William Penn was placed as if to remind any visitor that this station practiced brotherly love.

Jake, in his mind's eye, saw his own office: papers scattered about. Old paper cups decorating file cabinets. Case files piled willy-nilly on his desk and Chips' office not much better. He smiled as he remembered Bennie's routine admonition: Jake, for heaven's sake. I wish you and Chips weren't such slobs.

Ten minutes into his wait, Captain John Ellsey made his entrance, walking with measured steps. His uniform was fitted perfectly. Jake stood up, took one look, then concluded he was about to meet a martinet.

John Ellsey extended his hand. With a cheerful greeting, he gushed, "Mr. Lindsey, I gather. How do you do? I'm John Ellsey. Would you like some coffee? If you don't mind, I'll have some." He pressed the intercom. "Please bring two cups of coffee and a couple of doughnuts. I haven't had time for breakfast, Mr. Lindsey. Last night, we rounded up, it seems, every hooker in the fifth ward. We'll book 'em, feed 'em, and turn 'em loose. They'll be plying their trade again by midnight."

"Yep" Jake agreed. "Same the world over."

"If it was up to me, I'd let them do their thing. Oldest profession on the planet. We've got murders, muggings, robberies, all sorts of mayhem. But prostitution is out front. The ladies aggravate the preachers, the preachers jump on the mayor. The mayor screams at the commissioner. The commissioner orders me to bring 'em in. After all these centuries, Mr. Lindsey, shit still flows down hill." He passed a coffee to Jake. "Cream? Sugar?"

"No, thanks. Black's fine."

"What can I do for you, Mr. Lindsey?"

"Call me Jake. I'm a P.I." He showed his license. "My partner, Peter O'Donnell was murdered here in town, or at least his body was retrieved nearby. I hope you can share information with me."

"Boston, huh. Be glad to show you the file. We don't have much to go on at present. Will you do the same for me?"

Jake felt sheepish that he had anticipated Captain Ellsey incorrectly.

"You bet. I'll not ask to copy the file. Is there a place I can sit to read?"

"There's an alcove just off the records room. Has a couple of desks. Knock yourself out. If you need anything else, check with me or Detective Lieutenant Kulaski. He's handling the case."

Jake took fifteen minutes to read over the sparse information. He returned the file to the clerk. "Can you point me toward Detective Kulaski's office?"

"Next floor up. Third door on the left."

"Thanks," Jake said as he turned toward the stairs.

Kulaski's door was open. "Lieutenant Kulaski, may I talk with you a few minutes?"

"Sure, come on in. The Captain told me to expect you." He rose from his chair. "Have a seat. Want some coffee?"

"No, thanks. Just had some."

Kulaski glanced at his watch. "Then how about lunch. I converse better when my stomach's not growling."

"Okay by me," Jake replied.

Outside the station entrance a vendor had parked his cart. "This is my favorite restaurant, Jake. You have a choice. Philly cheese steak sandwich or Bratwurst dog."

"Cheese steak."

"Good choice, two steaks. You want coffee or coke?"

"Coke."

"And two cokes, Charlie."

Kulaski's office was disheveled. Jake felt at home.

"So, Ellsey tells me O'Donnell was your partner. You read the file. At this point, we don't have much beyond that."

"What about the two who discovered the body?"

"They're not your average rocket scientists. They called in anonymously from a pay phone. We checked houses near the phone booth. Didn't take long. We went to Paoli and picked 'em up the same day. They were a little behind the technological age. They had been fishing without a license; scared half to death when we brought 'em in."

"What about these names, Septo and Agles? The last I heard they were out on bail from that first encounter with my partner."

"Yep. We looked into that," Kulaski grumbled. "The damn judge threw out the charges. Said it was their word against O'Donnell's. We checked their last known addresses, but they had flown the coop."

"Have you ever heard of a town called Cedarville? My secretary said that Chips told her he was headed there. Perhaps the day he was killed."

Kulaski walked over to a large, detailed map covering one side of the wall. He looked first at the town and city list, then examined the towns and cities near Philadelphia. "Nope, no Cedarville in these parts."

"Thanks for your time, Detective. Could you give me the last addresses of Septo and Agles."

Kulaski pulled open his desk drawer to retrieve a notepad. "1617 Haley Way. That's out near the big bridge. We checked there. Nothing turned up."

"Thanks for your help. I'll keep you and Captain Ellsey posted on whatever I come across. I do appreciate what you put up with from liberal judges. I was Boston P.D. for many years."

———————————————

Jake drove slowly along Haley Way, checking house numbers. He stopped in front of a rundown, clapboard structure. A "For Rent" sign was tacked to the door. He pressed the doorbell and after the second ring, a scruffy looking man came to the door. Jake was greeted by the smell of sweat and bourbon.

"You here about the room?"

"The room?" Jake repeated. "I saw your sign. You don't rent the entire place, just rooms?"

"That's right. You want a room or not?"

"No, but I would like some information."

The renter smirked. "With me, information is in short supply. I don't get out much. I told the other cops all I knew about the bums who stiffed me for three months rent."

150

"I'm not a cop, I'm a P.I. My partner was murdered and I want to ask Mr. Septo and Mr. Agles some questions. Are we talking about the same folks?"

"Yeah, them bums stiffed me. If you find 'em I'll be happy to help you do a number on 'em."

"Do you know where they went, who came to see them. You know, anything at all that you remember?"

"Didn't ask and they didn't tell. Like I told the cops, I mind my own business."

Jake started the engine simultaneously slapping the steering wheel in frustration. "Son of a bitch. Nobody knows a damn thing!"

Two miles down Haley Way, Jake observed a sign pointing toward the expressway. As he turned right off Haley, from the corner of his eye, he saw another sign; that one blinked on and off CEDAR TOWN TAVERN. Jake pushed down on the brake pedal. "Well, I'll be damned." He backed up quickly then pulled into a nearby parking lot.

After checking the Glock in his shoulder holster, Jake ambled through the door of the saloon. The bartender busied himself washing beer steins. A lone customer sat at the end of the bar watching a baseball game that was decorated every few seconds by a horizontal line across the screen.

Jake eased onto a stool across from the bartender. "Gimme a Bud."

The bartender brought out the bottle and a refrigerated stein.

"That'll be two bucks."

Jake placed a twenty on the bar. "I'll trade you that bill for the beer and some information."

"Yeah, what?"

"Do you know a couple of cuties named Septo and Agles?"

The bartender resumed his dishwashing. "Never heard of them."

In a single motion, Jake leaned across the bar, grabbed the necktie of his server, and pulled the man half-way across the barrier.

"Wrong answer." He slammed the man's face against the mahogany bar.

"You broke my nose, you bastard!" he screamed, the blood oozing from his nostrils, "Billy, call the cops!"

Jake turned his attention to the customer. "Billy, if you go anywhere near that telephone, I'll shoot a hole right through you. Get over here and sit next to me."

Billy didn't argue.

"That's good. You just sit here and be good,"

"Now, Mr. Never Heard of Septo and Agles, let's try again. I won't break your nose next time. It'll be your neck."

Clete Doolin's face was beginning to match the color of the blood streaming from his nose. Jake pulled hard on the necktie.

"Speak up."

"Okay! Okay!" Doolin gurgled. "You're strangling me."

Jake ceased tugging at the necktie.

"Them two rented a room in back. They left three days ago. Said to forward their mail to a P.O. box in Pittsburgh. Don't know why they bothered. Septo was the only one who ever got any mail, and it was always from his mother. Told me to forget I'd ever seen them — or else."

"Very good. I want that P.O. box number. Oh, and the mother's address, if you have it. If you reach under there and pull out anything that isn't paper, I'll shoot you smack between the eyes,."

Doolin's hand shook as he retrieved a small notepad from the storage area under the bar. "I don't have the mother's address. Swear to God!"

Jake copied the information quickly. He moved toward the door, then turned abruptly. "If either of you sticks your head out that door before I'm long gone, I will shoot you. And, you Mr. Bartender, I'd advise you not to go to the police. You'll be investigated as an accessory to murder."

After a brief wait, Billy asked, "Should I call the cops? He scared the hell out of me!"

"Uh-uh, I don't think so. I'm guessin' he's a wise guy. I don't want no trouble with the mob. Just forget you saw the whole thing. Billy, help yourself to the beer. I'm goin' to the john to clean up my face. If a customer comes in, tell him I'll be out shortly."

Billy filled a stein with beer and shivered with the first swallow. He thought about what had happened. It didn't make much sense to him, but he was frightened.

As soon as Doolin returned from the restroom, Billy asked, "Clete, did you kill somebody?"

"No, Billy. I didn't kill no one. I don't know what the wise guy was talking about. "Doolin placed his arm around his brother. "Remember what I said. Forget you saw what happened. We don't want the wise guys puttin' out a hit on us."

Damon Kelly was not enamored of having to be called before the boss. He especially did not like the darkened room, nor the device through which the boss's voice was distorted. He sat, fidgeting, checking the luminous dial on his watch every few seconds, tiny beads of sweat forming above his upper lip. He had learned over the years that working for this organization was extremely stressful, even as it paid well. He knew the boss did not like loose ends. This day the boss's tone of voice communicated to Kelly that it was a season of loose ends. How he wished the boss would get on with it.

"Damon, what happened?"

"The son of a bitch wouldn't turn loose, after the boys got smacked around by that P.I. We had to start all over. He was a bulldog. We thought the P.I. would back off, but when he continued to snoop around, I put those two on his case again. They whacked him like they shoulda done the first time. Threw him in a river after they'd chained him up." Kelly shook his head. "The idiots tied the chains like you would a rope, so they said. To make a long story short, most of the weighting came off and he was washed up."

"You remember, don't you, Damon, that those two were on a blotter already. Damon, why didn't you hire someone here in Canada?"

"Sir, I couldn't just pick a hit man off the street. You know, gun restrictions and all that."

"Where are those two at present?"

"I got 'em a place in Pittsburgh. You want to know their exact location?"

"Why do you think I asked in the first place?"

Moving cautiously in the dark, Kelly handed a card to the boss. When the boss stood, Kelly recognized the signal that the conversation had run its course.

"Take care of it Damon. Clean it up."

As Kelly turned to leave, his boss directed a final question. "What about O'Donnell's partner? Didn't he interrogate your boy after the first incident?"

Kelly could feel the blood drain from his face. He'd never told the boss about Jake's questioning of Septo. "Yes, sir. I thought it insignificant. The boys never saw him again."

The days had begun to grow short along the Scottish coast. Weather pundits were predicting an early arrival of snow. The wind was unrelenting and Connie's quest for a family tree had been thwarted by several dead ends. Her anxiety over John Angus had not diminished, though Scotland Yard had not followed Jon and her for over a week. She failed to understand why she felt guilty. She kept telling herself that she had done nothing immoral, even if removal of the coded letter from Angus' wall was illegal. Her rationalizations fell upon a deaf conscience.

She peered out the window just as Jon drove up. She watched him sprint to the door and was there to open it for him.

"Jon, where is your coat? Do I have to treat you as if you're my child?"

He slammed shut the door, then embraced her. At the same time he kissed her full on the mouth.

"My God!" she exclaimed. "I hope you don't get pneumonia. You are shivering."

"Oh, my darling, it's not because of the weather. I'm doing it as an excuse to get you back in bed to warm me up!"

"You're a trickster, Jon LeFreaux," she giggled, "but I love it. Oh, and I've decided I love you!"

Jon was startled for an instant. She had never promised him more than being a partner in sex and ancestor search. For the moment, he was confused and speechless.

"Well?" she pressed him close.

"Oh, uh — I was blown away the first time I saw you. For the longest time, I just wanted to get in your pants. One day, I decided I wanted to be around you for at least twenty more years or 100,000 miles, whichever comes first." He tousled her hair. "And, I love you back."

"Good," she replied. "To the bedroom, kind sir. I want you to screw my brains out."

Afterward, Connie lay quietly in his arms, her angst having been subordinated to fifteen minutes to a wild, thrashing entanglement, culminating in a screaming convulsing orgasm.

"I love you," he muttered still breathing heavily.

"I love you back," she answered.

"Connie, I was able to use my cell when I stood on that nearby hill. Jake says he'll be occupied for some time back in the states. Said he had some leads he wanted to follow. He apologized for not being here to wet-nurse us. He made it clear that we should keep looking over our shoulders. Oh, and he said I shouldn't knock you up. He doesn't want another person to look after. I told him your eggs may or may not hatch out."

"Well, thank you for sharing my bodily deficits with Jake." Her retort was laced with sarcasm.

"I'll not tell anyone that you like your women unbathed and smelly, you pervert." She pinched his cheek.

"Okay! Okay! Uncle!"

Each became wrapped in their own thoughts until Jon whispered, "When are we going to see Mary Manion again?"

"I was thinking the same thing. Give George a call. Have him pick us up tomorrow morning. With Jake back in the states, we're left to our own devices. I know he thinks we ought not to expose ourselves to the cops or the bad guys. Too bad. I refuse to sit on my hands any longer."

Connie poured Cassidy a cup of coffee. "George, thanks for checking in everyday. How are things going with you?"

"Very well, thank you. I've bonded a bit with my probation constable. Nice fella. Quite a history buff."

"Aren't all Scots?" Jon offered.

"Well, yes, I suppose. I'll have my chauffer drive us all over. Constable MacCartney is the only person I've ever known who can talk seemingly without breathing. Ah, but he's a font of information." Cassidy sipped his coffee. "Let me tell you what I learned from him yesterday. We drove on A921 to Kinghorn. There's a monument at the spot where Alexander III allegedly fell from his horse and broke his neck. Roscoe - that's the constable — told me that the Stone of Destiny was brought to Scotland by an Egyptian princess name Scota, after she had wandered in the desert for twelve hundred years." Cassidy rolled his eyes. "If we are to believe that mythology, perhaps the first Scottish rulers were anointed above that Stone just before the birth of Christ."

"According to Roscoe, the Stone had been kept to seat Scottish kings for centuries. Then, the story gets muddled following the reign of Alexander III. It seems that after the death of ol' Alex, King Edward of England pilfered the Stone and hauled it away to Westminster Abbey."

"But," Cassidy pointed his index finger upward, "the seven-hundred year old rumor is that a fake stone was substituted when Scottish nobles uncovered the plot." He paused. "Makes a good tale."

"George," Jon asked, "Did your buddy know what happened to the real Stone of Destiny, assuming the legend has some truth in it?"

"Oh, there's lots of speculation. Some believe the true Stone of Destiny is not far from it's original resting place, the Scone Palace. Among the rumors, take your pick: it was hauled away to Ireland. It was hidden in a cellar in the highlands. It was shipped to the United States in the nineteenth century."

"What about the Stone that was returned to Edinburgh in 1995?" Connie asked.

"Some Scots believe it is a fake. Roscoe says most people see it as the real thing."

"Okay, George. Let's have your chauffer haul us to the abode of Mary Manion. This plot is getting thicker."

Chapter Twenty Seven

Bridgeville, Pennsylvania, a small suburb of Pittsburgh, was known for its magnificent golf course and several NHL notables who resided there. A police force comprised of a chief, ten officers, and a clerk, kept the peace mainly by issuing traffic tickets and keeping drunks off the street. Then for the first time in twenty years, a murder was committed within their jurisdiction.

Jake Lindsey poured over the documents Chief Tom Becker placed before him.

"Chief Becker, I see here that your search of the dead man's apartment yielded very little. Will you permit me to look through those items you found? By the way, how were you able to come up with the real names of the victims?"

"Easy. Both men had multiple ID cards, drivers licenses, and passports. Agles must have made a hobby of being someone else. He had seven — count 'em — seven fake driver's licenses, three fake credit cards and five club IDs. We hit pay dirt through our DNA data base. I immediately phoned Philly. You know the rest from there"

Chief Becker summoned the clerk. "Patrick, go to property and bring Mr. Lindsey that bag of goodies we collected from the dead man's apartment. And, I need some coffee. Whatever's in my cup is cold. Can't stand cold coffee."

Jake lit a cigarette and commenced a methodical examination of the items the clerk placed before him. He noted the fake ID cards. Nothing unusual, pen and pencil, slip of paper, pocket change, pocket knife.

"Chief did these numbers on that piece of paper mean anything to you? 87016174577E3DK?"

"Nope. We checked personal effects for bank check IDs. US telephone numbers, probation IDs, passports — nothing came up."

Jake copied the string of numerals into his notepad.

"Were there any fingerprints not belonging to the stiffs?"

"None. Whoever did 'em in were probably acquaintances. There was no sign of forced entry."

"Thanks, Chief. I'll stay in touch and let you know if I stumble across anything of value. May I ask the same favor from you?" Jake handed Becker one of his cards.

"Yessiree. I'm sure sorry about your partner."

That night as Jake tried to make sense of the number series, he felt a twinge of guilt for having omitted his own role in the events that cost Chips his life. That couldn't be helped, he rationalized. He learned early in his career as a PI that too much information and too many people in the know could muddle an investigation.

Shortly before dawn he awoke, having gone to sleep with his head on the desk, and no further along in deciphering the numbers. He showered, drank a cup of coffee, then dialed the number for British Airways.

Mary Manion, as was her wont each fall, was planting her bulbs when Connie and Jon drove up.

"Hello, Mary. I hope we're not interrupting your morning work."

"Not at all, lass. 'Tisn't work. I get a bit of joy from me flowers in the Spring. Makes up for the diggin' in the fall. I'll be needin' a wee tad of rest. And good mornin' to yer handsome Lad."

"Ah, Mary," Cassidy replied, "you do make a body feel good and young."

She turned her attention to Jon. "And you, lad, are ye fellin' good and young?"

"Now, Mary, how can I feel anything else in the company of two beautiful and charming women?"

The old woman placed her spade to one side. "Let's go inside afore the rain comes. I'll make a pot of tea."

"Sounds good," Connie said.

The three visitors sat, waiting patiently for Mary to prepare the tea and lay out the crumpets. The teakettle began to steam and whistle.

Connie passed a package to Mary. "I brought you some chocolates and teabags. I hope you like chocolate."

"Ah, indeed I do. I'm thankin' ye. 'Tis a treat which I can afford once in a blue moon," she laughed.

"Mary, when we were here last, you said you had knowledge pertaining to the Stone of Scone. Can you share that with us?" Connie leaned close to Mary.

"Surely. The words ha' been passed down through many generations."

She went into the kitchen and returned with three time worn, hard-back journals. "You see, now, I write things in me books. Been keepin' a diary since I was a wee sprout of a girl. Ye're welcome to read in me cottage. I don't let 'em out of this place for none save the Holy Father, should he show at me door. I know ye'll be wantin' to make further inquiry once you've read 'em over. I've placed a mark over anything about the Stone."

"Thank you, Mary. We'll try not to be a bother," Connie assured her. "George, how about you take this one," she handed a journal to Cassidy. "And Jon you take this one. I'll read from the most recent years."

Cassidy perused all entries, unlike Connie and Jon, who noted only the starred writings. "Mary," Cassidy remarked, "Your handwriting is beautiful."

"Ah, now, Lad. Could ye be puttin' me on? But thank you. Had a school marm who was always threatenin' to whale me if me script couldn't be deciphered."

Half-way through George's assigned journal, Mary's starred entry caught his eye. It read:

'Today on my 21st birthday, my granny told me of the Stone, I learned that it went all the way back to the book of Genesis and is what makes me a Scot. My Granny says that all Scottish kings dating from Macbeth and beyond were crowned while seated above the Stone. I was a bit taken aback when she told me that Alexander III was the last Scottish king to be crowned upon the stone in Scotland. I said to Granny that my teacher disagreed with her. My Granny then told me the Stone was to have been removed to England after the death of Alexander. Granny says a stone was taken to the Abbey, but it was not the real stone. Granny says the real Stone was taken from Scone and to this day is hidden from the bloody English.'

Four hours and many starred passages later, Connie and the others took their leave from Mary Manion, but not before she had elicited a promise from Connie that the three of them would visit again. "And Lass, never tell anyone about the journals. There be too many shenanigans around that blessed Stone."

"Well, what did you…" Jon never finished his question after Connie gave him the shush sign. She raised a finger from her lap. It was pointed toward the chauffer.

"What did you think of the drive across this magnificent country?" he asked, acknowledging Connie's stop signal.

"Oh, a great drive and I enjoyed visiting with Mary. She was very helpful in our search for lost ancestors. Didn't you two think so? Oh, and I loved her lecture on Scottish flora."

"Yes," George said, "She does know gardening."

Connie exhaled. George had recognized her signal to say nothing about the content of journals. She had decided to trust no one outside their circle for the time being.

Once Jake unpacked his travel bags, he joined the others seated around the table.

"Glad to be home, guys. As I was telling you, the trip to the U.S. was a wrenching experience. I wake up each morning knowing I'll never see Chips again. I finally had to give in to Bennie Rochelle, my office manager. She got her PI license a year ago and was bugging hell out of me to get on a case." He poured himself a cup of coffee. "So, I turned the Jon file over to her, reluctantly, I might add."

"Were you able to meet with my father or mother?" Jon asked.

"Nope. I wanted the bad asses who killed Chips. Never got a chance to see your people."

"What happened?" Connie inquired.

"Someone got to Septo and Agles before me. They had moved out of Philly over to Pittsburgh. They were staying in a suburb called Bridgeville. They had been whacked, execution style. Bullets to the back of the head."

Connie reached across the table to squeeze Jake's hand. "I'm sorry about Chips, but I'm glad you're back. I feel safer when you're around. The three of us are poor detectives."

"Thanks," Jake replied. "I intend to pick up where I left off. So the Mary Manion visit was successful. Tell me what you learned."

"Ladies first. We'll jump in," Cassidy said.

Connie placed her notepad on the table. "Mary Manion kept a diary from the time she was in her teens. She allowed us to read from three thick journals covering four decades of her life. She treats her entries as, to quote her, 'God's truth'. Outside of Scotland, her truths would be known as urban legends. Her early information about the Stone of Destiny came mostly from her grandmother, then in later years, from her mother and community gossips. George, tell Jake about the Alexander legend."

Cassidy referred to his notes. "Mary believes that a stone was taken to England following the death of Alexander. But," he raised his index finger, "it was not the real Stone. According to Mary, the tale passed down through the ages was that an ersatz piece of rock was substituted for the real thing; that the true Stone remains hidden to this day."

Jake interrupted. "Why all the fuss? After all, hasn't Scotland been a part of Great Britain for a few hundred years?"

"Yes," Cassidy answered, "but in the thirteenth century, that issue was not yet settled. Hardly a year passed that one clan wasn't fighting another, with England egging it on."

"And," Connie added, "the demise of Alexander III was a benchmark in the history of Scotland, plus," she grinned, "perhaps some light real or fantastic, has been shed on Jon's and my search for those ancestors from the dark regions of our collective unconscious."

"What do you mean by benchmark?" Jake asked.

Jon responded quickly, "The clan conflicts, the power struggle between Scotland and England, and the battles among the royals all contributed to a pot boiling time. It was during this time that Mel Gibson — er, excuse me, William Wallace worked over the British lion."

"Of special interest to Jon and me is the possibility that one or more of our ancestors could have been involved in the alleged murder of Alexander," Connie said.

Jake turned his attention to Cassidy. "George, what do you think? And I'm not talking specifically about the validity of those old rumors. I'm more concerned about the danger facing these two." He nodded toward Jon and Connie.

"We've been extremely careful. My probation constable says that Scotland Yard has discontinued surveillance on these two. I didn't quite understand their reasons for doing it in the first place."

Connie gave a subtle nod, first to Jon, then to Jake. Both men acknowledged her signal by giving a thumbs up.

"George, we're going to trust you as a member of this circle." Connie proceeded to give Cassidy a detailed account of the events involving Connie and Jon, and the reasons they were investigated.

"George, please don't be offended. We were at the point of not knowing whom to trust."

"Don't blame you at all. Since I'm being less than candid with Mr. LeFreaux…
I understand."

Bennie Rochelle checked her purse to make certain her newly acquired PI license
was in place. She gave a quick glance at her image in the foyer mirror then pressed the
elevator button.

She walked into the office, contrasting mentally Jake's office with the surroundings
before her: two receptionists; straight to her front a door over which read Raymond
LeFreaux, C.E.O.; to the left a hallway with offices on either side; to the right an enormous window out of which she could see the ocean and Logan Airport; classic paint-
ings decorating the entire area.

She approached the nearest receptionist. "I'm Bennie Rochelle. I have an appointment with…"

"They're expecting you. May I hang your coat?"

"Thank you. It is a bit nippy out today."

The LeFreauxes were standing near a semi-circular sofa fronting Raymond LeF-
reaux's desk. He extended his hand. "I'm Raymond LeFreaux. This is my wife, Eileen.
Pardon me if my jaw dropped when you walked in. I assumed Bennie Rochelle was a,
uh — man."

"Oh, I get that all the time," Bennie grinned. "Thank you for agreeing to see me."

"Would you like some coffee or tea, dear, or perhaps a soda from the cooler?"

"Thank you, yes. Tea would be nice."

"So, Miss Rochelle, you're following up on the visit from your colleague Mr.
O'Donnell, I believe. I presume I may have intimidated him. Could that be the reason
you've been sent in his place?"

"Regrettably, no sir. Chips is," Bennie struggled to keep from choking up, "Chips
O'Donnell is dead. He was murdered recently in Philadelphia."

"Oh, my God!" exclaimed Eileen LeFreaux. "I'm so very sorry. My husband was feeling a bit guilty when he told me of Mr. O'Donnell's visit. I assume that you, as was he,
are a part of the plan to protect our son."

"That's correct, Mrs. LeFreaux. So many things have happened both here and in
Scotland. But I assure you Jon is being kept safe by my partner, Jake Lindsey. By the
way, if you desired Mr. Cassidy to be incognito, Jake is now working with him. Jake
says George Cassidy is an able colleague. He's at Jon's side at all times."

LeFreaux cleared his throat while glancing at his wife. "I'm glad I sent George. I
knew he wasn't necessarily an effective gumshoe, but he was always competent and
loyal in every task I assigned to him."

Bennie Rochelle felt the discomfort of approaching a touchy subject. "Mrs. LeFreaux, thank you again for agreeing to talk to me. I must tell you I feel quite awkward at this moment."

Neither LeFreaux volunteered a response. "So… I, uh, let me see, how do I say this. Chips told me that your inheritance was the source of the LeFreaux fortune." Bennie paused, "We believe that Jon is in danger because of his inquiries relating to the Stone of Destiny."

"What might that have to do with us?" asked Eileen LeFreaux.

"We're not certain at this point. When Jon first started his search for the family tree, he was working with a woman named Constance Nordstram."

Bennie proceeded to tell the LeFreauxes the reason Jon had become associated with Dr. Nordstram: the parallel dreams; the dead ends in Scotland and Canada; the attack on Connie.

"So, I've laid out a hundred thousand dollars for Jon to go off on a wild goose chase," Raymond LeFreaux shook his head from side to side. "And, now his life may be at risk."

Eileen LeFreaux placed her hand on her husband's arm. "I've never told anyone this before now. I didn't think it very important. You know how stories are passed from one generation to the next. Well, in my case, Granny O'Shaughnessy always told me that I would someday inherit all of her money and property. She said it would be a gift from an ancestor who emigrated from Scotland in the eighteen hundreds. My mother died at an early age and my father was killed in an automobile wreck. One morning, at the age of twenty-three, I woke up a wealthy woman. Ray and I had been married for less than a year." She glanced at her husband. "Granny admonished me never to try to find the source of my wealth. You, uh, know, it was a situation of don't ask, don't tell. So, I didn't." She drew close to her husband. "This man turned two million dollars into a great deal more."

"Oh, yes," LeFreaux added, "about forty-nine million more at last count."

"Raymond, dear, I'm ashamed that I did what I did thirty-seven years ago. Please understand that I love you more than anything in this world, but I was afraid of the future."

Bennie Rochelle, for the moment, had become a spectator to a truth session between two people who had lived a white lie for more than thirty years.

"Afraid of the future?" LeFreaux asked, "What do you mean?"

Eileen LeFreaux squeezed the arm of her husband. "Darling, when we married, there was no such arrangement as a pre-nuptial agreement. God!" She exclaimed, "I feel so deceitful. My inheritance was worth not two million, but more like five million." She gave a sheepish look at her husband. "I placed three million in a trust for our son. It must be worth considerably more by now."

Raymond LeFreaux sat silently, for several seconds, then he rose from his chair and walked to the picture window. For what seemed an eternity to Bennie Rochelle, he stared out the window, then returned to sit beside his wife.

"It's okay, dear. I suppose that had I been in your place, I might have done the same thing."

He kissed her lightly on her cheek.

"Thank heaven you're not angry with me," she responded, as a lone tear made its way down her cheek.

"Now, Miss Rochelle, where from here?"

"Where from here?" Rochelle pondered. "I'm not sure. Perhaps if we ever know why Chips was murdered…" her voice tailed off. "Thank you both for receiving me. I'm glad that you understand our concern for your son."

As Bennie turned to leave, she gave parting advice. "If I were in your place, I would be security conscious."

"Agreed," LeFreaux answered. "My company has a security apparatus in place. We'll be diligent."

———————————————

MacTavish glared across the table at his visitor. "I do not appreciate your insinuation, Dr. LeFreaux!! I care very much for the safety of Dr. Nordstram. I'm not overly concerned for the man who has become her lover." He nodded to Jon. "As I have told her, I wished to scare her away from Scotland, I did not order an attack upon her. I had nothing to do with the murder of old John Angus."

"MacTavish, I'm not accusing you of anything. Not yet, anyway. You lost Dr. Nordstram and her trust when you tried to get her to leave Scotland. What were you thinking? What's all the furor over that damn stone?"

MacTavish rose from his chair. "I don't have to tell you a bloody thing. In fact, I chose to speak with you because of my concern for Connie Nordstram."

He pressed the call button at the end of the table. "Molly, please bring some tea."

A short time later Molly appeared with the tray.

"Thank you, dear. That'll be all." He gave a flick of the wrist. Jon felt a surge of disgust.

As he commenced to pour the tea, Michael MacTavish explained, "Dr. LeFreaux, I saw the look on your face. I know you yanks don't appreciate our social customs but let me tell you, ol' boy, these islands and our very polished caste system have survived several centuries and surely have made us the most civilized society on the planet."

Jon fought the urge to call MacTavish a pompous ass. At the moment, he needed any information MacTavish could provide.

"I'll not disagree, Lord MacTavish. I assure you my disdain was fleeting. Back to the reason I came here. The Stone. It seems to me from what I've learned that any inquiry about the Stone is a high risk venture. I find it hard to believe that people drive upon a rail track to commit suicide. And, why was Connie threatened after she became friends with John Angus?"

"Well, Dr. LeFreaux," MacTavish replied, "You have put your finger on the very reason I desired Constance to be gone. John Angus, over the years, has been a lightening rod for bad things happening to those who seek the truth about the Stone."

LeFreaux leaned closer to MacTavish. "And what might the truth be?"

"Ah, yes. And there's the rub, as Bill Shakespeare once said, all we've had over the years is one rumor after another. Whatever the truth, many Scots believe that John Angus was a central cog in the rumor mill."

Jon hesitated, framing a mental picture of the man before him. He was guessing that what he was seeing was not what he was getting.

"Lord MacTavish, are you involved in the Stone thing? Did you have anything to do with the murder of John Angus?"

"No! and No! How dare you be so impertinent? This conversation has ended. You can find your own way to the door! Oh, and by the way, dear boy, I was her lover before you came on the scene."

Chapter Twenty Eight

"How was your flight?" Bennie asked as she gave Jake an effusive hug.

"Long. Bad food. Boring. But no terrorists were aboard. Or, if they were, they chickened out."

"I'm parked out front. We'll get your luggage and hope my rental hasn't been towed."

By the time Jake placed his bag into the luggage compartment and Bennie Rochelle had received a lecture from the airport police, the two private investigators were ready to plan their forthcoming actions.

"So how did you talk your way out of a ticket?"

"Told him I was dyslexic, plus I couldn't read French."

She exited the airport and commenced the ten mile ride to the hotel.

"Ah, Bennie Rochelle, you are something!" Jake exclaimed, leaning across the seat to kiss her on the cheek. "Thank you for calling me. If you'd taken this on by yourself, I'd have been tempted to fire you."

"You would not, Jake Lindsey. You need me because I'm smart enough to untangle numbers that made no sense to you. Oh, and prevent the agency from going into bankruptcy."

Bennie weaved her way through the traffic while Jake sat quietly.

"So, what's our move, Jake?"

"Go over once more what you told me over the phone. I forgot to bring the notes," he replied sheepishly.

"Jake Lindsey," she teased, "If your ass wasn't attached to the rest of you, you'd forget to bring it along."

"But you know, young lady that Chips and I knew you'd…" Jake didn't finish his thought.

"Jake, I try to get past what happened to Chips. I moped around for a while, but then I got madder and madder." She sighed, "Anyway, I don't consider myself to be a rocket scientist because I was able to reverse those numbers and come up with the name, Sylvestre Gereau."

"It was his telephone number?"

"Yep. Unlisted here in Canada. I called the number. Told the lady who answered that I had a lottery winner check for Mr. John McCherin. She allowed as how John McCherin didn't live there; that it was the residence of Sylvestre Gereau. Then I said that made sense because Mr. Gereau coincidentally shares the ticket with Mr. McCherin. Then I told her I'd deliver the $900,000 share to Mr. Sylvestre, but I needed the address. That I would deliver the money before the week was out. I imagine she peed her pants at that point. She gave me the address and said she was always home."

"Bennie Babe, I can't believe you pulled that off," Jake laughed. "Chips taught you well. I'll clean up a bit and we'll pay a visit to Mr. Sylvestre."

"You'll remember me. I'm Sykes. Dr. Nordstram, please come to the station. I believe you're familiar with the location. If it isn't too much bother, please have Dr. LeFreaux accompany you."

"I've told you all I know!" Connie tried to remain calm, even as the receiver almost shook in her hand. "What do you want now?"

"Oh, we just need to start tying up a few loose ends, Mum. We have a new corpse on our hands."

"And what does that have to do with me?"

"Ye'll find out. I'd rather not discuss it over the tele."

"When do you want us to come there?"

"Soon, Mum. Today if possible."

An hour later, Connie and Jon sat across from Sykes.

"We've told you before," Jon said, "We know nothing about the John Angus murder. So why do you keep harassing us?"

Connie nudged Jon, hoping to short circuit further belligerence.

"Detective Sykes, you were not forthcoming over the tele. I'm sure you have a good reason for our summons."

"Perhaps," Sykes replied. "How well do you know Michael MacTavish?"

"I know him quite well. Dr. LeFreaux has met him once."

"Under what circumstances did you become acquainted with MacTavish?"

Connie became less tense. "He was the initial reason I came to Scotland. He and I are the end of bloodline cousins. I stayed at Sonsie for a time when I first began my genealogical research." She nodded toward Jon. "Dr. LeFreaux has been assisting me in that search."

"How did you get on with MacTavish?"

Connie paused, seeing no good reason to omit detail. "At first, we were very simpatico. He was a delightful host. Later I began to trust him less."

"And why was that, Mum?"

"After I was attacked outside Sonsie, I grew suspicious and wary. You might say even paranoid."

Sykes waited several seconds. "And your reason for not trusting him?"

"I had reason to believe that he had something to do with the attack on me. Later, in fact, quite recently I came to the conclusion he had nothing to do with the assault."

Sykes bored in, "And what changed your mind?"

"I believed him when he told me he was concerned for my safety and had planned to scare me out of Scotland."

"Did he ever say why your safety was important or who would wish to do you harm?"

"No."

"Did he express any sort of negative attitude about John Angus?"

Connie could feel her heart pounding. "He, uh, his comments about Angus were, at first, benign. In fact, he referred Angus to me. Michael said he was a gossip and a folklorist, but harmless. Later I was told that Michael was suspicious of John Angus; that he was a, uh, lightening rod for bad things happening to people who sought information about the Stone of Destiny."

"And were you seeking information about the Stone, Dr. Nordstram?"

"Only as it may have related to any of my ancestors," she answered.

"Dr. Nordstram, what would you think if I told you MacTavish may have been using you to get information about Angus?"

Connie sat silently for a few moments, in her mind recalling conversations with MacTavish about John Angus. "I wouldn't know what to think. Angus was always kind and helpful to me. I suppose it's possible Michael was using me."

"You said someone informed you that MacTavish was suspicious of John Angus. May I inquire as the identity of that someone?"

Connie clenched her fists to control a sudden shaking. "My bodyguard, Jake Lindsey, told me."

"Detective," Jon could contain himself no longer. "My patience is growing thin. Why in hell have you called us here?"

Sykes wagged his finger toward the officer outside the door. As the officer entered, Sykes directed, "Please escort Dr. LeFreaux to the waiting area. He's not needed here at present."

The uniformed policeman tapped Jon on the shoulder. "Be a good lad now and follow me. I'll seat ye and bring you a spot of tea."

"Jesus Christ! A man can never get a straight answer around here!"

"Wait outside, Jon. I'll be along," Connie urged.

The door closed behind Jon and his escort. Sykes referred to his notes. "Dr. Nordstram, were you and MacTavish lovers at any time while you stayed at Sonsie?"

Connie felt the blood rush to her face. "Yes, we were lovers for a very short time."

"Then I must assume MacTavish was in your bedroom during the evening hours?"

"That's precisely right. So what?" Connie hesitated. "Detective Sykes, do you believe Michael had anything to do with the murder of John Angus?"

"Oh, I doubt it, Mum. If you'll wait outside, I have a wee number of questions for your friend." Sykes signaled the officer.

Once seated, Jon became angst riddled, remembering as he did that day in Angus' cottage.

"Just a few inquiries, Dr. LeFreaux. May I call you, Jon, or perhaps Jonathan?"

"As you wish, Detective. What have I done? Jaywalked? Spat on the sidewalk? Dumped trash on the road?"

Sykes ignored the barbs. "Jon, did it make you jealous when you discovered that Dr. Nordstram had been bedding down with Michael MacTavish?"

Jon swallowed hard. "What are you talking about? I don't believe you."

"Why don't you ask her, Jon. Now, to my question. When you found that she was popping you and someone else, did you go into a jealous rage?"

Jon felt a slight wave of queasiness. "Why would I be jealous? I don't know the game you're playing?"

"I believe you, Jon, for now." Sykes motioned to the policeman, who opened the door for Connie.

"Dr. Nordstram, Dr. LeFreaux, Michael MacTavish was found dead this morning. He had been bludgeoned to death."

Jon watched for Connie's reaction. She inhaled sharply, struggling to keep her composure. "Is that why we're here? Am I a suspect? Or Jon?"

"Not at present, Mum. I do wish to have a statement from each of you. You may write it or do a recording."

"You mean now? Today?" Jon asked.

"Yes, please."

Once Connie had written her statement, she requested the right to modify it should she have additional recall. Jon's statement was brief; mostly hearsay.

As the two of them were preparing to leave, Sykes had another bit of information for Connie. "You're aware, Dr. Nordstram, that Michael MacTavish changed his will recently, and that you may be in his last will and testament since he has no other living relative."

"Mr. Gereau, I'm Jake, this is Miss Rochelle. We've scheduled a photo shoot at our headquarters. I represent the Silver Dollar Lottery Company. We wish to gain as much publicity as possible from this event. We'll transport you there, then give you a ride back to your place."

Jake extended his hand, which was ignored by Gereau. "You got I.D.? Who'd you say you work for?"

"Silver Dollar Lottery. We're well known in the states." Jake removed a card from his wallet. "Will this suffice?"

Gereau studied the card briefly. "Never heard of your company. I ain't gonna appear for no picture taking."

Before he could close the door, Jake had placed his Glock against Gereau's chest.

"I'll bet this toy convinces you to attend our photo session. My, my, let us examine that bulge in your jacket. Bennie, see what the man is hiding."

"Surprise!" Bennie mocked. "We have here a .38 special. In Canada, yet!"

"Where is your wife, Sylvestre?" Jake asked, as he herded Gereau to the car.

"She's running errands. If you dare hurt her, I'll…"

Jake interrupted. "Sylvestre, we have no interest in your wife. Get in the car. We're going for a drive."

There was a protracted silence in the auto until Bennie pulled off the road into a wooded area.

"Now, Mr. Gereau let's get to the truth of the matter." Jake saw the sweat forming above Gereau's upper lip.

"I swear to you! I don't know what happened. Those two just fucked things up and I had to go in with a cleaner. Before we could get rid of the bodies, we were about to be discovered and had to get out fast. I swear that's the way it was."

Jake gave Bennie a high sign wink.

"You know as well as I that the boss don't like messes."

Gereau began to moan, "Please don't kill me. Please. I've done some good jobs for the boss. Don't that count for something?"

"Give me your wallet," Rochelle ordered.

"This ain't right," Gereau begged. "I'll give you money. I don't know what the boss is paying you, but I'll go higher. I don't want to die!"

He passed the wallet to Rochelle.

"Yeah, Jake, before we erase this piece of shit, we need to know if he's left a trail to the boss."

"No, no! There's no way. For God's sake, I don't even know the boss's name."

"Bullshit!" Jake went nose to nose with Gereau.

"No! I swear on my mother's grave I don't know him! I get my orders from a bookie. We always meet at the track."

"So, if you don't know the boss's name," Bennie interjected, "then you don't know the bookie's name, oh, sure!"

"No, really, I don't."

"B.R., I think it's time we put this sonofabitch down."

Rochelle took her cue. "I don't know, Jake. Maybe we can use him. Mr. Gereau, how serious are you about wanting to stay alive?"

"What do you mean?"

"You offered us money earlier. As erasers and cleaners we don't get to bargain with the big boys. If you agree to tell us when you meet with the bookie we might be willing to make a trade. When is your next meeting with him?"

"Why would you want to meet with him?"

"Because you're not the big fish that muddied up the waters," Jake answered. "So, it was this bookie who created the mess."

"Yes, uh, yes. He was the two-faced bastard that gave me the orders to hire Agles and Septo. I ain't gonna take a bullet for him! I'm supposed to meet with him on Tuesday at the track. Fourth window, third race."

"Today is Tuesday, Sylvestre," Bennie noted.

"Oh, yeah. God, I'm so scared, I forgot what day it is."

"We'll buy you lunch, Sylvestre." Jake put his arm around the frightened man. "Then we'll drive out to the track."

"Jon, say something, say anything," Connie pleaded. "You've ignored me since we left the station. Why are you so angry?"

"You don't know, do you, Dr. Nordstram. You really don't know."

"Know what, Jon? What happened to you in there?"

Jon moved close to her. "So, you were fucking him and me. For how long, Connie? How long were you doing both of us!"

"Please don't yell at me. Yes, I was intimate with him before you and I became lovers. But I had ended that part of the relationship. Now, get the hell out of my face."

Jon backed away.

"You believe me, Jon? Tell me, you believe me. My god, you are all that I can handle. The two of us, I suspect, are at the top of the list again."

"He said you may be in MacTavish's will and he had no living family."

Connie walked by the corner table which contained a stack of unopened mail. She laid aside a flyer and an envelope from her ex-husband's lawyer. She unsealed the envelope from Morton, Elwood, and MacIntire, Ltd.

She read the message once, refolded the letter, then unfolded it to reread the contents.

"Jon, I don't understand any of this. Michael's executor has scheduled a meeting for this Friday."

"Seems to me pretty easy to understand," Jon retorted. "Guy dies, passes on his estate to his newly acquired lover and long lost distant cousin."

Connie clenched her fists in rage. "You bastard! Get your shit together and move out of here!"

"I'll do that, Dr. Nordstram. I regret that it has come to this. On the other hand, I'm pleased to disassociate myself from a slut."

Connie slapped him. Her blow was off center and landed flush on his nose.

Jon used a tissue to wipe away the blood. "Damn, lady. You do pack a mean wallop."

"I'm sorry, Jon," she exclaimed. "I wish I could take that back! What are we doing?"

"And I wish I could take back what I said." He dabbed at his nose to stem the bleeding.

"Jon, my darling, I have not been involved sexually with Michael since we... I don't know what is going on." She touched his cheek. "I love you, damn you."

As they embraced, Jon's cell phone buzzed. "Hi, George. I see. Yeah. No. Tomorrow is okay with me. Hold on. He says he's got a good lead for us, wants to pick us up at noon."

Connie shook her head to affirm.

"Okay, George. See you shortly."

"Sorry I acted like such an ass." Jon kissed her.

"Wonder what ol' George has for us?"

Chapter Twenty Nine

The cottage rested atop a ridge in the highlands. Inside four men sat around a table stained by years of spilled tea and haggis residue and felt the warmth from a blaze in the stone fireplace. Decades of smoke and neglect had basted the inside of the cottage.

Ray Ahern took a swallow of scotch from the glass placed before him.

"Mr. Ahern, how much longer shall we be in this pitiful place?" Alex Thornton asked.

"That's why I'm here. The heat is off for the time being. You may return to your homes. I'll not allow that bastard, Lindsey, to intimidate me further. I've arranged jobs for the three of you. You'll not be working for me, however, as company employees. Alex, you'll be at McCays Tool and Dye. Erin, you'll be servicing vehicles for Albertion Trucking. Pete, you'll be a bookkeeper for Levin Food products. Any questions?"

Erin O'Riley spoke first. "Thank ye Mr. Ahern. I'm beholdin' to ye. I've been a mite worried about me wife and young ones."

"Erin, you shouldn't have concerned yourself. I've seen to your family." He turned toward the others. "As I have with your wife, Pete Boone, and your mother, Alex."

"Mr. Ahern," Thornton inquired, "I don't know even a wee bit about tool and dye. Will ol' McCay give me a long leash?"

"The job's a cover, Alex. You'll still be working for me when I call on you."

"Thank the Lord," O'Riley added. "I ain't ever owned a motor vehicle. I'd be at a loss to work one."

The others laughed when Erin ruffled Boone's hair. "This lad a bookkeeper? Lordy! When he adds two plus two, half the time he comes up with an odd sum."

Ahern arose and walked over near the fireplace. He stared at the flame. All the while the others fidgeted, impatient but hesitant to push Ahern. After several moments, he informed them, "One of our Rite brothers has been killed. As usual, the Yard won't give out any information, nor will the constabulary."

"Might I inquire as to the brother's name?"

"Lord MacTavish, Pete. Someone apparently used a shillelagh to beat him to death."

"Good Lord!" O'Riley exclaimed. "Our own Grand Master!"

"The police ought to start rounding up papists," Ahern shrugged. "But they won't. The authorities are scared to death of the papists."

"Don't mean to be cheeky, Mr. Ahern, but can we be leaving soon?"

"Pack your belongings. We'll be on our way."

Fifty feet from window four, Jake and Bennie watched as Sylvestre Gereau awaited the arrival of the bookie. The racetrack crowd milled about, now and again walking to the betting windows, referring to their tip sheets before placing their wagers. The entire area reeked of cigar smoke and beer. The attendance this day was a microcosm of social diversity. At window four, a well attired man waited in line behind a raggedly dressed bettor; both hoping to pick the winner. One least able to afford losing.

Jake glanced at his watch. "Bennie, I'm getting antsy. Hope ol' Sylvestre's not taking us for a joy ride."

"Jake, you were never one to show the patience of Job. Relax."

Half an hour later, Jake nudged Bennie. "I've had it, kid. That no good bastard has fooled us."

At the same time Jake and Bennie commenced their walk toward Sylvestre, a scraggly looking individual tapped Sylvestre on the shoulder. When he turned, Jake and Bennie moved in quickly, each with a sidearm in back of the man.

"In a low voice, Jake said to the shoulder tapper, "You be real still and very quiet and I won't stick this knife in your ribs."

"Hey, man, I believe you. All I wanted was a light." He began to shake. "What do you want with me? I was about to bet my last two dollars."

Before Jake and Bennie could react, Gereau had melted into the crowd. Several steps away the bookie observed the scene, then lit his cigar and walked to the nearest exit.

"Which way dammit, Bennie? We've been had!! Did you see where that snake went?"

"No, I was too busy backing you up with this bum. I'll look around."

Jake grabbed the arm of the terrified man and escorted him to the nearest wall. "You got a wallet? Take it out."

Jake opened the billfold to find not two dollars, but rather two twenties.

"Okay, sport. Start singing! Who the hell are you? And how do you know Sylvestre Gereau?"

"Sylvestre who?"

"The guy you tapped on the shoulder."

"Never saw him before. Some other fella I'd never seen gave me the twenties to tap him on the shoulder and strike up a conversation."

"Jesus Christ!!" Jake responded.

"Weren't you the least bit interested in a stranger who wanted you to strike up a conversation with another stranger?"

"Ain't nobody offered me forty to do anything lately. I didn't ask no questions."

"What's your name?"

"They call me Long Shot. Long Shot Barbaro."

Jake took a step back. "Okay, Mr. Long Shot, can you describe the man who gave you the dough?"

"He was uptown. Coat, tie, the works. Had a, uh —" Long Shot made a pulling motion on his chin, "whadda ya call one of them beards that hangs down from your chin? He had one of them."

"A spade?"

"Yeah, yeah. It was a spade beard, you know."

"Long Shot, if you've lied to me, I'll track you down and break both your legs. If I need you for identification purposes, how can I get in touch?"

"Sometimes, I'm at the shelter, when I ain't sleepin' in the park. 'Bout half the time, I'm out here."

Jake fought an empathic surge, then reached into his wallet and took out a twenty. "On your way, man. Get a bath if it won't offend your body too much."

"Thanks, mister. But don't scare me next time. Please."

Rochelle walked up as Long Shot was leaving. "No sign of him, Jake. I looked high and low. Where from here?"

"We'll try his house, but I suspect he'll change his address immediately. He'll have his boss and us on his ass."

Chapter Thirty

Connie slid into the seat beside Cassidy. "So, George, what is this momentous discovery you've made?"

Before answering Connie, he asked his driver, "You know the best route to Aberdeen?"

"Yes, sir. We'll take a few wee passages, then enter road 817B. Barring misfortune, we'll be there by noon."

Cassidy pulled the lever that raised the window between the driver and his three passengers.

"Okay. Here's what I learned from my time at the Aberdeen shipyard. In examining some old manifests, I found the name Yolande Margaret Hamilton MacTavish Swanson. According to that record, she set sail for Sweden in 1822. The record shows that she was escorting a small child and a coffin which contained the remains of her late husband, whose name was recorded in the manifest as Baron Haakon Swanson."

"My God!" Connie exclaimed. "George, you may have discovered my missing link! Did the manifest show the destination?"

"Yep. Stockholm. No specific address, which wasn't unusual in those days. Someone probably met her at the ship."

"Then there should be a record of her arrival."

"Not necessarily," George replied.

"Stockholm harbor was not your average Ellis Island." Cassidy replied. "However, had she remained in the area, there might be a gravestone."

After receiving permits from the harbor record master, the three Americans began pouring over the manifest hoping to discover the last address of Yolande and Baron Swanson.

After three hours of manifest scouring, Jon announced, "Duh! Let's ask these folks if any other type of record could be around."

"Oh, yes," George said. "The forest and the trees. I'll check with John Fergus, the records fella who steered me to the correct manifest."

John Fergus wasted little time in locating the receipt record.

"Here 'tis. This shows that Yolande Swanson gave her address in March, 1823, as Markum, Scotland."

"Nothing more specific?" Cassidy asked.

"Not 'atall, Laddie. In those days, much as 'tis these days, folks were known in their villages. Now and again, a number might show up. Small villages rarely had street identification."

Connie pointed to the large map on the wall. "Can you show us the general area where Markum is located?"

"Sure, Lass." Fergus walked over to the map. "Markum is far up in the highlands." He pointed. "Here. And don't ye know, me guess is that the village to this day has no street names."

Connie, could not veil her excitement on the drive back to Edinburgh. "George, you're great! I feel I'm much closer to solving the mystery of our dream." She gave Jon an emphatic kiss on the cheek.

Jon put his arm around her. "I wish I could share your optimism. Oh, I believe things are coming together, but I'm concerned for your safety — and mine. I'll be glad when Jake returns."

"Yeah, me, too," Connie agreed.

"There's so much going on, I haven't had time to get really scared." She placed her hand on Cassidy's arm. "George, thank you, thank you! You say you're not a detective. I think you're one hell of a detective!"

"I must say," he replied, "I'm enjoying all of my adrenaline rushes. For years, I've sat behind a desk manipulating figures and watching bottom lines. Ah, but I do smell more danger than I'm used to."

———————————————————

Connie was confused by her feelings as she entered the conference room of Morton, Elwood, and MacIntire, Ltd.

"Dr. Nordstram, please be seated at the head of the table. You are, after all, the person of the moment."

"Thank you," she replied as Samuel Elwood pulled out the chair for her.

"I'll introduce those around the table. I'm Orland MacIntire." He pointed to each one as he called their names. "Our recorder, Mary O'Neal, Samuel Elwood, Tom Morton. At the other end of the table is Arthur Perry, who, also, has a vested interest at this meeting. Good, then let us get started."

He retrieved a folder from his attaché case. "First, as you know, we are here for the reading of Michael MacTavish's will, with a small number of caveats."

MacIntire's droning recital of the legal basis for the will heightened Connie's angst. She knew only what Scotland Yard had told her. The letter from the barrister had been an invitation to a hearing, not the contents of a will. What had Michael done and what were his reasons for doing it? She knew that in her short relationship with MacTavish she had experienced both his caring side and a part of him that frightened her. She wanted the Scottish lawyer to get on with it - whatever it was, caveats and all. She regretted that Jon was not seated beside her.

"And now," the lawyer looked directly at Connie, "I shall get to the meat of the matter, as you yanks say, Dr. Nordstram. In his will Lord MacTavish leaves his castle and his country estate in the highlands to Dr. Constance Nordstram. In addition, he wills his import-export business, his cattle and sheep farm in the highlands, and twenty million pounds in hard currency to Dr. Nordstram. Dr. Nordstram, the condition stated herein is that you must retain and be the benefactor of both the castle staff at Sonsie and the caretakers of the estate. This file will provide you with all the information you need to assume control of MacTavish's holdings.

The lawyer took a swallow of water before he directed his attention to Arthur Perry. "Lord Perry, as a Grand Master of the Free Masons, Scottish Rite, your organization is to receive one million pounds. I will read his exact words, "to be used for the betterment of mankind, and in so doing, serve as a counter to the I.R.A., the order of Alexander, and all others who wish to break up the Island Empire."

"Our business is concluded. Dr. Nordstram, Lord Perry, as Lord MacTavish directed, I have deducted the executor fee, you shall receive a receipt and a summary of the proceedings of this meeting. Do you have questions?" He waited. "If not, thank you for coming. Dr. Nordstram, will you stay behind very briefly?"

Connie nodded.

When the door shut behind the others, MacIntire walked to a small refrigerator.

"Would you like a drink, my dear?"

"Yes, please. Scotch over ice."

He poured himself a scotch, no ice, then gave Connie her drink over ice.

"Dr. Nordstram, the reason I asked you to stay after is because I wish to be your solicitor." He grinned, "Your lawyer. Lord MacTavish was always pleased with my service over the last thirty years. Should you choose me to be… I believe you Americans say, legal eagle; I should be pleased to serve you as loyally as did I your benefactor."

"Thank you. For the time being I'll say yes." Connie coughed. "Umm good scotch, Mr. MacIntire. My feelings are so jumbled right now, I'm not sure I know what day it is. Honestly, this was totally unexpected."

"If you'll forgive my presumption, Lord MacTavish gave me a few more details than were in the will." He ran his fingers through a thatch of grey hair. "Dr. Nordstram, he was in love with you. He had no other living relative save you. He said he wanted to make things right with you. Obviously, he had no occasion to do so before he was murdered."

Jon rose from his chair as Connie closed MacIntire's office door. He gave her a reassuring hug when he saw the look on her face.

"So?"

Connie struggled to keep from showing the emotions she felt. "I'll give you all the gory details when we're on our way to the cottage." The elation she felt was tempered by a veneer of guilt over her earlier doubts about Michael. Now, Sykes's suspicions would be the events of this day.

"Jesus," he said. "Must have been a bad session."

Connie ignored him until they reached their auto. She could hold it in no longer. She did an impromptu dance. She tried to prevent herself from shouting. "Jon, my love, earlier this year, I was your average college professor, working for the next promotion and salary increase. Now, I am so wealthy, it staggers my imagination." She proceeded to give Jon a blow by blow account of the will proceeding.

Jon held out his arms. "Hey, this is the first time I've slept with a rich female, who by the way, I love."

———————————

Damon Kelly waited for an invitation to take a seat. It never came.

"What happened, Damon?"

"As I told you, sir, I set up a meeting with him. When I got to the track, I headed immediately to our usual place, window four. I was about to greet him when I noticed him looking over his shoulder. I mean he was nervous. I waited and watched him for a bit. I hired a bum to tap him on the shoulder. All of a sudden the bum had a rod in the ribs. A man and a woman. Cops, I figure. I left immediately. That's the way it went down."

"Do you know where he is at present?"

"No, sir. He's gone to ground. I've got some people on it. We'll find him."

"Find him and erase him, Damon. Someone, somewhere, is causing me to have a headache. I don't like headaches."

"I understand, boss."

"That's all, Damon. Get it done."

"Yes, sir," he said as he left the darkened room.

A short ride later, Kelly knocked on the front door of the Gereau residence. After a second knock, a middle-aged woman answered.

"Is this where Sylvestre Gereau lives?"

"Yes, it is," she replied.

"Are you his wife?"

She laughed. "Do I look young enough to be his wife? Hardly. I've been hired to keep the house while the Gereau's are on vacation."

"Do you know where they went for their vacation?"

"Ah," she glowered, "You are the inquisitive one. No, I don't know where they are. They left, didn't even give me a telephone number. Said they would call."

Kelly pushed her into the house and braced her against the wall. "You're lying to me, bitch. Now, I want you to reconsider what you've just told me. It doesn't make a damn bit of sense that the Gereaus would up and leave you with zero instructions." He loosened his grip on her throat. "So, let me ask you again. Where did they go?"

Jenny Ortega began to shake and cry. "So help me God, they didn't say. They didn't say. Please don't hurt me."

He slapped her hard. "You're lying."

Blood appeared from the corner of her mouth. "They told me someone would come looking for them. They gave me money and told me to keep my mouth shut."

"Well?"

"Don't hit me again. I don't know why they told me to keep quiet. I don't know nothing."

Kelly thought for a moment, then released his grip on her. "Okay, bitch. I'm gonna look around. You stay right by my side." He pulled a pistol from his jacket. "If you make a move to a phone, you're a dead woman. Understand?"

"Yes, yes. I won't."

"Good. We'll start in this room." He began to look through desk drawers. He threw magazines and books asunder, cursing all the while.

After dismantling an armoire, he grabbed Jenny and pulled her behind him into the kitchen. There, he rifled every cabinet and closet, leaving clutter in his wake.

"What's upstairs?"

"Bedrooms — one bathroom," she answered.

As soon as they entered the master bedroom, Kelly picked up a notepad near the telephone. On it was written AMERICAN, 555-8419.

"When did they leave here?"

She hesitated for an instant. "Let me think. They called me four days ago. When I got here, they was packed and ready to go."

"What time was that?"

"About four in the afternoon."

"You're sure about that?"

"Yes. I know because I always watch Oprah. She was just coming on."

Kelly punched in the number for American Airlines. Following three automated instructions, accompanied by Kelly's cursing, a person came on the line.

"May I help you?"

"Can you list your flights out of Montreal during the time span from 6:00 to 9:00 p.m.?" He waited. After a while, he spoke into the phone. "Let me repeat back what you said: 6:05 to London; 6:30 to Los Angeles; 7:05 to Seattle; 7:50 to Philadelphia. Was that correct?"

He cradled the phone. "Now, lady, I want you to go into a state of amnesia. You don't remember that I was here. If you do remember, your life won't be worth a spit. Am I clear?"

"Yes! Yes!" she blurted. "I promise I won't say nothin'."

"What's your name?"

"Jenny."

"Jenny what?"

"Jenny Ortega."

"You got any ID that'll show your name and address?"

"My bag is downstairs in the kitchen."

Kelly copied the information from her passport. He gave his parting caveat. "You say anything, lady, you remember what I told you. I know where you live. Says here you have two kids. Keep in mind, I'll remember that."

He stroked his beard as he walked to his car.

Chapter Thirty One

Molly poured tea to the people gathered around the table.

"By the size of this table," Jon surmised, "the MacTavishes must have thrown parties for everyone in the kingdom. How many people do you guess could be seated?"

"Molly, how many persons can be seated around the table?" Connie asked.

"Don't rightly know, Mum. Once I counted thirty-four guests invited by Lord MacTavish," Molly responded.

After all members of the household staff arrived, Connie invited them to sit. For an instant they gave quizzical looks to each other. Molly asked, "Are you sure, Mum? We have always waited to be called upon, but we never sat with his Lordship."

"Well, now," Connie gave a soft laugh, "Try to enjoy the experience." She made a sweeping motion with her arm. "Please sit." She introduced Jon and George, then asked each staff member to raise a hand and be recognized.

"I've asked you to this meeting for several reasons. First, as you know, Lord Mac-Tavish has willed this place, uh, this dwelling, oh, hell, James Miller, what do we call my new home?"

"Tis a manor, Mum. Often 'tis mistaken for a castle. And, if I may be so forward, how shall we refer to your Ladyship?" he blustered.

The other servants twittered.

"You may call me your highness."

The servants grew silent very quickly, while George and Jon laughed aloud.

"Hey, I'm teasing, James. Please talk to me as an equal. Most of my friends call me

Connie. My students addressed me as Dr. Nordstram. My ex-husband last noted that I was a bitch." Laughter.

Immediately Connie sensed the group becoming more comfortable as the meeting progressed.

"You haven't asked the question, but I'll give you the answer. I want all of you to remain employed in the household, if you so desire." She pointed to James Miller. "Mr. Miller, you will continue to manage the manor. I see no good reason to alter any of your duties. Okay, now we've settled that issue. Three gentlemen will be residents in the manor. At least, for the time being. Mr. Cassidy is assisting in my research project. Mr. Lindsey, who is presently out of town and Dr. LeFreaux are my personal assistants, as well as my bodyguards. Each of them will require living quarters. Any questions?"

Molly's excitement caused her to stutter. "Oh, Mum! I'm s-s-so pleased that you're here. We have missed you!"

The others nodded their approval.

James Miller stood to address Connie. "About the others, Mum. We have other outbuildings. The tools for upkeep are there. Also, Mum, the living quarters for the grounds men."

Connie was surprised. "Oh, I didn't know. Where are those buildings?"

"About a kilometer from the manor."

"James, how many acres does this estate cover?"

"I apologize, Mum. I don't know 'acres.'"

Connie made a circle in the air. "You know, how much…"

Before she could finish, Cassidy interrupted. "How many hectares, Mr. Miller?"

"Aye. Let me see. Absent my file, about 500 hectares."

Cassidy glanced at Connie. "Over 1200 acres, Dr. Nordstram."

"Thanks, George. Okay staff, my first task is to learn the metric system. James, would you give us a tour of the grounds when we've finished here?"

"Yes, Mum. Delighted to show you around."

When Connie rose to leave, Cassidy asked, "May I stay to visit with the group. I promise I won't keep them from their duties. I want to get acquainted with them, oh, and learn more about this marvelous estate."

———————————————————

"Now lads and lasses," the commissioner began, "We're getting pressure from the top. 'Twasn't so bad until Lord MacTavish was done in. Don't you know, don't you know, that we took a bit of guff from Fleet Street when their lads collided with a locomotive? But that passed. Then we had the American woman assaulted. That created only a slight fuss. After that, John Angus met his maker from parties unknown. The Yard biggies are getting perturbed. When they get perturbed, I get perturbed. So, lads and lasses, I want you to get perturbed. We need to busy ourselves and get to the core. I'll hear from each one of you. Sykes, you've been looking into the Angus homicide. What do you have for us?"

"Not a whit to go on, sir," Detective Sykes answered. "We've looked at the possible lash-up between the two cases," he nodded to Sheila Morgan, the lead investigator on the Nordstram assault.

"Nothing. We've interrogated a number of the villagers. No leads, except that John Angus could talk a body to death. We came down hard on LeFreaux and Nordstram, but neither broke. We tailed them for a fortnight. We were able to visit more castles than we cared to. During one foray they visited a woman named Mary Manion. When we questioned her, she called us all matter of rubbish. Said we'd never find the real Stone."

Commissioner Adrean Montrose shook his head from side to side and emitted a long sigh. "You know, they'll never give us any peace. Her Majesty had the infernal rock returned to Edinburgh, but they remain to this day, convinced that it is a fake. Sykes, how did the Stone get into the Manion conversation?"

"We inquired as to why she received a visit from Nordstram and LeFreaux. Oh, and another fellow from America named George Cassidy. He's on watch from the local constabulary. Seems he was speeding, driving without a license and bribing a vehicle rental lad. He's a friend of Nordstram. Said he was in Scotland to help her genealogical research. We think he's a harmless bloke. Just a bit clumsy. In any case, Mary Manion is one angry Catholic. Mostly, when we made an inquiry, she would launch into a tirade toward every Royal from James to the present. The woman was of little assistance." He referred to his notes. "A fellow from the states named Lindsey is now a bodyguard for Nordstram and LeFreaux. He's a P.I. Checked in with us. Said he came over after Nordstram was attacked. He was a co-operative chap. We checked with Interpol and the Boston, Massachusetts, police commissioner. He's clean. A tough one also. Seems he was attacked in a local pub by three of Ray Ahern's employees. They came out on the short end."

"Ahern is an American, is he not?" the commissioner asked.

"Yes, sir. Heads his own company. Moves about. London. New York. Paris."

"Does Mr. Lindsey have a notion as to the reason he was assaulted?"

"He guessed it's because he's been asking questions relating to the Nordstram attack."

"What do we have on Ahern?"

"Nothing. We can't tie him to the Lindsey affair. We cancelled surveillance on him. Lindsey let it be known that he would keep us informed should he discover any dirt on Ahern."

Montrose directed his attention to Detective Morgan. "Sheila, what about the Nordstram case?"

"Sir, I've been unable to uncover anything that makes sense. No mugging. No witnesses. The only item of significance is what Dr. Nordstram reported the assailant said. The assailant, according to her statement, told her to quit snooping and to go home, or words to that effect," she reported.

"What about the usual club of suspects?" the commissioner asked.

"Oh, we've rounded 'em up. No luck."

"So much for all that folderol. I want all of you to concentrate your efforts and find who murdered Lord MacTavish. The only persons, at this juncture, with a motive are our visitors from America, Dr. Nordstram and her lover — or whatever he is, Dr. LeFreaux. Nordstram obviously had the most to gain from his death. Before she came on the scene, MacTavish in his will left the bulk of his holdings to a man named Perry, a grandmaster in the rite. We have determined that MacTavish changed his will two months before his death. Sykes, you will lead the investigation."

———————————————

As they entered the outskirts of Calgary, Bennie Rochelle teased her new partner, Mark Campbell, "I'll bet that if Jake had known you won't fly, you'd still be a class two detective in Boston. Do you know how many hours we've been on the road?"

Campbell glanced at his watch. "Two days and we're still alive. Sorry. I had a wheels up landing when I was in the military. That was the last time I came near an airplane." He changed the subject abruptly, "I know we've got work to do, but I want to visit their crime museum here in Calgary. The word is that it's quite a tribute to Canadian law enforcement."

"Jon was accurate about how the Laforges spend their time. God! It must be nice to be rich."

"Miss Rochelle, we'll never know."

"Unfortunately, you're right," she agreed. "What was that address?"

"Smack downtown, according to this GPS reading."

Twenty blocks later, they parked in the garage accommodating those housed in the Wheatland Office building. "They own all of this property?"

"That's what I was told back in Montreal. Fella named Jordan said the Laforges have assets all over Canada."

Bennie closed the car door and pushed the keyless entry. "Let's see what turns up when we do a bit of stirring."

The sixteenth floor of the Wheatland was occupied entirely by Laforge Enterprises, Ltd. The outer lobby housed three receptionists and a security desk. A semi-circle of TV monitors was set atop the desk.

Mark gave a cursory look around the area. He stopped in front of the desk, seated behind which was an attractive woman who Mark guessed was in her mid-thirties.

"May I help you, sir?"

"I'd like to see Mr. Lambeau."

"You would, eh," she responded with an expression, a cross between a smile and a sneer, "and your name, please?"

"Campbell. Mark Campbell."

She scanned a computer printout before her. "I don't see your name on my appointment log. Without an appointment, you'll have to go through security." She pointed. "Over there, and you ma'am?"

"I'm with him," Bennie answered.

As they walked toward the security desk, Bennie said, "Let me take this one. I'll lay some charm on him. Betcha he needs some TLC. Let's roil up things."

She smiled at the security guard and presented her newly acquired Canadian P.I. license. "Hello. How're you today?"

The guard examined her credentials. His response was curt. "What's your business here?"

"We'd like to see Mr. Lambeau."

"What's your business with him?"

Bennie smiled. "Murder. We understand that Mr. Lambeau might be able to help us."

The guard pressed an intercom button. "Lemme speak to Mr. Lambeau."

A moment later a deep voice responded, "Yes."

"Mr. Lambeau, there's a couple of P.I.s who want to see you."

"Did they indicate why they wish to see me?"

"Yes, sir. The lady," he paused reading from her license, "a Miss Benedette Rochelle, says it's about a murder."

A brief interlude passed before Lambeau spoke. "Have one of your men escort them to my office."

"Yes, Sir." The guard pressed another intercom button. "Charlie, I need you out front."

"Sooo — you got here an armed camp," Mark offered. "Y'all afraid someone's gonna run off with the entire building, eh?"

The desk guard ignored Mark's repartee. A second uniformed man approached the desk. "Take these people to Mr. Lambeau."

"Follow me," the second guard directed.

"Bennie, these are some grim folks. You suppose they start the day by having someone place their nuts in a vise? Oh, and so much for your charm."

Even as Mark spoke loudly enough for Charlie to hear the barb, Charlie paid no attention.

The man who greeted them did not fit the executive picture Bennie had envisioned. He was young, early thirties, late twenties, strikingly handsome. His single-breasted Italian jacket matched trousers that fit perfectly, and had not been purchased off a rack. His smile was the polar opposite from the greetings Bennie and Mark received from his employees.

He offered a well manicured hand. "Welcome to Laforge Enterprises. I'm Jacques Lambeau."

"Mark Campbell," he motioned toward Bennie.

"Benedette Rochelle. We're working on a murder case. We hope you can help us find a certain individual named Sylvestre Gereau."

Lambeau released his soft grip on Bennie's hand. "Gereau. Hmm. Sylvestre Gereau. Oh, yes. I do remember the name. Given some clues, I might even remember his face. Please take a seat." He pressed the intercom button. "Sue, please look into our files, active and dead. Anything on Sylvestre Gereau? What's this about a murder?" he asked Mark.

"Three murders. One of our colleagues was killed by two men who were later executed by Sylvestre Gereau, or we believe that to be the case."

A female voice came over the intercom, "Mr. Lambeau, a Sylvestre Gereau never worked here, but at one time was employed in the eastern division. That would have been from '99 to '03. Notes in his file show that he served in company security."

"Thanks, Sue. Yes, I do recall him now. I must have met him at a company event of some kind."

"I assume you haven't run into him lately?" Mark asked.

"No. I'm sure that I would remember had I been around him lately."

Bennie reached into her purse for a note pad. "Can you describe him? You know height, weight, age, any distinguishing features?"

Lambeau pondered briefly. "He was a big man. About forty to forty-five years old. Thinning hair, if I recall. Rather abrupt, you know, tart in conversing. That's about all I remember about him."

Campbell pointed to a picture hanging on the wall. "Are these individuals in your employ?"

"No, no. The men in the picture are from the Montreal division. That's me in the second row. I used to work in Montreal until I was promoted to this position."

Mark stood, ready to leave. "Thank you, Mr. Lambeau. We appreciate your time and information."

As they neared the lobby exit, Mark turned abruptly and walked back to the receptionist who had referred them to the security desk. "We really had a good meeting with Mr. Lambeau. I'm Mark Campbell. You must be the Susan Delgado Mr. Lambeau spoke to on the intercom while we were in his office."

Delgado's earlier icy demeanor morphed into a smile. "Yes, yes, I am. I'm glad you had a good meeting."

"Susan, that photo," Mark pointed to the group picture on the wall behind her desk.

"I think I know one of those fellows. That one with the spade beard. I can't quite recall his name, but I'm sure I know him from some other setting."

"Oh," she volunteered, "That's Mr. Kelly. He works with our company in Montreal, but he comes here occasionally."

"Sure!" Mark exclaimed. "Montreal. Yes, now I recall." He extended his hand to the receptionist. "So good to meet you. Have a good day, eh."

The two American private investigators strolled casually down the hallway to the main exit. "Bingo!" Bennie expressed in a low, excited voice. "The luck of the Irish, Mark Campbell. You are an observant schmoozer. I had forgotten I told you about a phantom bearded man. Bet you can't remember the name of the racetrack bum I described to you."

"Sure, I can. Long shot Barbaro. Same as the horse and I'm not Irish."

Chapter Thirty Two

Tired and rumpled from his transatlantic flight, Jake banged the door with the iron knocker hanging from the nose of the brass lion. A few seconds passed before Osgood, the butler, opened the door. "Good day, sir. You must be Mr. Lindsey, the private policeman; I suspect I'll be seeing a great deal of you. Now isn't that so? I'm Chauncey Osgood. I direct traffic from this doorway."

"Well, Chauncey, old chap how do you do?" Jake extended his hand. "Glad to meet you."

Jake reached for his luggage, but was disrupted by Chauncey. "Please, sir. I'll take care of that. I'll show you to your quarters. Follow me."

The stone stairway steps, worn from centuries of use, led to the third level. "You'll be quartered here, Mr. Lindsey. Your colleagues' rooms are down the corridor. Lady Nordstram requested that I invite you to her quarters as soon as you have been made a bit comfortable."

"And where does the Lady hang her hat, Chauncey?"

"Not sure I understand, sir."

"Where in this castle is she located?"

"Ah, yes." Chauncey nodded.

"Second level, third door on the left. It's a manor, sir, even though I like to tell my kin in the colonies it's a castle."

"Where in the col— er, the states do you have relatives?"

"Me sister's family lives in a province called Rhode Island. Two of me nephews fetch golf balls from the bramble for their masters. I believe these lads are known as Cadillacs."

"You mean caddies, don't you?"

"Sure, now. Caddies they are. They travel all over the countryside retrieving golf balls from the bush and bramble."

Jake laughed as he slapped Osgood gently on his back. "Chauncey, old bean, I like you."

"Yes, sir. I'm sure we'll be getting on famously."

Jake walked about the room, which in years gone by had been used by numerous ranks of royalty: lords, barons, dukes, marshals, and at least one prime minister. Jake stared at the painting of Winston Churchill, then shifted his gaze to Lord Nelson, flanked on one side by the Duke of Normandy and on the other side by the Duke of Windsor. "Damn! What has Connie stumbled into?" he muttered to himself.

Following a short bath in the largest tub Jake had ever seen, he changed his clothing. He donned a wool sports jacket and announced to the Queen, occupying one wall all to herself, "Your Highness, how do you keep warm in this oversized meat locker?"

At Jake's first knock, Connie opened the door and hugged him enthusiastically.

"God, am I glad to see you, Jake. I know you had a task back there, but I hope it'll wait. Things around her have come unglued. We needed you."

"I missed you three. No problem with my leaving. I turned that end of things over to Bennie Rochelle and I hired an old partner from Boston P.D. I'll concentrate on things Scottish. Which reminds me, do ye have a tad of that mountain dew? Over ice if ye please."

Cassidy and LeFreaux greeted Jake with effusive handshakes. "That's the worst imitation of a Scotsman I've ever heard! Damn, dog, I've missed you."

"Yeah, me, too. Bet you can hardly get along without me. Anyhow, I'm glad to be back. How about you guys catch me up."

"Same old routine," Connie said. "Oh, but I suppose you noticed we've changed addresses," she added, with a straight face.

"Any leads on who hammered his Lordship?"

"Not a whit so far," Jon answered. "As usual, their only suspects thus far are Connie and yours truly."

"Makes sense to me," Jake teased. "Guy dies. A conniving woman from the colonies inherits the estate. Who could ask for a better suspect?"

"So, which of us was commissioned to do her dirty work? Jon or me?" Cassidy asked.

"George, I'm kidding."

"Gotcha!" George guffawed.

"Okay, let's get serious. I had a lot of time on the flight to do some thinking. Somehow, I believe that the goofy dreams you two have," Jake looked at Jon and Connie.

"May not be as goofy as I once thought. Think about it. You start looking into family trees here and in the USA. Bodies start piling up. George, do you think that Stone has a darn thing to do with what's going on?"

The others were silent, waiting for George's response. "This may surprise. I don't believe our inquiries about the Stone are germane to our situation."

"You don't. I'm incredulous," retorted Jon. "What's your reasoning?"

"I don't believe the rumors that the Stone at Edinburgh is a fake. There's not one iota of proof. I'm a bottom line man. I must see proof. Jon, you can appreciate that, I'm sure."

"Yes, George. But these last few months have tempered my ideology somewhat."

"Why, George," Jake asked, "if all the mess we've encountered isn't about the Stone, then what?"

"Please don't laugh," Cassidy answered. "Do you remember the watchwords during the Watergate scandal? Follow the money."

"I've read about it," Jake replied. "We're young."

"Thanks a lot," George joked. "I'm not that old. It was a big event in my day."

"Hell, George, if that's our direction, Connie and Don Juan here," he countered, "top the list. So, where does that leave us?"

Cassidy answered quickly, "We quit perseverating over the Stone. No more inquiries about it, no more of our time wasted on it." He hesitated. "I'd like to know how MacTavish came by his money. I'd like to know where Jon's family money came from. Especially, how did the Laforges become so wealthy?"

Jake chided Cassidy. "George, you'll be a good detective sooner than I imagined. Okay, kids, I agree with George. We start tracking money. Connie, right at the moment, you're the only one who has a stash here in Scotland. Or the only one we know about."

"Does that mean…" Connie didn't finish her question before Jon interrupted.

"Yep. We start with the fortune of the dearly departed cousin Michael."

"Do you mean," Connie blurted, "that our ancestor search goes to the back burner?"

"Not necessarily," Jake replied. "My guess is that we'll turn up a legion of ancestors at the same time we're sniffing out money. Besides, you and Jon can continue your own agenda, okay? I'm going to hire a bodyguard for you two."

"Ah, come on, Jake. We've been able to survive while you were away. We'll be fine. Don't forget I'm packing."

"Uh, huh. And for God's sake don't get caught."

Chapter Thirty Three

The morning had been cold, exacerbated by a stronger than usual North Sea wind. Kathryn Digbe decided early that she wouldn't attempt to do any more repair work on her short picket fence. She put away her tools, then set about making a pot of tea.

She had not invited nor expected her early morning visitors. Now, she sat stiffly, anger roiling within her. The three masked men sitting opposite her sipped on the tea she had not invited them to drink.

"Who did you commission, old woman, to kill Lord MacTavish?" The intruder leaned in, close to her face. He had about him the smell of onion and sweat. She said nothing.

He slapped her. "We know you and your kind put the shillelagh to his Lordship. We want the names of them what wielded the club."

Digbe could hear only the wind outside. She could see only her precious garden, dormant now until the Spring. She saw the hill overlooking the sea and silently thanked Jesus, Joseph, and Mary and all the Saints for the vision they gave her. She said nothing. The intruder turned to one of his confidants. "Give me the torch."

The second man passed him the lighter. "Now, you papist bitch, we'll see if a wee bit of fire'll loosen your tongue." He grabbed her arm. When she fought him, the others pinned her against her chair. The intruder held the lighter flame to the back of her hand. She screamed in agony until he pulled the flame away.

"Lest ye want your hand well done, old woman, who killed him?"

Though in excruciating pain, Kathryn Digbe yanked one arm free from his grasp. In the same motion, she tore the mask from the face of her tormentor.

"You devil. I don't know you!" she screamed. "I'll guess you descend from John Knox!"

"Not a bit of fortune it'll bring ye!" He held the flame to her hand until the screams turned to a moan, then silence.

He slapped her once, twice. No response. "Wake up bitch! Ye're just playing dead!"

"Mon, she's unconscious. Don't burn her no more," his accomplice ordered.

"She ain't unconscious, she's dead"

The room became deathly quiet until the tormentor stuttered, "Wha — what did — what do we do now?"

"Don't know about you lads. I'm leaving this place," said the third masked man as he moved toward the door.

"Get back here, dang you! We must do something with the carcass!"

"I have an idea," said the second masked man. Let's place her on the floor near the stove. The coppers'll believe she burned her hand just afore her heart failed her. What do you think?"

The leader pondered the question, then answered, "Yes, good, good! Drag her over to the stove. I'll light the flame and set the tea pot to boiling."

"We're in for King Billy hell when we report what happened," the second masked man retorted.

"We ain't a gonna tell the real story," the inquisitor cackled. "Here is what happened. We asked the papist bitch for names. She didn't co-operate. She said she'd forget the visit from us. We left afterwards. Are we agreed?"

The others nodded their affirmation.

"Man, this is the only way to travel."

"Jon, I'm glad you're having fun with your new toy. I hope you don't displace your shoulder doing all that shifting," Connie said.

Jon downshifted as he entered the outskirts of Perth. "Where is the Scone Palace, George? We're here."

Cassidy checked his map. "About a mile ahead, turn right. Check your GPS to see if that satellite agrees with me."

"Yes," Jon answered. "Shows us turning right on to Warfield."

"Okay, George. Tell us all about Scone Palace," Connie requested.

"Glad to do so. According to the best sources I can find, a man named Kenneth MacAlpine set aside an area and named it Celtic Obertha, which he designated as the

Kingdom of the Scots and the Picts, who by then were unified. That was in 846. From that date, all Scottish kings were crowned over the Sacred Stone of Destiny. When Edward I of England took the Stone from Scone and parked it in Westminster Abbey, all subsequent British kings have been crowned above it. Even to this day. Sometime early in the 12th century, Alexander I founded the first Augustinian monastery on the same site. Early on, the monastery was used, also, to house the royal family. In 1210 William the Lion started a settlement which is today Perth. By the way, the monastery was ransacked by the overzealous followers of John Knox."

"Who was John Knox?" Jon asked. "I think I slept through that history lecture."

"Now you're awake, Jon," Cassidy grinned.

"He founded what is today the Presbyterian Church. He was rabidly anti-Catholic, and somehow lived to a ripe old age. Queens Mary and Elizabeth were fearful of the consequences should they have burned him at the stake."

"Would you say, George, that was anti-inflammatory politics?" Connie asked.

"Yes, you punster. Let me change the subject slightly. You remember what I said about following the money?"

"Yep," Jon replied.

"New data, you two. In my searching through records, I discovered that the rift between the Viking King Haakon and Alexander II was settled by the Treaty of Perth over who held title to parts of Northern Scotland. Anyhow, to cut to the chase, the king who replaced Haakon, fellow named Mangus, agreed to sell Norway's rights to those parts of Scotland in dispute. So the Western Isles reverted to Scotland for four thousand merks in silver."

"What's all that got to do with our present circumstance?" Connie asked.

"I'm getting to it. No one seems to have recorded what happened to the four thousand merks. I did some barnyard math. What would you estimate these coins to be worth today?"

Before either could answer, Cassidy raised his voice. "As much as one hundred million dollars, probably more. Connie, this may interest you. The man who managed Alexander III's money — not sure they had chancellors of the exchequer back then — was named John MacTavish."

"Are you saying that…"

"I'm not sure what I'm saying."

Cassidy interrupted. "I think we should try to find out what happened to John Mac-Tavish and the king's money. From what I could determine those silver merks never came into the hands of ol' Edward I back in England."

"Okay, guys, when we return to Sonsie, we are going to turn that place upside down. The genealogist who put me in contact with Michael had only Michael's word to track back. At least, that's what Michael told him. Said his was the accurate record."

Jon steered the Jaguar into the parking lot at the bottom of Moot Hill.

"There it is," he muttered softly. "The very building that housed the rock that's caused so much fuss."

"No, no!" Cassidy corrected. "Neither the monastery up there, rebuilt in 1804, nor the palace ever housed the Stone. But somewhere on this site is where MacAlpine set the Stone. The exact location is unknown."

As they approached the palace, each member of the trio remained eerily silent. There it was, a monument to another time, now almost covered by creepers, its battlements rising above great stanchions of Scottish history, its grounds the nesting places for pheasants; now but an important stop for serious tourists and an occasional student of history.

"Scone Palace," George continued, "the magnificent edifice which was built by the first Earl of Gowrie, was constructed from the stones of an old abbey. After Gowrie was found to be a part of a conspiracy to kill James IV, the Gowrie property was returned to the English Crown. David Murray, history records, saved King James from death. Subsequently, the estate was presented to the Murray family, one of whom restored the castle to its present day lustre."

The three Americans strolled into the long gallery, half a football field in length. While Connie gazed at the Gothic ceiling, Jon knelt to touch the oak floor, upon which numerous sovereigns had trod.

"Connie," George said, "that ceiling was once covered with fresco scenes depicting the hunting exploits of King James VI."

"I prefer the present ceiling," Connie stated.

"The Gothic pattern is awesomely beautiful."

"George, how did this inlaid floor survive the centuries?" Jon asked.

"They used peat bog. I'm not sure exactly how it was done. But it is amazing how it has stood the test of time," he hesitated, "and feet."

George led them to the ambassador bedroom. On the wall hung portraits of Lord Starmont and his daughter Lady Elizabeth. The pièce de résistance was a four poster bed which overshadowed all else in the room, bearing the coat of arms of George III. The bed had been given to Lord Starmont by the king to honor Starmont's service to the crown.

Jon placed his arm around Connie. "How about I get one of those for you and me after we're, uh — married?"

194

"Are you proposing to me?"

"Are you proposing to her?" Cassidy echoed.

"Well — yeah," Jon stammered.

"I'll think about it," Connie answered as she winked at George. "In the meantime, I want to visit the site where Alexander either fell from his horse or was murdered by God knows who."

Kathryn Digbe propped herself up in the hospital bed, more comfortable now that tubes no longer were attached to her body.

"Ten minutes, no more," the nurse directed, closing the door behind her. The four Americans gathered around the bed.

Connie spoke first. "Oh, Kathryn, I'm so sorry." She bent down and kissed Digbe on the cheek. "I understand you suffered a heart attack, but what happened to your hands?" Connie asked as she lifted Digbe's right arm.

"Ah, lass," she answered in a tired voice. "That's the reason me heart went on the blink. MacTavish's runnin' boys did a bit of roastin', they did."

"What did they want from you?" Jake asked.

"They wanted the names of them who killed the MacTavish devil. I would ha' to make up a story. I dinna know who put the shillelagh to him. But them that did it will sit beside St. Peter one day. Would you," she pointed to Cassidy, "please pour me a tumbler of water?"

Cassidy eased the glass into her bandaged hand, then patted her gently on her head. "You're a tough one, Kathryn Digbe."

"Oh, I doubt that! You shoulda heard me wailin' when that bastard son of John Knox put the fire to me."

"Did you recognize any of your assailants?" Jake asked.

"Nae. There were three o' them. All wore masks. I managed to tear away the mask of me main tormentor. I had ne'er seen the dog before that day."

Jake held up three photographs. "Was he one of these men?"

She stared at the photos of Boone, O'Riley, and Thornton. "Nae, wasn't any of them. But I swear before all the saints, I'll ne'r forget his face. Oh, and by the bye, the constable showed the same pictures to me."

Digbe's eyes grew tired. The pain killer was taking effect. "Ye know, don't ye, they'll never stop until they find where the Stone is..." Her voice trailed off.

Connie placed a box of chocolates on her bed stand.

"God be with you, Kathryn Digbe."

"Did you have an appointment with Mr. Kelly?" The receptionist smiled at Mark and Bennie. "If so, I've had to cancel all of his appointments. He'll be out of the office for several days."

"Do you know his whereabouts or when he may return?" Bennie asked. "We have important business to discuss with him."

The receptionist lifted the telephone and punched one key. "I have two people here to see Damon. They say they have important business to discuss. Can you meet with them?" She listened briefly, then said, "Mr. McGill will see you. He's Mr. Kelly's assistant. Down the corridor, second door on the left."

The secretary greeted the P.I.s and escorted them into Carlyle McGill's office. He stood to greet them. "Welcome. I understand that you wish to discuss a business deal."

For Bennie, it was now or never — let the devil take the hindmost. "Mr. McGill, my partner," she nodded toward Campbell "and I are private investigators." She extended her I.D. "We have reason to believe that Damon Kelly has information relating to a crime in the United States. We wish to interview him."

McGill walked quickly to close the door to his office. "A crime? What crime, if I may be so bold as to ask?" His demeanor reflected his surprise at the suddenness of Bennie's statement.

Mark watched as McGill began to fidget with the buttons on his jacket. He sat for an instant, then stood behind his desk. "Murder, Mr. McGill. We have reason to believe that Damon Kelly has either killed or commissioned someone to kill a colleague of ours, among others."

"You have to be mistaken. Mr. Kelly involved in a murder. That's absurd."

Bennie moved in closer to McGill. "Where is he? Surely, as his assistant you know how to reach him."

"I don't know where he went!" McGill's anger punctuated each word. "And even if I did know, I'd not reveal it to you!"

McGill was on the run. Mark could smell blood. "Then perhaps you can tell us who might know the location of one Damon Kelly. The RCMP, I'm sure, would be pleased to help us find him. I suggest you think real hard and try to remember his instructions to you when he departed for places unknown."

McGill had begun to sweat. He dabbed at his brow with a handkerchief. "You can't bluff me! Who the hell are you to barge in here and…" As his voice increased in volume, he began to cough. When the spasms stopped, he returned to his chair slumping, placing his head in his hands.

"Europe. That's all he told me. I didn't ask about a specific location."

"Did he give you a fax number, a telephone number, anything at all?"

McGill looked to Bennie. "Nothing. Said he didn't wish to be bothered on his vacation time. He admonished me not to tell anyone that he was going to Europe."

"Mr. McGill, who does Kelly report to in the organization?"

"I assume that would be the CEO."

"And who is the CEO?" Mark asked.

"Why, Mr. Laforge, of course. Martin Laforge."

"Dr. Nordstram, you'll remember me, I'm DCI Sykes. I have some questions for you." He signaled his assistant to start the video camera.

"Detective Sykes, would you and he," Connie nodded toward the other detective, "like tea or coffee?"

"Why, yes. Very kind of you, I'm sure."

Connie pressed a small button under the table. Molly answered the call soon thereafter.

"Yes, Mum?"

"Please bring, oh — tea or coffee?"

"Tea please for the both of us."

Connie broke an awkward silence. "Now, gentlemen, get on with the interrogation. I'll try to give you as much information as I'm privy to."

"Where were you on the night of September 18th?"

Connie paused for a moment. "I believe that was the day the three of us, Dr. LeFreaux, Mr. Cassidy, and I, toured the Dunrobin Castle. That night we stayed at the Norbert Inn near Nairn. We planned to tour Cawdor Castle the following day, if I recall."

"And did you?"

"You're asking if we toured Cawdor?"

"Yes."

"We did, sir. I was surprised to discover that Cawdor is associated with Shakespeare's Macbeth."

"I see," Sykes appeared bored as he responded. "Tell us about Cawdor Castle."

"Well, it was very impressive, as are many of the castles in Scotland. I was especially enthralled by the greenery, the gardens, you know." Connie gave a nervous giggle. "I doubt the castle was built by a mule, as legend tells us."

"Whose coat of arms is on the wall of the castle?"

"Why, the Thanes of Cawdor, of course." Connie's initial anxiety was being replaced by pique. "If you wish to have me lead you on a vicarious tour of the castles I have visited, I'll do so. I suspect, however, that is not your intent. So, let us get to the meat of the matter. Am I still a suspect in Lord MacTavish's murder?"

"Ma'am, you need not be saucy. We are simply doing our job. If you were in my stead, would you not be a bit suspicious that a fortune was willed to you two months before Lord MacTavish's demise?"

Connie hesitated for an instant. "Perhaps, but, I would also be following any other lead in my files."

Sykes raised his voice abruptly. "What did you and Dr. what's his name, your lover, use to bludgeon MacTavish to death?"

Connie responded angrily. "I've had about enough of your inane questions. If you intend to arrest me, do it!! If not, I have important things to take care of!"

Sykes lowered his voice. "I repeat, we're just doing our job. If your alibi holds up, that is, if the Norbert has a record of your stay…" his voice trailed off. "Turn off the camera. Please go about your business, Dr. Nordstram." Sykes turned to his assistant. "Escort Dr.," he glanced at his note pad, "Escort Dr. LeFreaux to this room."

After a brief wait, Jon took a seat opposite Detective Sykes.

"Now, please sir, where were you on the night of September 18th?"

"Jesus Christ!" Jon exclaimed. "That was the week, I think, that I was with Connie, er — Dr. Nordstram in the Highlands, ancestor hunting and castle touring."

"What castle?"

"We visited a number of them. I don't remember exactly. During the week of the day you mentioned, it might have been Dunrobin or Cawdor or maybe Urqubart. We've toured so many, after a while they begin to mesh."

"I assume," Sykes leered "that you continue to serve Dr. Nordstram."

"If you mean, do I co-operate with her in our search for ancestors, yes, I suppose you could say that I serve her."

"Are you her lover?"

"That's none of your damn business!" Jon retorted.

"Yes, 'tis, when Scotland Yard is investigating a murder."

"You know, Inspector, I think you don't like Americans. First, your people try to connect Connie and me to the John Angus killing and now this. To answer your question, yes, I am in love with Connie Nordstram and yes we are lovers. Are you titillated enough or do you wish graphic detail?"

Once again, Sykes bore in. "What did you use to beat Lord MacTavish into a bloody pulp!"

Jon laughed. "Good try, Inspector. If I were to kill anyone, I'd probably do it the old fashioned way. I'd more than likely have shot him, stabbed him, or strangled him in his sleep."

The instant Jon said it; he wished he could have retrieved the words.

The Inspector straightened up. "I assume from that remark that you possess a firearm."

Jon breathed in. "Are you kidding? In this gunless country? Absolutely not." He became more relaxed as he remembered having removed the pistol from the Jaguar and having hidden it in the manor.

"Then you'd not mind our searching your person and your auto?"

Jon forced a smile. He felt certain he would be at their mercy until a proper murder suspect turned up. "Not at all, Inspector." He raised his arms.

Detective Inspector Sykes ignored the gesture. "Please remember, Dr. LeFreaux, that we are holding your passport."

"Am I free to resume my search for ancestors?"

"I do have further knowledge about the Stone of Scone. Have you believed all the many rumors floating about?"

Jon became wary. "Haven't had any inclination," he lied.

"Do you believe the Stone at Edinburgh Castle is the real one?"

Jon declined to fall into the trap the detective had set. "Oh, I have to assume it is real. It looks real. It's a nice piece of rock. Though to tell you the truth, I wouldn't know one old rock from another."

The DCI bristled. "Do you know what the Stone means to Scotland?"

"As I understand it," Jon replied snidely, "a two thousand year old woman brought it to Scotland from somewhere."

"Egypt, it was." Sykes's reply seethed with anger. "You are a typical yank. No respect. You live in an MTV, one-syllable world."

Jon was riding a crest of witty repartee that was by his silent estimation, witless. "Perhaps so, Inspector. But we don't wear dresses and eat sheep innards."

"I have no further questions," the CDI blurted. "Turn off the camera."

Chapter Thirty Four

Jake Lindsey had visited the local pub for three nights in a row. His theory that birds and humans tend to return to their old nests had so far proven invalid. He sat now, sipping his ale, scanning the room, glancing at the door. He had begun to enjoy this particular pub and returned to it often. Thus far, with each visit he had managed to pick up a lady or a trollop for some late night solace. On this night, the pub crowd was sparse and the female pickings were lean.

Jake, unlike Jon, was beginning to blunt his cynical view of Scotland and the Scots. He looked around him: the bar, polished by centuries of woolen clad elbows; the slate flooring worn from thousands of revelers; the rock walls covered by scores of clan banners and coats of arms. As he listened to the raucous laughter, followed now and again by toasts to the queen or some long departed kinsman, he was struck by the realization that his own country was less than three-hundred years old. It made him feel young, but less important on the world stage.

He signaled the bartender for his tab, paid up, and was about to leave the premises. Across the room, he spotted Thornton greeting a group of the patrons. His patience had paid off.

He slipped out the back entrance, then stationed himself across the street from the front entrance. He had no desire to encounter Thornton amid a number of his friends. If Jake's guess was accurate, Thornton had dropped in for a late night mug. Jake lit a cigarette. He glanced at his watch: 12:45. O'Malley's pub would close at 2:00.

Years of surveillance work had taught Jake how to be patient. One of the ways he helped the time to pass was by seating himself in the dark next to the nearest wall. He would smoke and when sleep threatened to intervene, he would walk, slap himself, or drink coffee from the thermos he kept in his automobile. Tonight he had neglected to bring the thermos. So it was walk, slap, sit.

Shortly after 2:00 a.m. the pub began to empty. Jake watched Thornton emerge with three of his friends. After last minute farewells, the four men went their separate ways. Thornton had parked his car on the street opposite the pub. Jake moved into an alley abutting the building where he waited. Thornton crossed the street and walked toward the lone vehicle, fifty yards away. Jake ambled cautiously toward the tipsy Thornton. As he placed the key to unlock the car door, Jake eased up behind him.

"Well, well, Mr. Thornton, I've missed you." Thornton winced from the Glock jammed against his back.

"You be real quiet. I have a very nervous trigger finger. You see that Toyota three cars down. Move slowly toward it. If you let out a peep, I'll pass you on to your ancestors."

Thornton started to enter from the passenger side. "No, no, Mr. Thornton, you're going to drive."

"But I'm in me cups. I wouldn't be safe. 'Tisn't me carriage."

"Oh, I'm not worried. I don't intend to enter you in the Grand Prix. You just drive out of the village very cautiously. I'll navigate you."

"Are ye gon' to do me in? I'm sorry I jumped on ye that time. I got a sweet and lovin' family — I'm beggin' ye not to kill me."

"Keep your voice down or I'll whack you right here," Jake directed, as Thornton's voice rose with each plea.

They rode in silence for a few kilometers before Jake said, "Turn here."

Thornton began to babble. "The sea. Lordy! We're a goin' to the sea. Ye're gonna shoot me and dump me in the sea! Ain't it a fact!"

"Depends," Jake answered.

"Depends. What are ye sayin', depends?"

"Shut up and keep driving." Jake placed the pistol close to Thornton's face.

The cliff overlooking the sea rose fifty meters above the water. An early morning fog obscured the sea, then cleared to reveal a glimmering glass-like surface. No wind this night.

"Okay, sport, out of the car. Walk over there to the edge and look down." Jake nudged Thornton with the pistol.

"Please mon, if ye're gon' to kill me, don' throw me to the rocks. Shoot me afore ye do it."

"I'll let you live if you answer my questions truthfully. If you lie, you're a dead man," Jake bluffed.

"I'll tell what ye want to know if I know it. Swear on me mother's grave."

"Why did you and those others attack me that night?"

"We were given twenty pounds to rough you up. The boss said you'd been askin' too many questions."

"Such as?"

"Aboot the Stone."

"What about the Stone?"

"All the boss said, you and the lass were getting too close to it."

"Close to it?"

"Yes, indeed." Thornton lowered his voice and in a conspiratorial pose, "None of the papists believe the real stone is at Edinburgh. The boss, God bless him, is loyal to the Queen, and so is meself. The Boss says that if it ain't the real stone, then where would it be?"

"The boss. What's his name?"

Thornton didn't answer until Jake reminded him. "It's a long way down to those rocks. I'm waiting."

Thornton dropped to his knees and commenced to plead. "Mister, ye've got to promise me ye didn't hear the words from me mouth. The boss wouldn't like me stoolin."

"Your boss is Ahern. Right?"

"You said it, not I," Thornton responded.

"Did Ahern pay you and the others to kill John Angus and Kathryn Digbe?"

"Lord no!" Thornton stood up. "I've done some dirty deeds in me lifetime, but I'm not a murderer."

"Does Ahern employ other runnin' boys besides you, O'Riley, and Boone?"

"Not to me knowledge. Now, don't ye know, Mr. Ahern may be a bit shady, but he'd never kill a body."

"Do you know of other folks who might have killed Angus and Digbe, and who want Connie Nordstram out of the country?"

"Surely," Thornton replied, "Most them who serve the Queen and have no truck with the papists."

"Give me some names," Jake ordered.

"I swear to you, I know only one bloke they talk about. He's a mean one. Folks say he'd send his mother to the hereafter for a few shillings. Folks call him O'Feely. Like I say, he's a real mean one."

"Who does he work for?"

"Word is, he's a lone wolf, I believe you yanks call him." Thornton relaxed, feeling less threatened.

"And where does this O'Feely reside?"

"Me friends say he lives in the bad part of the burgh, on Abbey Way."

"You mean the ghetto?" Jake inquired.

"Aye. What ye want, ye can come by in there."

Jake holstered his weapon. "I'll drive you back to your car. If this fellow, O'Feely is waiting for me, I'll whack him and come for you. Are we on the same page?"

"You know, Bennie, I've about had enough of the countryside between here and Montreal." Campbell whistled. "Wow! Now we're looking at a ranch! Hell, the place is manicured. I'll bet the cattle are washed down each day."

"Just goes to show you what a few dollars can buy," she replied. "And by the way, if you'd fly, we wouldn't have Canada memorized."

The driveway to the main house was set inside a line of trees, perfectly spaced. On either side, white split rail fencing was the border for grassland as far as the eye could see. Cattle, fat from patches of fescue, grazed in small herds, oblivious of all about them.

Mark eased the SUV onto the circular driveway. The main house rose above the other outbuildings, three stories plus battlements.

"All this place needs is a moat. Have you ever seen anything like it?!" Mark exclaimed.

"Have you been to Rhode Island? Mark, the robber barons built many of these at Newport."

"Okay. So you're well traveled. I got down to New York once. You ring the bell."

The butler who opened the door was straight from the nineteenth century, set incongruously in a Canadian mansion. "May I say who's calling?" his accent was upper London, with a slight practiced British edge.

"I'm Mark Campbell. My partner is Benedette Rochelle. We have an appointment with Mr. Laforge."

"Ah, yes. Please follow me. I'll announce you to Mr. Laforge."

Martin Laforge put aside the book he was reading and greeted the private investigators. "Welcome to the Circle L. May I offer you a drink?"

"Yes, thank you," Bennie replied. "I'll have scotch and water, ice, if you…"

"And you, Mr. Campbell, I assume?"

"Yes, sir. Do you have a Moosehead? I love Canadian beer."

"You bet. So you two are American P.I.s, eh? Right off the bat, I hope you're not here to bring me to justice for calling George Bush a war monger." He laughed heartily.

"Not at all," Bennie said. "Before we get down to business, I must say I admire your riding outfit. You appear to be ready to lead a charge of the Light Brigade, rather than round up cows."

"Why thank you, Miss Rochelle. It is miss, isn't it?"

"I'm sure you already knew, Mr. Laforge." Bennie took the drink Laforge offered. "Before I moved to Massachusetts I grew up on a horse farm in Tennessee. Tennessee Walkers."

"Delightful!" Laforge responded. "What say the three of us conduct our business on horseback?"

"Not me." Mark waved off the offer. "You two go right ahead. I'll wait here and read or drink Moosehead while you're yippee coyoting out on the range. I don't know one end of a horse from the other."

"Miss Rochelle, you look to be about the size of my wife. Clarmont," he motioned to his butler. "Show Miss Rochelle to the master room. Help her select a riding outfit."

"Very well, sir," Clarmont replied.

As Bennie disappeared up the stairs, Laforge asked, "Let's get to it, Mr. Campbell. You didn't come all this way to drink Moosehead beer, did you?"

"No sir. We're here on a murder investigation. We have touched base with Northwest Mounted and received their permission to move about the Province."

"And what," his ire began to show, "does that have to do with me?"

"Not with you, Mr. Laforge. We're inquiring about one of your employees. A man named Damon Kelly."

Laforge poured himself another drink. "Damon Kelly is one of my most trusted employees. He's a young man who made his way up the management ladder through hard work and keen intelligence. He emigrated from the U.S. fifteen years ago. At present, he's the Vice President in charge of corporate expansion." Mark chose not to interrupt Laforge's pacing around the room, sipping at his drink. "I can't imagine he would know anything about a murder."

"Where did he reside before Canada?" Mark asked.

"If I recall, it was Pennsylvania. Philadelphia, I think."

Laforge shook his head in disbelief. "Is he suspected of murder?"

"Perhaps of orchestrating a murder."

Laforge pulled open a drawer in his desk. He lifted a notebook. "Damon is scheduled to be at our Calgary office this week." He lifted his telephone and touched the speed dial. "Put Mr. Kelly on, please." He waited. "He's not there you say. Where in hell is he?" A short wait. "I can't believe what I'm hearing! Try to locate him and get back to me!!"

Laforge slammed the telephone down. "He's out of pocket. Nobody seems to know where he is or to give a damn. Someone's head is going to roll!"

He picked up the phone once more. "Please put Mrs. Laforge on." After a short wait, Annette Laforge answered. "Damon has disappeared. Did he leave any word with you? I see. If you hear anything, call my cell. Okay. I'll be back in Montreal the day after tomorrow. Bye."

"Damon worked closely with my wife on a couple of her community projects. She has no idea where he could be."

Rochelle bounced down the stairs. She was attired in jodhpurs, boots, and a blouse that barely accounted for Rochelle's tiny bosoms. "Alright, gentlemen. Let's ride to the sound of the hounds."

"Very good. Clarmont, please tell the groomsman to saddle Hannah and Attila. We'll be out shortly. Mr. Campbell, make yourself comfortable. We'll return before sundown."

Chapter Thirty Five

Jake had seen it all before now. In Southie; in the slums of Brockton; ill kept streets and yards, houses that had been ravaged by years of neglect and salt spray. It was a place of refuge for those who sponsored the illegal and the decadent. It was the seedy side of Edinburgh.

His wait had paid off. In his rear view mirror he watched a man enter the run-down cottage. Jake surmised that O'Feely was the man as described to him. Jake was hesitant to confront an individual who, by all accounts, was a tower of brawn, not to be taken lightly.

Jake checked his rear pocket to make sure his leaded slapper could be pulled easily. He rammed a clip into his Glock, walked to the door and knocked. No Response. He knocked again. At the same instant he heard footsteps behind him. O'Feely moved in close to Jake's back. As he started to place his chokehold, Jake's elbow smashed into O'Feely's rib cage. He doubled over in pain and reached again for Lindsey. This time, he felt the sting of Jake's slapper. His knees buckled under him. Before he hit the ground, Jake's Glock was next to his nose.

"You know, fella, that's a most inhospitable way to greet a visitor. Now, get your ass up and let's go inside."

"Whoever you are, you're a dead man! You hear! You're a dead man!"

Jake brought his pistol down across the bridge of O'Feely's nose.

"Let's try again. Get off your knees and open the damn door and do it quickly."

That time O'Feely opened the door, but not before he had damned Jake to the nether regions in one verbal tirade after another.

"Mr. O'Feely, your reputation precedes you. I have a few questions. If I understand correctly, you're muscle for hire. Is that true?"

"I don't know what ye're talkin' about," O'Feely sneered. "If ye're smart ye'll go back to where ye come from, you damn colonial."

"Guess I'm not smart, Mr. O'Feely. May I call you Orley?"

O'Feely ignored the question. He extracted a cigarette and a lighter from his shirt pocket. After lighting the cigarette he commenced to flick the lighter case in a rhythmic motion, all the while staring hard at Jake.

"Orley, I was told that you were orange at one time. So, I did some checking. You see, Orley, that's what I do to put groceries on the table. I dig. Guess what I found. In Ireland, you were not Orley O'Feely. You were Sampson Learmus Smith, to this day wanted by MI-5 and a slew of other British agencies, not to mention the IRA. Shall I continue to give you your own personal history lesson?"

O'Feely's hand began to shake. His face turned angry red. "What do ye want from me?"

"Well, let's start with John Angus. Did you know him?"

"I did. So did all the papists in Scotland. If ye're about to ask me if I put him under, I did no such thing."

"What do you know about John Angus?"

O'Feely smirked, "He allus played the fool, but he was not to be stitched with that. He was the conniving one. Every bloke in Scotland knew he was the one behind the taking of the Stone from Westminster."

"But I'm under the impression that four young people did the dastardly deed."

"Oh, but 'tis a fact that John Angus was the buckeen of that charade."

"What's a buckeen?" Jake asked.

"He was, you might say, the topper who guides things along."

"John or Sampson, whatever your name is, if you had nothing to do with Angus' murder, do you hear rumors?"

By now, O'Feely had begun to be less wary.

"Aye, in this cursed land, rumor feeds the beastie. The talk is that Lord MacTavish put Angus under the sod."

"MacTavish?"

"Aye. The Lord himself."

Jake was incredulous. "Why would MacTavish want Angus dead?"

"Sure. Every bloke knows that Lord MacTavish says the Stone at Edinburgh is the real one. The rub is that he don't believe it."

"What might he believe?" Jake asked.

"That John Angus knew the whereabouts of the real stone."

Jake shook his head. "Why would Angus do that and why should MacTavish give a damn?"

Jake was playing the game of possum. He knew most of the information O'Feely was offering. The part that came as a surprise was O'Feely's suspicion that MacTavish had caused Angus' death.

"Have you ever done muscle work for a man named Ahern? Did you assault Connie Nordstram and Kathryn Digbe?"

O'Feely flared up. "Hell no! I ain't ever popped a woman!"

Jake reached inside his coat pocket. "Smile for the camera," he directed as the flash went off.

"You can't do such a thing!" O'Feely yelled, "I don't like me picture snapped by strangers!"

"Tough shit, old bean. Any other complaints?"

"Yeah! If ye don't do me in this day, I'll track ye doon and put ye under the sod!"

"I'm terrified, Mr. O'Feely," Jake said. "I'll make you a counter offer. Should I see you in my presence ever," Jake jammed his finger into O'Feely's chest. "I'll assume you're out to kill me. But, just in case, I'll be watching you. You won't know when or where. Keep that in mind, ye old chum."

"Are you sure, George? You're telling us, that beyond all doubt, you've cracked that code we found at the Angus cottage?"

"Connie, I appreciate your skepticism. I've come at it from several angles and every computer program I know about."

Connie read aloud the words Cassidy placed before her. "The saint guards pillow."

"Sounds like gibberish to me," Jon said.

"Makes more sense than what Lindsey's buddy came up with," George replied.

"Oh, come on! Dave Darlink is the foremost code breaker in the world."

"Okay, okay," Cassidy interjected. "I've done some more digging. You'll be pleased to know that our girl Yolande left Sweden, supposedly with the body of her husband on board a ship bound for Boston. However, the Stockholm hall of records shows that the man she was married to, Ole Swanson, interred in Stockholm. No burial record in Massachusetts."

"My God! Are you sure, George?" Connie exclaimed.

"I had the curators of interment at both Stockholm and Boston search their records. No Ole Swanson is listed."

Connie arose from the chair, walked a few steps, then returned.

"Are you okay, Connie?" Jon asked.

"Just a tad queasy. I'm in a state of elated confusion as of this moment. George, you have stirred the ancestral stew." She kissed him on his cheek. "Based on what you've found, are the coins back in play?"

"I'm not following you," Jon said. "What are we talking?"

"It's a long shot, but let's assume that after old Alexander's trusted bursar absconded with those extremely valuable merks, those coins made their way into the hands of John MacTavish's great, great grandfather — oh, and possibly your great, great grandfather — one and the same. Now," George paused to light his pipe. "Let's assume, also, that your great, great grandmother, Yolande, who as we think we've discovered, descended from Alexander III, became privy to the merk theft. From all we know, she was not a favorite around Sonsie; treated, perhaps, no better than a servant to that old tyrant, MacTavish. Now, stay with me. What if she decided on some payback? What if she was made pregnant, not by old MacTavish, but by the groomsman whose name we've never uncovered."

"George," Jon said, "As the Scots say, do you have a hole in your riding britches. That's pretty farfetched."

Connie jumped in. "Maybe not, Jon. We need to find the name of the alleged paternal groomsman. If his name was Ole Swanson, well…" she hesitated. "Guys, we need to get our passports. I'm going to put some pressure on Scotland Yard. After all," she preened, "I am among the landed gentry with perhaps a wee bit of influence. In the meantime, George, I have a task for you. On the third floor, there's a room with all sorts of records and files. Would you be willing to start going through those stacks and see what turns up?"

George smiled. "Right up my alley. I'll get on it."

"And Jon, my dear," Connie placed her arm around LeFreaux, "Since Mrs. Manion thought you were a cutie, would you pay her another visit?"

"Hey, young lady," Jake declared with enthusiasm. "You seem to be ready to do battle with the bad guys again. Am I correct?"

"Indeed ye are," Kathryn Digbe replied. "What's in the box?"

"Connie asked me to drop these goodies off to you. How are you feeling?"

"Good, lad," she grumped. "But these agents of William the devil won't allow me up and about." She smoothed her bedcover. "Now, I just know ye didn't come this way only to fetch me chocolates."

"I was worried about you and yes, I do have an ulterior motive." He pulled up the one chair in the room. "I have a photograph I want you to look at." He extracted the enlarged picture of O'Feely from a manila folder. He held the photo up. "Do you recognize this man?"

Digbe reacted quickly. "That's the son of Satan who put the torch to me. I'd never forget his ugly face. Do ye have the mon in ball and chain? If he be, I want a turn at him!"

"Do you know him, Kathy?"

"Nae. Until he put the fire to me, I'd never seen him."

Jake placed his hand on her arm. "What was he after, Kathy?"

"The masked ones, they were, believed I was the one behind the killing of the Mac-Tavish devil." She gave an impish grin. "If I was, I'd be prouder than a swordsman at Bannockburn."

"Kathy, do you have any notion as to who set this man on you?"

"Could be any one of the Freemason bastards."

"Freemasons?" Jake was taken aback.

"Aye," she replied. "The Lordship devil practiced their witchcraft."

Jake lowered his voice. "Witchcraft?"

"Aye," she sat upright, "Ye ain't one of them, are ye?"

"A Freemason? No. I'm a Roman Catholic in hiding. Haven't been to mass in years."

"My, my, Jake Lindsey! I'll say a rosary for ye."

"I'll be going now." Jake rose from his chair. "But I'll be back. Connie and the others will come, also."

"How about the old bloke, George, he was."

"Oh, I'm sure he'll be along," Jake answered.

210

Chapter Thirty Six

The morning traffic in Montreal was filing down Mark Campbell's nerves. After he sounded his horn for the third time, Bennie gave him a gentle nudge. "You're not going to get there any faster by tooting that horn. You're lucky some Canadian hasn't become irate."

Campbell inhaled deeply. "We're gonna be late to meet the ol' girl if this damn traffic doesn't thin out."

"Won't matter, Mr. Clock-watcher. If anything, maybe a little waiting will be good for her. Might even upset that icy demeanor I detected over the telephone. God! How I hate for someone to condescend to me!"

"So, I'm cool," Mark responded. "How do we approach her?"

"I want to know if she dens up with Damon Kelly. If so, for what reasons. I've rarely heard of a middle manager type taking time away from his job to help Mrs. Community Dogood."

"What are you saying?"

"I suspect," Bennie said, "that there may be some hanky panky. And if she uses him in her community projects or for stud service…" her voice trailed off.

"Do you think she'll know Kelly's whereabouts?"

"Yes, I do," Bennie answered. "I expect her to become flustered by our visit. She'll deny knowing where he is. We'll see. You be good cop. I'll be bad cop."

The butler observed the auto moving onto the circular driveway. He spoke into the intercom. "They've arrived, Mrs. Laforge."

"Yes," she replied, "And damnable late. I detest people who make appointments, then show up late. Send them into the study."

Campbell had barely removed his hand from the brass knocker when the door opened.

"Hi, there," Bennie's greeting was accompanied by her best smile. "We have an appointment with Mrs. Laforge."

"And you're half an hour late. Madam will meet you in the study. Please follow me."

Annette Laforge wasted no time. She was obviously angered by the tardiness of the American private investigators. "You're late. State your business. I have other places I should be at this very moment."

Both Americans presented their credentials.

"In case you're wondering, Ma'am, we have checked in with your local authorities. I apologize that we failed to meet your timeline. Bad traffic." Campbell extended his hand, which was left hanging in mid-air.

Bennie stared hard at Laforge. "Well, Madam, since you have so little time for us, I'll get right to it. We're looking for Damon Kelly. The gossip around town is that you two are very close."

"What do you mean by that?" she answered, her face growing red as she fidgeted with her watch.

"What do you think I mean?"

"Are you insinuating that I'm having an affair with Damon?"

Campbell became the good cop. "Of course, we have to assume that you are faithful to your husband." He paused, "unless proven otherwise."

"My husband sent you, didn't he?" She raised her voice. "My husband has hired you. Isn't that the case?"

Bennie ignored the question. "If Kelly is not your lover, what is your relationship with him?"

"That's none of your damn business!" Laforge flared. "I don't like you. I don't like the way you dress. I don't like your perfume. I don't like your attitude."

"Bennie, Mrs. Laforge, please. I'm asking you both to calm down a tad," Mark offered, knowing that a Laforge nerve had been touched. "Miss Rochelle, please be civil to the lady," he winked at his partner.

"I hardly know Damon Kelly." Laforge said, her voice calmer than before. "He helped me arrange a charity event once, as I recall."

Rochelle turned a page in her note pad. "Mrs. Laforge, you should know a private investigator rarely asks a question to which he doesn't already know the answer. For instance, we know that in June, 2002, he accompanied you on a business trip to Brazil. He assisted you with two charity events in 2003. He helped you close a beef selling deal in Pennsylvania in 2005. Shall I continue?"

"Get out!" Laforge yelled, pointing to the door.

"Do you know where he is, Mrs. Laforge? Damon Kelly is either a murderer or an accessory to murder. I'll leave my card. Should you learn his whereabouts, I would appreciate your call, and I'm sure RCMP would, also."

As the Americans drove away, Bennie slapped the dashboard. "Jackpot!" she exclaimed. "Where from here, partner?"

"We're going to ask some low level assistant to McGill for Kelly's business travels, emphasize Europe."

"A low level comely assistant blonde, no doubt," Bennie teased.

"No doubt," Campbell responded.

George Cassidy had poured over ancestral records for a fortnight. He rubbed his eyes and was ready to call it a day. At that moment, a footnote caught his attention. It read:

For further information on the John MacTavish family history, go to Volume III, 1800-1875.

A new burst of energy and Cassidy stood before the curator. "MacTavish, 1800-1875, please."

Cassidy crosschecked names, places and events. When "MacTavish, John" turned up, Cassidy felt a surge of elation. It read:

Lorraine MacTavish nee O'Shaughnessy, descended unknown father 1791-1846 perhaps from Mangus, 1704-1751, Isaac, back to Christian MacMangus, perhaps 1275? From MacAlpine clan?

Cassidy returned the volume to the curator, then requested any material on the King's court, Alexander III.

"Not all the court can be verified," the curator said. "The lower members may not be identified. Ye know, they were doon in the servants' quarters, more than likely."

Several crosschecks later, Cassidy muttered "Bingo!" There before him, recorded over seven hundred years before was the name Christian MacMangus, under which was written:

"Ah, Mr. Fergus, where would I look to find the names of the King's groomsmen?

"Aye, surely," Fergus replied. "Do ye have the name of the benefactor of groomsmen?"

"MacMangus, it says here."

The curator went into the stacks and returned a short time later. "Ye know, we're about the business of putting all here on computers. I donna think much of it meself. To get the full meaning of an entry, ye've got to see it and smell it," he laughed. "Let's see what comes up from this book. If MacMangus is here, no king's groomsmen may be tallied."

After finding the name MacMangus, Cassidy checked the dates of tenure. Another hour of crosschecking and he read the entry for which he was searching.

MacMangus, John. 1251-1298. King's Groomsman keeper, hanged for treason. Four Groomsmen (no names) drawn and quartered for treason. Charges were brought by Mac-Tavish, John. The five conspirators absconded with $4000 merks paid to King Magnus by Alexander.

When Cassidy returned the materials to the curator, he asked, "These records indicate that John MacMangus was hanged for treason in 1298. Executed, also were four of his groomsmen, but their names were not listed."

"'Tis true. In those days groomsmen were nobodies, you might say. The records of the day may or may not have listed names or the records may have been lost. Wasn't good, don't you know, to be just a mere human being."

"Nathan Fergus, you've been a great help to me. I'll come by one of these days and buy you a nappy. You do drink ale, do you not?"

"Indeed I do."

"Thank you again."

The Sonsie kitchen staff concluded the removal of the dishes, followed by the usual request that sent Molly and the others into a state of ambivalence. "We're ready for our coffee now, if you please, Molly. Tea for the Inspector."

"Yes, Mum," she said and walked away muttering under her breath.

"You know, guys, they don't believe we're developing our taste for tea as quickly as they would like." She smiled at her guest from Scotland Yard.

"Thank you for accepting our invitation, Chief Inspector. I'm aware that Jon and I may continue being suspects. We thought we could share information and just possibly alleviate a bit of your suspicion about us."

"Thank you for a marvelous meal, Lady Nordstram. Your are correct in assuming that you are considered suspects. I will say that my suspicions have been tempered somewhat. Perhaps this night you'll be able, as you say, to alleviate my remaining doubts." He nodded toward Jake. "I have appreciated the co-operation of your bodyguards, Mr. Lindsey and Mr. Cassidy."

"Would you like a cognac with your tea, Inspector? Jon asked.

"No, thanks."

"I'll have some," Jake said.

"And I," Cassidy agreed.

"So," Jon remarked casually, "Let's get through this rone, if possible."

"Ah," said DCI Sykes, "Ye know a bit of Erse."

"Very little," Jon replied.

"What's a rone?" Connie inquired.

"A thicket. A mess to get through."

Connie gave a thumbs up to Jake.

"You go first." Then she turned toward DCI Sykes. "If that's acceptable to you, Inspector?"

"Of course, proceed," he answered.

Jake referred to his notes. "On the sixteenth of this month, I visited with a fellow over in the fifth district. Took his picture in the process. His name, O'Feely, was given to me by an acquaintance I met in one of your local pubs, fellow named Thornton. As I told you earlier, Inspector, O'Feely is known as an enforcer for whoever is willing to pay. As I also told you, I showed his photo to Miss Digbe, who identified him as the man who assaulted her.

"Recently, I received a message from my partners in which they believe a man named Damon Kelly is possibly in Scotland. And…" Before Jake could continue, Sykes interrupted, "And what about this Kelly bloke?"

"He is a murder suspect in the U.S."

"And what, pray tell, does that have to do with anything in Scotland."

"My partners discovered that he has traveled frequently to Edinburgh! I believe he may be here at present."

"I see," replied Sykes. "Please continue."

"A man named Ahern heads a business here in Edinburgh. He hired three of his thugs to beat up on me."

"And why would he do that?"

"For the same reason that Dr. Nordstram was attacked. When we commenced to inquire about ancestors, the Stone of Scone began to come into play. Someone, or some people, want us out of Scotland," Jake answered.

"Ah, blarney! That Stone pops up once more. Will ye and the others never give in? That Stone is in Edinburgh and 'tis the real stone!" Sykes shook his fist emphatically. "Now, what about this Ahern?"

"It goes like this, Inspector. My partners found that Ahern, Ltd. with many layers between, works for Laforge Enterprise in Canada. I think it possible that Damon Kelly is here to contact Ahern. Kelly is an official with Laforge Enterprises."

"I'll not ask ye how you come by your information, nor will I ask ye about that firearm you carry. I do advise ye to watch your step."

"Oh, I intend to do that," Jake grinned.

"Now, Dr. LeFreaux, you've been a bit tart with me afore now. How do you fit into this folderol?"

"Well, sir," Jon answered. "As you know, I'm ancestor hunting, but each turn I make, the stone seems to enter into the equation."

"Ah, come now, Dr. LeFreaux."

"No, no! I mean it, Inspector. Dr. Nordstram and I befriend John Angus. Next thing we know, he's dead. We find a great source person in Kathy Digbe and she's almost killed. We've told you before now that the Stone came up in their conversations."

"And that man, Ahern, came into the picture in an oblique sort of way," Jake interrupted. "I have a theory that Mr. Ahern not only hired thugs to work me over, he also was behind the attack on Dr. Nordstram."

"Your proof, sir?" Sykes glowered at Jake.

"I'm working on that, Inspector. For the present, my intuition is guiding me."

"Well, now, P.I. Lindsey," Sykes chortled. "The Yard does not give a sassennack for intuition."

"So, where from here, Inspector?" Connie asked.

"First, hear me now, especially you, Mr. Lindsey. If you impede the Yard in our investigations, you'll be in a bit of trouble."

"I understand," Jake said. "And I'll continue to share with you my findings."

"And be remembering, lad, that does not include your intuitions." He turned to Connie. "Lady Nordstram, I'll remind you and Dr. LeFreaux that you continue to be under a veil of suspicion, a formality only. At this point we have no reason to target you primarily. I'll remind you to keep me informed of your movements. I'll not retain your passports." He smiled. "Now I'll take my leave."

Connie was, once more, filled with a sense of dread. She had hoped the inspector would dismiss her as a suspect in the MacTavish murder. She revisited in her mind the bloody scene in the Angus bedroom, and felt a wave of nausea. She had wanted to recount to the inspector the events of that day. Jake and Jon had squelched that notion.

Jon placed his arm around her. "Yeah, I'm disappointed also. But, God, I'm glad you didn't get a surge of conscience about the Angus thing."

"We're in a mess, guys. When at first we chose to deceive…" She shook her head slowly from side to side.

"Come on, Connie!" Jake exhorted her. "Suck it up. Don't cave now!"

She stared at Jake. "I may be fearful and ambivalent, but I'm not stupid."

"Until we know the people we can trust," Jake said, "We'll continue to be selective with the information we share with anyone. Scotland Yard included. Does that make sense to you two?"

Connie and Jon nodded their affirmation.

Chapter Thirty Seven

George Cassidy rubbed his eyes, then sent his latest check-in message to Raymond LeFreaux. He closed his laptop, thanked the archivist, and made his way to his chauffeured automobile. As he opened the rear door, two men eased up behind him. Before he could react, he felt a stinging blow to the side of his head, then everything went dark.

When he regained consciousness, he found himself bound to a chair, facing a well-dressed, middle-aged man.

"By God!" George exclaimed. "I know you! What's this all about?"

"Let's make this as cheery as possible," his captor said. "To answer your question, I believe you told someone in a local pub that you had deciphered a code."

"I don't know what you're talking about!"

"Ah, but surely you do. All we want from you is the message you deciphered. Tell us that and you'll be free to go."

"Why did you do this? I trusted you," Cassidy said to one of the men.

"Ah now," the chauffer replied. "Ye were a bit of a fool to get yourself all involved in this."

"You're damn well dismissed here and now! You'll no longer drive for me!"

The men ringed around his chair laughed uproariously, slapping the back of the chauffer. "You're fired, me friend! Mr. Cassidy'll surely have to procure himself another driver!" More laughter, then there was silence.

"Mr. Cassidy, you can make this easy or difficult as you wish. Where is the code and how did you come by it?"

"Fuck you!" Cassidy screamed, feeling a rush of bravado.

"As you wish. Mr. O'Feely, take charge."

O'Feely moved quickly behind the chair, where Cassidy's hands were bound. George Cassidy heard the click of the lighter, followed by the searing pain. Out of body, but tormented by the reality of the pain, George heard himself screaming.

"Talk, you old bastard," Damon Kelly ordered, "or I'll turn loose this arsonist again."

Cassidy said nothing. Again the fire was applied. The room was filled now with the odor of burnt flesh.

"I'll tell you, please! I'll tell you! Please don't hurt me anymore."

The masked man pulled the flame away from Cassidy's hand. Cassidy repeated the code. The other masked man copied it onto his note pad. "And how did you come to have this information, Mr. Cassidy?"

"John Angus gave it to me before he was killed," Cassidy lied.

"What do you think it means?"

"I don't know. John Angus just said it was about the true Stone."

Even as he cringed from the pain, Cassidy knew he would not be alive after this night. At that instant, he wished to die. Shortly thereafter, his wish was granted.

"Kill him," the masked man ordered.

A garrote was placed around Cassidy's neck. After a bit, his eyes glazed over and his lurching against the chair ceased.

Bennie Rochelle read from her folder, then looked up at her partner. "From the information I have, this has to be the place."

Mark Campbell pressed the doorbell. The woman who answered the door looked to be in her seventies, possibly early eighties.

"Are you Mrs. Conners?"

"Yes, I am. To what do I owe the pleasure of your visit?" Her demeanor put Mark at ease. Her gray hair enhanced an attractive face that had never been lifted or botoxed. She had a slight limp and a widow's hump that caused her to be less than five feet tall.

"Ma'am, I'm Mark Campbell and my partner," he gave a nod, "is Bennie Rochelle. We're private investigators."

Laura Conners chuckled. "Well, don't just stand out here. Come inside and tell me why I'm being investigated."

Bennie felt the memory of a grandmother long since deceased. She placed her hand on the arm of the old lady.

"Oh, Mrs. Conners, we're not investigating you." Then Bennie teased, "But you might fit the profile of a gun moll. No. We're here seeking information."

"Make yourselves to home while I pour some tea."

The apartment was well ordered: a lamp in each corner; throw rugs showing the ravages of age; an ancient TV set, in front of which was a sofa and an easy chair; two unlit candles set on a coffee table; a book shelf lining one wall. The room was devoid of sunlight and gave off a faint mothball smell.

The old woman placed the tea service before them.

"Well, now. I suppose you're here to ask me about my great, great, grandfather and how he came to be obscenely wealthy."

Mark was taken aback. "Mrs. Conners, that, indeed, is one part of our inquiry. But to tell you the truth, that's only part of the picture. We're trying to bring to justice a murderer and possibly more than one accomplice. Oh, I'm sorry, I cut you short. How did your ancestor, as you say, become obscenely wealthy?"

"Oh, he was a bit closemouthed, or so my grandmother always said. Now and again, he would get into his cups and start blubbering about his Scottish ancestors. My grandmother would tell us that he would talk regretfully about having cheated a friend out of a great deal of money." The old lady gazed into the past. "My granny said he never gave any details. Said he stayed drunk the last years of his life. Pity."

"Mrs. Conners, you assumed we were here to ask about your family background. Have you had other people…"

"Oh, yes," she interrupted. "Had two policemen asking the same questions."

"Two policemen?" Bennie asked.

"Oh, yes. Nice fellows. A Mr. Septo and a Mr. Agles. Nice fellows." She shook her head as she repeated herself.

"Do you have a family?" Mark asked. "Any children?"

"Had a daughter, her name was Matilda. My father adored her. She was alienated from me by the time she was sixteen. She left home at the behest of my bastard father, never saw her again."

"So you have no idea where she may be at present?"

"Maybe up east. Once I saw a postmark on a letter to my father. Buffalo, I think it was."

Bennie leaned toward the old lady. "My dear, you don't seem to be very wealthy, when I consider what you've told us."

"Oh, I'm not. But I have a clear conscience and I'm not a blubbering drunk," she twittered.

"Did your father leave you out of his will deliberately?" Mark asked.

"Sure did. Didn't like my lifestyle. Thought I was a floozy just because I wore tight dresses, danced the Charleston, and uh," she hesitated, "knew a number of men."

"You mean…" Before Bennie could ask, the old lady blurted, "Yep, knew'um in a biblical sense."

"Your daughter," Mark switched the subject. "Did she marry?"

"Surely. One of her childhood friends came by to visit me once. Asked if I was going to the wedding. Wasn't invited, I told her."

"Mrs. Conners, do you remember the name of the man she married?"

"O'Shaughnessy, it was as I recall. My daughter's friend didn't know anymore about him."

"Laura," Bennie asked, "I know you don't look a day over sixty and I know I should never ask a lady her age, but…"

Before Rochelle could finish, once more, Laura anticipated the question. "I'm ninety-six. Owe it all to rambunctious living, though I did quit smoking when I was eighty-five." She arose from her chair. "I've surely enjoyed my visit with you. Now, it's time for my nap. Please call on me again, anytime."

Bennie Rochelle embraced the old woman. "Thank you for helping us. I hope to see you again."

As the two detectives walked to their car, Bennie queried, "Why do you suppose she was so ready to give us all of that info?"

"Payback," Campbell replied. "She'll take revenge any way she can get it."

Bennie slid into the passenger side seat. "I wonder why Septo and Agles needed information from her. If, as Jake suspects, those two were tied up with Laforge and Kelly, it doesn't make sense that they'd be snooping into stuff."

"Yep," Mark agreed. "We're going to shuffle off to Buffalo and look for some O'Shaughnessys."

Bennie lowered her voice, "You wouldn't consider flying, would you?"

"Nope."

"I'll accompany George's body back to the states. I need to check in with my father. If that's okay with you two."

"Makes sense," Jake said, "We'll try to keep out of trouble until you return."

"I'll trust you two to do just that."

Jon moved close to Jake to give an exaggerated whisper, "And don't you try to get into Connie's pants while I'm gone. On the other hand, stick close to her. Okay?"

"I'll be sure to do thing two. No promises on thing one," Jake laughed.

Jon hugged Connie. "The lorry's waiting. I'll see you two in a week or so."

As Connie walked Jon to the taxi, she said, "I know you were teasing, Jon, but that was not very sensitive on your part. Made me feel like a slab of meat."

"I'm sorry, Sweetheart. I won't do that again," Jon agonized. "Forgive me?"

"Of course," she replied "and besides, I'm not his type. He's more of a get-in-get-out-move-on kinda guy."

"I'll worry about you, Connie. Be careful and for God's sake, don't move around by yourself."

When Connie re-entered Sonsie, Jake met her at the door. "I've got to see a man about a dog. The local constabulary is sending over a fellow to make sure nobody does you in."

A short time later, Jake parked his car across the street from Ahern Enterprises, allowing him a good view of people entering or leaving. He looked at his watch — 5:30 p.m. He knew that if Ahern followed his usual routine, he would enter his chauffeured limo near 6:00 p.m. At 5:45, the ivory colored, elongated vehicle pulled up to the curb. The driver exited and walked to the nearby diner. Jake walked quickly to the limo and tried the second rear door. The driver had not bothered to lock it. Jake glanced over his shoulder, then slipped into the spacious seating area. He lay on the floor behind the driver's side and removed the Glock from his shoulder holster.

He didn't have to wait long before the chauffer opened the rear door and found himself staring at Jake's pistol.

"Get inside, ol' boy and pour me a drink from this mobile pub." Jake emphasized his demand with a wave of the Glock.

"Be careful with that gun, Lad," the chauffer cautioned. "I'll be comin' right in."

"Lower your hands. I don't want anyone to think you're being held up. And that bulge in your coat, take the weapon out and place it on the seat beside me."

The chauffer followed Jake's order. In a calm voice he asked, "And what would ye like to wet your whistle?"

Jake chuckled. "So, you Scots know that expression. Scotch straight up."

"Aye."

Jake placed the chauffeur's Luger into his jacket. "You were an officer in the Wermacht?"

"No, No. Me father brought it home as a souvenir from the big war."

His hand shook as he poured the tumbler of scotch. "What is it ye be wantin'?"

"I want to converse with your boss. So, get out of the car now and take up your station as you would normally do."

Jake watched the chauffer through the darkened rear window. A few minutes passed before Jake observed Ahern moving toward the car. As he drew near the limo, the chauffer opened the door.

"John, take me to…"

Before he completed the request, Jake ordered, "Get in the car. You and I are going to have a little talk."

"You bastard! I'll do no such thing."

"Then I'll shoot you here and now, then I'll shoot your girlfriend and…" he looked to the chauffer, "I'll steal your driver and your car. Now, get the hell in. John, get behind the wheel quickly or I'll put a bullet in your gut! Move!"

Once they were seated, the chauffer asked, "Where shall I drive?"

"Just drive," Jake answered. "And don't do anything stupid that'll cause the local gendarmes to pull us over."

They rode in silence until they reached the countryside. Each time Ahern started to say something, Jake would tell him to "shut the hell up". After his second attempt Ahern slumped in his seat and did not speak again until Jake ordered the chauffer to pull to the side of the road.

"You're going to kill me, aren't you?"

"Maybe, it all depends."

"Depends. Depends on what?"

Jake placed the Glock against the side of Ahern's face. "I'm looking for a man named O'Feely, or at least that's the name he gave me. If you know his whereabouts, you better spit it out now. I'm pretty sure that SOB murdered my friend and that disturbs me."

Though the weather was brisk, Ahern had begun to sweat. "I swear on my mother's grave. I don't know anyone named O'Feely."

Jake tapped on the chauffer's shoulder.

"How about you, John boy. Do you know an O'Feely?"

The chauffer commenced to turn to face Jake. "Straight ahead, John boy. You keep your gaze straight ahead. I'll tell you when I want to look at your pretty face. Back to my question. Do you know O'Feely?"

"Nae, I don't know the mon personally, but I have heard tales about him."

"What kind of tales?"

John MacBarr hesitated, "Uh-uh-that he's a mean one. Heard that he killed two men with his bare hands."

"So, you've never been around him?"

"Didn't say that. Once I was having a dram or two with me friend. This big mon came through the door. Biggest mon I ever did see. Me friend told me not to look at him.

"And that's the only time you saw O'Feely? Can you describe him to me?" Jake asked, testing the chauffer.

"Surely, he was a mountain of a man. A beard. Had a mean look about him. I wasn't about to go over and introduce meself."

Jake wanted to laugh, but realized it would take him out of his present character. Satisfied that the chauffer was truthful, he redirected his attention to Ahern. "Mr. Ahern, I have reason to believe that you know a man named Damon Kelly. Have you seen him recently?"

Ahern waited a few seconds then answered. "Yes. He and I have certain common business interests. I met with him last week."

"And those common interests?"

"We're, uh — we're both connected to Laforge Enterprises, a Canadian concern."

"I see. Do you know where he is at present?"

"He's back in the states as far as I know."

Jake continued to press Ahern. "What day, what hour did you meet with him?"

"It was, I believe," he paused. "May I look at my Blackberry?"

"Go right ahead. No sudden moves." Jake raised his voice, "That goes for you, also, John boy."

"Ain't a movin' a muscle," the chauffer replied.

Ahern activated the blackberry. "Ah, here it is. We had lunch twelve days ago at a local restaurant. Met for two hours."

"What did you talk about?"

"A possible business deal."

"What kind of business deal?"

"It was," Ahern stammered, "uh, the thing was, uh…"

"It was what?" Jake asked.

Ahern lowered his voice almost to a whisper. "He wanted to come up with a way to get around the beef import regulations."

"And?"

"I told him no way."

"That was the extent of your meeting?"

"Certainly. Swear on my mother's grave."

"My, my," Jake retorted "your mother's grave must be covered with oaths. John boy, drive us back to Mr. Ahern's office."

Chapter Thirty Eight

"Dad, did George have a family?"

Raymond LeFreaux placed his hand on Jon's arm. "A son. No other relatives that we knew about. George never bothered to re-marry after his wife died. Now and again, he would bring a woman to our company events. George was married to his work. I met his son once. An obnoxious ass, he was. George was pretty much alienated from him." LeFreaux smiled, "But old George got even with him. When that wayward lad swaggered in to the will reading, he got a big surprise. George was very penurious with his money. Managed to save a bundle. Guess what? George left all of his money to the local cancer prevention chapter. If you recall, his wife passed away after a long struggle with breast cancer."

"I didn't know that, Dad," Jon said. "George didn't talk much about his personal life. Didn't matter to me. He and I became close in Scotland. I shall miss him even though at times he would entwine me in Scottish history when I had other things to worry about."

For the next half hour Jon walked his father through his experiences in Scotland. Occasionally, Raymond LeFreaux would frown skeptically as Jon explained how he met Connie and became immersed in the search for ancestors.

"Where do I go from here, Jon?" LeFreaux asked.

"And Jon," his mother interrupted "can't you just stop this dangerous nonsense, marry Connie and come home?"

"I can go for the last part, but the contingency at that juncture is I'll live in Scotland. Did I mention that Dr. Nordstram is now the proud owner of a castle near Edinburgh? Furthermore, the bad guys will know my whereabouts whether I'm here or some other place."

"So what do you do now?" Jon's father asked.

"I'll check in with Jake and Connie."

"And what does that mean?" Raymond LeFreaux asked.

"I'll share information with them and I'll continue to dig into that code."

"What code?" his father was surprised.

"Uh, oh, I neglected to tell you about a code that may tell us where the Stone of Scone is located at present."

Jon's father sighed. "Do you really believe that nonsense?"

"I'm not sure, Dad. I do know that when the ancestor hunt crossed paths with the Stone lore, all hell broke loose for Connie and me." Jon placed his arm around his mother. "Mom, does the code mean anything to you?"

He passed a slip of paper to his mother.

———————————

On their way to the solicitor's office, Connie directed a barb at Jake. "I know you're a close-mouth about your pub conquests, but will you please tell me why we're going to see the estate lawyer?"

Jake ignored her briefly then said, "It occurred to me, Lady Nordstram, that this drama may have players that haven't come out from behind the curtain."

"You're talking in riddles. Give me a translation?"

Jake drove the car into the parking garage. As they walked to the elevator, he said, "I've done some in-house detective work with your Sonsie staff. Molly told me that a Sir MacIntire and Sir Perry were frequent visitors to Sonsie. She referred to them as 'sirs' though I suspect any living organism with more status than a monkey, would be a 'sir' to Molly."

"And what, Jake, does that have to do with anything?"

"Did you get a copy of the will?"

"No. Once it was read, I asked the lawyer to place it in my file, uh — the Sonsie file."

Entering the elevator, Connie asked, "Did Molly elaborate on anything she may have observed about those visitors?"

"She said that once a couple of months ago, she heard them talking in loud voices. Molly said they were using, quote, unquote, bad language."

"Okay, so what?"

"When we announce ourselves, I don't want to deal with Sir MacIntire. If you're willing to engage in a bit of chicanery, I want you to have me meet not Sir MacIntire, but Mr. Lavin. I was referred to him. You are to distract Sir MacIntire. I want to see that MacTavish file and that will."

"I'm confused," Connie responded.

"Three months ago, almost to the day, you inherited the MacTavish estate. My detective brain has gotten lazy. When the paranoid section of my brain woke up, I recalled that you said a smaller portion of the estate was left to Perry, a Grandmaster in the Masons. My guess is that when the will was changed, Grandmaster Perry may not have been a happy camper."

"God, you are paranoid. The guy got quite a bundle."

"Yeah, but you got the big bundle."

The receptionist informed Connie and Jake that Sir MacIntire was out of the office, but that Mr. Lavin would be happy to listen to their concerns. A short time passed before Lavin walked from his office. He smiled when he saw Connie.

"Dr. Nordstram, how good to see you again. Sir MacIntire is on another case. May I be of service?"

"Thank you for seeing us," Connie said. She turned to Jake. "Mr. Lindsey is in need of a solicitor. You were recommended."

Jake extended his hand which was gripped and shaken with enthusiasm. "Please come into my office, oh, and Dr. Nordstram, you may accompany him if you wish."

"Thanks," Connie replied. "I'll wait here. I haven't read the <u>Telegraph</u> this morning."

A disappointed expression came over Lavin's face. "As you wish."

As soon as Lavin closed the door behind him, Jake wasted no time.

"Sir Lavin," he was interrupted by Lavin.

"I am not a Knight of the realm, thank you, sir."

Jake shrugged. "Doesn't matter. I'll get right to the point. I want to see the MacTavish file, including any will written before the most recent one."

Lavin was flustered for an instant. "I am not - - I can't - - I'm sure you understand that I can do no such thing."

"Oh, Mr. Lavin, I strongly disagree. Please bring the file forthwith."

Lavin pointed to the door. "Please leave or I shall call security."

Jake smiled and took one step toward the door. "Oh, by the way, I'm a private investigator. I'm sure your client, a Mrs. Collingsworth, will not be pleased that you kept over ten thousand pounds of the insurance money you recovered for the loss of her jewelry."

Lavin's face turned pale. "Wait! Wait! Perhaps I can answer any question you may have about the file."

Jake wagged a finger at Lavin. "No, no. I'm fully capable of reading a file. Let us not discuss alternatives. Am I clear?"

Without answering, Lavin left his office and returned with a strong box. He placed it on the desk. "Do what you will. You know, of course, I could be fired and my certificate to solicit could be revoked. I beseech you to keep this confidential."

"I'll do that. Now, you just sit there and be available should I have questions. Oh, and I'm not in the habit of breaking a confidence. I'll trust you, also, to keep this event between you and me."

Page after page of transactions, investments and balance sheets covered the item Jake was looking for. He pulled the paper from the file.

"Mr. Lavin, I have here in my hot hand an old will. How about you cut through all the mumbo jumbo and give me the bottom line. These parties of all the parts make me dizzy. Okay?"

Lavin gave a nervous glance over his shoulder. "Sir MacIntire is due to return at any moment. I won't bother to read this document. It was Michael MacTavish's original will."

"And?" Jake made a tugging gesture. "Who benefited in the old will?"

"Grandmaster Sir Arthur Perry. Please, Mr. Lindsey. Sir MacIntire handled all of the MacTavish estate. I never was privy to any of the transactions." Lavin clasped and unclasped his hands.

"Was Sir Perry the only person named in the will?"

"Yes," Lavin replied. "Please allow me to return the file from whence I took it."

"Very good. But before you do that, make me a copy of this sheet. Okay?"

The woman greeted Bennie and Mark with a harsh, "What do you want?"

Mark showed his license for a brief second. "Are you Matilda O'Shaughnessy?"

"What is it to you?"

"Mrs. O'Shaughnessy, my partner is Detective Rochelle. My name is Mark Campbell. Recently, we interviewed your mother. She was able to direct us here." Mark rubbed his hands together. "Ma'am, could we please come in out of the cold. We won't keep you long."

"How is the old bitch?" she snarled as she motioned them in. "Leave your shoes in the foyer. I'll not have you tromping snow and mud on my carpet."

"She is well. She was quite cheerful. Talked at great length about the family."

"Oh, I surely bet she did. No doubt she was bitter because Granpa cut her out of his will."

"No," Mark replied. "She seemed content. Her attitude toward life was very positive. She's ninety-six. Looks sixty. A beautiful lady."

"She was a slut. And to this day, more than likely if she could juice up the mechanism, still be a slut."

"May we sit?" Bennie asked as she moved toward the sofa.

"If you wish," Matilda answered. "But I want you to get on with your business."

"Mrs. O'Shaughnessy," Bennie stared at the floor as she asked, "Where is your husband?"

"That bastard! In hell for all I know!"

Mark waited, then asked, "Do you have children?"

"One conning bitch daughter, who sends me a pittance now and again."

"Is she here in Buffalo?"

"No, she lives in Canada. Montreal. She got her father's money after he had stolen what Granpa left to me."

Bonnie noted a lone tear creeping down the cheek of the old lady.

"I loved the sonofabitch. Turned over all our business, money, and other assets for him to manage. I trusted him. I was a fool. After he left, I woke up one morning with no money, no husband, and no daughter." She made a sweeping motion with her arm. "This pitiful residence is a far cry from Park Avenue, Miami, San Francisco, and the Riviera. We had places in all those cities."

"So, you never remarried?"

"Hell, no! All men are evil and not to be trusted. My ex-husband died ten years ago. I assume he left everything to my daughter."

"Do you know how your grandfather became wealthy?"

"Nope. Never asked. I just know he loved me. Left everything to me." She slapped her thigh. "And that bastard took it from me!"

"About your daughter ma'am," Mark asked. "Is she married?"

"Some frog named Laforge. If justice be served, he'll eventually steal my daughter's fortune."

"Is your daughter's name Annette?" Bennie asked.

"Yes. But I never refer to her as anything but slut, or bitch," Matilda smiled.

"Thank you Mrs. O'Shaughnessy. You've been very helpful," Bennie said.

"By the way, detectives, are you with the city police?"

"No," Mark squirmed, "we are private detectives."

"Whatever," the old woman responded. "I hope you catch the slutty bitch doing something illegal."

As Mark drove away, he smiled at Bennie. "Ain't poetic justice a frightening thing."

"Agreed," Bennie answered. "God! I'm freezing! Why would anyone choose Buffalo as a place to put down roots!"

"Wings and Bills," Mark replied.

Chapter Thirty Nine

"Too bad George never got to rummage through all this stuff," Connie said.

"Oh, yeah," Jake agreed. "He would have been a kid in a toy shop. So, how many more rooms do we search through?"

"Three more," Connie answered. "And if we continue to find nothing of interest, I'll have to assume that my cousin, Michael, either didn't have the merks or at some point cashed them in. Jake, it was a long shot in any case. In seven centuries, God knows what happened to that silver. The one thing we do know, if George's reason was valid, those coins never made it to King Edward."

Three rooms later Connie and Jake ended their two day search through MacTavish memorabilia.

"Let's have a drink, Jake. I'm worn out. I need to just sit and contemplate where I fit into this crazy universe."

"Good idea, girl. But I also want to invite the staff to join us."

"The staff? Why the staff?"

"You can appreciate this, professor," Jake offered. "It'll be like a seminar. I've learned from my years in business of tracking people that the more you gather the more you uncover."

Connie was puzzled. "From the hired help? Come on, Jake."

"Well, now. I see that since you own a castle, you've developed an elitist attitude to go with it," Jake chortled.

"That's not fair, Jake. You know I don't treat the staff in a condescending manner!!" Connie, didn't bother to hide her pique. "Okay, Mr. Gumshoe, when do we meet with them?"

"How about now?" Jake asked.

"You mean…"

Before Connie could finish her sentence, Jake said, "Yeah, now."

After the staff had assembled, Connie announced, "Hey, guys, thanks. I know all of you are quite busy. Mr. Lindsey has some inquiries. Molly has placed some tea and cakes on the table. Mr. Lindsey insisted also that the beer fridge and the liquor cabinet be available to you. Anyone for that?"

The Sonsie staff seemed frozen in their seats until Molly said, "I'll have a wee taste of that Scotch in the cabinet."

Once each member made his/her choice, Connie nodded toward Miller, the manager of the household. "Won't you have something?"

"No, thank ye, Mum. 'Tisn't the proper thing we're doing. We're here to serve you. 'Tisn't right that you should serve us."

Connie felt her cheeks grow warm. "As you wish. Mr. Lindsey, proceed."

Jake walked around the table and placed his hand on Miller's shoulder. "I understand your concern, Mr. Miller. Next thing you know, Lady Nordstram will be dusting and I'll be cleaning the toilets."

The laughter that followed brought about an immediate attitude change in the room.

"We'll be glad to help ye, Mr. Lindsey, if the Lord be willin'," Mrs. Marley affirmed.

Jake gave selected pieces of information relating to the threats toward Connie, the work of Scotland Yard, and the death of John Angus. After a while, he paused to light a cigarette, then placed the pack and the lighter on the table. "Help yourselves, any of you who engage in the filthy habit. Now, I assume that each of you has been questioned by Scotland Yard. Am I correct?"

Each member of the staff nodded in agreement.

"What about the groundskeepers?" Jake continued. "Have they been questioned?"

"As best we know," Miller replied.

"I want each of you to think back over the past months. Can you recall any suspicious activity that caught your attention?"

Molly raised her hand. "Only what I've told you and the coppers."

"Let me be blunt," Jake said, "Do you have any notion as to who murdered Lord MacTavish?"

There was a protracted silence. Then Jennifer Harrigan blurted, "I think it was the papists and their ilk."

"That's a lie!" Oma Springs countered. "Ye got no proof. Lord MacTavish made no difference in the way he treated Catholic or Protestant!"

"Okay, okay!" Jake interjected. "Let's not get into a religious war."

The two adversaries glared at each other, but said no more.

Jake resumed his questioning. He directed his attention to Harrigan. "Why do you believe a Catholic killed Lord MacTavish?"

Harrigan hesitated before answering. "Because they hated him. 'Tis a fact that he was the Lord of the countryside. Anyone here this day will swear that he was in league with the Free Masons. And don't ye know, they got no love for the mother church."

None at the table offered a rebuttal. "And why would he, you know, be so angry with the Catholics?"

Harrigan looked around the table before answering. "Because of the Stone. The Masons know that the Stone housed in Edinburgh is a fake. They'll stop at nothing to find the real stone and, uh, have every Royal Arse crowned above it."

Jake went over his notes, then said to the group, "Does anyone else have anything to say?"

All remained quiet. "Good. Dr. Nordstram, anything more?" Jake looked across the table to Connie.

"No, but I wish to thank all of you for taking time from your duties."

The group rose to leave. Before they reached the doorway, Jake called out, "Oh, Mr. Miller, would you stay, please."

With a scowl on his face, Miller returned.

"Please sit, Mr. Miller, unless you feel more comfortable standing."

Miller remained standing.

"Mr. Miller, I'll get right to the point. I'm sure you have some suspicion about who did your boss in."

Jake observed his reaction, which was manifested as a slight facial tic, followed by a dabbing of his sweaty forehead.

"I know nothing. May I return to my duties, sir?"

"Not yet," Jake answered in a low voice. "I have one more question. Do you know of any secret passageways in this place?"

"'Tis an unusual question, sir. I do not." Miller answered and left the room abruptly.

"What do you think, Connie?" Jake reached for his drink.

"I think our house manager is awfully upset about something."

"Connie, I want to talk to the groundskeeper and the groomsman. Shall we take a ride to the south forty?"

William McSwain, stable keeper, removed his cap as he greeted them. "Evening, your Ladyship. Are ye here for a turn around the pasture?"

"Not today, Mr. McSwain. I don't believe you've met Mr. Lindsey. He would like to talk to you about some of our concerns."

McSwain extended his hand. His grip was firm, his brogue pronounced. "I trust we be doin' work that pleases yer Ladyship."

"Oh, certainly, Mr. McSwain. You keep the horses well attended."

"And me mucker, Mum. He's a good one."

"I know," replied Connie. "He seems to be very young and good at what he does. The stables are well kept."

"Oh, he is, Mum. He's a good lad."

"Mr. McSwain, may I call you William and I'm Jake. I'm a private investigator. I want to ask you some questions."

McSwain smiled, but said nothing. "Your late boss, Lord MacTavish, must have made a few enemies over the years. Do you know who they might be?"

McSwain adjusted his cap. "As I told the Inspector from Scotland Yard, it'll take a wee tad of time for me to make ye out a list. His Lordship was not the sort ye'd take a dram with. He was a hard man. Not like her Ladyship, who treats us well." He tipped his hat to Connie.

"And how did he treat the groundskeepers?"

"The same, they say. They'll be comin' in any minute now. Ye can ask them."

"William, do you know a man named O'Feely?"

"Met him once. A scary man, he was. The coppers never asked me about him. His cousin," McSwain glanced toward Connie, "is a grounds man. James Partridge, he is."

Jake closed his notebook. "Thank you, William, you've been very helpful."

"Your Ladyship, ye know, ye don' ha' to drive down to yer horse. All ye need to do is ring the tele and I'll have old Jumper to you faster than you can say Tam O'Shanter."

"Thank you, Mr. McSwain. I'll remember that."

On the short drive back to Sonsie Jake pulled into the yard of the groundskeeper. For a moment, he kept his hands on the steering wheel and stared straight ahead.

"What?" Connie asked.

"Just thinking."

"Do you think Michael was killed by one of the staff?"

"Can't say. I do know, however, that your worker bees know more than they're saying."

"Jake, why would they not be forthcoming with us?"

Jake paused before answering. "Fear. Think about it, your Ladyship; journalists run over by a train. A couple of bodies discovered at the edge of the nearby firth. Old Angus butchered. You, yourself attacked. MacTavish bludgeoned. An old lady torched. In their shoes, I'd be a bit concerned."

Connie grinned and tapped him on the shoulder. "Ha! We're in their shoes, matter of speaking."

Jake's knock on the cottage door was answered by a comely woman appearing to be in her mid-forties. Several steps away Thomas Jenkins and five children were seated around the dining table.

The woman's face lit up when she saw Connie. "Ah, your Ladyship." Anna Jenkins did a slight curtsey. "Please, Mum, won't you come in."

"Thank you. It's Mrs. Jenkins, am I correct?"

"Yes, Mum. Would you take a bite with us? We're just lickin' our plates, as they say. I have a bit more haggis in the oven." She moved closer to Jake. "And yer man friend is welcome, also, don't you know?"

Connie touched Jake on his arm. "This is Mr. Lindsey. He is my guest at Sonsie. He is a private investigator. He has some questions for Mr. Jenkins."

Anna Jenkins made a shooing motion to the children. "Upstairs all of you. Do your numbers and your spelling."

Jake tousled the hair of the lone son in the group.

"Beautiful children, Mrs. Jenkins. What are their ages?" Connie asked.

"Stair steppers they are — ten, nine, eight, seven and six."

"I bet you're Catholic."

"Why sure, now. How did you know?"

"Just a guess," Connie answered as Jake rolled his eyes upward.

Thomas Jenkins motioned to a chair. "Please be seated. You're welcome to our house, your Ladyship. Goes for your friend, indeed."

"Mr. Jenkins, I understand that you oversee," Jake checked his note pad. "Three other groundskeepers. Is that correct?"

"Certainly, sir, and they be the best of the lot."

"Before Lord MacTavish was killed, do you recall seeing any suspicious activity or person around the premises?"

"No, sir. Not at daylight. Told the coppers."

"Not at daylight? How about after dark."

"Well, now, Mr. Lindsey, I wouldna been out and about unless his Lordship called upon me service."

Jake leaned toward Jenkins. "Who do you think killed Lord MacTavish?"

Jenkins looked toward his wife, but said nothing for several seconds.

"Tell him, Thomas, what we be thinking," she urged.

More time elapsed before Thomas Jenkins blurted, "Sir, I'll be at odds with me kin, but there is a lady named Manion up the road a bit. She was the talk of the pubs. She hated his Lordship and always spoke up about it."

"Do you know why she hated him?" Connie asked.

"The rumor, Mum, is that she grew mean after his Lordship dismissed her from service."

Connie bolted upright. "She served in Sonsie?"

"Yes, Mum. She oversaw the kitchen and the old house staff," Anna Jenkins said.

"Do you know the reasons for her dismissal?" Connie continued.

Anna Jenkins twittered. " 'Tis said that she consorted now and again with Mr. Miller."

"So, Mr. Miller was a party to the hanky panky but kept his position. Very interesting. How do you suppose Mr. Miller got off Scot free?" Jake asked.

" 'Tis said Miller held the Sword of Damocles over his Lordship."

"Meaning what, Mrs. Jenkins?"

"'Tis said Miller dug up some skeletons," she replied.

Connie tugged at Jake's jacket. "Thank you, Mr. and Mrs. Jenkins. We'll be going now. Mrs. Jenkins, have the children had occasion to go through Sonsie?"

"No, Mum, nor have the Mister and myself."

Connie reached for her hand. "Then I want you and the children to come to Sonsie. Shall we say tomorrow morning?"

Anna Jenkins gave a quizzical glance toward her husband. He nodded.

"Thank you, Mum." She curtsied as Jake and Connie exited the doorway. "We'll surely be there. And, Mum, might me husband take a bit of time away from the hedges. He's never been inside the castle."

"Oh, absolutely," Connie answered over her shoulder.

Several steps out of earshot, Jake teased, "Are you trying to screw up the entire social system, your Ladyship. Next thing I know ye'll be burring your words and bootin' your abouts."

"You know better, Jake. And by the way, why didn't you ask Jenkins about that groundskeeper, Parrige or some such?"

"Partridge," Jake answered. "I want to see if our stable keeper, McSwain, gives Partridge a heads up. I'm fishing and I've just baited some hooks to stir things up among the hired help."

Chapter Fourty

"M rs. Laforge, thank you for giving us some of your time again."

"I guess I was a bit rude when last I talked to you. I was angry that you thought I was having an affair with Damon Kelly." Annette Laforge pointed to the chairs. "Please have a seat. Would you like some coffee, or perhaps a cola?"

"Yes, thank you," Bennie responded.

"None for me," Mark said.

Laforge pressed the intercom button: "Tommy, two coffees, please. Bring cream and sugar."

"Mrs. Laforge, since we saw you last we've visited with your mother and your grandmother and…"

Before Mark could continue Annette interrupted. "I guessed you would do that. And, I suppose you now know how a dysfunctional family looks."

He ignored her remark. "To be honest, we believe that a number of murders have something to do with an individual, or individuals, within your corporation, Damon Kelly for one, and Sylvestre Gereau for another. Since we spoke with you last, we have been trying to track both men. Haven't had much luck. We believe that Kelly was in Scotland recently and may still be there."

Mark examined his notes while Bennie continued the questioning. "We suspect, also, that the source of your wealth may be part of the picture."

"What do you mean?"

"Annette, do you know how your father acquired his estate?"

"Yes, I know. My father married into the money," she answered, "and saved it from the impulses of my mother."

"Impulses?"

"Yes. Had my mother been left to her own devices, my grandfather's fortune would have been squandered in Paris, Brazil, Monaco, and in any other ports of bacchanalia. By the time my father took control of the corporate affairs, the liabilities were almost equal to the assets."

Mark resumed his inquiry. "Your mother told us that you send her 'quote, unquote' a pittance now and again."

"Ha! So she considers ten thousand a month, a pittance! My God! She hasn't changed one iota!" Laforge walked to her desk and extracted a journal. "Here's my proof that I haven't turned her into a bag lady." She passed the journal to Mark. "The cancelled checks are there, also."

"Annette, on another subject, the last time we met, you believed that your husband had sent us. By the way, he did not. Does he suspect you're having an affair?"

She laughed. "God no! In the first place he wouldn't care and in the second place, I'm too damn busy running things from the Montreal office. No, I was angry when I blurted that. Should he ever start monitoring my behavior, it would probably have to do with my business travels. He thinks I use business to justify my world travel."

"Did you do a pre-nup when you married?" Bennie asked.

"No. Our holdings, personal and corporate are subject to the nuances of Canadian law. And, you probably know already, I'm an attorney, licensed to practice in all Provinces. Got my law degree from Georgetown."

"Do you know how your grandfather came by his fortune?" Mark asked.

"Granddad didn't talk of it in any great detail. Once, he said his grandfather had a stake when he arrived in this country from Scotland."

Bennie drank the last of her coffee. "We understand that a Dr. LeFreaux was a guest in your house sometime last year."

"True. He claimed to be a long last cousin." Laforge tapped on the table before continuing. "He and I have a night terror that's very similar in its details. I checked on him because I thought he was a gold digger."

"And what did you find?"

Annette smiled sheepishly. "Among other attributes, he comes from a wealthy family and is an archeologist. Haven't seen him since."

"Mrs. Laforge, do you know anything about the Stone of Scone?" Mark asked.

"Stone of Scone? Never heard of it."

"Thanks for meeting with us. You've been most helpful."

Jake walked across the pasture toward the man stacking bales of hay under a three-sided shed. As Jake came closer, James Partridge paused from his work, eyed Jake, but said nothing.

"Are you Mr. James Partridge?" Partridge walked to the edge of the building and gave several nervous glances before he answered. "Yes, I be, what kin I do fer ye?"

"I'm Jake Lindsey. I have a question or two for you."

Partridge motioned Jake into the hay barn. "Ye're a bodyguard fer her Ladyship, ain't it true?"

Jake smiled as he heard Connie referred to once again as a Ladyship. "Sure is." Then abruptly, "Where is your cousin O'Feely?"

"Oh, Mon," Partridge whined, "I ain't got time to keep up with his whereabouts."

"Well now," Jake continued, "I want you to think real hard and perhaps you can give me some options."

"What do ye mean options?"

"Oh, such as locations he might be inhabiting." Jake moved in close to Partridge.

"I told ye, Mon. I have not a notion."

"Mr. Partridge, I have a wee bit of knowledge about clans and such. Now, I'll ask you again. If you don't know exactly where he is, I want five — count'em — five places he could be. If you don't come up with five, I'll stomp your ass and hang you to that rafter." Jake pointed toward the ceiling.

Partridge commenced to beg. "Mister, you don't know what they'll do to me person."

"Who are they?" Jake asked. He reached for the pitchfork leaning against the wall.

"The royals."

"Is your cousin a papist?"

"Lardy, no! May the saints preserve me if I ever called him a papist. He is a true Orangeman."

"And you?"

"I be wi' the crown."

"Okay," Jake said, "back to my first question. Number one."

"What? Number one?"

"Yep. Then there'll be only four other addresses I'll be checking."

"Ye've got to give me your solemn promise not to tell me cousin."

"You've got my word." Jake placed his arms across his chest. "Cross my heart and hope to croak."

Partridge gave Jake a puzzled look.

"Let's see. Mike O'Malley's pub."

He began to count on his fingers.

"He's got a lady friend near Sterling."

"Where near Sterling?"

"A burgh named Castle Rock."

Jake copied the information into his note book. "Her name?"

Partridge tugged at his ear, "Maggie, I think. I don't know her last name."

"My cousin lives in Edinburgh. Some place. I don't know exactly."

"Continue," Jake said.

"He was on a job or two for a laird, so me cousin said."

"A laird?"

"Certainly. A land owner. A rich bloke."

"His name?"

"Don't know. My cousin never said his name."

"That's four," Jake held up four fingers.

"Ye're a hard mon, mister." Partridge thought but said nothing for a few seconds. He lowered his head. "He mayhaps went back to Erin. But I think not. The yard would have him in prison before a body could say Tam O'Shanter."

"Thank you, Mr. Partridge. You've been most helpful. My lips are sealed."

As Jake walked to his car, he posed a loud question to no one in particular, "Who the hell is Tam O'Shanter?"

Ed had dreaded his next appointment. He had been unable to accomplish the task assigned to him. On the elevator to the executive suite, he worked mentally to frame his report in the best possible light.

Now, he stood before his superior, one who, as Wallace had learned, did not suffer incompetence readily.

"So what happened, Ed?"

Wallace cleared his throat before he answered. "We did as you instructed, but while we were looking for the document, we were surprised in the act. He recognized us and we were forced to kill him."

"And, why, Ed have you not reported this before now?"

"I've been on the run, don't you know. The damn papists have a reward on my head."

"And why," Kelly asked, "Did you not dispose of the body?"

Wallace shook his head from side to side. "We panicked. No other reason. We had reason to believe that he would not be at his residence. But he was. The old bastard wouldn't tell us a thing."

"Ed, I'm giving you one more chance. If you do not find Sylvestre Gereau and that document…"

"Sir, we have scoured Scotland. We know he's here. We'll get him eventually."

"Please take care of it. The organization does not like messes and you have left a messy trail."

"Yes, sir. I'll take care of things."

Wallace felt the sweat as it dripped from his forehead to his nose.

"I'm adding another task for you."

Wallace perked up. "Yes, sir. I'm ready."

"You'd better be ready — you're on a short leash as things stand. I want you to grab Dr. Constance Nordstram. Take her to the castle. Get all the information you can from her. I don't care how you get it. If you have to erase her, make damn sure nobody will ever discover her body." He waggled his finger at Wallace. "Do not kill her unless it's absolutely necessary. Any questions? If not, good luck, Ed."

Wallace started to speak, then overcame the urge. He remembered once again that he was responsible for small details. Damon Kelly concerned himself with the big picture.

Upon leaving, he muttered under his breath, "Bastard. He doesn't care how I get the information, but don't kill the bitch unless I have to. But make sure I dispose of the body if I kill her. He should try to follow those directions, with Scotland Yard, and the damn papists breathing down my neck. Good luck, Ed, my ass."

"Connie, my love, I've missed you." He hugged and kissed her, first on her cheek, then full on the mouth.

"Me, too," she said before he kissed her again. "Tell me all about it. You were pretty vague over the phone."

"It's about a Swedish saint. It seems that a few centuries ago, a monastic order was founded and St. Briggette was the patron. Okay, bottom line, the order went south until the nineteen-sixties, but was re-instituted at that time. Presently, there is a monastery near Amity, Oregon, which houses a small number of monks. It's the only one in existence." Jon kissed Connie again. "What if, my love, that stone is buried in Oregon?"

"Could be," Connie answered. "or the stone could be in Sweden. Or, the damn code is a hoax intended to get all of us killed." Connie squeezed Jon's hand. "Where do we go from here?"

"Have you ever been to Sweden?" Jon asked. "But before we decide anything, I'm going to soak my weary body. I'm grungy. After that I want to screw your brains out."

"You could have said, 'Connie, I want to make love to you.'"

"Same, same," he said and started toward the stairs. "I miss George already. The service was simple. The only family that showed up was a sister."

"I miss him, also," Connie rejoined. "He was our minutia man."

"By the way, I'm guessing the lad who met me at the door is your bodyguard. Right?"

"Yes. He trails me around like a lost puppy. I've felt very safe."

"Okay, dear one," Jon exclaimed, bounding up the stairway. "Be back in a jiffy."

Jon gauged the temperature of the water, then poured himself a tumbler of scotch as he waited for the nineteenth century tub to fill. He watched the steam rise from the water as he tried to sort out the events that had changed his life. Six months before, he had been out of work, barely able to pay the rent and treat himself to an occasional steak. Now, he was in love with a psychologist who had the same nightmare as he and, for reasons unknown, he was at risk by persons known and unknown. Scotland Yard was a known entity. Veiled threats for reasons unknown came from persons unknown.

By the time Jon pulled the plug and stepped from the tub, the water had grown tepid. He shivered as he dried himself. "God!! I hope I can talk Connie into putting a central heating system into this place."

Two layers of clothing later, he went down the stairs to Connie's quarters. He rapped gently on the door, waited, then knocked again. He pushed the door open to find an empty room. He walked to the head of the stairs and called out, "Chauncey!"

From the ante-room the butler appeared. "Ah! Master Jon. What may I do fer ye?"

"Have you seen her Ladyship and the constable recently?"

"Indeed. A gentleman and a lady came by. I escorted them, along with the constable to her Ladyship's quarters. Wasn't but a short time later, her Ladyship and the others left the manor."

Jon could feel his heart pounding. "Did Dr. Nordstram tell you their destination?"

"No. Nor did I ask. Her Ladyship did seem nervous. 'Twas a bit unusual. Her custom is to give me a big smile and say 'Chauncey, I'll return soon. Hold down the fort.' Of course, I know this is no fort."

"Is Mr. Lindsey in his quarters?" Jon asked.

"Indeed. He entered the premises at eight bells. He's usually cheery. Sometimes, a bit cheeky."

"Thanks, Chauncey."

Jon bounded up the stairs to Jake's room. After a brief greeting, Jon said, "I'm afraid we may have a problem."

Chapter Fourty One

"What was your impression of Martin Laforge on horseback or otherwise?" Mark asked.

"I believe that he is a nerd with a playroom full of toys. I don't see him as the head of an organization that includes murder incorporated. And you?" Bennie replied.

"I'm withholding judgment. I have to admit that my snooping around has turned up no dirt on the man. I was granted access to the RCMP records. Show he's clean as a nun's underwear. He lucked up by marrying into a stack of money, though he was not in a breadline when he married Annette. His income tax records are above board. Seems he gives a lot of queenies to good ol' socialist Canada."

"Then why do you withhold judgment? From what you say, he's not a resident of the dark side?" Bennie queried.

"My instincts as a cop have taught me to doubt the good nature of mankind. Somewhere along the line, Laforge was unable to dodge the Big Ten."

Bennie gave him a puzzled look. "The Big Ten?"

"You know the script ol' Moses brought down from the mountain. Such as, why would a guy who is about as handsome and charming as Henry Waxman end up with a rich fox like Annette?"

Mark waited for the light to change. "What makes you think Laforge is without sin?"

"Mark, I'm a people person. The people I've interviewed love the man," Bennie replied, "and I'm not giving him a pass just because he lets me ride his horses."

"Uh huh. More than likely he would like to ride you."

Bennie jabbed him lightly on the shoulder. "So, are you jealous?"

"God no," Mark interjected. "The closer you get to him, the more we'll learn about Laforge Enterprises. But, on another subject, how are we going to approach Mr. Lambeau. Oh, and why, my dear colleague?"

"Mark, the man was too smooth for my taste. When we enter his office, I want you to observe the way he has everything laid out." Bennie pointed, "There's a parking spot. Grab it before that vehicle up ahead takes it."

As they entered the lobby of Laforge Enterprises, Ltd, Bennie said, "Are we agreed that I take the lead on this one?"

"You got it, kid. His manicured nails and dandruff free jacket made me nervous when we met with him last time."

Susan Delgado stood to greet them with a practiced smile. "Good to see you again. Mr. Lambeau is expecting you. You'll not need an escort this time around, eh."

"Thank you," Mark replied "I'm glad to see you again."

Mark walked behind Bennie into Lambeau's spacious office. As she had advised, Mark commenced to itemize the office accoutrements. An inkwell was set in the right corner of a well polished desk top. A small stack of papers occupied the exact center of the desk. Telephone and intercom were placed at the right corner of the desk. On the wall to the right of Lambeau's desk was a Rembrandt centered exactly. On the wall to the left of the desk, slightly off center, was a Dega. Fresh flowers were centered on the coffee table. Conference chairs were arranged in a near perfect semi-circle. Lambeau's desk was elevated so slightly that Mark almost missed the subtle furniture power statement.

"Well, once again we meet," Lambeau said while kissing the hand extended by Bennie. "Since you are P.I.s, I assume you have questions regarding Mr. Gereau."

"Perhaps," Bennie answered, "But first we wish to know how long you've known Damon Kelly?"

"I, uh," Lambeau stuttered, "I don't recall — I, uh…" He tugged at his tie. "At a casual estimate, three or four years."

"How about Sylvestre Gereau?" Mark bore in quickly.

"As I told you before, I barely remember the man." Lambeau's tone became tart, his face red.

"Just a couple more," Bennie said. "How long have you been with this company?"

"Ten years as of last January."

"And before that?" Mark continued.

"Let me see, I worked for a mining concern in Quebec for a short while, then a dry goods distributor in Montreal."

"And before that?" Bennie queried.

"I was in school. What does that have to do with anything?"

"Where in school?" Mark raised his voice.

"University of Northern New York. Please excuse me. I really must get to my next appointment."

"What did you study in college, Mr. Lambeau?"

"Human resources management. Now, please leave my office."

"Did you graduate?" Bennie asked.

"I've asked you politely to leave," Lambeau flared as he pressed his intercom.

"Send security to my office!"

"Thank you Mr. Lambeau. We'll leave now. If you recall any details that may assist us, call me," Bennie chided as the tossed a card to his desk.

"Mr. Lambeau, your Dega is not quite centered. You should fix that," Mark grinned.

"Get the hell out!"

Driving back to their hotel, Bennie began to giggle, then laughed uproariously. "Did you see his face when you laid the Dega thing on him!! I thought he was going to burst!"

"Yep. I can just hear him now. 'Delgado, who hung the Dega crooked?'" Mark laughed. "I'll guarantee you we could drive him crazy by moving a few things around in his office."

"Mark, you're not saying…"

"No, no," he interrupted. "It was a rhetorical possibility. But, back to the task at hand. Mr. Not-a-hair-out-of-place was all shook up when we came down on him."

"I've an idea," Bennie suggested. "What do you say we check into Mr. Lambeau's academic history?"

"We're on the same page."

"But not before I do some horsing around with Martin Laforge," Bennie teased.

The room was dark, dank, and reeked of rat dung. Connie could barely make out the figure next to her. He spoke for the first time since their abduction.

"I'm terribly sorry, Mum. They were upon me before I knew what was happening. I'm very sorry."

"It's not your fault, Mr. McMann. Who would have thought anyone would be so brazen as to enter the manor and perform a kidnapping in broad daylight."

"Mum, things of this nature rarely happen." His voice came through the stench and the blackness. "And not when the sun is up."

"Do you have any idea where we are?" Connie felt a wave of anxiety, but tried to keep her voice even.

"Aye," McMann answered. "If I were a betting man, I'd say we're in a basement or a dungeon of some kind. I'll try to find a wall and perhaps beyond that a door. Speak out now and again, Mum. That way I'll know where ye be."

Several steps later, his arms extended to the front, he found a wall. "Walk to me voice. I've encountered a barrier of some sort."

Slowly, Connie made her way to the sound of McMann's voice. Not a shred of light anchored her existence. The only sounds came from McMann, rodents scurrying across the floor and her scream when a large rat crawled across her foot.

"Are you okay, Mum?" McMann yelled. "Are ye hurt, Mum?"

"No, no. I'm sorry I yelled. A damn rat crawled across my foot. I get goose bumps just thinking about it."

"Ye're almost to me. Just reach out and I'll reel ye in."

Connie breathed in, exhaled, repeated the process. She would need all of her training in psychology to deter a panic attack. At the very least, she thought to herself, I'm not alone. I have Atticus McMann and the rats to keep me company.

"Mum, me friends and the Yard will be a'searchin fer us, no doubt. Don't let your heart be troubled. We'll leave here and we'll pay back them what done us wrong."

Connie felt McCann's grip on her forearm. For an instant her existence was re-affirmed.

"Thank you for being here with me. I'm not sure I could endure, were it otherwise."

"Oh, come now, your Ladyship, ye're the queen of the manor. Ye'd be just fine even if I was lifting a tankard in John Champion's pub." Connie held on to his arm. "Mum, I daresay, your grip is firm."

Connie gave a soft laugh as she loosened her hold. "My God, Mr. McMann. I didn't mean to dig my nails into you."

"Mum, lets move about." He guided her. "You walk along the wall to the right and I'll go about the left. Just keep talkin' and I'll do the same. We'll get a notion of the size of this place if you count your paces."

As Connie moved along the wall, McMann's voice grew less loud with each number he pronounced. Every five steps, Connie announced the sum of steps she had taken.

"Mr. McMann, I've reached a corner!" she shouted.

"Good Mum. Now keep walkin' and countin'."

After a bit, McMann let Connie know that he too had reached a corner. Several steps later the two prisoners converged.

Once more Connie felt comforted when she touched the jacket of McMann. "I counted 125 steps," she said.

"And I 147," McMann added. "Mum, we are in a dungeon, sure as ol' Bill Wallace got quartered."

Both were startled by the screeching sound of a door being opened. For an instant, a ray of light pierced the darkness.

"Where are ye, now? Come quickly to the door!" the masked man ordered.

Connie and McMann stepped rapidly toward the light, and the muzzle of a pistol.

"I've a bucket the two of you'll share as a loo, and a jar of water to go along with your bread. If ye demand better accommodations, ye'll have to speak to the management."

"Why are we in this black hole of Calcutta?" Connie asked. "What do you want from us?"

"I know not," their captor chortled. "And I don't ask. Me job is to bring you a wee tad of nourishment and empty your crap."

"Would you please leave us a torch?" McMann asked.

"Surely, you joke," the masked man replied.

The door closed and once more the two captives were in total darkness. Connie bit off a piece of the bread. "Mr. McMann, extend your hand and feel for the bread. I'm not very hungry, but I could use some water."

"Here 'tis, Mum."

Connie reached cautiously toward his voice, then felt the water container. Her hands were shaking; her energy sapped by fear. I can't give up. I know Jon is searching for me. Hunger pains were replaced by overpowering nausea and she retched uncontrollably.

Mark and Bennie identified themselves to the college registrar, after which she invited them to her office.

"What were those names again?"

"Damon Kelly, Thomas Lambeau, and Sylvestre Gereau," Bennie answered.

The registrar booted up her computer, punched in the names and waited for the PC to print out the information.

"Okay. Let's see. Damon Kelly was graduated in June, 1988, with a degree in police science. Thomas Lambeau attended from 1984 to 1986. And Sylvestre Gereau attended from 1983 to 1985. Neither graduated."

"What were their majors if you're allowed to tell us?" Bennie asked.

"No problem," the registrar replied. "Let's see. Ah, here we go. Both Lambeau and Gereau were police science majors."

"So, the picture, my dear, is beginning to clear up," Mark said.

"Yep, they had their own little fraternity. I don't believe in coincidences." Bennie smiled at the registrar. "I hope we're not making you anxious over those fellows. They may or may not be involved in a crime," she lied. "Thanks for your help."

Later over lunch, Mark flipped the pages of his note pad, pausing occasionally to read an entry. Bennie waited for him to converse, respecting the intensity of his concentration. As their meal was placed before them, Mark closed his note pad.

"Bennie, Babe, here's my conclusion. If we start with Agles and Septo, move up to Gereau, then to Kelly and on to Lambeau, or possibly the reverse order…"

"You mean…" Bennie started to say.

"I mean I'm not sure who the big tuna is. I'm not ready to give either Laforge a pass, not yet, anyway."

"So, where do we go from here?"

Between bites, he answered, "There has to be a reason for the trail of dead bodies, here and in Scotland."

"Oh yeah," she said. "And if my hunch is correct, there was some chicanery many decades ago. Jake thinks the silver merks are the cause for the blood and gore. Jon believes the Stone of Scone is the problem."

Mark drank the last of his wine before responding. "What if there's another reason or reasons, for this mess? What if the events have nothing to do with that damn rock and old Edward's loot?"

Chapter Fourty Two

"Jon, I was allowed to sit in on the first task force meeting. Scotland Yard has gotten big time serious in their search for Connie and McMann. Naturally, they're doing it by the book. My book is different, I don't intend to tippy-toe through their maze of civil liberties. I suggested they haul in a legion of shady folks and commence to knock 'em around. Pissed 'em off when I offered to bring in an Irish consultant from Boston P.D."

Jon paced back and forth, smacking his fist into the palm of his hand. "Why did I have to take a damn bath? If I'd been with her, maybe I could've stopped the bastards!!"

"Oh, yeah," Jake answered, "And get yourself deep-sixed."

"Jake, do you believe she's alive?"

At first, Jake didn't answer.

"Well, do you?"

"Jon, I don't read tea leaves. I'm not gonna bullshit you. She may be dead by now. But..." he hesitated, "No bodies have turned up. The folks from Scotland Yard have interrogated boat owners. As far as we know, from their information, nobody reported any suspicious activity along the docks. We have to assume that no bodies were dumped in the North Sea. It's been five days since they were abducted. That's a positive sign."

"God, Jake you are an optimist. I'm scared to death!"

Jake placed his hand on Jon's shoulder. "If she's alive, ol' buddy, we'll find her. I have an idea that she wasn't the only one the kidnappers were after."

"What do you mean?" Jon asked.

"Think about it. Whoever grabbed her was more than likely after you, also."

"Then why didn't they get me. Hell, I was quite naked, soaking in a bath. All they had to do was a quick search."

"Because you were out of the country. Or, that's what they believed."

Jon was silent; engrossed by the possibility. "How did anyone outside our little circle know my whereabouts?"

"Come on, Jon. Shall I list 'em for you? How about the Sonsie staff? Or the local dicks? Or any passerby you just happened to bid goodbye?"

"Do you really think I'm at risk?"

"Yep," Jake answered, "and I believe we should take advantage of that situation."

"What are you thinking, Jake? You insidious rascal."

"If you're willing, I want to use you as bait."

"I'll damn well do anything to save Connie. So, tell me more."

As Jake outlined his plan, Jon was aware of the long shot possibilities. He knew, also, that in looking for an artifact, you first clear away the dirt. He realized, beyond his initial bravado, that he was no Jake Lindsey. If Jake was right, they might get beyond the barriers thrown up by the Scottish courts. Time was of the essence. He was not in the habit of being the goat staked out in a jungle filled with predators. But he knew, also, that rescuing Connie was worth the risk.

"How do we go about it, Jake?"

Lindsey lit a cigarette before he answered. "You're going to go on the market with information you're willing to sell."

"You mean advertise in the local papers, or some such?"

"Nope," Jake explained, "You'll do it by word of mouth. You'll contact a fence or two, whose names I procured through devious means. You'll get drunk in a few pubs and mouth off about a secret code you're willing to sell."

"What if it's not the code ol' Angus was hoarding? What if someone is just pissed off about Connie inheriting a castle? What if someone thinks we killed MacTavish?"

"Jon, we don't have time to examine every single scenario. It is possible that the Angus connection is a red herring. As a start, my friend, it's the best thing we have going for us." He paused, "I'm going to keep you safe. I have no desire to explain to your old man any shortcomings of my guardianship. At every juncture, when you're vulnerable, I'll be covering your back. Okay?"

Spring in western Canada was late in arriving. The winter blizzards had ravaged the land until late April, then torrential rains had flooded the lowlands. But this day in May, sunshine blanketed the countryside and shone on the two people riding horseback.

"Mr. Laforge, I truly appreciate your hospitality. I enjoy our outings." Bennie patted the neck of her mount. "And I have grown so fond of Attila. He is a magnificent horse."

The two horses cantered a short distance before Laforge asked, "Miss Rochelle, I know you love to ride. I suspect, also, that you have other reasons for the visit."

"Yes, Mr. Laforge. I believe you should be apprised of something about two more of your employees."

"And please, Miss Rochelle, Bennie, call me Martin. You make me feel older than I am. Now, what, my dear, am I entitled to know about two of my employees?"

Bennie proceeded to tell him of the visit to the University of North New York. She omitted Lambeau's name from her account. As she outlined the facts and the suspicions, Laforge became agitated, occasionally shaking his head as if in disbelief.

"I should have known when Damon Kelly was out of pocket. But I didn't want to believe that he was anything but ethical and honest. I intend to put my own security people to work on this mess."

"Who's in charge of your security personnel?" Bennie asked.

"Thomas Lambeau. Good man."

Bennie felt a slight touch of discomfort caused by her omission of Lambeau's name. She remembered the teaching of Jake Lindsey — "Never show your hole cards until you win the hand."

"Martin, would you hold off getting your security people involved. If there are others in your organization involved in murder and conspiracy, and they know the heat's on, they'll sure as heck go to ground. If you agree, Mark and I will keep you informed, and I'm sure RCMP will do the same."

For an instant, Laforge was startled. "RCMP? My God, how did they become involved?"

"We had to tell them."

"Bennie, if the press gets wind of this, it could be devastating. We're on the Canadian and the New York market!!"

"I promise you, Martin, we'll be discreet. I believe also that RCMP will investigate quietly. Mark and I are working with only one of their special case detectives."

Bennie was surprised that Laforge did not extend his usual invitation to a post-ride cocktail.

"Miss Rochelle, please come again. In the meantime," his voice cracked slightly, "keep me informed."

As she drove away, she touched the speed dial on her cell. "Mark, I'm not so sure about Martin Laforge after the ride today. I'll fill you in."

"How many days have those two been in the hole?" Kelly asked.

"Seven days," Elaine responded.

"Have you two followed my orders about no conversations with Dr. Nordstram and her puppy dog?"

"Yes." Her reply was tart. "The bitch tries to get Arthur to converse. He has told her nothing."

"Does she show any signs of breaking?"

"No. I would have guessed that she'd go bonkers by now. After the first time Arthur brought her food and a crap bucket, she's said nothing. She takes the bread and water and blinks when the light shines for a bit, then goes back into the darkness."

"How about her puppy dog?"

"Oh, he curses Arthur in English and Erse."

"Let's leave her in the dark for two more days. If she hasn't talked by that time, I have other plans for her. Frankly, if I had my way I'd put her tits in a vice. She'd beg to talk."

"What is she supposed to tell us?" Elaine asked.

"That's none of your concern. You were paid to bring her here and make sure she doesn't leave. The less you now, the better off you'll be."

Kelly turned toward the door then stopped and asked, "You were supposed to nab a guy named LeFreaux. What happened?"

"He wasn't there. We had word that he was out of the country."

Once Kelly closed the door behind him, Elaine called out to her husband. "Arthur, get the hell over here."

"Yes, my Queen of the dungeon."

"I had a visit from that American sonofabitch. He blew me off when I asked why we were holding those two. He said that we should keep them in the dark for at least two more days." She paced angrily. "Who does he think he is? We take the risk of having Scotland Yard on our case and that bastard tells us nothing."

"Don't get your haggis in an uproar. Ye'll get indigestion, lass. So long as the mon keeps the guineas coming, he need not tell us a thing."

Across the wall, Connie fought to maintain her sanity. She had used every weapon in her arsenal of psychology: self-hypnosis; breathing exercises; self talk. She had learned to do walking laps in the darkness. She had memorized one part of her inky environment. Each day she knew, also that she must give emotional support to McMann. As each twenty-four hour period passed, he became less talkative; more withdrawn. Connie had grown less fearful of the rats. Once in the midst of growling hunger pangs, she wondered how raw rat might taste. But nothing she did mitigated the physical discomfort. The most difficult part of the incarceration for Connie was trying to sleep on the dirt surface. Each time she grew tired enough to lie down, she would commence writing her next book. She would bring up an imaginary computer screen, then talk and see the words appear to her minds eye. She fantasized about Jon. She imagined green pastures and sandy beaches. But the tormenting darkness would override any pleasant emotion; then she would return to her purgatory in a dungeon.

The door opened and the welcome shaft of light penetrated the dungeon dark.

"Come get your gruel. Fer your enjoyment today, ye'll have a wee bit of fish to help ye wash doon your bread. Oh, sure and some toilet paper and a few female stoppers. Me yankee wife told me not to bring those goodies, but I sneaked them out. She said you could rot in your filth for all she cared."

Connie and McMann moved quickly to the door. "Thank ye, thank ye!" McMann groveled before his captor.

Connie recognized the first sign of the Stockholm Syndrome. She became concerned immediately.

McMann went to his knees. "I'll do whatever ye want. I don't know what ye desire from this woman, but I'm willing to help ye. I don't want to go back into the darkness!"

Connie's anger boiled to the surface. "Get up, Mr. McMann! It'll be alright! She extended her hand and helped him to his feet. "We'll get through this. Don't lose your nerve. They want something from me. If you and I cave now..."

She never finished before Arthur slapped her hard. "So, bitch, ye're an expert on what's gonna happen to ye!"

McMann bull-rushed Arthur. The sound from his pistol deafened Connie for an instant. Before her eyes, she saw McMann's skull explode.

"You bastard! You didn't have to kill him!" She commenced to scream hysterically.

"I didn't mean to shoot! Oh, Jesus, Joseph and Mary. It was an accident."

Elaine rushed to the side of her husband. "What the hell happened, Arthur?"

"He attacked me, he did. I had to do it, don't ye know."

"Okay, okay, quit whining!" Elaine directed her attention to Connie, "Shut up, bitch! You want some of what he got?"

Connie ceased her screaming. She glared at her captors. "You don't scare me anymore. You're a pair of scum! Now, you've committed murder and you'll spend the rest of your lives in prison!"

Elaine slammed the door in Connie's face. Once more she was engulfed in darkness. But she knew the name of one of her captors.

"Quite a pad you've got here, Jake," Bennie gushed. "I always knew you'd rise above your humble beginning."

"Good to see you, too." He kissed her cheek.

"Thank you two for coming over. I hate to take you away from the Laforges. Mark, it's good to see you again. Mark was my partner long ago in the Boston PD," he said to Jon.

"Glad to be here on the ground — out of the air. If I didn't love Bennie and owe you, I'd never put myself through that ordeal."

Bennie laughed. "Jake, from the moment he got on the plane, he didn't say three words until we landed. Sat like a statue."

"I was certain half the passengers were terrorists," Mark added.

"Chauncey put you up, okay, I assume?"

"Yes," Bennie replied, "God! I feel like I'm back in the eighteenth century."

"In a way, you are," Jon said. "Wait'll you start looking for the central heat switch."

"Alright, let's get down to business."

Jake placed two folders on the table. "I've kept you informed about this mess. Any questions before I assign duties?"

Mark and Bennie said nothing.

"Bennie, I want you to put some pressure on Mr. MacIntire, the lawyer." Jake passed a folder to Bennie.

"Mark, you're going to track a fellow named Ahern, American. As I've told you he's tied up with Laforge Enterprises, and possibly with our buddy, Damon Kelly, on the side."

"Jon, I want you to get drunk at the Dumbarton Pub and keep mouthing off that you know a secret and that you're willing to sell it. I'll be covering you as usual."

Jon reacted. "Jake, we've been over this. I can take care of myself. Besides our baiting system hasn't turned up squat. We need to spread our efforts. If I recall, you have some leads. Now, by God, you do your thing and I'll keep staking myself out where the bad guys can see me!!"

"Okay. I give up. At the very least, I've placed a GPS on your car. And, dammit, put me on your speed dial." Jake cuffed Jon on his shoulder.

"Jake, I know what you promised my father. Things have changed. I have to believe that Connie is alive. We may not have the luxury of time."

"Keep me posted, all of you," Jake directed. "I've told Scotland Yard and the local constabulary that Mark and Bennie are helping us. I've not given them details. I'm paranoid as hell; still trying to figure out who to trust."

Chapter Fourty Three

Mark Campbell felt completely out of his element. The buildings were old. The streets were narrow and, as with most Americans, he believed the natives drove on the wrong side of the road. Though his rental was equipped with voice direction GPS, the road and street numbering system continued to confuse him.

After two trial runs, Mark located Ahern's office building and his residence, then drove two rehearsal routes between the two. For three days, Mark observed Ahern leave his house and drive straight to his office, then at the end of day back to his villa. No stops along the way.

On the fourth day, as usual, Ahern drove to his office, but two hours later returned to his chauffer driven limo. Mark watched the auto drive away and enter a roadway heading north. Mark commenced to follow, staying a safe distance behind his prey.

Ten kilometers later, the limo turned onto a secondary road and increased speed. "Damn," Mark slapped the steering wheel, "I think I've been made!" He pressed down on the accelerator and watched the speedometer climb to 100 KPH. As he topped a crest in the road, the limo was not in sight. After a half kilometer he came to a side road. At the entrance was a sign, "No Throughway." Mark turned onto that road and began his search. He touched the speed dial on his cell.

When Jake answered, Mark said, "I followed our prey out road C221. He turned off on a country road and I lost him. I'll keep looking. Jake, I think he made me. Sorry. I'll see what I can do."

"Don't fret, pal," Jake responded. "Do what you can. I'm not surprised that he may have discovered your tail. I've been on his case. He's probably paranoid by now. Keep me posted and for God's sake don't put yourself at risk."

Mark drove slowly, looking left and right for the limo. He was ready to give up the search when from the corner of his eye, he spotted a cabin near a hillock two hundred yards away. The limo was parked to one side of the cabin. Mark drove several yards down the road and parked behind a small copse of trees, retrieved his binoculars from the rear seat, and walked to a vantage point on the small rise. Minutes later, Ahern returned to his vehicle, then drove back toward the city.

Mark pressed the speed dial to Jake.

"Hey, Mark. What's up?"

"I caught up to our buddy, Ahern. He came to a small cottage, stayed about twenty minutes, got back in his stretch and left. What's my move, Jake?"

"Meet me on that main thoroughfare. What's the number?"

"C221. I'll be parked at the turnoff."

Before he broke off, Mark exclaimed, "Hold it! A Land Rover just pulled away from the house. Shall I follow?"

"Yes, keep your cell on. Give me an update every ten minutes, and, Mark, watch your step."

"Jake, you haven't changed one iota. Still wet nursing me. I'll be fine and dandy."

Mark waited a short time before emerging from the copse. He followed the Rover, maintaining a gap of several hundred feet between the two vehicles.

Upon entering the city, Mark pressed his speed dial. "Checking in old buddy. I'm on the tail of the Rover. Can't tell whether man or woman." He paused, "Just turned on Euclid Avenue. I don't think I've been spotted."

"I'm not too far away," Jake replied. "I'll catch up to you if the traffic doesn't do me in."

"Jake, the target just turned on Arbor." Mark waited. "Okay, he stopped in front of the Cassidy building. Do you know where we are?"

Jake laughed into the phone. "You bet! If you need a lawyer, you're at the right place. I should be there in five minutes or so."

"The driver is a male. He just got out of the car and entered the building. Looks to be forty-ish. Has a beard. About six feet," Mark guessed. "Do anything for you?"

"Oh, I'll take a wild stab. The guy has a spade beard?"

"You got it. I think the sumbitch may be Damon Kelly."

"Mr. MacIntire is with a client. Shall I tell him you're waiting?"

"Yes, I'm in a bit of a hurry," Kelly replied, glancing at his watch.

Five minutes later Bennie walked from MacIntire's office, acknowledged the receptionist and tried not to panic when she recognized Damon Kelly.

Kelly rushed immediately into the office.

MacIntire looked up from the folder he was reading. "What are you doing here!" he exclaimed. "I told you not to leave the cottage."

"Ahern drove out to the place. He thinks he was followed." Kelly tugged at his collar and wiped his brow. "He's worried about Interpol and the Yard."

"Were you followed here?"

"I don't think so," Kelly answered. "I'll need a new safe house."

MacIntire hesitated before responding, obviously upset as he scribbled an address and handed it to Kelly.

"Take the back stairs in case you were followed. I'll contact you. Do not, I repeat, do not call me. Do not come here again. Am I understood?"

"Yes, sir."

"Do not return to your vehicle. When you rented it, did you use your own name?"

"No, sir. I'm not stupid."

"That remains to be seen," MacIntire grumbled. "Now leave before anyone knows you're in my presence."

Kelly took a step toward the door and then paused. "Two people saw me enter your office. Your secretary and a blonde haired woman."

"My assistant is discreet. The lady to whom you referred was looking to invest a bit of money and needed advice. I have her address in case we need it. She's harmless."

While Kelly made his way to the back entrance, Bennie was surprised by Mark and Jake as she exited the elevator in the lobby.

"Hey, Blondie. Fancy meeting you here."

"I just saw Damon Kelly in MacIntire's office!" Bennie said.

"You're sure?" Mark asked.

"Yep. That beard, whether he likes it or not, is his passport to trouble."

Mark deferred to Jake. "What's our move?"

Jake thought for a moment. "We'll wait for him to come to us. Mark, check around. I think this is the only elevator area in this building. He'll have to go to us or through us when he leaves the premises."

"What about a service elevator?" Bennie asked.

"If I remember," Jake answered, "It's not too far form here. Mark, you bird-dog it, okay?"

"Check," Mark acknowledged as he walked away from the others.

Ten minutes. Twenty. Half an hour passed before Jake said, "Enough of this waiting. Bennie, stay here in case he's going down while we're going up."

Jake and Mark emerged from the elevator and hurried down the corridor to MacIntire's office.

"May I..." the receptionist didn't finish her greeting before the P.I.s burst into the barrister's office.

"If you have a weapon in that desk," Jake ordered, "keep your hands where I can see them."

"What's the meaning of this! You have no right to invade this property!" MacIntire glared at Jake. "I know you. You damn colonials have no sense of propriety!"

"Where is the sonofabitch?" Jake inquired, his voice raised and angry.

"I don't know what you're talking about."

"Oh, I think you do, Mr. Shylock," Mark said. "Kelly. Damon Kelly. He met with you within the hour."

Jake yanked open the closet door, then peered into the offset kitchenette.

"I've never heard of anyone named Damon Kelly," MacIntire replied.

"And, I suppose you never heard of Roy Ahern?"

MacIntire did not respond even as his face began to pale.

Mark made the "V" sign toward his eyes. "We're watching you, amigo. You make one misstep and we'll be on you like stink on shit. Do you get my drift?"

MacIntire tried to remain calm. "If you don't leave immediately, I'll call security."

"Good," Jake bluffed. "And while you're about it, you may wish to summon Scotland Yard and Interpol. Oh, who by the way have you on a watch list."

"What do you mean?"

"I mean," Jake moved chin to chin with the lawyer, "if you're involved in the kidnapping of Dr. Constance Nordstram, you are going to be in a world of hurt. Need I repeat myself?"

"I don't know what you are talking about."

Mark opened a door leading from the kitchenette. "Dammit, Jake! There's a stairwell back here!"

Jake seized MacIntire by the front of his jacket and braced him against the wall. "I ought to cut your nuts off and stuff 'em down your gullet. And I will do so if I discover you're in league with Kelly and Ahern."

Several kilometers away, Damon Kelly entered a small house and locked the door behind him.

Chapter Fourty Four

Annette Laforge, tired and disheveled from her recent flight, entered her limo and directed, "Gordon, drive me to the ranch. Is Mr. Laforge there?"

"Yes, ma'am. He arrived from Montreal yesterday afternoon."

"Did Mr. Laforge get the hay in before the monsoon?"

Gordon Carter smiled at the idea of Martin Laforge working the ranch. "Yes, ma'am. The boys made it just ahead of the rain."

"Did Mr. Laforge tell you his reason for going to Montreal?"

"No, ma'am."

Annette reached into the bar for the vodka. "Gordon, please replenish the ice in the fridge. Not too much remains."

"Yes, ma'am. I'll take care of it."

Gordon Carter knew the drill. He drove the limo into the Laforge driveway as the first rays of sunshine broke over the Canadian landscape. He extracted Annette's luggage from the trunk. By the time he reached the doorway, Annette Laforge had joined her husband in the dining room.

Martin Laforge rose from his chair to give Annette a perfunctory peck on the cheek. "You want coffee?"

"Yes, please."

He signaled the kitchen maid.

"How was your trip, my dear?"

"Most profitable, Martin. We worked out the details on the contract. We'll be helping to pave over most of Japan by the end of the year." She motioned to the kitchen maid, "Marina, please bring me toast and marmalade."

Laforge discontinued reading the <u>Times</u> which he placed to one side. "Good job, Annette. You must be exhausted. Did everyone on the other side seem pleased?"

"I think so. There was a lot of bowing and smiling. Most important, the signatures are on the contract. We have to deliver within sixty days."

"No problem," he answered.

Annette nibbled at her toast, working mentally to frame the question she had dreaded to ask.

Martin Laforge resumed reading his newspaper.

"Martin, if I may be so bold as to inquire, how was your trip to Montreal?"

Annette was startled momentarily by his response. "It was okay, if it's any of your business!! If you're inquiring into my reason for the trip, that is my concern!"

"Martin," Annette's voice was calm. "I don't give a damn if you move in with her. I'm not enthusiastic about the idea, but I'll not have you embarrass this corporation. I don't intend to divorce you for the same reason. Should I ever hear of you being seen in public with her, I'll ..."

"You'll what, my dear? I know all about you and Damon Kelly. I've known for a long time! Touché!"

"I have absolutely no idea what you're talking about!" Annette exclaimed. "I've worked with Kelly. Mostly, I've looked over his shoulder. I don't trust him one iota! He's crooked, evil, conniving, and mercenary. Did I miss anything? I can't believe you'd think I'd bed down with that slime!"

"You mean to tell me, dear wife, that in all of your business travels, you never... "

"Hell, no!" she interrupted. "I've had men come on to me who were far removed from Damon Kelly, but I never cheated on you."

Martin stared at his wife, but said nothing.

"I have more important matters to discuss with you, Martin. I had an auditor go over our books. How could security cost ten million dollars a year? Nothing was itemized, and speaking of people I don't trust, add Lambeau to that list. Isn't he your Chief of Security?"

Martin moved around the table and placed his arms around Annette. "Okay, Okay. I'll tell you all about it. I have the same suspicions about Lambeau, but I need proof. I'm working on it."

––––––––––––––––––––

Jon LeFreaux was beginning to understand Scottish pub society. That epiphany was the direct result of three nights of raising toasts to every Scottish hero from Macbeth to Bruce. He had come to realize also that in his special way he, too, was a spinner of fiction. During the first night at the pub he was the victim of a broken love affair with a woman named Maggie. The second evening of Scottish bacchanalia, he bragged that he had found a secret code which could alter the history of Scotland.

This night Jon was ready to hold forth at the MacGregor Pub. In spite of Jon's reluctance, Jake Lindsey was seated in a corner away from the raucous crowd of which Jon had become a part.

"Hey, yank!" a reveler called out to Jon. "We got a Maggie for ye!" The inebriated Scot, half escorted, half pushed Maggie MacDaniel before Jon.

"Ye see, Lad, for every Lass who breaks your heart there be another by the same name who's ready to make ye forget. Maggie, this yank needs a bit of bed warming."

The drunken Scot weaved his way back to his group. All raised their mugs to a broken hearted yank who knew a secret.

"Ah, yes!" the Scot yelled. "Next, he'll be tellin' us of his kinfolk from Atlantis!"

His declaration was met with uproarious laughter.

Jon placed Maggie's hand in his own. "Hello, Maggie, my name is Jon." He kissed her hand as the bar patrons guffawed. "My heart was broken by another Maggie, another time, another place."

"Ah, now," she purred. "Ye mustn't be burdened by a bad memory. Would ye like to buy me a dram?"

She led him to a booth away from the raucous crowd. One booth away, Jake Lindsey sipped his scotch and water.

"Now, me sad yank, tell me all aboot yourself. What brings ye to our land?"

"Maggie, I came here to forget my past and to find a new woman."

The woman to his front was not new. Jon estimated she was in her late forties, early fifties, and worn down from overuse. Jon continued his charade. Every few minutes between sad stories, he would sip his drink, then pour most of it on a floor that reeked from earlier drinks.

Half an hour later, he blubbered through his drunken pretense, "Maggie, my love, I have a big, big secret." He spread his arms wide. "So big, so heavy, I grow tired of carrying it."

"Well now, dearie, I can help you, but we must go to me cottage. There ye can free yourself of the weight you carry. Too, laddie, I'll help ye forget the Maggie who broke your heart."

Maggie MacDaniel assisted Jon to his feet and led him from the tavern.

"Now, Laddie, where is your auto?"

Jon pointed to his Jaguar. "Can you drive, girl? I'm wasted, don't you know."

As soon as Maggie drove away from the curb, Jake Lindsey eased his auto onto the street a short distance behind the jaguar.

"I like your carriage, Laddie," Maggie gushed.

"I'm glad," Jon replied, checking to make sure Jake was tagging along. "Just you drive carefully. Go slow. No sudden turns, lest I throw up."

Several kilometers later, Maggie parked near an apartment complex. Jake eased to the curb, exited his auto, and watched his prey go through the main entrance. The building was in a dilapidated state, its dry walls flaking, decorated with dust and graffiti.

Jake waited briefly then knocked on the door over which was a sign, MANAGER. After a second knock, a middle aged woman in her nightclothes opened the door.

"What do ye want this night?" she shouted. "It ain't even sunup. Make it quick."

"The apartment number of Maggie MacDaniel, if you please," Jake answered.

"Now, let me guess. Ye be her long lost brother," the woman leered. "Ye're likely a member of Parliament lookin' fer a tumble in the hay."

"Perhaps," Jake replied, as he tried to control his impatience.

"She's a bit of slut, don't ye know."

"The apartment number, please. I don't have all night."

"Well, now! Ye don't have to be so cheeky."

Jake removed a ten pound note from his billfold. "Will this speed things up?"

"Apartment 31, third floor." She placed the money in the pocket of her housecoat.

Jake hurried to the stairs. He failed to hear Betty MacGuffy's parting shot. "Damn Colonial!"

Jake didn't bother to knock. He backed off two steps then slammed his two hundred pound body against the flimsy door. When he crashed into the room, the first thing he saw was Jon duct-taped to a chair. Orley O'Feely was behind him, a lighter poised in his right hand. Jake glanced at the Uzi on the bed next to Maggie.

"Maggie," he ordered in a calm voice, "if your hand moves toward that Uzi, I'll make you one-armed for the rest of your life. Now, Mr. O'Feely, free up your prisoner and seat yourself in his chair. Do not reach for the pistol you strapped to your ankle."

O'Feely commenced to laugh. "You smashed a good door when all you needed to do was twist the handle and walk in."

Jake kept his weapon trained on O'Feely while he moved to the bed and retrieved the Uzi.

"Maggie, dear, you help your friend free the captive."

He glanced at his watch. "I'll give you two minutes to get that damn tape off. Jon boy, are you okay?"

"Yep, but I was beginning to think you got lost. I hope I haven't soiled my underwear. Jesus, this bastard was getting ready to burn me with that lighter." With the tape removed, Jon rubbed his hands together to regain circulation.

"Please sit, Mr. O'Feely. I have some questions for you. Jon, relieve him of the ankle piece." Jake grabbed Maggie and pushed her toward O'Feely. "You bind him to that chair, girl."

O'Feely started to arise from the chair. Jake shoved him back, at the same time bringing his slapper hard against the side of O'Feely's head.

"Jon, help Maggie seat her buddy in a more permanent position."

"You bet," Jon replied as he commenced to wrap the tape around O'Feely.

"Don't hurt me, please, Lado. 'Twasn't my idea!" Maggie pleaded.

"Shut your mouth, bitch." O'Feely directed a barb at Jake. "Ye think ye're so damn smart. This scrubwoman came to me about a mon runnin' his mouth in the pub!"

"Jon, take my lighter and stand behind Mr. O'Feely. Now, Maggie, where was Mr. Scumbag planning to scorch this fellow?"

She looked down at O'Feely. "I don't know exactly, mayhaps his hair or his hands."

Jake gave a soft laugh. "I'm not a copycat. Jon, when I give you the word, we'll have us a facial barbeque."

"Oh, God! No!" O'Feely screamed.

"Then tell us where Lady Nordstram is being held," Jon directed.

"I don't know any Lady Nordstram. I swear it on me mother's grave! I swear it."

"Next question: What were you hoping to gain by roasting ol' Jon here?"

"The mon who hired me wanted to know if this lad," O'Feely nodded toward Jon, "knew about a code that would tell the whereabouts of the Stone. That's the honest to God truth. We don't know nothin' about a lady named Nordstram."

"For some odd reason, I believe you," Jake said.

O'Feely gave a sigh of relief.

"Okay. Different question. Jon get the lighter ready. Who hired you?"

"I don't know that! I got me directions from ol' Maggie! Swear on me mother's grave!"

"Maggie, dear," Jake cooed, "This piece of flotsam on the chair is going to prison for attempted murder. If you wish to help yourself, please tell us who hired you as the go between."

Maggie commenced to sob hysterically. "They'll kill me if I tell, don't ye know?"

Jon broke in, waving the lighter, "Maggie can you imagine the pain if I decide to roast the bottoms of your feet? Now, I want you to take the easy way out. If you cooperate with us, we'll go to bat for you with Scotland Yard."

"I don't know his name. He gave me the money and a note for him," she pointed to O'Feely.

"Describe him," Jake directed.

"He was a yank, I suppose. He spoke like a yank. He was a spiffy dresser. Had a beard," she motioned to her chin in a downward motion. "'Tis all I remember."

Chapter Fourty Five

Connie recalled her rat running revulsion when she was an undergraduate at Notre Dame. Today, sitting in the darkness, alone since her bodyguard was murdered, she plotted a maze for a human rat. She prayed silently that Arthur would continue to be the bearer of her meager food ration. Her analysis of the woman led her to believe that of her two captors, she was the psychopath. Connie was sure that Arthur merely followed the woman's directions and that he possessed some semblance of a superego.

The shaft of light was the signal that food and water had arrived. Connie lifted her waste bucket and moved quickly to the door.

Through the light to which her eyes were not accustomed, she smiled and said, "Thank you, Arthur. What's on the menu today?"

"Some bread and cheese. And I brought ye some tea."

Arthur reached for the bucket of waste. He paused in mid-stoop. "How do ye know my name?"

Time to place this rat into his first maze. "I remember your voice from a night in the pub."

"I never seen ye in O'Bannon's. That's me usual place of business when I go for a dram. I never saw ye!"

"Oh," Connie teased, "I don't know your looks, but I do remember your voice."

Arthur tugged at his klan-like mask. "I don't like ye're knowing me name."

Now Mr. Rat, work your way around the next corner. "Arthur, I believe you killed McMann in self-defense," she paused.

Arthur became agitated. "Ye saw what happened. He came at me like a mad dog. The pistol blew off by accident, don't ye know. I ain't never done nobody in afore. I didn't mean to shoot the bloke. I ain't no killer."

"Arthur, I'm guessing that this kidnapping was not your idea." He removed his mask. "You're correct, your Ladyship. Me loving mate got the money. I ain't seen a farthing of it."

"And you're angry as hell, aren't you?" Connie placed her hand on Arthur's arm.

He flinched. "Don't confuse me, your Ladyship. I need to think. I need to think. Too much going on in me head."

"Arthur, I'll testify for you when Scotland Yard arrests you."

Connie's captor slapped himself several times, as if trying to de-jumble his confusion and ambivalence. Concomitantly, Connie prayed he would not remember his wife repeating his name earlier in her presence.

"You'd tell Scotland Yard it was an accident?"

Connie could feel the weight of her own moral code. "Arthur, I'll tell them what I saw. I'll tell them you've been kind to me. I'll tell them whatever I can that will help you."

Arthur became more agitated. He raised Connie's anxiety level when he placed the mask back on his face.

"Arthur," Connie worked to keep her voice even, "You know that you'll bear the responsibility for my kidnapping. Your wife will more than likely not be charged. But you'll be charged with kidnapping and murder."

"But it was her idea."

"Doesn't matter, Arthur. You're the man of the family. All she has to do is testify that you, as her husband, forced her into this escapade. Her word against yours."

Arthur tore off the mask again. "I'm so confused, don't ye know. I don't know what to do."

"Let me go, Arthur. Scotland Yard will take note of such action."

Arthur slapped his forehead, "Mum, ye'll promise to help me?"

"I shall do so, Arthur."

"That's it! That's it! I don't gie a rotten sey what that bloody bitch thinks! I'm fed up wi' her bossiness! She sets it so any blame will fall at me feet!"

He handed his pistol to Connie. "Make it look good, your Ladyship. Right through me shoulder. Then run like the wind!"

"I, I," Connie stammered, "I've never fired one of these things. What do I do?"

"Ye place your hand around the butt, and your finger here." He eased her finger into the trigger housing. "Shoot it here." He pointed high up his shoulder. "Keep a steady hand." In spite of the queasiness she felt, Connie moved closer to her captor. As she started to pull the trigger, she said, "Arthur, do you have a cell phone?"

"Yeah."

"Give it to me. I'll call the emergency room to let them know…"

"No! No! Elaine will suspect. Just shoot and be on your way!"

"Thank you for responding to my call so quickly, Inspector." Martin Laforge moved to the wet bar. "May I offer you a drink?"

"Thank you, no. You reported over the phone that your wife came home from Japan the day before yesterday and was scheduled to fly to Montreal today. Is that correct?"

"Yes. I assumed that she went to the airport to board the 6:35 flight. She would have left, I assume around 4:00."

"What do you mean, you assumed she went to the airport?"

"I don't arise that early. With all the airport security precautions, she said she would set her alarm for 4:00 a.m."

Inspector Morrissey made notations on his pad.

"Does your wife drive herself to the airport as a general practice?"

"No, our chauffer, Mr. Gordon, usually drives her. Today, however, is his day off. I assume she drove herself. The Mercedes was not in the garage when I opened it. I would have to believe she drove it."

"Mr. Laforge, we checked every parking lot at the airport. No Mercedes fitting your description with the license number you gave us was in any of the parking areas."

Laforge paced back and forth. "Do you think anything…"

"I don't know what to think at this point. We've put out an APB on the auto. Do you have a photo of your wife? We'll commence the missing persons process."

Laforge placed his hands to his front. "Whoa, Inspector. Is there any way you can keep this event below the radar? If it becomes a cause celebre, my company's stock will take a beating."

The inspector frowned. "I'm not sure I understand your concern. I should think you'd want all of RCMP's resources brought to bear."

"I certainly do so. I'm just asking for a bit of discretion. You see, Inspector, my wife, as you may know, is the mover and shaker in the organization. She's been written up in Forbes, the Times, Time Magazine, U.S. News, and Newsweek. In a sense, she is the Jacqui Kennedy of Canadian commerce. Can you imagine the stir it would cause should it hit the newsstands?"

"Tell me, when did you receive the call from your Montreal office that your wife had not arrived there as scheduled?"

"Her ground transport was to meet her at 3:25 eastern standard time. When she didn't exit the plane, I got a call from the Montreal office. Shortly thereafter I telephoned your office."

"Sergeant Johnson," he turned to his assistant, "have six of your Mounties report here. I want you to start the ground checking ASAP. And if you don't mind, Mr. Laforge, I'd like to inspect you wife's living quarters. I assume those quarters are the same as your own."

"Inspector," Laforge snapped, "If you're asking about our sleeping arrangements, we have separate bedrooms."

"Do you have a stable relationship with your wife?"

"What the hell kind of question is that?" Laforge blurted.

"Mr. Laforge, I'm sorry. I have to ask these questions. There is the possibility that something bad has happened to your wife. But I must also consider the possibility that she simply drove off, ok? If such is the case, Canadian and US authorities will spot the car sooner or later." Inspector Morrissey closed his note pad. "And you're sure she never checked in at your Montreal office?"

"Oh, yes. She is meticulous about time — she keeps to a schedule."

"Inspector, why are you having your men check the grounds?"

"Just routine. In case someone was waiting outside the house when she opened the garage. Okay, let's go through her bedroom."

––––––––––––––––––

"Where am I?" Connie raised her head to look around the room.

"You're in a hospital, dearie. Some lads found you, half frozen, with a touch of pneumonia." The doctor placed a stethoscope on her chest. "But you're much better now. Are you hungry?"

Connie managed a weak smile. "Oh, am I hungry. I'll eat whatever's on the menu and lots of it."

"Well, now," the doctor answered, "I'll have the kitchen prepare you a bit of porridge and a muffin. Perhaps some tea."

"If I have a choice, I'd like eggs, steak, toast, milk and coffee."

"Let me explain, Dr. Nordstram. We can't overtax your system. I know you're hungry, but if you gorge yourself…"

Connie interrupted before the MD could continue. "I know, doctor. I forgot. I'll do your bidding. How do you know my name?"

"Well," he grinned, "I could tell you I'm psychic. Fact is, there are two lads waiting outside to see you. I've had the devil's own time keeping them at bay until I could give your morning exam."

"How long have I been here?"

"Three days, your Ladyship. We've been feeding you through a tube, don't you know. So, my dear, are you ready for visitors?"

The MD didn't wait for an answer. He opened the door. "Okay, lads. You may see her now. Fifteen minutes, if you please. Don't exhaust her."

Jon walked quickly to the bedside and planted a light kiss on Connie's cheek.

"You can do better than that," she said. "I'm not Typhoid Mary, even though I've spent several days with rats as my only company. Now, give me a kiss."

Jon fought to hold back the tears he felt welling up. "God almighty, lady, we had almost given up. Jake and I could find not a trace…" He kissed her full on her mouth.

Jake moved close to the opposite side of the bed. "Your Ladyship, if you're passing those out willy nilly, I'll take one."

"Oh, Jake!" Connie's voice rose. "On my worst days in that damn dungeon I was sure I'd never see either of you again."

"To tell you the truth, I'd given up hope. But your poor little rich boy never doubted."

"So, you two, in my absence, what has transpired?"

"Connie, we don't have time to go over everything," Jon replied. "Suffice it to say, it's like pulling teeth to get the proof we need on the designated culprits. But we're working on it. One Orley O'Feely alias Smith and his girlfriend, Maggie O'Toole are in the slammer. O'Feely is charged with kidnapping and deadly assault on Miss Digbe and uh, my body."

"Connie," Jake asked, "How were you able to escape the dungeon?"

Connie grinned wickedly. "I shot my way out."

"You did what!" Jon exclaimed.

Connie then launched into the account of her experience with Arthur Hooshman.

"And I can say, absolutely, that had he not helped me, I'd still be sleeping with the rats."

"Nevertheless, he was responsible for your kidnapping," Jake said, nodding toward the door. "A man and a woman from Scotland Yard are waiting outside. You'll have to tell them what you told us. I hope to get to this Arthur fellow before the Yard puts him on ice. I want to know who put those two on the payroll and what they wanted to know."

"Oh, I know what they wanted from me. The code. If I had remembered it, I would have confessed immediately. You can't imagine the horror of living in total darkness. I'll never again doubt the value of light."

The MD cracked the door, "Gentlemen, time's up. We have some food for Dr. Nordstram. After that, she'll have visitors from Scotland Yard."

Chapter  Fourty Six

Jake started the engine of his auto, then let it idle for a moment. "Jon, the Yard checked every hospital and clinic in Southern Scotland. No forty-year-old male with a bullet in his shoulder, checked into any of those places.

"So, where now?"

"I'm gonna start looking for MDs who don't work during the daylight hours. Those who have had their licenses revoked."

By the afternoon, Jake had the names of six individuals who, for one reason or another, were not allowed to practice in Scotland.

"Jon, I'll assume that ol' Arthur will need someone with surgical skill to treat that shoulder. There are two surgeons on this list." He passed the list to Jon, "You pick the one we visit first."

Jon perused the list. "How about ex-Dr. Thomas Quinton Jones. Says here he lives in South Barringteen."

"Good choice. That'll be the one nearest the old castle ruins where Connie was kept."

Jon opened an atlas. "We're not too far from that hamlet. If he's the one, how do we get the information from him?"

"Finesse, dear boy. Finesse," Jake replied.

Following two hours of inquiry, Jake and Jon were directed to a local fish market owned by Jones. "Hey, fella," Jake sidled up to one of the employees serving customers in the open air market. "Is the boss around?"

"Around what?" the man replied, puzzled.

"Let me try again. Take me to Mr. Jones."

"Aye. His office is over there." He pointed to a door several feet away.

"Thanks pal," Jon said. "Ice me about five pounds of herring." He turned to Jake. "I'll wait for you out here and cover your back."

Jake nodded his affirmation.

Jake knocked on the door. A loud voice responded, "Enter!"

Jake walked through the door and announced "Dr. Jones, I'm a private investigator in the employ of Dr. Constance Nordstram." He presented his credential. "You treated a man recently with a bullet in his shoulder. I want his name and his address."

"I say, chap, you do get quickly to the heart of a matter." Jones smiled. "I like that about you colonials. You know, I did my surgery internship at Johns Hopkins. Fine education I received." He invited Jake to sit.

"Let us assume that I was his attending physician, though I'm not admitting such, what might you want from the lad?"

"Did he tell you," Jake asked, "that he and his wife held Dr. Nordstram captive in a dungeon for near two weeks?"

"He did that, indeed, though he never mentioned her name. He told me the story of how he allowed her to escape. I treated him. When he left my office he was on vicadin for the discomfort. He was quite ambulatory."

"Do you know where I might locate him?"

"Indeed. Two days ago his body was discovered in a waste bin outside the village."

"And his wife?"

"Her name is Elaine Hooshman, wife of Arthur Hooshman. She's in the local hoosegow, as you colonials say — arrested for spousal homicide."

"You're kidding!" Jake could not cover his surprise. "Connie was right. She is a psychopath." He sat silently a moment before he continued. "Dr. Jones, I know that you have been decertified to practice, yet you seem to do so openly."

James lit his pipe. "True, true," he puffed. "The local constabulary realize how difficult 'tis to support a physician in our small village. And, by the way, I haven't left a sponge in another patient since that fateful day. Had she lived, I would not be selling fish. I'd more than likely be practicing in Edinburgh or Dunbar."

After a short drive, Jake parked in front of the jail. "Jon, you have a choice. Go inside with me or baby-sit your herring."

"Unless you need me for good cop, bad cop duty, I'll remain in the car. When you turn your charm on her, I'll bet she'll sing like a diva. But she may be intimidated if two colonials come at her all at once."

Scotland Yard plus several special constables surrounded the house. Jake stood beside the chief inspector waiting for the events to unfold.

"Chief Inspector, how do you know Damon Kelly is inside?"

"We don't know for sure, laddie. According to one of our street boys, he was seen with Wallace. We know, surely, that Kelly on the go needed a safe house. We believe Wallace has provided him a haven."

"What about this Wallace?" Jake asked.

"He's an old orange operator. We've pinched him a few times. Ne'er were able to make anything stick. Everyone in place?" the inspector queried his assistant.

"Yes, sir. We're ready."

At that point the inspector activated his bullhorn. "Ed Wallace, your house is surrounded. Please exit through the front door and raise your hands above your head."

Jake had offered to confront Wallace one on one, but had been rebuffed. Now, he could only observe what he considered to be overkill.

After a short wait, the inspector made a second request. "Ed Wallace, you have one minute to come out. If you do not, we shall commence firing."

The door opened. Wallace ran outside, firing wildly with a submachine gun. Within the space of a few seconds, his body was riddled with bullets.

"Don't kill…" Jake never finished his request. "Dammit, inspector! I thought we were going to take him alive!"

"And what would you have me do!" the inspector replied angrily. "The bloody bloke comes out shooting as us!"

"With all due respect, Sir, he committed suicide. He was firing into the air."

"We couldn't be sure of that. If you wish Scotland Yard to continue working with you, please control your outbursts."

Jake said nothing for a few seconds. "I apologize inspector, I'm extremely concerned for Dr. Nordstram."

"As is our department. I have assigned two of our people on a twenty-four hour watch. In addition, we'll have cruisers in the area all night."

"Thank you, inspector."

"Need we assign someone to Dr. LeFreaux?"

Jake gave a light chuckle. "I think not, inspector. He gets grumpy when I get overly protective. As I told you, he is the reason I'm here. He'll not get far from my sight. You know, don't you, that Damon Kelly will not be in the house."

"We'll see," the inspector replied.

The ambulance arrived as the detectives were cordoning off the scene. Jake watched the body of Wallace being loaded into an ambulance. Jake muttered under his breath as he walked away, "Same the world over. Everybody with a gun has an itchy trigger finger."

The SWAT team leader exited the house. "Inspector, there's no one else in the hoose."

For the second time in a fortnight, Connie experienced her night terror. She awakened in a high state of agitation. Her scream brought her bodyguard, Jon, and Molly running into the bedroom.

Jon held her tightly. "Its okay babe, we're here." He stroked her sweaty forehead.

"Would ye like a tad of spirits, Mum?" Molly asked.

"Yes, that would be helpful. Thank you. I want you three to stay safe." She began to sob. "I watched McMann get his head blown off. The same must never happen to you."

"Oh, I shant let it happen, your Ladyship. Two of us will be looking after you. And we'll be watching the back of each other."

Molly returned with a tumbler of scotch. Connie took a large swallow, then placed her hand on Molly's arm. "Thank you, dear. Now, I want you and the detective to leave us, okay, and Molly, I want a great, big breakfast within the hour."

"Yes, Mum. Eggs, bacon, muffin, coffee. Yes, Mum! Ye're feeling' well!"

"Your Ladyship," Harrigan said, "my partner will be relieving me after a bit. Any instructions?"

"No, enjoy your day," Connie replied. "Tell detective Smith to check with me."

As soon as the door closed behind Harrigan, Connie moved to one side of her bed. "Please hold me," was all she managed to say.

"Connie, I'm not sure I can ever let you out of my sight again. I know the dark terrifies you, but we'll get through it."

"I've thought about it: Jon, you know how much I hated having to teach psychology from a behaviorist frame of reference?"

"Oh, I remember. You told me."

"Well, my darling, get ready for an academic shock." She paused. "I'm going to condition myself back into the darkness."

"How?" Jon quizzed.

"A little bit at a time, and you're going to help me. I'll deal with a dark bedroom for fifteen minutes the first night, thirty minutes the second night and so on. You get the idea."

"How do I fit in?"

"You'll be outside the door timing the process. At any point should I have a panic attack, you'll rush in and turn on the light."

"And if you're successful? I remember my Psych 101. How will you reward yourself?"

Connie grinned and kissed Jon on the cheek. "Take a wild guess!"

"Elaine, if you want to help yourself, say, cut some time off the sentence you'll receive, I want you to help me again, okay?" Jake waited for her response. Nothing.

"Did Damon Kelly tell you who he was working for?" Once again Elaine Hooshman refused to answer.

"If you refuse to cooperate, I don't give a damn if you rot in prison. And, lady, you ain't lived until four or five big dykes stick something twelve inches long up your ass."

Jake waited for the idea to sink in. No response. He raised his hand "Guard!"

He turned to walk away. "Wait, mister."

Jake signaled the guard, "Never mind." He sat back down at the table across from Elaine.

"Once I heard him talking on the tele. He said the name Limbaugh, I believe that's the name he said."

"You're sure it was Limbaugh?"

"Yes, it was and he asked if all was well in Canada."

"Could the name have been Lambeau?"

"Maybe. What I heard was Limbaugh."

"Elaine, you've been a big help. I'll vouch for you when the time comes," he lied.

Two hours later, Jake was back at Sonsie, where he called immediately for a council of war.

"I want this meeting to be secure. Mark lock the door over there," he pointed, "and Bennie the one over there. Connie, has anyone been snooping around since I ran a bug check?"

"No, I requested of the staff that anyone claiming to be a service person should report to Detective Harrigan. No one of that ilk has attempted to enter Sonsie. And I trust my staff, Jake."

"Connie, at this point, I trust my mother and all of you. Otherwise, just call me paranoid." He removed a note pad from his jacket. "Let's get started."

He gave an account of Scotland Yard bringing down Ed Wallace. He told the group of his sessions with Elaine Hooshman.

Mark interrupted Jake's monologue. "Shouldn't we have inspector Sykes at this meeting?"

"Mark, Detective Harrigan will be with us to make sure we stay within Scottish law. Okay, Steve?" Jake shot a quick glance at Harrigan.

"Surely," Harrigan said. "If our activities are connected a bit with my duty to her Ladyship."

Connie shook her head from side to side. "Jake, I can't believe that Sykes could be a central character in this mess. I just can't."

"Dr. Nordstram," Jake retorted, "you're not back in an ivy covered building writing a book on dreams. You are the target of some bad people." He glanced at Jon, "and so is Jon."

"I know he is, but why?"

"Because, my darling. I'm spending a great deal of time in your company," Jon answered. "I haven't told you before now, the Hooshmans intended to grab me at the same time you were kidnapped. I was lucky, because someone mistakenly informed them I was out of the country. They want that code. Already they have killed and kidnapped for it."

"Mark, give us a rundown from your end," Jake directed.

"The Scottish boys checked out that house in the country. Belongs to Ahern. When the Yard questioned him about Damon Kelly, he never wavered. Said he did some business with Kelly and had allowed him to use Ahern's place in the country. He knows by now that he's under surveillance.

"We believe Kelly's left Scotland. The Yard checked departing flights at Heathrow and Edinburgh. No Damon Kelly. If he left, he has a false passport. No one fitting his description. Mr. Ahern is making no sudden moves. Bennie said." Mark glanced at his partner. "Bennie says Ahern hasn't come near the barristers since we tailed him that day."

"Bennie, are you still tight with that law firm?" Jake asked.

"Do they suspect anything?"

"I don't think so," she replied, "I've kept a low profile. The main man, MacIntire, is putting moves on me. Yuk!"

"Yep," Mark laughed, "she dangles herself before him like a carrot to a horse."

"No! No!" Bennie countered, "more like a carrot before a donkey. He's semi-ancient, folks."

"Connie," Jake stood, walked around the table to her, "any thoughts? Instructions? Marching orders?"

"No," she said, "I'm trying to get my strength back. Jon is helping me learn to sleep in the dark again. No, you guys seem to have things under control. That is, as much as this dreadful situation can be controlled."

"Jake, if it is okay with you, Bennie is going back to Canada to work from that end," said Mark.

"Sounds good. Bennie, be careful."

"Mr. Miller, how about you and I go for a walk," Jake gave him a stern look.

"Sir, I do not take instructions from you, nor do I wish to walk with you," Miller replied angrily.

"Her Ladyship gave me permission to walk with you. Unless you wish me to tether you and pull you along, start moving to the door."

"How dare you!" Miller exclaimed loudly. At the same time he began moving toward the door.

Outside, Jake said nothing, but pointed the way through the garden. Once again he was impressed by the Scots' love of flora. On either side of the main path were well manicured bushes, and standing out from the field, a variety of roses. Every shrub and flower had been treated with loving care.

When the two men emerged from the garden, the North Sea loomed up before them, wisps of fog swirling like a miasmic chorus line.

For a brief interlude, Jake said nothing as he stared at the sea. Miller could stand it no longer.

"What do you want of me? You could have, you know, seen the water without my company."

Mr. Miller, chances are you can be of great assistance to me," Jake countered. "Tell me all about a lady name Mary Manion."

"I barely remember her. She was on his Lordship's staff many years ago, before his Lordship hired me. As I was the new manager of the castle, she oriented me before she left his Lordship's employ."

"Mr. Miller," Jake admonished, "you have lied to me. My associate followed you to Manion's place of residence. My associate reported to me that you visited Mary five times over a thirty day period. Now, let's start over. How long have you been reporting to her the activities at Sonsie?"

"I, uh, uh — I don't care to honor your question with an answer," Miller replied, wringing his hands.

"Very well, Mr. Miller. I'll tell her Ladyship about your spying. I'll tell her, also, about that shenanigan years ago that cost you a year in the slammer, where you met Ed Wallace. Now, the way I see it, B follow A and C follows B. Ed Wallace had Dr. Nordstram kidnapped and kept in a black hole where she suffered rats, hunger, and terror. I believe Wallace worked for Mrs. Manion and I intend to see that she's brought to justice. Do you understand me, you piece of shit?" Jake's voice rose with each word. "Dr. Nordstram won't sleep in the dark because of what was done to her!"

Jake turned his gaze back to the garden, and beyond the manicured hedges. For a brief moment, the sunlight cut through the clouds to illuminate the battlements of Sonsie.

Miller breathed deeply. "She's a powerful woman, she is."

"Are you afraid of her?" Jake asked.

"I'm afraid of everything and everyone." His voice was low and pleading. "I thought, perhaps, when his Lordship gave me a position, I could leave the muck behind me. Do you know, Mr. Lindsey, the burden of being found out? When Wallace was released from prison, he found me and threatened to expose my past. I didn't realize until much later that he, too, was a minion of Mary.

"Tell me about her. Did she order the abduction of Dr. Nordstram?"

"I don't know that for certain," Miller stared downward.

"Then what do you know about her?" Jake's voice betrayed his impatience.

"I know that she wants a cache of coins she believes is hidden at Sonsie."

Jake snapped to attention. "What type of coins?"

"Merks. Scandinavian merks. Ancient coins. Ed Wallace told me to search every inch of the manor."

"Have you done so?"

"No. Sonsie is not a cottage on the countryside. I have looked about, but so far found nothing."

"Mr. Miller, do you know who killed Lord MacTavish?"

Miller was momentarily stunned. "Great God, no! I swear before Jesus, Joseph and Mary and all the Saints!"

"I'll put it another way. Did Manion have MacTavish murdered?" Jake asked.

"I think not!"

"And why do you believe that, considering the perception that she ordered the kidnapping of Connie Nordstram?"

Miller hesitated before answering. "I've known her for many years, quite intimately, you understand. She believed that Lady Nordstram knew a secret code, which told the location of the coins."

"I'll be damn! And all this time Connie believed the code related to…" Jake stopped in mid-sentence.

"If you thought perhaps the code was the key to the whereabouts of the Stone of Scone, no truth to it," Miller countered.

"And why…"

"Because Mary already knows the code. She told me that John Angus secreted the code away. She said the sacred stone was safe from the royals."

"Mr. Miller, who, besides Manion and Angus knew there was a code of some sort?"

"There are rumors," Miller replied.

"Such as?"

"A small fraternity. Rumor has it that a small group, no more than ten or twelve blokes, are pledged to keeping the Stone safe. Rumors, you see."

"Do those folks have the code?"

"No, no," Miller answered. "Mrs. Manion and John Angus were protectors of the code. So 'tis said."

"Mr. Miller, I want to make a deal with you. Since you were spying on Dr. Nordstram and up to no good otherwise, I want you to be my informant on the activities of Mrs. Manion. If you agree, I'll not turn you over to Scotland Yard, nor will I tell Dr. Nordstram of your infamy. I assume you haven't taken Mrs. Manion to raise."

Miller was puzzled. "What do you mean about raising the woman?

"What I mean is, are you madly in love with her, or was it simply a working arrangement?"

"Ah, yes. Now I see your point," he didn't answer immediately.

"So, what'll it be?" Jake asked.

"I do say, I shag the old girl now and again. She gave me a few pounds each month to keep her informed about Sonsie. No, I'm not, as you say, madly in love with her."

"Is it a deal, or not?"

"Yes," Miller responded.

They walked in silence to Sonsie. Jake ended the conversation with a caveat. "If you cross me, you'll be out of a job and back in prison before you can say Tam O'Shanter."

Chapter Fourty Seven

"So, what do you think of Scotland?" Bennie asked as they walked to the entrance of Laforge's mansion.

"I enjoyed it I suppose, when you were with me." Mark answered. "Otherwise, it was a tour of castles and such. How was your flight? I'm sorry to put you to work before you've had a chance to overcome jet lag."

Bennie placed her hand in his. "The flight was long. You really missed me?"

"Yep." He squeezed her hand. "Had nobody to cover my back."

He waited for her reaction. It was quick in coming. "Are you messing with my head?"

"Not at all, partner," he laughed. "As they say among the Brits, you're shaggable."

"Jerk!" Bennie removed her hand from his and gave his shoulder a light swat.

"Jeez, lady! Ouch! Use some of that energy to knock on the door."

The butler opened the door. "Mr. Laforge is expecting you."

Martin Laforge greeted them. Without enthusiasm, he pointed to the sofa. "Please sit. Thank you for coming."

"You were pretty vague over the telephone, Mr. Laforge. I must admit I was surprised by your call."

"Let me get right to the point. I'm a suspect in my wife's murder. Not a suspect, exactly. As you say in the lower forty-eight, I'm a person of interest. The way we do it in Canada is quite civilized and quite tedious. Almost daily I'm questioned by a new interrogator. They never handcuff me. They just call on the phone and invite me to RCMP headquarters. They keep asking me the same questions over and over. I suppose it'll be convenient for them if I simply confess to my wife's murder." He paced about before continuing. "I admit, Annette and I haven't been very close these past few years. But I cared for her. I want you to find the people who murdered her. I'll retain you at whatever the cost."

"If you are innocent, Martin, we'll consider your case," Bennie offered. "There are conditions. You must be honest with us. If there are skeletons in your closet…"

"I promise you both. I'll answer any questions to the best of my memory."

"Have you bared your soul to the Mounties?" Mark asked.

"Not entirely," Laforge grimaced. "I've been involved with another woman for the last four years."

Silence. Bennie spoke first. "We'll need her name and place of residence."

"Do you have to bring her into this mess?"

"I'm afraid so," Bennie replied. "Just a matter of time before the police know about her."

Laforge walked to his desk retrieved paper and pen, wrote "Maria Anton, Legacy Lane, Montreal."

"We noted from news stories that your wife's body has not been recovered," Mark said.

"No, it hasn't been found. The Mercedes was located at some depth in the lake fifteen miles outside the city. The car was discovered using technology I don't understand. Doesn't work on humans."

"Why is foul play suspected?" Mark asked.

"The Mounties found Annette's jacket in the car when the auto was recovered."

"Mr. Laforge, what's the status of your company, assuming Annette is dead?"

"Surprise," he responded sarcastically. "Her shares were supposed to fall into my portfolio in the event of her death." Laforge slumped in his chair. "So, you see, that's motive number one. I did not know that she changed our pre-nup without my knowledge. That's motive number two. You see I killed her in a fit of anger, not knowing according to RCMP, that her shares reverted to me only if she was not murdered."

"Martin," Bennie said, "To state the obvious, you are in one hell of a predicament. Please give Mark and me time to confer. May we use your library?"

Molly placed coffee, tea, and cake before each person seated at the table.

"Thank you, Molly. I'll ring should I need you." Connie smiled at her favorite servant.

"Inspector Sykes, you have the floor."

"I thank your Ladyship. As of yesterday, MacIntire, Perry and Ahern were arrested. All are out on bail. We have charged them with conspiring to bring illicit beef in the country. Thanks to Mr. Lindsey," Sykes nodded to Jake, "we are on the lookout for an un-indicted person named Damon Francis Kelly. We were unable to associate the other chaps with the kidnappers of her Ladyship."

Jake gave a heads up glance at Jon. Sykes continued, "We believe that Michael Mac-Tavish sponsored the murder of John Angus. Animosity had existed between the MacTavish group, clan if you will, and the Angus group.

"We believe, also, that John Angus was murdered by persons unknown in order that those persons become privy to the secret that Angus carried. We hypothesize that the secret was buried by Angus in the wall of his domicile, and is now in the possession of those hired by Lord MacTavish."

Connie felt a surge of anxiety. "May I interrupt, inspector? Do you have any idea as to what's contained in the secret?"

"Just a guess, Mum. I would say the directions for a wild goose chase."

"A wild goose chase?"

"The Stone. Don't you know, now. That infernal stone that is safely ensconced at Edinburgh Castle."

"Inspector, any clues about the murder of Michael MacTavish?" Jon asked.

The inspector emitted a hearty laugh. "Well, now, since you mention it, you and her Ladyship are no longer suspects in either case, MacTavish or Angus." He drank a swallow of tea. "We are operating on the assumption that confederates of Angus did in his Lordship. Payback, you might say."

Jake eye-rolled Jon before he said, "Inspector, you're holding O'Feely or whatever his name happens to be, I understand he's confessed to the murder of George Cassidy."

"Yes, that's true."

"I wish I'd got to him first. Maybe I could have convinced him to give us the big dog."

"Mr. Lindsey," Sykes countered. "you're in Scotland and we're not the Earps. Be careful as you skirt our laws. I'm on to you, as you yanks say. Don't let me catch you with your knickers down."

"You made a bargain with O'Feely, did you not?"

"Yes, we did so. We dropped all other charges against him."

"What charges, Inspector?"

"His crimes as a revolutionary against the Crown," the inspector answered.

"Revolutionary crimes?" Jake countered, "We call it treason in the USA."

———————————————

"Molly, you wished to talk to me? Please have a seat," Connie offered.

"Thank you, Mum. I do believe ye ought to know about something what caught me eye. May the Lard help me. I been burdened."

Connie waited for Molly to continue.

"Well, Mum, I was needin' some things from the kitchen stock room, don't ye know. Well, now, I couldna' find her. Right aways I started to look fer her. 'Twas a day when ye were oot and aboot."

Connie interrupted. "When you say her, you are referring to?"

"Mrs. Harrigan, Mum. I saw the door to your Ladyship's room, it being open. When I looked in, she was rummaging through your Ladyship's belongings."

"Did you confront her?"

"No, Mum. Quite truthfully, I knew not what to do until this day."

"What day did you observe Mrs. Harrigan in my quarters?"

"The day afore yesterday." Molly lowered her head. "I'm ashamed, Mum. I shoulda come to ye right away."

Connie placed her arm around the young woman. "It's okay, Molly. You did the right thing."

"Mum, please don't tell her that I came to you. All the other staff will see me as a tale carrier. We Catholics have enough trouble as 'tis."

"I'll keep your confidence, my dear. Have Dr. LeFreaux and Mr. Lindsey come down for breakfast?"

"Yes, Mum. They're dinin' now, don't ye know."

Connie placed a shawl over her shoulders before entering the dining nook. Both men rose from their chairs when she walked to the table.

"Well, now, what a pair of gentlemen."

She kissed each man; Jake on his cheek, Jon full on his mouth.

"We've decided not to be boorish, now that you're here, Ladyship," Jake teased.

Jon grinned impishly. "Connie, last night was the first night you slept with the lights off. I thought about sneaking under your covers."

"Darn good thing you didn't, I might have considered you a rat. Okay, down to some dirty business. Mrs. Harrigan was caught going through my room looking for something. Any ideas?"

"Yes," Jake answered. "Merks, I'd say."

"Or," Jon ventured, "a mysterious code known to Connie."

"If I recall correctly, when I first confronted the staff about the murder of MacTavish…"

"Yes! That lady was quick to blame any Catholic."

Chapter Fourty Eight

The day had been cool, with just a whisper of the upcoming spring. Bennie and Mark, for the past two days, had engaged themselves in the least palatable of P.I. rituals: surveillance. Their target of the moment was the security chief for the Laforge Corporation.

The home of Jacques Lambeau was built atop the highest hill in the area. Four other upscale homes were located nearby. For the third consecutive day, Mark and Bennie sat inside a rental auto different from the one a day before. From their vantage point they could observe those who entered the gate of the Lambeau compound.

Bennie passed the thermos to Mark. "Coffee's still hot."

"Thanks," he said, lowering his binoculars to the seat.

"Are you still okay about taking on Martin Laforge?"

"Yeah. Why do you ask?" He poured coffee from the thermos. "I'll ask you the same question."

"I guess I feel a bit unclean," she answered. "After all, he was not on our suspect radar that long ago."

"Whoa!" Mark exclaimed. "Mr. Lambeau has a visitor." Mark called out a series of numbers. "We got us a Pennsylvania license plate! Run it, detective Rochelle."

A few minutes passed before Bennie read from the computer screen. "Says here the automobile is registered to a rental outfit in Paoli, PA." She commenced the search for the name of the renter.

While Mark kept his binoculars trained on the Lambeau residence, Bennie read aloud the information coming over her wireless.

"Okay. The car was rented to a Samson Garfield, address, Sao Paulo, Brazil."

"Good job, Benedette. Now, we'll wait to see what happens."

An hour passed before a male figure, emerged from the house. Mark passed the binoculars to Bennie. "Can you make him?"

"Oh, yeah," Bennie said. "That's our boy, Mr. Sylvestre Gereau. How creative was he, indeed! Samson Garfield!"

The detectives drove behind Gereau to the Grand Hotel near the center of Montreal. They waited briefly before entering the lobby, then each took up stations and commenced to read the morning newspaper.

From the corner of his eye, Mark watched Bennie approach the concierge. She showed her credentials in a flash and conversed briefly with him.

"What was that all about?" Mark asked.

"A little hedging our bet," she responded. "I told him we were detectives and would make an arrest when our man exited the elevator, that he would probably create a ruckus. Didn't tell what type of detective."

Mark grinned, "Girl, you do take the cake. I was agonizing over how I was going to put my Glock in his ribs and not have hotel security make a fuss."

The P.I.s didn't have a long wait. Gereau walked from the elevator and headed straight for the exit.

The detectives moved in on Gereau, one to either side of their prey.

"Gereau, you are under arrest. Now, move quietly through the door."

"What the hell…"

"Don't argue," Bennie directed as she gave a thumbs up to the concierge, who by that time had alerted hotel security.

"That sensation you feel near your spine is my Glock. You do something stupid and…" pause, "I need not tell you the consequences. Place your hands behind you. This time you won't have the luxury of a race track to cover you."

"You bitch!" Gereau yelled. "I thought I recognized you!"

"Keep your voice down and get the hell into that SUV," Mark ordered.

Once inside the car, Mark pressed down on the accelerator and shortly thereafter was on the road to Ahern's cottage in the country.

"You're not going to get away with this!"

"We'll see. Bennie responded. "And if you don't shut up, I'll duct tape your mouth and nose and make you breathe through your ass. Got it?"

Gereau slumped in his seat. He remained quiet until Mark drove up to the Ahern cottage.

"Bet you didn't know we knew about this place?" Mark turned to Bennie, "Keep him in the car until I check out the place. Mr. Samson Garfield, please give me those keys in your pocket. Uncuff him, Bennie."

"I don't have any keys!"

"So, you rode to the hotel on mass transit. Give me the damn keys before I put some hurt on you."

Gereau reached into his trousers and handed the keys to Mark.

"Which one opens the front door?"

Gereau pointed to a brass colored key.

After a quick check of the house, Mark walked back to the auto. "Okey dokey, let's all go inside and have a cozy get together. Sylvestre, you'll do most of the talking, Miss Rochelle and I will do most of the listening."

"I was only following the boss's orders. Why would the boss want me dead? I'm just a worker bee. Please tell him I'll do anything."

Bennie rose from her chair. "Mr. Gereau, what would you like for your last meal?"

"Oh, God, No!" Gereau began to sob.

Mark moved in close to Gereau's face. "Who wants you dead? Who's the big guy?"

Beads of sweat appeared on Gereau's forehead. "I swear to you I don't know the name. I always got my orders from Damon Kelly. Once, he told me the boss was a big cheese in a powerful organization. That's all I know. Said he didn't know the boss's name; that he always met the boss in a dark room."

"Who arranged this safe house for you? Who owns this place?" Mark asked.

"Roy Ahern," Gereau muttered in a low voice.

"Who do you suspect as the big cheese?" Bennie asked.

Gereau became agitated squirming in his seat. "If I tell you, I'm a dead man."

Bennie chuckled. "If you don't tell us, you're a dead man."

"Can we make a deal? You know, I give you my best guess and you set me free."

"No deal," Mark countered. "But we'll arrange an extradition back to Pennsylvania, where there's no capital punishment."

Gereau sat silently, puzzled, pondering the offer.

Suddenly, he blurted, "Annette Laforge!"

"I'll be damned!" Jon shouted across the room. "Who would have dreamed the object of our searching would be located in this ol' rusty knight."

Connie stepped gingerly across the suit of mail Jon had laid out piece by piece.

"I almost quit looking before I got to this fellow's metal foot. Take a look, your Ladyship." Jon passed a piece of paper to Connie.

She scanned the paper and read aloud, "Received from Kimball MacTavish/million pounds services rendered." It's signed Jorge Amundsen dated October 23, 1878."

"How about this!" Jon exclaimed, "My mother's maiden name, if you recall was Amundsen. Connie, babe, this plot gets thicker and thicker! Are you thinking what I'm thinking?"

"Only in spades, Jon. Can you believe it! Tell me now, my love, that you don't believe in Carl Jung."

Jon paced back and forth, before he asked, "Where, from here?"

Connie was circumspect for a moment. "Somewhere in this castle is a stash of merks worth a great deal of money. That's assuming Michael didn't sell 'em."

"Or the other possibility," Jon added, "someone stole the coins and placed 'em on the black market."

"If I were to gamble my life on it, I'd bet that Michael was not murdered by some angry nationalist. I think he was killed by an angry coin collector. Where is Jake at present?"

"He said he was going to do some background on Mary Manion and Katy Digbe," Jon answered.

"Jon, I want you to hire a building inspector to go over every inch of this place. I want to know of any secret passageways, or dungeons. If those coins are here, by God, we'll find 'em."

She smacked her palms together.

"I'll take care of it," Jon said. "I want you to be safe. Promise me you'll never do anything stupid, like wander off without your bodyguard."

"Sometimes you irritate the hell out of me!" Connie flared. "Each time I think you're different from most men…"

"Hey, I'm sorry." Jon crossed his arms over his chest. "Cross my heart. That was condescending." He placed his arms around her. "Now and again, I forget that you held your own in the black hole of Scotland."

"Okay. Sexism noted and forgiven. I'm going to double check the records that George never finished."

Jake had watched the cottage of Mary Manion for three days. He had witnessed mail deliveries, milk deliveries, and grocery deliveries. In each case Manion had met the men at the door, conversed briefly, then shut the door behind her.

On the fourth day, Jake decided to take up station after nightfall. His new schedule proved to be fruitful. At ten-thirty p.m. two men were met at Manion's door. They followed her inside. At eleven-fifteen the two Manion visitors left the house, entered a late model Volkswagen and drove away. Jake followed them, lights out, using moonlight and the beam of the auto.

A short distance from Manion's house, the two men exited their vehicle, then entered a rundown cottage.

Jake waited until the lights came on in the cottage. He walked the one hundred yards from his car at a casual pace. He peered in the front window, and observed five men and a woman seated around a table.

It was decision time for Jake.

From the looks of the group inside Jake concluded they were not members of the choir in the local church. He decided to shorten the odds by waiting until the meeting broke up.

As the moon rose higher and higher, Jake, once more, peered in the window of the cottage. He never knew what hit him. By the time he regained consciousness, he was prone on the floor of the cottage, his arms bound behind his back.

When he was able to focus on his surroundings, he saw before him one man dozing in a nearby chair. He commenced to wriggle his wrists, all the while keeping an eye on his captor. He remembered how he had freed himself from the Iranians two days after he was captured in the American Embassy.

Strain against the rope. Relax. Strain against the rope. Relax. More than fifteen minutes into his struggle against the rope, he eased one hand free, waited, then pulled his other hand through the carelessly tied bonds.

He rolled from his side to his back and soon had worked his arms free. No sooner had he cast aside the rope than the man guarding him realized what was happening and moved quickly toward his pistol on the nearby table. He was a second too late. Jake came to his feet and overturned the table. The pistol skidded across the room with both men charging after it. The guard, smaller in stature to the burly American detective, provided scant resistance when Jake wrestled him to the floor.

"Where the hell is my Glock?" Jake asked while holding his adversary in a choke hold.

"Fuck ye, damnable royal!"

"Okay. Let's try another inquiry," Jake grumbled as he yanked the man to his feet. "What was the meeting all about?"

"Ye're carrion. I'll not tell ye a bloody thing!"

Jake twisted the man's arm behind his back and pushed him to the kitchen sink. Jake then placed a plug in the sink drain and turned on the faucet. "So, how do you feel about breathing water?"

"Y'd not do that to me! Ye're workin' fer the royal devils. They wouldn't stand fer it!"

Without answering, Jake pushed the man's head into the water, held it there for several seconds, then brought him up for air.

"Don't do me again, mister!" The man gagged and coughed. "We are a cell of the Roy Society! We aim to be free from the damnable royals."

Jake looked at his watch. "When will your friends return?"

"After daybreak. And ye'll have hell to pay."

Jake shoved the man into a chair.

"Now, sport, I'll show you how to tie up a man. Were you a Boy Scout? When I was a scout I had to earn a knot tying badge. What's your name?"

The man said nothing.

"Fine. Let's go back to the water." Jake wrenched the man to his feet.

"MacClardy. They call me Babe. Babe MacClardy, I be."

Jake pushed him back into the chair. Many wraps and knots later, Jake placed a dish rag in MacClardy's mouth and tied his legs to the bottom of the chair. Jake then hung three pots and pans on the front door handle before he twisted the inside lock. "Is there another door to this place?"

"Umm," MacClardy shook his head from side to side.

"Now, why don't I believe you?" Jake walked into a narrow hallway at the end of which was a rear entrance. He returned to the kitchen to get more pots and pans for his jury rigged alarm systems.

"Mr. MacClardy, I'm going to nap a bit. I'm a light sleeper. If I hear you move so much as an eyelash, I'll do surgery on you with your own Uzi."

Jake lowered the shades before he lay down next to MacClardy's chair. Jake had managed three hours of sleep before a loud knock on the door awakened him.

"Babe, let's open the door. The sun's up and a burnin'."

MacClardy tried to warn, but the only sound he could make was a muffled scream, "ummmff."

Jake came to his feet, unlocked the door, then stepped to one side behind the door. As soon as Morris Dempsey made a clanging entrance, Jake pushed the Uzi against the back of the unsuspecting man.

"What. What?" At that instant the situation became clear. He saw MacClardy, bound and gagged.

"Get over there on the sofa after you've dropped your weapon to the floor," Jake ordered.

"Doon't have a weapon, mister! What are ye doin' to us?"

Jake reached inside Dempsey's jacket to retrieve the Glock taken when Jake was captured. "You know, of course you're carrying around stolen property, my property. My pistol."

By now, Dempsey was shaking as if he were chilled. "I wasn't gonna keep it," he whined. "I was gonna gi' it back to ye. I swear to all the saints!"

"When are your buddies coming back?"

"They'll not be a comin'."

Jake slammed his fist into Dempsey's midriff. As the man struggled for breath, Jake shoved him onto the couch and repeated his question.

"When are the others returning?"

Before Dempsey could answer, a car pulled up and parked in front of the cottage.

Jake pulled the curtain to one side and saw three men and a woman walk to the door. Jake greeted them before they could enter. "Please do come in. Leave your weapons on the floor. Seat yourselves comfortably and let us have a meeting."

As they disarmed themselves, one of the men, in a measured tone, stated, "My friend, you are in serious trouble. Surely you don't believe that you'll live to see your next birthday."

Jake ignored the threat. "You, lady," he motioned to a chair. "Please sit. You sir," he ordered the man who made the threat, "tie her to the chair and gag her. I'll not have her screaming and disturbing the neighborhood when I start to roast her tits." Jake placed an iron skillet over a gas flame atop the stove. "What's your name, lady?"

"Joan Murphy," she whimpered. "You wouldn't do that, would ye?"

"Try me," Jake replied. "I'll not roast your tits if you and your friends give me some information."

"Don't tell 'em nothing, Joan!" Norris Beckham glared at her. "He's a colonial. He'd never do that to a lady."

"You," Jake pointed to John Abernathy. "Undress the top part of the lady. Do it quickly!"

"Don't hurt her, mon!" Bob Murphy screamed. "She's me wife! I'll tell ye…"

Before Murphy could complete his thought, Beckham interrupted.

"Shut your mouth!"

"It ain't your mate he's about to burn!" Murphy responded angrily. "The boss is a mon named Reardon."

Beckham moved quickly toward Murphy. "Ye're a traitorous bastard!"

Before he could strike Murphy, Jake brought the Uzi across the bridge of Beckham's nose. He fell to the floor, semi-conscious.

Murphy did as Jake dictated. Jake then bound Murphy and placed a rope around the neck of each person and tied the other end of the rope to the feet of the person. Following that, he bent each person's legs to a 90 degree angle and tightened the rope. Any attempt to escape would bring about choking.

After Jake left the cottage, he removed his false beard and a blonde wig. He punched in several numbers on his cell phone. "This is a friend. If you go to 13 North Mark, you'll find a group of revolutionaries and a cache of weapons."

Chapter Fourty Nine

Martin Laforge sat, his head lowered, shocked by the news he had just received.

Bennie placed a hand on his shoulder. "I'm sorry, Martin. You had no idea that Annette was stabbing you in the back?"

"None. Not a doubt about her loyalty. After her car was recovered from Twin Lake, I was sure she was dead. We had our differences, but…" His voice trailed off. "The bitch wanted me pinched as a murder suspect. Do you see it that way?"

Mark listened intently before he ventured his thoughts. "Mr. Laforge, where do you think she may be? Gereau said she left town but he didn't know her destination."

Laforge's telephone rang. He picked up the receiver, listened, mumbling "uh-huh," occasionally, while his face grew pale. He slammed the receiver down and shouted, "She has ruined this company! My CFO reports that there is minimal liquidity. Yesterday, she," he stopped in mid thought, "I assume it was she, sold our fifty-one percent of the company."

"You mean…" Bennie received an answer before she completed her question.

"Yes, my dear, I'm belly up. To add insult to injury, she sold this ranch outright. My CFO says that the new owner is expecting me to be out within sixty days. If she thinks I'm giving up easily, she had better rethink. I'll ask for a court restraining order."

"Martin, we were under the impression that all decisions concerning Laforge Enterprises were treated as joint ownership by the two of you."

"Let me tell you, Bennie," he explained. "When we married, I was the one with his hat in hand. Oh, I had a section of land and a modest home. I trusted her, and," he looked from one to the other, "she trusted me until recently. But the breach of trust on my part had to do with another woman, not with the company. I always interpreted 'breach of trust' as a caveat relating to company business."

Bennie and Mark exchanged uplifted eyebrows. When Laforge didn't continue, Mark said, "Mr. Laforge, can you think of anything that would give us a lead into her behavior and subsequent disappearance? Anything. No matter how insignificant it may appear to you. Habits. Hobbies. Obsessions."

"Obsessions?" Laforge gave Mark a quizzical look.

"You know, conversations she started again and again. Something of intense interest to her, aside from the company."

Laforge arose from his chair, paced about, said nothing as he appeared to be trying to recollect. When he returned to his chair, he looked first to Mark, then to Bennie.

"Come to think of it, she never acted the same after Jon LeFreaux visited us. She seemed more anxious. She would engage me in conversation about something called the Stone of Destiny. I wasn't especially interested in that rock, though it did make a good story."

Bennie's and Mark's attention became immediately more focused. "Martin, can you remember what she said about the stone?" Bennie asked.

"Let me see," Laforge thought for a moment. "Once, last week, she came to me one day and rambled on and on about a saint and that piece of rock. Oh, and once I referred to the stone as a piece of rock, she admonished me on the spot."

"Can you remember the name of the saint she talked about?"

"It was something like Bridges or Brind or Breene. I can't remember exactly. I had my own problems. She had found out about my lady friend."

"Briggette," Bennie prompted, "did she say something about St. Briggette?"

"Yes, that was the name. And believe you me, Annette was in a high state of excitement about that saint," Laforge sighed. "I wish now I had shown more interest in St. Briggette."

"Mr. Lindsey, I daresay you are the cheeky one."

Inspector Sykes smiled mischievously.

"I'm not sure I get your point," Jake answered, keeping his voice even.

"Oh I'm sure you certainly do. We received an anonymous call aboot a cabal involving Scottish Nationalists. When we arrived at the domicile, we found six persons bound up in most uncomfortable positions. The lot of them are wanted for all sorts of treasonous activities. Seems, also, they implicated a bloke who manages Dr. Nordstram's manor."

"Good work Chief Inspector. Any other details you can share with me?"

"Ah, surely. Two of the lads sang like canaries. Those two gave us the names of the persons who murdered John Angus and Lord MacTavish."

"The killer was O'Feely?" Jake surmised.

"Not in both cases, it seems. We have an all points on a woman who worked in Dr. Nordstram's kitchen. Her name is Harrigan. We suspect she may have fled to England."

"Is she a Nationalist?" Jake asked.

"No, no," Sykes replied. "According to the manor manager, Mr. Miller, his Lordship caught Mrs. Harrigan rifling through his possessions, searching it seems for valuable coins of some sort. We are holding MacIntire and Perry for questioning. The manor manager informed us that Harrigan was an agent for those two beauties."

"Does Mary Manion fit into any of these shenanigans?" Jake asked.

"Not to our knowledge. Why do you ask?"

"Just curious," Jake responded.

Inspector Sykes stared hard at Jake. "Mr. Lindsey, we're on the watch for a bloke about your size. Blonde hair. Blonde beard. American accent. He has led us to a breakthrough in those cases. Also, we have recovered enough weapons to outfit a king's regiment."

"Good for him," Jake said.

"Mr. Lindsey, I don't believe your methods are in keeping with Scottish jurisprudence. I must continue to advise you to be careful in your investigative endeavors." He extended his hand, which Jake gripped in a firm shake.

"Oh, I am careful, Chief Inspector. Sometimes, I do admit, I stir the stew to bring the meat to the top."

"Connie, are you okay with the way things have washed out?"

"If you mean," Connie answered, "Am I pleased that Scotland Yard no longer suspects us as the killers of John Angus, yes, I am."

Michael MacTavish's library covered three walls, with volumes floor to ceiling. "Your Ladyship, why are we doing this? MacTavish obviously hid those coins too well."

"My darling," she proposed, "we're doing this because I'm obsessive-compulsive and this library is the only stone left unturned."

"Couldn't we at the very least have the staff help us?"

"Are you nuts! After our experience with Miller and Harrigan, no way," she groused.

"Connie, during your intimate moments with ol' Michael, did he ever talk about his hobbies, what he read. You know, things such…"

"You never quit," she interrupted. "I don't remember. I've tried to forget that time."

"I'm not ragging you. I'm simply asking you if you recall any parts of the conversations that might give us a clue about hiding places in books."

Connie didn't respond immediately. Finally, she said, "The only writers he mentioned were poets."

Jon wheeled the ladder to the center of the wall behind MacTavish's desk. "Yep. He did seem to like the poets. I'm looking at an entire row. Connie, the man was orderly. The poets are arranged in alphabetical order. Jesus, he didn't have enough to occupy his time and wealth. I'll start at the end with Mr. Yeats." Jon removed a volume. "Great Caesar! First edition! Connie, this library may be worth another fortune to you."

Several volumes and two hours later into his task, Jon said, "Connie, the man has three Tennyson's, all leather bound."

"Thanks for your ongoing observations," Connie replied. "I'm ready to do something else. My God! We'll be here all month! Are you ready for lunch?"

"I'm starving," he replied, but first… Hey, Babe! Guess what? I'm holding a Tennyson that's not a Tennyson. It's a journal."

From her sitting position on the floor, Connie sprang to her feet, as Jon came down the ladder. Connie opened the journal to the first page.

"Jon, apparently Michael started this journal in 1970. March 15, 1970." She began to read silently, turning the pages quickly as she speed read the contents.

"Hey, how about letting me in on the journal secrets," Jon requested.

"So far," Connie said, "nothing salacious. I'll be sure to turn the journal over to you when I get to the part about me."

"Connie, I'm going to look for first editions while you read. You want anything? Tea? Coffee? Anything stronger?"

"Thanks. Have Molly bring me a diet soda."

By late afternoon, Connie and Jon were prepared to call it a day. Connie was poised to mark the journal page number when she exclaimed suddenly, "Here it is! Here it is! I'll read it to you!"

'August 16, 2006, the Merk Decision. This day I decided to return the merks to the Crown. I do so with great trepidation. When I consider the route taken by those silver coins, through countless ancestors, from the time of Elliot MacTavish, who passed on the collection, one to the other, over these centuries, my reluctance nearly overpowers me. I cannot undergo further the stress of every thief and renegade who suspects I have the coins. I am especially wary of MacIntire, even though he is my solicitor. I believe he knows the contents of the strong box in his bank. I cannot continue to endanger my distant cousin, Constance Nordstram. I am desperately in love with her. I wish the feeling were reciprocal. August 18, 2006, I transferred the coins to the Minister of Finance in Edinburgh. He was taken aback, had no knowledge of missing coins. I feel cleaner now. The merks, I trust, will become a mere snapshot in Scottish history. The story will never merit a modicum of attention, even though it is a significant part of Connie's and my bloodline.'

The two lovers, brought together by an archetypal dream, stared one to the other before Jon punctuated the moment: "Well, I'll be damned!"

Chapter Fifty

"So, if I'm to believe Mary Manion and Katy Digbe, the real Stone of Destiny is buried somewhere on this one-hundred and eighty acre spread," Jon said.

"The caretaker was quite amused when I explained our reason for being here. In fact she gave a hearty laugh. Said a woman and two men came around asking questions earlier this week. Said they were tourists from Canada," Mark said. "This place being a monastery, silence among the monks is golden. Can't question them."

The vineyards in central Oregon appeared as well manicured patches of grape vines. Horses and cattle grazed in pastures abutting the vineyards. Only a small plot of monastery land has been set aside for personal growing of grapevines.

"Hey guys, did you sample that candy? Those monks really know how to make it. I wish I had their recipe. The caretaker told me their products are shipped all over the world." Bennie recounted, between bites of chocolate truffle.

"Yep," Mark replied. "But I have an appetite for some folks name Laforge, Kelly and Lambeau. They're close by, I just know it. The information Mary Manion gave to Scotland Yard, plus the caretaker seeing three tourists from Canada, it's pretty obvious."

"Where do we go from here, Jake?"

"You won't like this, Bennie, we're going to do some P.I. drudge work. Twenty-four hour surveillance on this place."

Jon walked to the edge of the tree line, looked about, then returned to the others. "Jake, that'll be a tough task. Hell, we'd need a dozen people. There's a lot of land out there."

Jake smiled and cuffed Jon's shoulder. "You know, pal, I haven't made a good detective out of you, but I'm working on it. You didn't notice that there's only one entrance and exit to this place?"

Jon grinned sheepishly. "Okay."

"We'll watch in six-hour shifts around the clock. If you noticed when we came in, an adequate observation point is that clump of trees to the left of the entrance. A vehicle can be hidden from view. I've placed binoculars in the trunk and extra firepower should we need it." He glanced at his watch. "It's almost two o'clock. Bennie, you'll take the first shift. Jon will relieve you at eight. I'll go from two until eight. Mark, you'll be the anchor from eight to two. Everybody okay with that plan?"

"Where will you guys be when I discover Madam Laforge and the boys who operate the guillotine?" Bennie asked.

"We'll be at the motel in Amity. I checked the mileage. Two miles from here. Should you give a signal, the cavalry will be here swiftly. And Bennie, please don't do anything on your own. Wait for us. Okay?"

"Got it," Bennie answered through uplifted eyebrows. "I wish you'd think of me as a miniature Arnold Swartznagger and not a sorority sister."

"Sorry," Jake responded.

As the three men walked away, Mark inquired in a low voice, "Jake, I wouldn't mind doing a double shift with Bennie. I don't want anything to happen to her."

"Ah," Jake intoned, "so it's that way."

"What do you mean?" Mark flared.

"I mean she seems to be more than a P.I. partner to you."

"Yep."

"Well, my friend, if you wish to maintain that relationship, you'll not condescend about her ability. She's tough."

The Sonsie staff took their places around the table, giving nervous glances, one to the other. Connie launched quickly into the speech she had rehearsed.

"By now, I assume all of you have heard about Mr. Miller and Mrs. Harrigan. Both are fugitives by order of Scotland Yard. The authorities believe that Mrs. Harrigan bludgeoned Lord MacTavish to death, under orders from Mr. MacIntire of the Peoples Bank and Lord Perry, a Grand Mason. Apparently, their greed led them to commit that horrid crime. As you may or may not know, the conspirators were searching for rare coins, which they believed to be in Sonsie. They were wrong about the location of the coins. Lord MacTavish had returned those coins to the Crown. Mr. Miller, our previous house manager, was not a part of the MacTavish murder, but…" Connie raised her finger, "it is alleged that he, in cahoots with Damon Kelly and Ray Ahern orchestrated the John Angus murder and the George Cassidy murder. We believe, also, that others in Canada and the US were involved. To put your minds at ease, all other members of our household are not under suspicion."

"Now to the changes, Mrs. Scarborough will now become the new kitchen manager and Molly will be upgraded to fill Mrs. Harrigan's old position. The new overall manager of Sonsie will be Mr. Marley. I'm bringing in his wife to assume Molly's former duties." Connie went over her notes hurriedly. "Any questions or concerns?"

Molly raised her hand. "Mum, is Cahoots near Edinburgh?"

One-thirty on the second night, under a full moon, Jake sipped coffee from his thermos and fought the urge to sleep. He turned on the car radio, waited for the scanner to pick up a Portland station, then slapped himself twice on each cheek.

The road leading from the main highway was devoid of traffic. The night was still, except for the occasional howl of a coyote.

When Jake first spotted the oncoming auto, it was fifty yards from the entrance to the monastery grounds, being driven with the headlamps off. Jake pressed the speed dial on his cell. When Mark answered, Jake said simply, "Time to dance," to which Mark responded, "We'll be there in a jiffy."

"Mark, drive to the entrance as quietly as possible. Keep the headlights off."

Jake slammed a clip into his Glock, and grabbed his flashlight. In the moonlight the intruders were but shadowy figures; the voices indistinguishable. As he moved closer, he detected the sounds of digging; first pick, then shovel.

Though the night was cold, Jake could feel the sweat on his forehead. As they had practiced, his confederates were moving quietly through the grounds entrance within fifteen minutes of Jake's alert.

"Jake, is that you?" Bennie whispered, reaching out in the darkness to touch him.

He grabbed her hand, but said nothing until Jon and Mark moved up.

"Let's back off and make a plan," he directed in a low voice.

"The bad guys seem to be doing some excavating. I'm guessing they're near the statue of St. Briggette and I don't believe they're digging for chocolate truffles. We'll ease up on them and, hopefully, have them on the ground before they know what's happening. All of you packing?"

"Yep," Jon answered.

"Okay, let's move. Stay to the side of the driveway."

Jake and the others were a few steps away, when a booming voice cut through the stillness. "Who's out there? What are you doing?"

Quickly the old priest was shoved to the ground. "Shut him up!" came a command from a voice Jake recognized.

"Well, now! What do we have here!" In an instant Jake's flashlight illuminated the excavators. "Everyone stay exactly where you are. We have four high powered weapons trained on you."

Bennie placed her arm around the old priest. "Forgive them Father, for they have sinned. On the other hand, if you choose not to do so, that'll be okay."

"Mr. Ahern," Jake ordered. "Face down on the ground. That goes for the rest of you. Do it now! Roy, you were double dipping. Wanted everyone to believe you were a royalist. And all this time you doubted the authenticity of the Stone at Edinburgh."

"I don't know what you're talking about," Ahern argued.

"Come now, Roy boy. You had MacTavish and his cronies believing you were a simple beef broker from the good ol' USA. All the while you were working like a beleaguered squirrel to find the real stone. Why, old chap?"

Lambeau interrupted, "I'll tell you why. Whoever finds the real Stone will suddenly be very rich."

"You sniveling bastard!" Kelly yelled.

Jon stood over Damon Kelly. He pointed his pistol at Kelly's head. "I think I'll shoot this bastard right here. So, you're the SOB who kept my fiancé in a dungeon for two weeks." Jon cocked the hammer of his revolver.

"My God! No!" The old priest screamed. "This is a sacred place! Please, I beg you!" The old man walked into the light near Jake. "What is the meaning of this outrage?"

"Father, we're private investigators. Mr. Kelly, Mr. Ahern and Mr. Lambeau are wanted for a number of crimes. Not the least of which is murder."

"I see," the priest said. "I'm grateful that you came to my aid. What were they digging for?"

Jon proceeded to enlighten the priest about the Stone of Scone.

"Ah yes! I came to this country from Ireland forty years ago. I remember the story of how Jacob's pillow came to rest in Scotland." He chuckled softly. "The Scots are even more superstitious than the Irish."

"Father, we need some rope. Do you have any such lying around?" Mark asked.

"Surely, follow me to the work shed." Jake turned his attention to the men on the ground. "Which one of you is going to tell me the location of the female viper? How about you, Mr. Kelly?"

"I'll not tell you a damn thing! I don't know who you're talking about."

"Well, now," Jake shifted his attention to Ahern. "Roy, ol' boy, where is the lady?"

"Don't you say shit!" Kelly blurted. For his effort to stifle, he received a kick in the ribs from Jon. "Shut your face, scum! When Mr. Lindsey asks a question, someone had better speak up."

Jake walked around Lambeau, who was shaking with fright. Jake placed his foot on the neck of the fourth man. "I don't believe I know you, sir. What's your name?"

"Don't say anything!" Kelly ordered. "My lawyer will have us out of this as soon as I notify him of our circumstances."

Jake ignored Kelly's outburst. "I asked you a question. You look young. I hope you're smart and young. These three you're running with will be either executed or spend the rest of their lives in jail."

"Please, mister, you're hurting me. My name is Rodd, James Rodd. I met them two days ago. I'd never seen them before that. They asked me to do some work for them. I swear to you, 'til a short time ago I didn't know what kind of work I'd be doing."

"Boy, you talk, you'll regret it!" As Kelly was set to continue his tirade, Jon kicked him again.

"James, where is the woman who's traveling with these men?"

Before he could answer, Bennie walked up with a flyer in her hand. "Jake, I have here a menu from a restaurant in Newport."

James Rodd was quick to answer Jake's question. "They are staying at the Beach Heaven Hotel. That's where I work."

"Good enough, James. You may stand up now."

Rodd arose and dusted himself off.

Jake continued, "Take the rental car. Turn it in to the police in Newport. Miss Rochelle will follow you. Bennie, you know the drill. We'll be not too far behind you."

Kelly, Ahern, and Lambeau were bound and placed in the back seat of Jake's auto. Before Jon could start the engine, Father O'Flargerty rushed up with several boxes in hand. "Please take some candy for your trouble. It's been blessed."

Bennie rapped gently on the door. "Housekeeping. I have extra towels."

Annette Laforge opened the door to face two private investigators and two sheriff's deputies. Intuitively, she moved to close the door, but Mark's foot blocked her attempt.

"Good to see you again, Annette," Mark said. "Deputy Gardoski, this lady is Mrs. Annette Laforge, thought to be at the bottom of a lake in Canada, but now brought miraculously back to life. Please read her rights."

Before Deputy Gardoski could say, "You have the right to an attorney," Annette was on the telephone to her lawyer in Montreal.

She appeared nonplused even as the deputy placed handcuffs on her. She smiled at Bennie. "One woman to another, will you bring along my toiletry bag from the next room, please? So, how fares my dear husband? Was he sad at my death? Did he console himself by fucking that slut in the front office? I suspect he did." She directed her next question to Mark. "Was the Stone buried near St. Briggette?"

"We don't know for sure," Mark answered.

"If I may be so bold as to ask, how did you know I was here?" Annette asked.

"Pretty simple. We just trailed ol' Damon, your partner in crime."

Epilogue

"I wonder what Carl Jung would make of these two dreamers," Mark said.

Connie was quick to respond. "Oh, it wouldn't be a big deal to him. Just one miniscule bit of proof to support his theory of the collective unconscious."

"Oh, come now, my darling," Jon retorted. "I thought our dreams went above and beyond his theory of synchronicity and symbols. Hell, girl, we discovered three long lost ancestors who assassinated a King, and whose offspring later turned against each other." He tousled Connie's hair. "Truth be known, your Ladyship, you and I are Jungian enemies."

"True. But all of our kin got screwed by the kin of Annette Laforge. I'm not sure I'll ever share with our children that the same blood runs through the three of us."

"May I change the subject?" Bennie chimed in. "Why were so many people all steamed up about the Stone?"

Jake answered. "Bennie, babe, remember the adage, the rich are not like the rest of us. They don't know what to do with their wealth once they have a castle in California, or a mansion in Newport, or a million acres of land. So, they'll pay a ton of money for a certain stamp or an old coin." Jake paused. "Had the real Stone of Destiny been buried in Amity, Oregon, anyone who recovered it could have sold it for millions from some collector. And those merks were the same story, different plot."

Connie laughed. "You know, I never cared much for the teaching of Freud. If I had, I would say that coin collectors, stamp collectors, et. al. hated to flush their shit when they were growing up. At least Freud thought so!"

"Regardless," Jake said, "Each time those coins passed from one to the next, money was made. Most of it by Annette Laforge's ancestors."

"I wonder what'll happen to all the folks who filled out the details of Connie's and Jon's dream?" Bennie asked.

"Scotland was kind enough to allow the US to deal with Kelly, Ahern, Gereau, and MacIntire. Lord Perry and a few minor leaguers will be handled by the Scots." Jake frowned, "At this moment, Martin Laforge has refused to press charges against Annette."

"What about Mary Manion?" Connie asked.

"She's being investigated. She may or may not have been involved in the Angus and Cassidy murders."

"Oh, I think she was," Jon remarked.

"One more kinsman of ill repute. Good God! I worry about my own genes and yours. Our children will get a double shot."

"And the Stone. What about the Stone?" Mark asked.

"What about it?" Jake answered.

"Is the real Stone of Destiny in Edinburgh Castle?"

"Doesn't matter to those who believe otherwise," Jon said. "I don't believe the Egyptians built the Great Pyramid even though the majority of my peers believe so. But hell will freeze over before the history books are rewritten. Same with the Stone."

"A nation of people who accept the notion that a two-thousand year old woman transported a huge rock to Scotland... well you get the idea."

"Okay, gang. Those of us who work have to catch a plane to Boston," Bennie said, as she hugged Connie and Jon. "Are you two going back to Scotland immediately?"

"Yes," Connie responded, "but not before I buy more candy from the monks. You guys stay in touch."

As Connie and Jon drove from the coast to Amity, the clouds drifted away to reveal a great white mountain, named Mt. Adam.

"Jon, do you believe the real Stone is buried somewhere near that monastery?"

"It was not beneath the statue of St. Briggette. That's for sure." Jon replied. "Old John Angus believed it was on that property. Regardless, urban legends don't die easily."

For thousands of air miles, Bennie consoled Mark through the flight. While she read, or chatted, or ate, Mark usually sat straight, his body cemented to the seat around him.

When they exited the Calgary Airport, Mark bent down to kiss the pavement, much to the amusement of nearby onlookers.

"I'm hungry," he asserted.

"No doubt," Bennie replied. "I'll get a car. You handle the luggage."

Soon Mark was wolfing down breakfast as Bennie tabulated a set of figures on her note pad.

"Mark, our boy, Laforge owes us a tad over ten thousand dollars plus expenses for a total of twelve thousand, one-hundred and seventy-six dollars."

"Not bad for a few days work," Mark said.

They were met at the door by Laforge's butler. "The boss will be with you shortly. Perhaps fifteen minutes or so."

"It's early. I would guess he's in the shower," Mark said.

"No, no," the butler replied. "He's out back. He has a dark room in his work shed. Often, he meets with people in that room. His hobby is photography."

"Never mind, we'll not disturb him." Mark handed the butler a card. "We'll come back later."

A few steps short of their auto, Mark gazed back toward the portico. "Are you thinking what I'm thinking, Bennie?"

"Yes, I am," she replied. "What now?"

"We'll go to Mountie headquarters."

"And tell 'em what? We've got no proof, except the word of Gereau."

"Not so, my lady. We tell RCMP about the quote, unquote, dark room. They should be able to find the voice scrambler." He paused, "And perhaps other goodies linking old Laforge to the crimes."

"So," Bennie exclaimed, "For all the fake hostility toward his wife, they were in it together. All well and good, but what about our $12,176?"

"Hadn't considered that," Mark replied, as he turned down the driveway.